3-19-07

THE RIGHT OF THE PEOPLE

To Johnna Dunlap,
Thanks for all your
help with the Foundation's
work and your strong support of
our Second Amendment freedoms
and our rural heritage.

Best wishes,
Ed Gentry

THE RIGHT OF THE PEOPLE

Edwin F. Gentry

Library of Congress Number: 2005903263

ISBN: Hardcover 1-4134-9282-7

Softcover 1-4134-9281-9

This is a work of fiction. Names, characters, places and incidents either are the product of the author's imagination or are used fictitiously, and any resemblance to any actual persons, living or dead, events, or locales is entirely coincidental.

This book was printed in the United States of America.

To order additional copies of this book, contact:
Xlibris Corporation
1-888-795-4274
www.Xlibris.com
Orders@Xlibris.com
23325

To my family and friends
each of whom make life worth living.

In Memoriam

Harry L. (Lenny) Beasley, Jr.
(1953-1992)

His strength, his smile,
His character, his courage,
His humor, his heart,
There is never a sunrise
Never a sunset
Never a day in the woods
Or on the water
That he is not remembered.
That he is not loved.

ACKNOWLEDGEMENTS

THIS BOOK WOULD not have been possible without the love and understanding of my wife Faye and my son Eddie. Both of them were very understanding of the many hours I spent away from them while writing and re-writing the manuscript. Nor would it have been possible to produce this book without the hard work of both Cathy Jean Andino and Wendy Michelle White Lybrand. They, collectively, spent many hours transcribing the original text of the book from cassette tapes. They, together with the many re-writes of the book done by Ashley Brown, derserve my heart-felt thanks. Thanks also to Dawn Smith of Kerriville, Texas for her time, advice and encouragement to see this book through.

To Lou Messa, Fine Artist, from Madison, Virginia, my gratitude for his wonderful watercolor which appears on the cover. Lou is an extraordinarily talented artist whose work captures the heart and essence of that part of rural America that is today disappearing so rapidly. Thanks also to Robin Smith, my editor, for her help in both substantive and technical areas.

The seeds of this novel were planted early in my life by my father Garland Conrad Gentry. He took the time to show my brother Garland and me the true worth and meaning of the outdoor sports. It was his love of the law and writing that first encouraged me to put pen to paper. And he taught me to follow my heart. There can be no greater love, no greater gift, from a father to his son.

Last but not least, my heart-felt gratitude to my brother Garland, my cousins Fred and Johnnie Gentry in Mountain Park, North Carolina; my great friends Terry Minnick, Steve White, Steve Dudley, Dave Dunwoody, Jim Wynn, Bo Martin, Dave Smith, Paul Walther, Mike Stephenson of Four Oaks, North Carolina, Chris Anthon, T.C. Lea and his sons Davis and Cal, and a host of other family and friends who have, over the years, allowed me to share so many wonderful days in the outdoors. Truly, friends of a lifetime.

INTRODUCTION

WELL, I'LL BE damned, he thought smiling to himself. *It's still up there after all of these years.* Looking up between the triangle of trees, he saw the wooden platform now weathered gray with age, nestled comfortably against the oaks about twelve feet off the ground.

"Five years," he said aloud, "five years since I've been here. I can't believe it's been that long."

Yet, he thought, *it seems in some ways like a lifetime. Wonder if it'll hold me?*

Pulling on the wooden steps he had nailed up almost fifteen years before, he decided that they seemed solid. *Well, solid enough. I didn't come all the way down here not to climb up and see.*

Slowly, gingerly, he pulled himself up, testing each step as he went. On the top step, he hugged the tree with his right arm and swung himself up and over the edge of the platform. Ducking under the arm rail, he stood on the deck of the stand that he had hunted from so often in the past.

Brushing the leaves off the platform with the toe of his boot, he pulled a rusty folding chair away from the corner where it had been wedged. The plastic padded seat had long since worn off, the stuffing pulled out by squirrels and mice for nesting material. Pushing and pulling, he slowly opened the chair and placed the four uneven legs in the middle of the platform. Testing it by pushing on its back, he was fairly sure the chair would hold him. As he eased down on the seat, it groaned audibly. But as it had many times in the past, it held his weight comfortably.

Glancing to his right he saw the initials his son Allen had left on the tree over a dozen years ago. The letters ARR were awkwardly-carved, little-boy block letters. John remembered the afternoon well when that was done. A bright, sunny, cold December afternoon he and his son had spent there. Watching, sharing, their faces turned against a cold northeast wind. The laughs and smiles, the anticipation of things to come; a memory of an afternoon in the woods.

Leaning back, his eyes closed, his mind took him swifly back from those pleasant memories to that autumn five years ago. "We could have seen it, should have seen it," he said aloud. "If I'd paid more attention all of it would have added up. Things could be so different."

CHAPTER ONE

A FEW MILES outside Miami near a gravel road paralleling a canal along the Florida Turnpike, a blindfolded man knelt on the ground that was to become his grave. His hands and arms were tightly bound and bleeding. In the heat and humidity of the spring night, the hard glare of the headlights gleamed off the sweat and blood that ran down his shoulders and arms and dripped from the tips of his fingers onto the dust. A runner who had skimmed both drugs and money from Raphael D'Angelo, his pleas to be spared fell on deaf ears.

"Please! Please! My wife, my children! Who will take care of them? I will give you the rest of my life . . ." he begged.

"Shut the hell up!" D'Angelo hissed as he pushed the man over on his stomach with the toe of his boot. "The rest of your life already belongs to me!"

"Madre de Dios!" the man whispered, his breath blowing small puffs of dust from the ground.

"Here, my friend. You do it," D'Angelo said, handing the semi-automatic pistol to Sterling. "You got to start somewhere. And don't forget to cover the top of the barrel. You don't want this asshole's brains all over your face."

No stranger to guns, Sterling liked the feel, the heft of the pistol. He stepped up behind the man, cocked the pistol, and without hesitation, fired a bullet into the man's brain. It had been easy for him to kill, painless. D'Angelo had seen the dark gleam in Sterling's eyes as he pulled the trigger and he liked what he saw.

The man's lifeless body lay still, his tears evaporating in the evening breeze, his blood staining an expanding circle. Raphael put his arm around Sterling's shoulder. "No flinch. I like a man who can kill and not flinch. Now, how about those stone crabs you've been wanting?"

On their way back to Miami, Sterling was unusually quiet.

Even he was surprised at the depth of his dark side. This seed of evil had developed early in his life and was unknown to almost everyone, even members of his family. Certainly he understood the family business functions of maintaining, strengthening, and expanding the business. But excitement and adventure had been lacking in his life since the beginning. Everyone knew he would succeed. Everyone knew he would continue the good works of the company. What no one could have foreseen was the flaw in his character that had developed because of the certainty with which everyone viewed his life.

He had always been aware there was a part of him no one else could see or understand. He was always testing the system, pushing himself into areas where he knew he shouldn't be. Indeed, where he had no reason, right, or need to be, yet he had to go there.

Its earliest manifestations were petty thefts from household servants and guests. Taking coins here, a few bills there, something out of a wallet or an unattended purse, always seemed to make his day more memorable. As he grew older and had access to more resources, his forays tended to become more serious and more dangerous. Mindless vandalism and breaking into homes when the residents were there excited him, made him feel more alive. The sheer lawlessness of these acts brought a euphoria he craved. Knowing the exposure of his criminal activity would put an end to his expected lifestyle made these acts even more compelling.

It was not until his college years that this compulsion began to gain prominence. Isolated use of marijuana and then cocaine led him into contact with an element of society he had never met before. While his family's wealth and position insulated him from fear of capture or conviction for any of these offenses, his contacts with this criminal element were like the first taste of whiskey to a future alcoholic. They provided a thrill which took on a life of its own.

The drugs led to violence and he soon learned the advantages of carrying a weapon and being accompanied by a body guard. He saw his first murder victim at nineteen and had been surprised at the morbid curiosity it had aroused in him. It had happened on a drug deal gone bad and he examined the lifeless victim closely. The two shots to the back of the head had rendered the man unrecognizable. *Damn*, he thought, *what a way to go! Never saw so much blood.* Only the approaching police sirens made him leave and even then, reluctantly.

"I'm going to do that to somebody sometime!" he said to his companion, as they turned to leave. *What a rush!*

Through his college years, he quietly associated with those who had criminal connections. His weekend trips to New York, Chicago, Washington, and Miami would bring him into casual contact with some of the most infamous underworld figures in the country. He was unerringly discrete about these contacts. Generally they would occur at popular clubs or restaurants and look like chance meetings. However, additional meetings were often arranged at private residences and he soon became an accepted and active member of this underground society.

When he assumed control of the corporation from his father, the business itself stayed free of any infection from this unseen side of its new president. Sterling Enterprises, Inc. was known and well-respected throughout the world. He was so careful that investigation of its business practices, associates, and financial resources would have disclosed no blemishes.

Though only a few years older in experience and viciousness, D'Angelo was ages ahead of Sterling. D'Angelo was a trusted assistant of one of the country's biggest drug and weapons dealers but he had no intention of remaining an employee any longer then necessary.

This weekend in Miami that led to Sterling's first killing had been carefully planned by D'Angelo. As smart as he was dangerous, he recognized early that Sterling was the kind of man who could be useful in many ways. He was always glad to see his young, rich friend, and he encouraged Sterling's sorties into the world of crime, drugs, guns, and death. Sterling usually needed little prodding to participate.

The lights of Miami brought Sterling back to the present and he asked, "Where do your friends go when they need to hide out?"

"Well, I guess that depends on how much money they have and how much trouble they're in. The members of the organization can usually help, and most everyone has their own thoughts about what they would do and where they would go if things got too hot."

"Wouldn't it be good," Charles thought aloud, "to have a safe house—a place you could go and really be comfortable? To wait until things cooled off a bit, to supply your men with hard-to-get items, or a place to help you get out of the country if you needed to?"

"Sure, all of us know places here and there where we could stay for a few days or a week if we have to. And there are people scattered around who can help you with ID's, transportation out of the country, and all that. What are you getting at?"

"I don't know just yet. But I've got a couple of ideas. You guys will be in Miami around Easter, won't you?"

"Sure. You know where we'll be."

"O.K. Give me a while to think about it and put something together. If it goes anywhere, I'll tell you about it then."

Where it went was Rapidan County, Virginia.

CHAPTER TWO

IT WAS JUST a slight motion, half-hidden by the scrub oaks, but unmistakable. More motion and, as John squinted through the early light, the entire silhouette of the deer materialized. First the head and neck, graceful, tapered, and still with a hint of that reddish-brown summer coat. It was a small deer and it had moved off before he could see the five-inch spikes which it had grown. He wouldn't have shot it even if he had seen the horns. He had killed bigger deer in other years and meat wasn't the reason for this hunt. Besides, it would have been a long drag up out of the river bottom for anything other than a real trophy. One like his friend Roy had taken three years ago.

No, on this day this hunt was for the memories. It was a day to relax, to escape town and family and phone calls—all of those responsibilities that demanded so much. "Just as well," he murmured. "If I'd shot him I'd have to go look. And at this range it would have been hard to miss. Then all of this fine relaxation would end and all of the hard work would start." *Better*, he thought, *to just ease back, settle in, and hope that no other deer disturbs me.*

As the sun rose higher, the temperature reached sixty degrees and the mist burned off the Rapidan River. The few flies that hadn't been taken away by the recent cold snap in central Virginia droned lethargically around the tree stand. John had built this stand nearly ten years ago and it had been a good one. Sitting twelve feet up between three pin oak trees, he found if he stayed long enough and was quiet enough he would usually take one or two whitetails a year. Not necessarily deer with large antlers but more than enough to supplement the meat supply in the freezer.

Since it was built only fifty or so yards from the Rapidan River, the noise from the rapids upstream were loud enough to hide any small noise he might make, yet not so loud as to let a deer sneak up on him. Besides, even when the deer didn't cooperate, the timeless movement of the river could hold his attention for hours. It was comforting to him to know the river had been there long before he was born and would survive long after he was gone. To experience a place like this, to share it occasionally, made him feel immortal. As long as he could come to the river, everything would be okay.

"Eleven o'clock—damn!" he muttered. If he was going to get back to the bank for his one o'clock meeting, he would have to leave. Leaving was always the hardest part; he never knew, with his schedule, when he would get back. Lowering his bow to the ground by a string that stayed tied to a limb at the tree stand, he grabbed his day-pack and climbed slowly down the seven steps to the ground below. All of his tree stands had seven steps; he thought it was lucky for him. At thirty-nine years old, it took him a bit longer than it once did to walk the mile up the ridge and back to his car. Sitting behind a desk five days a week didn't help either, though he tried to work out at least a couple of times a week. Usually he felt pretty good if he kept the lawn mowed.

Reaching his truck he loaded his gear and again thanked the powers that be that no respectable-sized deer had come by. *The morning was perfect just as it was, thank you very much*, he thought. *If I hurry, I have just enough time to swing by the house, shower, dress and get to my meeting.* It was always a shame to have to leave the woods to go to work, but at least his job gave him some flexibility.

Brenda, his wife of seventeen years, taught at the middle school in Rapidan County. They had met in college in Harrisonburg and married soon after he graduated. They had both grown up in Charlottesville, but hadn't met until his sophomore year at James Madison University.

Like most good relationships, theirs had developed slowly. John couldn't remember just when he had realized he loved her. The recognition of that love seemed like a slow burning fog lifting off the river; he knew it was there—something was there, but it had taken time and light and a little breeze to make it clear. Brenda had been more sure of her feelings but she'd had the good sense and patience to temper her emotions until his caught up.

A business and finance major, banking seemed like the right route for him to take. He liked working with people, and they, in turn, seemed to respond to his interest in them. Brenda had never wanted to do anything but teach. Since she was from a large family, caring for children came naturally to her and teaching them was an outgrowth of the love she harbored for all the children.

When their son Allen was born in 1987, their life together was on the way to being perfect. They had both agreed to settle in rural Virginia since even Charlottesville had gotten too large, too urban for them. Rapidan County, one of the smallest counties in the state, seemed ideal. Lying on the Rapidan River near its junction with the Rappahannock River, it was located centrally between Frederickburg, Culpeper, Charlottesville, and Orange. If they wanted any big-city entertainment, Richmond was only an hour and fifteen minutes away and Washington only an hour and a half.

Primarily rural, the county had many small and medium-sized farms and a few large dairy farms. There was some light manufacturing, mostly clothing and plumbing supplies. Its county seat, Clarkton, had the usual complement of an Ace Hardware, Revco, Food Lion, and three 7-11's. The new three-screen theatre was a real leap forward for Clarkton.

With a population of almost 17,000, the county gave a good account of itself and seemed to produce its share of hard-working, solid citizens for the Commonwealth. And it was still small enough so that you were expected to know at least half the people you met on the street by first name and wave at everyone you met on the road, whether you knew them or not.

Driving back to town, John thought he could tell the degree of kinship or affinity one person had for another by the wave they flashed as they passed. For someone who was unknown or a mere acquaintance a stiffening of one or two fingers was sufficient. If it was a business connection or someone called by their first name, all five fingers could come up and the hand might come all the way off the steering wheel.

Now if it was a good friend or someone on whom you relied or to whom you were indebted, or if it was the sheriff or the judge, a full-fledged wave was in order. Something like a salute, only with more feeling. Of course there were special waves for wives, lovers, and hunting buddies. And the teenagers' waves were a whole different category. Their waves, depending on the degree of hormonal activity associated with the recipient of the wave, varied from the simple raising of an arm to an apparent suicide attempt out the car window at a speed of at least sixty miles an hour.

Entering the bank with only a few minutes to spare, he stopped by Grace's desk. "Any messages?"

"Only a few—nothing important. Did you get all of your errands done?" she asked with a not too subtle wink.

"Yes, a real productive morning. If I'd gotten anymore accomplished, I couldn't have stood it."

"Fine, but before you go into the board room, you'd better get the rest of that camouflage paste off your neck." Handing him a handkerchief, she pointed to the bathroom.

"Sure can't fool you, can I?"

She smiled, "Don't even try."

CHAPTER THREE

ALLEN WOULD BE seventeen that fall and John didn't know it was possible to love a child the way he loved his son. An only child himself, he hadn't grown up with other children. He had good friends in school, but with no siblings, he had missed the closeness that comes with a large family, especially a large family in a rural community.

Allen was the first baby he had ever even held and, quite frankly, the experience had terrified him. The noise, the smell, the dependence of the child on him and Brenda was so foreign to him it was almost overwhelming. He had only gotten up with Allen the first few nights he had been home from the hospital. After that, Allen was Brenda's responsibility.

Brenda had seen all of this before. Growing up for her included an endless parade of babies being cared for by an equally endless troop of aunts, uncles, boyfriends, girlfriends, and neighbors. She knew, if she trained him right, that John would take to being a father and would probably do well at it. Subtle suggestions, a few hints here and there, a nudge in this direction, a poke in that, and every once in a while, a well-directed and well-deserved tantrum, served to mold her husband into a more than passable father. She took pains at the same time to encourage him to think he had figured out the process all by himself.

"I suppose you're going to teach him how to shoot too?" Brenda knew the answer to that question. John and Allen would do those kinds of things together and she wouldn't have stopped them even if she could have. She knew they would be cautious and careful.

"Now, Brenda, you know I grew up hunting and fishing and dad and his brother hunted much more than they fished. We had plenty of rabbits, doves, and squirrels to eat. And after a big game trip to the deep woods for a week or more we'd have venison too." Brenda knew that John loved the outdoors and had a deep respect for nature and all it can provide. And she knew he wanted Allen to be exposed to these same experiences.

"Just promise me you won't push him too much!" she said.

"I won't. It's just really important that Allen realize the value of this part of his world. If we don't teach him how to value his heritage, who will?" Brenda only nodded. It seemed natural for John to want his son to appreciate what he felt was worth having in life.

Seeing the look on Brenda's face, he said, "I know everybody develops different ideas about what's important. And I know I can't control what Alan ultimately will want to do. But I am going to see that he gets a good taste of hunting and fishing. Hopefully," he said with a wink, "some of that will stick." He knew if it did, Allen would be a better person for it.

Brenda had known for a long time, even before they were married, that a son of hers and John's would be introduced to all of this at an early age. She accepted that as part of life with John. She had even gone hunting and fishing with him a few times early in their relationship, but the thrill of these pursuits eluded her.

Growing up on a farm, she had become a more than adequate pistol shot. If she was going to be home by herself, she was going to be able to protect herself. She and John agreed this was especially important in rural areas where the police could be half an hour away when an emergency occurred. The Ruger .357 Magnum and the extra twelve-gauge shotgun were out of sight but never far away. Their presence was a comfort to her especially when John and Allen were away overnight.

John and Allen went on their first hunting trip when Allen was three. While he had only an air gun that fired no projectile at all, Allen was proud to be included and dutifully held the muzzle of the "rifle" toward the ground as he had been instructed. They hunted and fished together more and more as Allen grew older and he had progressed easily from his first lessons with a .410 to shooting uncommonly well with the .22 single-shot Winchester. This old rifle was one his grandfather had owned and had put more squirrels in the stew pot when John was growing up than he could remember. In the hands of his grandfather, had it done more than a little to see the family through the Great Depression. It helped John learn the art of the long shot many years go and it now was teaching its third generation of Richters.

Allen had killed his first deer when he was twelve, taking a nice four-point buck over the Thanksgiving holiday with one shot from his grandfather's old double-barrel sixteen-gauge Sterlingworth Fox. He was very proud of that hunt and had helped with the field dressing, dragging, skinning, and butchering. They had fried some of the tenderloin that night with some green peppers and onions, and, with hot biscuits, gravy and mashed potatoes, it was a meal to be remembered. At nearly seventeen, he had taken two more whitetail deer last season with the Winchester Model 70 John had given him for his sixteenth birthday.

John was proud of his son's ability and skill with firearms. Not because that proved him a competent teacher, but because it made Allen more confident, more self-assured, and brought him one step closer to being able to care for himself. And he was proud Allen understood and appreciated the sense of tradition that hunting with these firearms brought.

But tradition only held water for so long, and, with the opening day of the firearm season for deer fast approaching, Allen had made a request.

"Dad," Allen said, not quite able to look his father in the eye because he knew of his father's affinity for the bolt-action rifle, "can I trade my .270 in on another rifle?"

John took a quick look in Allen's direction. "Why would you want to do that? We just got that new scope on and got it sighted in good."

"Well, it takes so long to get off a second shot, I thought one of those new five-shot semi-automatics would be better. I'd be less likely to miss if I could get off two or three shots instead of one."

"You really think so?" *Well,* John thought to himself, *I guess I should have expected this. He's grown up with all these Rambo, Chuck Norris, Matrix, and Uzi-toting, automatic-weapon action movies. He'd believe the more shots you can get off in a second the more likely that you are to hit something. This needs to be nipped in the bud.*

"Do you remember all we talked about back when you were first starting this shooting business?"

"Sure, but I've learned all that and know how to get off a good first shot. I just thought . . ."

"If you get off a good first shot," John interrupted, "most of the time you won't need a second and third shot. For hundreds of years single-shot rifles were all people had to use. Then, whether it was for food or protection, if you missed with your first shot you went hungry or got shot by someone who was a little better and more patient than you.

"Now modern semi-automatics are excellent weapons and probably just as accurate as most bolt-actions. But you don't need anything else just now. Any fool can spray the woods with bullets. Better to stick right now with a rifle that makes you a better marksman.

"Besides, semi-automatics can be real expensive to shoot. You've heard Grandpa talk about going to the store in the late 1920's and 1930's to buy five twelve-gauge shells for a quarter and how stingy he had to be with those. Twenty-five cents was a powerful lot of money in those days, especially for a boy. He had the privilege of doing that because, of all his brothers, he was the best shot. With any luck he'd take those five shells and parlay them onto a week's worth of groceries."

"How could he do that? I don't think I've heard this one yet." Allen realized he had opened the flood gates and he might as well sit back and listen. He was going to get a lesson whether he wanted one or not.

But that lesson would be delayed. "I'll let Grandpa tell you all about that at Thanksgiving. Okay? But let's keep the .270 for now."

"Sure," said Allen, glad to have escaped with only a five or ten minute lecture on the advantages of bolt-action rifles. Besides, they would be at the hunting camp all next week and he'd have plenty of time to make his arguments then.

CHAPTER FOUR

SOME PEOPLE ARE like a cancer within a community. Most are open, obvious, and dangerous. Usually the criminal justice system removes them from society. But some of the deadliest are hidden, seemingly benign. These are the worst kind because the injury they cause and the damage they do isn't apparent and they grow, become more dangerous, more lethal every day they go undetected. So it would be with Charles Foster Sterling, III.

Born in Georgia fifty-one years ago into a well-respected, successful, and wealthy family, he was polished, well-educated, progressive, and seemed genuinely interested in the welfare of his adopted communities. The apparent epitome of an economic and social blessing on any city or community into which he came.

"Mr. Sterling, your three o'clock appointment is here—the reporter from the Washington paper."

"Thank you, Melinda," Sterling responded. "I'll be out in just a minute." *Damn*, he thought, *don't these groups ever get enough?* "Oh well," he muttered out loud, "free publicity—I'll take all I can get!"

"Come in, Mr. Baker. Thanks for being on time." Showing the reporter to a comfortable chair in the corner of his spacious thirty-fourth floor suite near 10th and K streets in downtown D.C., he turned on the Sterling charm for what he hoped would be an important interview for his company. Sitting comfortably next to the reporter, he smiled and said, "Fire away."

"Thanks, Mr. Sterling. I appreciate your time. I'd like to get some background information first, before we get to the future plans of the company. Can you start with your grandfather? I understand he's the one who began the company."

"That's right. You've done your homework. I like that. Charles Foster Sterling immigrated to the United States from England just after the turn of the century. He didn't have much formal education, but he did have an innate sense of timing and an uncanny ability to be at the right place at the right time with the right materials. Using those abilities, he created an international building supply empire by the late 1920's.

"He realized early that the devastation caused in Europe by World War I would require huge amounts of raw building materials, so he organized investors to control the supply of these materials. His intuition was correct and the European demand for those products materialized. In the 1920's, Sterling Enterprises, Inc. became one of the world's leading suppliers of American building materials. It not only met European needs but gained inroads into the development of the last American frontiers as well as the fledgling Asian and African markets. I've never known a man with a better vision of the future than my grandfather."

"But your company is much more than just building supplies now. Isn't that correct?" Baker interrupted.

"Of course." Sterling continued, "Our expansion into transportation industries was a natural by-product of the need to move these goods to and from all points of the globe. We concentrated primarily on providing these materials and on international maritime shipping and did that in a cautious, pay-as-you-go manner. Granddad was a really smart man, and, contrary to the excesses indulged in by many of his competitors in the 1920's and the euphoria which infected many businesses, he remained conservative and well-positioned, and the company stayed profitable. He made sure that we were one of the few international American industries not seriously harmed by the 1929 crash of the stock market and world-wide depression which followed."

"Do you think that was one of his greatest achievements?" Baker asked.

"Absolutely," Sterling agreed. "His vision and tight rein on the company enabled it to survive the depression and be well poised to respond to the world-wide demands for raw materials during the 1930's. By this time we had expanded the business to provide the raw materials to the European markets for the production of the weapons of war."

"And that brings us to a point I wanted to cover. What about the allegations that your company supplied raw materials to the Third Reich? Materials that were ultimately turned into weapons that were used to kill Americans?" Baker knew the danger of asking that question and looked curiously over his half-frame glasses to see Sterling's reaction.

Sterling too knew this issue would surface and kept his anger and temper where he always did, hidden from view. Leaning forward and staring intently at the reporter, very much like a fox would look a cornered rabbit, Sterling replied. "My grandfather knew the export of such materials to the German government was prohibited and he obeyed the law! He couldn't help it if many of the materials shipped to other countries ultimately found their way to the factories supplying weapons to Germany. Was it true that in the first years of the war many of the weapons aimed at each other across battle lines were there because of materials supplied by Sterling Enterprises? Yes, but we weren't responsible for those materials after they left our hands. We weren't responsible for where they ended up!"

"That's a convenient explanation, Mr. Sterling, but isn't that a little like an ostrich sticking its head in the sand? Your grandfather had to know."

"Just a damn minute!" Sterling interrupted. "There hasn't ever been any proof, any evidence whatever, that there was any intentional wrong-doing on this company's part before or during the war. And if this is where this interview is going, it's over!" Sterling knew the value of showing some anger at the appropriate time, and as he reached for the phone to call his assistant to have the reporter escorted out, his anger had the desired effect.

"Wait," said Baker. "I know that question was out of line. Can we continue?"

Relaxing, Sterling pulled his hand away from the phone. He nodded regally and continued, "We were heavily involved in the war effort in the United States and our role in supplying materials to any Axis powers before the War was never proven. By 1943, my father, Charles Foster Sterling, II, was running the business and he was among those specially honored by the White House after the end of the war for his contribution to the country's victory. And our stock remained strong and unblemished through the depression following the war. I'm sure you know that during the Korean War we served again as a major supplier and transporter of necessary war materials. Our company has been a cornerstone of every war effort this country has been involved in since 1917."

Taking his questions once more to the brink of the insulting, Baker said, "Yes, but all of this patriotism came with a price, didn't it?"

"Of course," Sterling snorted. "How long would we have stayed in business if we'd given all of this away? There had to be a profit and the wealth generated by four decades of successful management was substantial. We left Boston shortly after the beginning of the depression and resettled near Savannah, Georgia. We did keep a home on Cape Cod and a residence on the peninsula near the shipyards of Newport News, but Savannah was home to all of us after the 1960's.

"I was born in Savannah in March, 1942. And yes, I grew up with all of the advantages that wealth and position could give me. I was educated in private elementary and secondary schools, went on to Harvard, and got a degree in business management."

"Wasn't all of that expected of you? I mean, didn't you ever get tired of always having to live up to these expectations?"

"Well, sometimes. But I'll tell you, I've been lucky because I've always been just as at home at a private dinner table at the country club as shooting eight ball with classmates at a local bar. I'm really just a down-to-earth kind of guy. And yes, it was assumed that I would be the successor to my father. I seemed to take naturally to running a company and came quickly up through the company ranks until, in the autumn of 1979 when Dad retired, I was unanimously elected president and CEO by the board of directors."

"A real American success story then?" Baker asked.

"Yes, I guess you could call it that. And yes, I've been very fortunate. My father and grandfather laid a great foundation and I hope my legacy will be to continue their good work."

"Well, from the price of your stock and the dividends they pay, I'd say you were right on track."

"I hope you're right. And speaking of profits, I'd better get ready for my board meeting this afternoon. Will you excuse me?" Sterling asked, rising to usher the reporter out.

Leaving the room, Baker again looked around at all the trappings of wealth and power that surrounded Charles Sterling. *Yes*, he thought, *a real American success story. But there's more here. My radar is going off big time.*

CHAPTER FIVE

JOHN RECOGNIZED THE peculiar, rapid steps coming down the hall to his office even before he heard Roy's voice. "Hey, Grace, is John awake?"

"Well, I haven't heard any snoring in the last few minutes. I guess the phones are turned up too loud today." She knew Roy well and appreciated the special relationship he had with John. Roy was the kind of guy who could keep you young—or kill you, one or the other.

"Tell him to come on in. It'd be useless to try and stop him," John yelled. "Hi, Roy," he said, extending his hand. He always smiled when he saw him because Roy always looked like he had just gotten away with something and couldn't wait to make you an accomplice.

Slightly built, only 5'7" in his hip boots, he was wiry and could walk the shorts off everyone John knew. They had met right after he and Brenda had moved to Clarkton and had been hunting and fishing together ever since. Their relationship was solid because Roy was ten times the woodsman John would ever be. He knew that, accepted it, and took pleasure in learning from Roy. Roy, on the other hand, didn't hold his expertise over John's head. He didn't have to. He knew what he knew and he knew a lot. What's more, he wasn't stingy with it. Roy listened a lot, and when he spoke, you could count on it as gospel.

"I got a bite on the Fitzgerald place!" Roy exclaimed.

"You're kidding! Belleview? The one just up river from my favorite stand?"

"You got it."

"God, that's got 2,000 acres in it."

"2,187 to be exact."

"Hasn't it been on the market for almost five years? Ever since John Fitzgerald died, and his cousins in Michigan decided they didn't want to live in Virginia," John asked.

"Yeah, bless their hearts. If they wanted to live there I wouldn't be up for my commission. Six percent of the sale price. Whew! I can take a lot of time off next hunting season!"

"Wait a minute. You said you had a bite. Define bite. I've been fishing with you enough to know that a bite may be a glance, a nibble, or a full-fledged strike. Which is it?"

"Let me say this: I sent the contract to the buyer today with the Fitzgeralds' signatures already on it, at the price the buyer had indicated he would pay. Can't tell you what that price is. You'll know soon enough anyway."

"Damn, you lucky bastard. You'll be off all next season. There won't be a deer left in the woods. Wasn't the asking price over three and a half million dollars?"

"True, but they came down some. Still, it'll be my best commission ever. Maybe you and I will get that sheep hunt in British Columbia after all."

"Can you tell me anything about the buyer?"

"Not yet. He's a nice enough guy. Real quiet. Wants to get out of the city, away from the crime and drugs, but be close enough to run his business."

"What business?"

"I'm not sure. Manufacturing of some kind. But his bank references are as good as gold. What this guy wants, he gets. I'll fill you in later and I can get you introduced next time he's down. He'd be a great account!"

"Thanks. Hey, what's he going to do with the old home? It could be a real show place with some work."

"He seems inclined to fix it up. I gave him the historical information on it and he really seemed impressed. Boy, wouldn't the folks in the historical society love that. Another old home to add to the spring garden tour."

"Don't knock it. Places like that are part of what Rapidan County is all about. They're real treasures."

"I know. I'm just not as much of a history buff as you are. Listen, I gotta run. I'll call you about opening day."

"Okay. Hey, don't forget to hit this guy up for a permit to hunt. That farm's got a lot of deer on it."

"Yeah, I'll try later."

John always felt that the silence seemed quieter after Roy left the room. Maybe it was his intensity. Maybe it was just that they got along so well together that he felt his absence more strongly.

The Fitzgerald place, he thought. *God, I've always loved that place.* Shortly after they had moved to Clarkton, John was learning the county and riding some of the back roads when he came on it. Old Mr. Fitzgerald had long since let the entrance grow wild, but there was still something stately, even timeless, about the gravel road leading up on the knoll where the old plantation home stood. It was nearly half a mile from the main road to the house and the oaks that once lined the entrance road were memories now. Only huge stumps here and there were left to recall their glory years.

The house itself was still in reasonably good shape. Mr. Fitzgerald had always had the good sense to keep the roof repaired. Built in 1804 on part of an original land grant, the farm, which would have been called a "plantation" back then, had always been in the Fitzgerald family.

From the outside it looked like a typical house from the period—English basement and all, except it was larger then usual. The bricks were made from clay that came from down by the river and had aged well. The stone chimneys on each end of the house were immense. However, the remarkable feature of the house was not evident from the outside. Inside, instead of a center hall dividing the two halves of the house right from left, a hall ran the entire length of the front and stairways curved upward to the second floor at either end of the house. There was only one other like it anywhere within fifty miles that John knew about.

He had only met Mr. Fitzgerald a few times. Those had been pleasant meetings and he had really liked the old fellow, except that he wouldn't give him permission to hunt. Mr. Fitzgerald had shown him through some of the house and had given him a pamphlet about the history of it that had been published by the historical society during the Bicentennial in 1976.

The part that had fascinated him most was the history of the house during the War Between the States. John had learned early not to call it the Civil War. The proper Southern view was that since the South had seceded from the Union and formed a separate country, the war did not fit the definition of a Civil War. That is, it was not an internal struggle between two factions of the same country, but a war between two separate countries. Obviously, Mr. Lincoln had taken exception to that position and a lot of good men from both sides died to resolve the question.

Belleview lay on the east side of what had been a main road between Fredericksburg and Charlottesville. It fronted the Rapidan River for more than two miles and had a commanding view across the river, over much of Culpeper County, and all the way to the Blue Ridge Mountains over thirty-five miles away. During the war, whoever held the high ground on the plantation controlled the railroad and a lot of the land west of the river.

The early war didn't touch the plantation. The farm was too far south to be directly affected by the battle of First Manassas, though some of the cannon fire could be heard on the plantation that day. And it was way too far north and west of McClellan's disastrous Peninsula Campaign of 1862.

But a little later that year, the war finally came to the home. Another Union army under Nathaniel Banks had occupied Culpeper and General Lee didn't plan to let him leave there unmolested. To protect the rail connection between the Shenandoah Valley and Richmond, Lee sent Stonewall Jackson and 20,000 infantry to make the Union's stay in Culpeper as unpleasant as possible. Contact was made on August 9, 1862, near a small prominence just a few miles from Belleview called Slaughter's Mountain or Cedar Mountain.

For the better part of one of the hottest days that year, those Confederates and 10,000 Union soldiers did their best to kill one another. And they did a fair job of it. Jackson's numbers told and by nightfall the Federals were back across Cedar Run, retreating toward Culpeper. Banks had lost another battle to Jackson and would never live it down. The next day Federal reinforcements forced Jackson to retire back toward Orange but the wounded from the battle, hundreds of them, flooded local homes for miles, including Belleview.

Mr. Fitzgerald had shown John the darkly stained kitchen table used by the surgeons for an operating table. The table had long since been retired and stood, unused but revered, in a special corner of the parlor. Nothing was allowed to be placed on it except a small Confederate flag and an old tintype of Captain Isaiah Fitzgerald.

Captain Fitzgerald had been killed at the Mule Shoe during the battle at Spotsylvania Courthouse on May 14, 1864. His body was recovered after Lee shifted away from Spotsylvania toward Richmond and was sent by the Federal soldiers to Belleview, only sixteen miles from where he fell. The Captain was buried behind the house by his wife and sisters and every year since then, on May 14, fresh flowers had been placed on his grave. Every year until old Mr. Fitzgerald's passing. Since then, there was no one to remember.

As he turned back to the stack of loan applications on his desk, John wondered aloud, "I'll be real interested in seeing what becomes of that place."

CHAPTER SIX

"THIS IS EXACTLY what I had in mind," Charles Sterling said to Roy as he and his staff inspected the grounds at Belleview. "A perfectly beautiful rural setting, a restorable home and out-buildings. Close enough to New York, Washington, Tidewater Virginia, and Savannah so that I can be anywhere I want to in two hours or less, and, best of all, no crime."

"Well, Mr. Sterling, I'm glad you feel that way. When I got the inquiry from your office about the setting you were looking for, this place was the first one I thought of. You know the manor house was built well before the Civil War?"

"Yes, I read the history on the plantation that you sent me. The boarding school buildings were built, though, in the early 1920's?"

"Yes, the great-grandson of the original builder felt that a small private school for young men on their way to college would be very successful, given its proximity to the metropolitan areas. Unfortunately, the founder didn't count on the Depression and the school was only open for six years."

"Well, that was a bad investment for him, but it is absolutely perfect for what I need."

"What would you do with these buildings?"

"Well, I've been wanting to move my personal headquarters from the Washington area for a long time. I don't plan on moving the administrative offices here but I need some place out of the city. Some place quiet and peaceful. Some place where I can bring management and administrative people for conferences, seminars, things like that. I can't believe how perfect this is! The old dormitory over there behind the manor house will remodel nicely into suites for my people. I expect many of them will be coming for a week or two at least. The old building off to the side," he said, pointing to the right of the dormitory to a low two-story brick building, "will be perfect for lecture rooms, conference rooms, a dining hall. Didn't you say that there was already a kitchen in that building?"

"Yes, the old classrooms were upstairs in that building and the dining hall and kitchen were on the lower floor. So what you're really talking about here is a sort of convention or conference center for Sterling Enterprises?"

"Well, the manor house would be my personal residence, but it will serve the other purpose well too. I can't believe that we found a place so right this quickly."

"I'm certainly not trying to talk you out of buying the place, but isn't this going to be a bit large for that kind of operation?"

"Not at all. Sterling Enterprises employs, world wide, over eighteen thousand people in twelve different countries. We have the main office in Washington and three primary subsidiary offices in Los Angeles, Dallas, and New York. My concern is that this place might not be big enough."

"Well, I . . ."

"Do you have a contract with you?"

"I have the original ones signed by the Fitzgerald's. The asking price is three million, two hundred thousand. What did you want to offer them?"

"Three million, two hundred thousand," Sterling said without blinking.

"No counter-offer?"

"No. I think that's a fair price and I want to make sure that this place doesn't get away from me. Is a hundred thousand dollar deposit enough? I have a certified check with me."

Incredulous, Roy managed to stammer, "No problem. Would you like for me to introduce you to a local architect and some local builders about the renovations?"

"Not right now. I certainly want to use local people if I can. I know what a benefit that would be to the community, but you have to remember that I'm in the building-materials business and I expect we we'll use our own people for most or all of this."

"What about financing?"

"That's already taken care of, though I'll need to meet someone at a local bank for our local accounts, line of credit, and wire transfers."

"I can arrange all of that. Just tell me when you'd like to meet them."

"We can talk about that later. I need to see your local airport and I need to meet your people in Planning and Zoning as well as the head of the local Chamber of Commerce. I guess all of these renovations will have to go through them, plus I want to find out what I can do in the community to help out."

"Well, let's take care of this paper work first. How long will you be in town?"

"Two more days, at least. I'd like to get this closed as quickly as I can. I've notified my attorney in Arlington already. If you know who's representing the Fitgeralds and they can get us a signed deed this week, I can close on Friday."

Jesus Christ, thought Roy, *he's paying three-million-two for this and he's gonna close Friday. I think I may take the rest of the month off. With any kind of luck I may be able to make a career out of this guy.*

"Mr. Sterling, the Fitzgerald's lawyer is William Brown over in Clarkton. He's done a lot of work for them in the past and I'm sure he'll get right on this."

"Well, here's my attorney's card. Pass that on to Mr. Brown and have him contact them so that we can get this done this week. For the price I'm paying, the commission you're making, and the fee Mr. Brown will make, I'd think that he can overnight a deed to the sellers and get it back by Friday. Tell Mr. Brown that I know he's required to have certified funds to record a deed and I'll have that to his office by noon on Friday."

"Absolutely. I'll go by his office right now and then stop by and talk with the directors of the Chamber and Planning and Zoning."

"Fine, have them get in touch with Melinda here. She'll make all of the appointments. She always lets me know where I'm supposed to be and when I'm supposed to be there." Melinda, Sterling's personal secretary, gave Roy that kind of helpless, sideways look that told him that was never the case. She was, however, charged with making sure everything he wanted to get done got done.

Leaving Sterling and his entourage at the farm, he drove down the driveway toward the main road, thinking, *I can't believe this. This is a gold mine! Nothing this good has happened to Rapidan County in twenty years.* It would be a long time before Roy realized just how wrong he was.

As the realtor's car stirred up the dust on the gravel drive, Sterling said, "Sam, what do you think?"

"Well, Charles, I'm not at all sure why we're here. You wanna fill me in?"

Sam had been with Sterling Enterprises for over ten years. He had come to work there shortly before Charles had taken over in 1979 and had quickly become indispensable. Melinda had been with Sterling since he started to work for the company after his graduation from Harvard in 1964. They were two of only a handful of people who were aware of Sterling's other activities. Their devotion to him was not hampered by scruples involving the legality of what he wanted to do. Sam had, on more than one instance, cleaned up little messes Sterling had created and had always been both successful and discrete.

Both Sam and Melinda, and those few others in the organization who were aware of Charles's criminal forays, were inalterably committed to helping him complete whatever project he embarked on. This project was no exception.

"Sam, did you ever hear of the Underground Railroad?"

"You mean like a subway?"

"No. During the Civil War, the abolitionists would set up safe houses from inside the southern states to lead slaves north to freedom. It was called the Underground Railroad because once the slaves got in the system of safe houses, they wouldn't surface until they were far enough north to escape capture."

"O.K., but I still don't understand why we're here?"

"Well, you know that I have some friends who, every once in a while, find it advantageous not to be able to be found."

"O.K., but, like I said, what's that gotta do with us and this old farm?"

"Well, I want to help them out but I don't want to risk anyone finding out where this is or what we're doing. This is going to be a wonderfully restored private residence with a private conference center for Sterling Enterprises. It's also going to be something else, very different. You know I've wanted a central location to run the weapons/bootlegging operation we've been talking about. Well, even with Clinton's gun-ban not being extended, the demand for explosives and automatic weapons is always high and the legislation since 9/11 and the war on terrorism will keep demand up. And hell, we can get as much of that stuff as we want, when we want it, and name our own price. Circumstances have created a huge black-market opportunity for us.

"What we're also going to have is one-stop-shopping for my friends who need extreme changes or need to make themselves scarce for a while. Not only are we going to have some deluxe accommodations but if somebody needs new identification, a new identity, we'll do all of that right here. Print shop, plastic surgery, professional make-up artist, all of if right here. And if someone just needs to disappear for a while but still wants the advantages of a metropolitan area, we're going to be able to provide that too."

Sam slowly shook his head. He knew he couldn't change Sterling's mind but he was amazed at the scope of the project. As illegal and risky as it was, he knew he would become involved and do his best to see Belleview became what Sterling wanted it to be.

"And, as far as anyone at the company is concerned, this is just going to be my private residence. We'll be able to use the other facilities on the property for guests of the company, family, and all that, and they'll be able to stay at the main house or the guest house out back.

Sam look perplexed, "But there isn't a guest house out back."

"But there will be soon."

"Oh," he said aloud. *I should have known.*

All of this went just as quickly as Charles expected. When he put his money behind a project it usually was completed well ahead of schedule. While John Richter did not meet Sterling, since people like Sterling dealt only with presidents of banks and not vice presidents or loan officers, he had heard of the plans for Belleview and still hoped he might get a permit to hunt on the property. But the more he heard about what was being developed there, the more he figured Belleview would remain as inaccessible as it had always been.

Given the economic boost the town fathers expected from the development of Belleview into the headquarters of Sterling Enterprises, the zoning changes were quickly made and the necessary building permits issued.

As was his custom, Sterling accomplished all of this without seeming to impose his will on others. He had long ago developed a style which allowed others to believe that they were operating on their own volition. That while they were doing a favor or eliminating an obstacle for him, they were doing so not because he was who he was, but because there was significant and substantial advantage to them in doing so.

Sterling quickly made it clear he hoped to be a contributing member of the local society. He established the right contacts and made it obvious, by word and deed, that the community would benefit substantially by his presence. His demeanor made this conclusion obvious but at the same time, did not leave the impression that everyone should be humbled before him. He had a great deal of charm, an attribute he had developed and honed to a sharp edge. As construction continued at Belleview, these skills didn't fail him in Rapidan County.

CHAPTER SEVEN

OPENING DAY OF deer season in Virginia has a way of making equals out of all hunters. Men who ordinarily wouldn't have much contact with each other come together on common ground. Despite differences in their education, economic status, and profession, these friends enjoy each others' company and respect the varying points of view, skills, abilities, and shortcomings.

The group that always hunted together the first week at Judge Collins' farm in the southern end of the county were like that. Judge Collins was a retired Circuit Court Judge who had been on the bench in Rapidan, Orange, and Madison counties for almost thirty years. He had retired six years before, and with the heightened problems related to the increased drug activity in the area and unlawful use of firearms, he was sorely missed.

Judge Collins had also been very hard on game law violators who made the mistake of appealing their misdemeanor convictions to his court. He was always of the opinion that such a person, if convicted, was a disgrace to the fraternity of true hunters. A conviction of any such crime in his court always resulted in a stiff sentence.

Though he lived in Clarkton, Judge Collins had purchased his farm out in the country over forty years ago. While he had never farmed it for profit, he did see to it that it was managed carefully to promote habitat for wildlife. The populations of deer, dove, rabbit, squirrel, and quail always seemed to be better in his part of the county than anywhere else.

While there was an old farmhouse there when he purchased the farm, he soon built a proper hunting lodge on the land. Large enough to sleep a dozen or more, it was built far enough off the main road to be the perfect place to spend the opening week of deer season.

Nestled among a large stand of beech trees, the two-story cabin had a large stone fireplace and chimney and a twelve-foot wide covered porch that ran the entire length of the front and back. It seemed to have sprung naturally from the ground where it stood.

The cabin was built out of foot-thick oak logs which had been cut and shaped on the property. The walls on the inside had been left rounded, bark peeled off, and unfinished. While it had electricity, running water, and indoor plumbing, the heat needed was supplied by the fireplaces and by the huge, old Majestic wood cooking stove in the kitchen. The stove was off in the opposite corner of the large room which made up the entire front half of the downstairs. Judge Collins had always been amused when someone called his front room a "great room". Those hadn't been the style when he built the cabin. It was built simply to accomplish his purpose of bringing all of his friends together in one place to enjoy the companionship of friends who hunt together.

The front room was a museum of prior hunts. Several mounted deer heads hung silently from the oak logs. Framed photographs, large and small, sent to the judge by successful hunters over the years were scattered randomly across the walls.

These photographs, some black-and-white and so old they were tinged with yellow, were not necessarily of trophy animals. Many times they were of a boy's first small buck or a particularly elusive deer that had been especially difficult to harvest. Many of the photographs were simply pictures of hunters who had commemorated their trip, successful or not, in a photograph, so they could remember the pleasures of the camp in future years. The history of the cabin was told in these photographs. They spoke eloquently of the hundreds of fires which had burned in the fireplace, the meals cooked on the wood stove, and the endless stories, some true, some half-true, and some laughably false, which had been told and retold within the secure walls of this refuge.

The furniture which had accumulated in the cabin over the last four decades was a mix of castaways from homes all over Virginia.

Any old sofa, armchair, stool, or other semi-useful piece of furniture which no longer served a purpose in its original home seemed to make its way to the cabin. There was never any shortage of furniture and the mismatch of furnishings seemed to reflect, even complement, the diversity of the hunters who regularly stayed there.

Saturday, two days before every opening day of deer season, those hunters who were fortunate enough to be included in the hunt on the judge's farm would begin arriving. Most were locals, though every once in a while out-of-town guests would be invited.

This year would be John's fifth year spending opening day at the camp and Allen's second. Judge Collins was particularly interested in having young hunters included in this traditional hunt and had been impressed by Allen's skill the prior year. What had pleased him more than Allen's knowledge and safe handling of firearms was his ability to get along with the adult hunters in the group. While Allen was duly respectful he was not above defending himself if made the butt of a joke because of his youth or inexperience, and he would immediately take issue with anyone who felt that his Winchester was not *the* perfect deer rifle.

John and Allen had spent the better part of the week getting everything ready for their stay at the camp. It was only seventeen miles from home and they could, in reality, go home for anything they might forget. But once they got there, they preferred not to leave. This self-imposed isolation seemed to enhance the wilderness experience that was so much a part of hunting on the Collins farm. Anyone who made the mistake of needing to run back into town for a knife they had forgotten, clean underwear, or for any other reason not life-threatening, had to endure a great deal of abuse from the other hunters for the balance of the week. Not wishing to face any such ridicule, they had packed, unpacked, and repacked again to make sure they had everything they needed.

They also spent time at the rifle range sighting in and practicing with their rifles. Allen always hunted with his Winchester .270 caliber and John favored his Winchester Model 88 .308 caliber lever action. It was the first rifle his father had given him and it had served its purpose well for almost twenty years. As long as he kept a good scope on it, the rifle was one of the most accurate he had.

The variety of food which the hunters brought was also eagerly anticipated. Judge Collins had long ago dictated that since he provided the cabin and the farm, everyone else could provide the food. With the variety of hunters who came, the judge found there was always more than he could even sample. John decided to bring several dozen dove breasts from a successful hunt several months earlier in Culpeper. He had a special way he wanted them prepared and made certain all of the ingredients were safely tucked away in his truck before he and Allen left.

By two o'clock on Saturday afternoon, John and Allen were ready to leave. Brenda knew, once they left, she would not hear from them again until the following Friday evening. They might as well be in Alaska as at the other end of the county.

She had grown accustomed to the look in John's eyes that appeared every fall and she was beginning to see the same expression in Allen's. She knew if John didn't get away from the everyday routine, sooner or later she would have to make him go. When he was around too many people for too long his mood changed. She could sense in him an air of dissatisfaction, not with her but with his life. She would miss him, but understood that he needed to go. She recognized these trips were almost a religion to him; they gave him a sense of inner peace and self-reliance that comes with the solitude of the woods.

As the truck pulled out of the driveway she almost felt envious of the experience they were going to share. That feeling didn't last long when she remembered how many men were going to be staying in the cabin for an extended period of time and what the collection of them would probably smell like by the end of the week. She thought, *I wouldn't go there on a bet. I'd much rather know that they are there, together, being rude, crude, and socially unacceptable than to wonder what bar he's in, how much he's had to drink, or who he may be with. Its not something I want to do and it sure is something they need and it seems to keep them off the streets and out of trouble.* Besides, between her job and the other hunting widows, she'd have plenty of company if she wanted it during the week.

CHAPTER EIGHT

THE TRIP FROM home to the camp was short in time but long in anticipation. Traveling the last several miles on gravel roads and turning down the lane which led to the cabin, both John and Allen could feel their excitement growing. The final half mile to the cabin was through stands of mature oak, several grainfields, and an area of cut-over hard woods. This thick growth was almost impenetrable but was some of the best hunting on the farm.

As they pulled into the clearing around the cabin, the warmth and hospitality of the setting reached out for them. There was just enough room in the clearing for the cabin, the meat house, skinning shed, and half-dozen or so vehicles.

As he and Allen got out of the truck, they could smell the smoke coming from the chimney and see the soft glow of the lights inside the cabin. As they got closer, they could hear the voices of some of the hunters already deep in conversation.

The inside of the cabin was a cloud of sensations. Wool jackets, many different styles of camouflage clothing, fluorescent orange caps, and safety vests were scattered about. The aroma from the contents of several pots on the wood stove coupled with the smell of freshly oiled rifles in the gun rack and the warm scent of leather boots, belts, and shell pouches all seemed to reach them at once.

As they closed the door behind them, some of the conversations halted briefly as the other hunters acknowledged their presence with a wave, a smile, or a hello. But there was a swirl of discussions, all different but related to the hunt, that went on uninterrupted.

"Bullshit," Roger said, "that's just plain bullshit!"

"You're trying to tell me that a regular Remington Power Point Bullet is just as effective as Winchester's Fail-Safe bullet?" Dave asked.

"Have you even tried any of the new Fail Safe bullets?" asked Dave.

"No," said Roger, "I haven't and I don't need to! I know in the 90's they were forced to take the pistol bullets off the market but you can still get the rifle bullets. My point is that the loads that we've been shooting for the last ten years are all you ever need on whitetails. All of this new designer ammunition is just bullshit. You don't need all of that controlled expansion, penetration, and all that other crap for whitetails."

"Maybe not, but think about two things. First of all, there are a couple of deer around here that are head and shoulders above the rest. You're trying to tell me that if you got a shot at one of those really huge bucks through some thick brush you wouldn't want all the power and penetration you could get?"

Before Roger even had an opportunity to speak, Dave went on. "Besides, you keep talking about going to Alaska bear hunting. If you're really serious about that, are you trying to tell me that It wouldn't be good to hunt with the same kind of bullets here that you would be hunting with there? You'd be crazy to go on a hunt like that and not be familiar with what your bullet can do. When you're forty yards from a thousand-pound brown bear, there isn't time to wonder whether or not your bullet is going to work."

"Well," Sam chimed in, "I've shot the Power Points and Fail Safes and I still like the Nossler Partition Bullet better than either of those. The Fail Safe's expansion and ability to do a lot of damage are great, but the Partition Bullet has been around longer. If I were going up against a grizzly or brown bear, I'd want to use that bullet."

"What do you think, John?" asked Dave, one of the county deputy sheriffs. "I know you've shot some of the new Fail Safes in your .308 and I know you like them. Don't you think they're the best thing since sliced bread?"

"Oh no—you're not going to get me into that discussion. I think you should shoot whatever your rifle shoots best and whatever you have confidence in. If you don't think you're going to hit anything with a Fail Safe or Partition or Power Point then you probably aren't. Any of those bullets will do a better-than-average job on a deer, and if you're thinking about larger game, then that's just something you need to be comfortable with." Having satisfied Dave and Roger that they both were right, John and Allen went over to pay their respects to Judge Collins.

The arguments about velocity, penetration, calibers, and types of bullets seemed to trail off and be enveloped by other conversations. The next loudest seemed to be one comparing the relative merits of traditional walnut stocks on high-powered rifles versus the weather-resistant composite graphite stocks so popular now. John couldn't see which hunters were involved but the conversation was, like the others, animated.

The judge was sitting in one of the easy chairs near the fire, talking with several other hunters. As they approached the chair it was clear he was holding forth on an issue particularly important to him. It was always easy to tell when not to interrupt the judge. Just as he had done when he was on the bench and was making a point he considered to be critical, he leaned forward, cocked his head slightly to the right, and stared intently at the individual to whom his comments were directed. John and Allen stood listening from a respectful distance until the moment Judge Collins noticed their arrival. Breaking off the conversation he stood quickly and greeted them with a warm, "Hello."

"Well, Son, its good to have you back. I see you're still carrying that old Model .270. You think you can hit anything with it this year?"

"Yes sir, I hope so," Allen said with a shy grin. He knew the judge was just teasing him because he had seen the one-shot kill he made on the four-pointer opening day last year. Judge Collins knew Allen could shoot and knew how to handle himself in the woods with a firearm. To Judge Collins it was more important for a man to know how to relate and react to others than it was for him to kill the biggest buck in the woods. Allen was mature enough to take the kidding that went on in the camp and laugh at himself along with everyone else. It didn't pay to be too thin-skinned around this group. Judge Collins got the reaction from Allen he expected and his appreciation for the young man grew.

"John, it looks like you haven't ruined this boy. Maybe if he gets old enough and moves away from you quick enough we may save him yet," the judge said with a hearty laugh. Bill and Jim, two of the regulars at the cabin, came over and joined in the conversation, welcoming John and Allen to the camp and offering to help unload John's truck. That chore taken care of in short order, everyone's attention turned to the pots on the wood stove.

CHAPTER NINE

AS WITH ANY group of hunters, no matter how small the group, there is always at least one person who is, or believes himself to be, the camp cook. In this group it was Rick Bannister. Rick was a production-line worker at a local plumbing parts manufacturing company, and he was without question the finest cook in camp. Rick had grown up in the hills of West Virginia. Losing his father at an early age in a coal mine explosion, his mother and two older sisters all had to work to keep the family together. Rick, the oldest of five boys, was left with the duty of watching the younger children as well as having dinner on the table every evening. Out of necessity, he had learned to use bits and pieces of whatever was available to improvise meals that were at least edible. While he admitted to many early mistakes, through his teenage years he had mastered the art of making a decent meal out of little or nothing.

Married and with three children of his own now, he continued to do most of the shopping and all of the cooking at his home. To him, getting in the kitchen and preparing a meal was therapy. It was an opportunity for him to do something creative; to do something different, something he could watch others enjoy. Since wild game had been a staple in West Virginia, he was extraordinarily adept at fixing meals at the cabin which were indeed memorable.

For this particular Saturday night, Rick had gotten several tenderloins from a young buck his brother killed bow-hunting the month before. This particular buck had been feeding in an apple orchard and in clover fields nearby. *This ought to be prime material,* Rick thought, as he sliced and floured the meat.

Taking the backstraps and trimming them carefully, he sliced the lean, dark red meat into half-inch thick rounds which were about three inches wide. Getting about thirty slices off each loin, the sixty or so slices were piled on a large platter and covered with a paper towel while the rest of the meal was prepared.

Food at the camp had to be good, solid, stick-to-the-ribs stuff. In addition to the tenderloin, Rick had precooked some sliced red potatoes and had layered them in a large Dutch oven with thin slices of carefully reserved Videlia onions from last spring's crop along with generous portions of whole milk, butter, and grated sharp cheddar cheese. Liberally sprinkled with cracked pepper and other seasonings he wouldn't reveal, this casserole went in the oven of the wood stove to bake.

Rick would only serve green beans the way his mother had taught him. Not blanched, undercooked, crunchy, and unseasoned as in many restaurants, but cooked over a two-day period with pinto beans, chunks of salted pork, smoked hog jowl, and ham hock thrown in for good measure. Rick had started this pot of beans the morning before at his house and now they sat on the back of the wood stove to simmer for several hours. This double cooking, Rick knew, insured a great pot of beans. *True*, Rick thought, *these guys wouldn't want to have their cholesterol level checked after a big dish of these, but once a year I figure they owe it to themselves.*

While the biscuits were rising, Rick sautéed the green peppers and onions that would cook along with the tenderloin. Using a huge fourteen-inch Griswold cast iron skillet, he began talking to anyone who would listen about the advantages of cast-iron cookware.

"I don't care who you are, how much money you got, or what you cook with, you can't do better than a good ol' Griswold skillet. My grandmother used one to fix some of the best meals I ever ate. She used it to keep my grandfather in line too. Believe me, sometimes he really needed it. I've got my grandma's eight-inch Griswold skillet at the house and it's as good as the day it was made. I'd like to think I was going to last as long as that skillet will.

"I've tried some of the fancy new stuff. The, what do you call it, Calphalon. My wife gave me a piece of that for Christmas last year. It works okay, but food just don't taste the same if it's not cooked in a well-seasoned iron skillet. I see on TV all the fancy chefs in their nice clean jackets and hats usin' real bright copper pots and pans, and I guess that's okay if you're going to pay $100.00 a piece for a meal. But if you want just good ol' plain American food, there just ain't nothin' better to cook it in."

And sure enough, on the walls on either side of the wood stove hung an enviable collection of cast-iron skillets in various sizes together with muffin and corn-stick pans. On the shelf next to the stove sat two huge cast-iron roasters complete with covers. All were well-seasoned and veterans of hundreds of some of the greatest meals ever served in the county.

On the back of the stove was one of the most important pieces of equipment in camp-the twenty quart cast-iron soup pot. On the first night in camp it had only water, onions, bay leaves, a bit of cracked pepper, garlic salt, a stick of butter, and three or four beef bones in it. This simmering pot contained what would become the soup stock which would be added to after every meal for the entire week. The mixture which would evolve in this pot would change on a daily basis, depending on what scraps and left-overs there were from each meal. After breakfast, any left-over bacon or sausage would go into the pot. There usually weren't any left-overs from lunch, but after dinner, any remaining potatoes, rice, meat, or vegetables would be scraped into the pot. Occasionally it was necessary to add additional water to keep the soup from turning into a thick gumbo. For years, every dinner at the cabin, beginning on opening day and ending at the end of the week, began with a steaming bowl full of what all the hunters called Rick's Evolution Soup. It was never the same twice and was never allowed to run out.

By the time everyone had unpacked their duffel bags, placed their rifles in the rack in the corner of the front room, and said their hellos, Rick was well on the way to having sautéed all of the peppers and onions. The vegetables were drained while the tenderloin, previously floured and sprinkled with pepper and garlic powder, was seared briefly on both sides. Once all the venison had been browned, it was added to the skillet with the peppers and onions. The tenderloin, vegetables, rolls, potatoes, and beans all matured at about the same time and when Rick announced, "Soups on!" there was no hesitation in anyone's step to come to the table.

Rick could always judge how good a meal was by the amount of conversation around the table. He was especially pleased tonight to hear total silence from the group. Everyone knew the best compliment they could pay Rick would be to eat everything he had cooked and he wasn't disappointed.

One of the nice things about being the camp cook was that he didn't have to worry about any of the clean-up. It was everyone else's responsibility not only to bring food to camp but, after the meal, to do the cleanup. With a dozen or so hunters in camp, this was never a burdensome chore. This particular night, John and Allen agreed to go ahead and get their kitchen duties over with.

In many camps it wouldn't be unusual for many of the hunters to pour a stiff after-dinner drink, or perhaps more than one. Judge Collins had never prohibited alcohol at the camp, and most of the men there did drink. However, the experience of hunting at the cabin was generally more than enough to keep everyone excited and on their toes. All of these men had found that the hunters who tended to over-indulge while in any camp were generally there to drink first and to hunt second. Everyone in camp this week had long since learned to avoid the heavy-drinking hunters. Judge Collins had said many times that if a man needs to use hunting as an excuse to drink, you'd best stay away from him. First of all, that person was not a hunter; second, he was not a sportsman and third, he may kill you and not even know it.

As he and Allen worked on the dishes, John could still catch the gist of the conversation by the fireplace.

"Most of 'em are road hunters anyway. Their idea of hunting is to get in their jacked-up, four-wheel drives, turn on the CB's, and chase each other around the county all day. It sure makes it tough on the real hunters when some road hunter gets permission to hunt on a two-acre piece of land, turns his dogs loose, and then spends the rest of the day chasing them through ten thousand acres of woodland."

Dave, the deputy sheriff, joined in. "That's really true. They're the real black sheep in the hunting community. And they're really hard to catch. There are more of them than there are of us, and what usually happens is they'll put one truck at one end of the road and another truck at the other end with their hunters in the middle and wait for the dogs to chase a deer across the road. If one of us or a game warden goes down the road past either of the trucks, a quick call on their CB radio gets everybody back in their trucks and their guns unloaded. By the time we get there, they're not breaking any laws. They know they're criminals, we know they're criminals, and all of the landowners know they're criminals, but catching them and getting them convicted is tough to do."

"Yeah, and they're making it almost impossible for us to find places to hunt," said Rick, who had now taken off his apron and joined the crowd. "I remember twenty years ago when I moved here, you could hunt almost anywhere you wanted to. All you had to do was be polite, show some respect to the landowner, maybe bring them a hind-quarter every once in a while, and you had the run of the county. We've had a real problem with people moving into the county from the city. Those people think now that they live in the country, they can go wherever they want to and do whatever they want to and not worry about what the landowner thinks. Those folks aren't real hunters. They're either city folks who happen to own a gun and a truck, or country boys turned into outlaws.

"Now there's one local bunch and that's just what they are, outlaws. They've lived here all their lives, they've always hunted wherever they wanted to, and they're not going to let anybody else tell them where they can hunt. These guys aren't hunters either. They're just plain poachers. We've always had people like that and I guess we always will. The only thing we can do is try and correct the image that they project and try to make other folks see that we aren't all like that. The problem with that is the road hunters are usually all the non-hunting people see because those cowboys are always up and down the roads."

"That's true, Rick," said Judge Collins. "Don't get me wrong, I truly love to hear a well-trained pack of dogs run deer, coons, or rabbits. I grew up on that kind of hunting. And I've been lucky enough to go on several trips out west to hunt bear and mountain lion with dogs. It's a great, challenging hunt. And those anti-hunters who have stopped the hunting of bears and mountain lions are reaping what they have sown because now the animal populations are up and the lions are killing more people.

"And," the Judge continued, "let's not forget the great heritage of bird hunting with dogs. It's a method of hunting that goes back centuries and it's just about as exciting as hunting can get. Besides, the conservation groups associated with hunting with dogs, like Ducks Unlimited and Quail Unlimited, have done more for wildlife conservation than all the anti-hunting groups combined.

"The real problem with deer hunting now in our part of the state is we don't have the large farms and open space we used to. Even twenty or thirty years ago, the dogs could run a long ways without coming near a subdivision. Now we just don't have the luxury of that much land.

"The kind of guys that you're speaking of, the road hunters, the kind of people that I convicted for years whenever we could catch them, are the ones who are making it easy for the anti-hunting groups to make the progress that they have. If we aren't able to correct the image of the American sportsman, we may have a difficult time in the future continuing to hunt."

"Well, that's depressing enough. What do we need to do?"

"What would be real helpful would be for the real hunters to make more and better contact with the farmers and other land owners. I know that my family and I are always impressed when someone comes up to the farm, politely introduces themselves, and asks for permission to hunt. While we don't always give it, those people who show up and make a good impression and are polite stand a better chance of getting a day out on the farm. These roughnecks who come thundering up in big trucks spraying mud and gravel all over everything, dribbling tobacco juice down their chin, and with a pickup bed full of beer cans don't stand a chance of hunting on my farm—and they never will."

The conversation continued for hours in front of the fire. As the evening wore on, the number of hunters dwindled as did the flames in the fireplace. Ultimately, only Judge Collins and John remained. Both were quiet, lost in the timelessness of the firelight and silence.

Sunday, the day before opening day, was spent doing camp chores—splitting firewood, cleaning the meat house and skinning shed, and sighting-in all the rifles. That was always an important part of the pre-season ritual. It was an opportunity for all of the hunters to demonstrate their ability as marksmen, and it was an unfortunate hunter whose scope was not properly sighted-in or who flinched as he squeezed the trigger. Many an excuse for a missed opportunity at a deer began at this sighting-in ceremony, and it was with great satisfaction that John noted he and Allen both shot acceptable groups at the one hundred yard target behind the cabin.

Roy had come to camp that morning and as usual, had shot a tighter group than anyone else. He had missed the Saturday evening dinner, putting the finishing touches on closing the sale of Belleview. Given the magnitude of that deal, everyone forgave his absence. Roy was the best shot in camp and had earned his expert marksman badge during his military career. It was seldom any deer he shot ran far after the trigger was pulled.

"Good optics and a slow squeeze," said Roy, "that's the best thing for you. You should sit around the house and practice squeezing the trigger. Dry-firing, you know. If it's too tight you should get the trigger pull reduced. Any good gunsmith can do that. The gun companies now are so afraid of law suits for accidental or unintentional firings that they set their trigger pulls too heavy. There's no way you can squeeze a trigger softly enough to get off a good shot when you have to put so much pressure on the trigger. I'm not advocating hair triggers but three pounds is pretty good. You have to exert less pressure but can still get a nice crisp shot off."

On Sunday everyone chose stands for opening day. When their alarms went off at four o'clock Monday morning, it seemed that everyone's feet hit the floor at the same time. Everyone, that is, except Rick, who had already been up over an hour to start breakfast.

Strong coffee, bacon, eggs, white bread toasted on the stove, and left-over scalloped potatoes were on the menu. Everyone was responsible for their own lunches and they had been packed and bagged the night before and put into the refrigerator. All had learned long ago to use the magic marker hanging from the string on the refrigerator to put their name on their lunch bag. Few of their tastes in lunches were the same and being disappointed at lunch once was enough to convince everyone to identify their own bag.

Opening morning dawned cloudy, misty, and cooler than usual for mid-November. It was not a perfect opening day but still there were several deer taken. Judge Collins usually asked the hunters in camp not to shoot anything smaller than a big six-pointer or a small eight-pointer. Early in the season, however, he would usually ask one or two people to take a small young buck for camp meat and for his freezer back in town. With these requirements filled on opening day, everyone settled in for the rest of the week, trying to tag a whitetail with a better-than-respectable set of horns. There were plenty of does, but doe season wouldn't come in until late December and no one was about to shoot one out of season. That would be a sure-fire way to never hunt with the judge again.

The weather got better as the week went on. While Roger, the high-school teacher, killed a nice ten-point buck on Wednesday, John and Allen hadn't seen anything large enough to use up any ammunition on.

On Friday morning, the last day of this week's hunt, Allen had taken his portable tree stand up on a high ridge covered with oak trees. He had seen several round, muddy scrapes along the ridge that told him a buck was marking the territory for the fall mating season. Further, he had seen the heavy acorn crop for this year, some of which was already falling. He and John had talked about it and they had decided it would be an excellent spot for the last morning's hunt. John had another similar ridge in mind and they separated early that morning to hunt on their own.

Allen had only been in his stand for about an hour when the eight-point buck came down the ridge. Three does had crossed in front of him about twenty minutes before, and though the mating season had not begun, the buck seemed interested nonetheless. When the buck stepped out from behind two large oak trees about a hundred and ten yards away down the ridge, Allen had put the crosshairs of the scope behind the deer's front leg and slowly begun squeezing the trigger. The report of the .270 echoed through the woods and he temporarily lost sight of the deer. A fraction of a second after the shot he picked the buck up running down the ridge. Thinking he might have missed he began to chamber another round for a second shot, but before he could, the buck collapsed and slid a few yards downhill.

It was easily the largest buck Allen had killed and made a great finale to the week's hunt. He found his father and together they field dressed the buck and slid him down the hill to a logging road where they could pick him up with the truck.

As he helped Allen, John thought, *I haven't seen a deer all week large enough to shoot and I don't even care. Seeing Allen take a nice buck is more than enough satisfaction for me for this week.* He had learned long ago that the memories of his son's successes that he had shared were just as precious as any luck he might have on his own.

John and Allen got back home shortly before noon on Saturday. Even though they could have hunted on Saturday, it always seemed to take several days to get over this opening week hunt. That was especially true when either one or both of them had taken a deer. And Thanksgiving was the next week and John's father would be coming to visit from South Carolina. Besides taking care of all of the hunting gear from opening week, getting Allen's deer into the freezer, and getting ready to hunt over Thanksgiving, John was sure Brenda would have a long list of honey-do's for him too. With winter coming on he wasn't looking forward to the chores, but knew their completion would put him a couple of steps closer to getting back to the woods again.

CHAPTER TEN

THE ECONOMIC BOOM that some had expected with the renovation of Belleview never developed. Though there was a great deal of activity on the old plantation, local contractors, builders, and building-supply houses saw little economic benefit from it. The public explanation was that since his company was in the building business, it was much more economical to use thier own company labor, materials, and supplies. That, to most people, was logical, and Sterling assured everyone that the county would benefit secondarily from increased traffic to and from the farm, purchases made by employees, and supplies purchased for guests. The true reason for not using local labor was the need to keep the real purpose of the renovation hidden from public view.

Roger Brownley, a company architect and close associate of Sterling's, was one of the few company men who knew the plan behind Sterling's presence in Rapidan County. Spreading his plans for the manor house across a sheet of plywood suspended between two saw-horses in what was to be the dining room, Roger spoke intently to his boss.

"Charles, you know you can do what you want to do here without spending a fortune on this old home. This ground-up restoration is going to cost a mega bucks."

"I know, but it has to be done this way. I don't want a hint of suspicion about why I'm here or what we're doing. If the manor house and guest house are not completed with historical accuracy, people may look too closely at the conference center. I want the locals to be able to visit the manor house on occasion and see that there's nothing odd about our presence here."

"O.K.," said Roger, "but you'd better be ready to spend some serious dollars on this place. I think we can save the floors but all of the interior walls have to be stripped, reinsulated, and replastered. These twelve-foot ceilings are going to be a real bitch. The plaster molding is going to be incredibly difficult to copy, but I think I know someone who can do that. Needless to say, we'll have to rewire and replumb the whole house."

"But I want all of that done so that the modern conveniences are as unobtrusive as possible. It's important that the home appear to be as it was in the 1800's. I need the locals on my side and doing an historically correct renovation of this place will get a lot of the old fogies in my corner."

"That goes for the bedrooms upstairs too?"

"Absolutely! I have Sam lining up a couple of local folks to scour antique shops for period furniture, beds, pictures, and all that crap. This house has to be a showplace to deflect attention from the other buildings. Like I told you, you've got a blank check."

"Music to my ears. When we get through with this house and the guest house, you'll think it's 1860."

"That's exactly what I need. Now let's go over to the old dorm. I want to see your plans for the heart of this little venture."

Walking out of the back of the partially-remodeled manor house and across the lawn toward the old dormitory, it would have been difficult for anyone to imagine what Sterling had in mind for the other buildings. Separated from the main house by several hundreds yards and a good number of large old oak and walnut trees, work had not yet begun on what the public would believe was an elaborate center for Sterling to house and entertain business associates.

Looking down the darkened center hall of the old dorm, the damp, musty smell of aging wet brick and wood seemed to make his vision of the property impossible. The dormitory and other outbuildings had been abandoned for three-quarters of a century and, though structurally sound, showed the ravages of time. Ceilings and walls had large holes and cracks in them, exposing the old lath boards.

Pigeons, rats, and mice had taken up residence in every nook that would shelter them. Wind-blown rain had long since saturated the wooden floors, making it dangerous to walk without being extremely careful.

Unrolling the plans on an old table propped up in the corner of one room, Roger explained his vision for the building.

"It's about the perfect size for what you want to do. At two stories and fifty feet wide by a hundred feet long we have five thousand square feet on each floor to play with. Like you wanted, I've designed the ground floor and second floor into eight one thousand square-foot-plus suites. While they'll all be a little different in design and all be decorated differently, they'll be state-of-the-art accommodations. We'll give the Waldorf a run for their money.

"There's a master bedroom in every suite. In a couple of the suites there are two smaller bedrooms for other guests, but in six of the suites there is only one additional larger bedroom. I thought probably most of your guests would be bringing at least one or two extra folks with them and some even more."

"That's true, and if anybody wants to bring more people than one suite can hold, then they can rent two."

"We've put in every conceivable amenity. There's a wet bar in every suite, sauna, Jacuzzi, intercoms, and cutting edge sound systems. We'll also have topnotch security systems installed. Cameras and audio and motion detectors will be installed and monitored twenty-four hours a day from the control room downstairs."

"Good, good. For what it will be costing these people to come here, I don't want them to have anything to complain about. What about the private exits?" asked Sterling.

"That's been one of the fun parts of this job. If you look at the plans for the first and second floors, you'll see that the master bedrooms in each of the eight suites are in the four corners of each of the two floors. In each of those four corners there appears to be a large walk-in closet. What we'll do is put a false wall in each of these four corners. This will conceal a hidden stairway that'll provide a private exit for each of the eight suites to two tunnels, one at each end of the building. These tunnels will run from each corner of the building down behind the dorm, connect about a hundred and fifty yards below the dorm, and then lead another two hundred and fifty yards off the back ridge to an underground garage about a hundred yards from that gravel road along the back of the property."

"Roger, you know I don't care what this costs, but how are we going to hide all of this construction from all the local folks who'll be in and out of here?"

"I don't think we're going to have a problem with that. First of all, the tunnels are going to be behind the dorm so that people who drive up to the main house or even come over to the dorm won't notice the excavation. Besides, the ground behind the dorm is going to be torn all to hell anyway putting in the septic field large enough to accommodate this size facility. We'll use precast concrete tunneling. We can probably do all the excavation we need within forty-eight hours. We can lay the foundations for the two tunnels in another two or three days and probably have everything in place and covered back up in less than two weeks. During that time we'll need to restrict access to the property. I know you're doing that already anyway but maybe even be a little tighter."

"My people can handle that. I think if we could get all that installed and camouflaged within two weeks there shouldn't be any problem. How many cars will the underground bunker at the end of the tunnel accommodate?"

"That depends of the size of the cars, but I'm figuring at least eight large vehicles or ten small ones."

"Make it big enough for twelve large cars. Though most of the people who come here won't be going anywhere else, they'll all want to know that they have transportation available if they need it. Besides, I want to make sure I have a couple of extra vehicles ready if we need them.

"This really looks great," Sterling continued. "The hotel part of the plan would pass anybody's inspection. What about the basement?"

"That's where I've had the most fun. Once you told me what you needed down there I spent a ton of time making sure that everything's perfect. You're not going to believe what can be accomplished there."

"Well quit bragging about it and show me."

Rolling up the plans, Roger said "Let's go outside and around back where you can see a little better,"

They walked out the front entrance of the dorm and around the south end of the building. Looking at the old dorm from the front, the presence of a basement couldn't be detected. And given the age and size of the building, the presence of a full basement was remarkable. It had primarily been used for storage though no one really knew why the original builder had gone to such extra expense. However, it was a tremendous advantage for Sterling's plan becase it was the heart of his clandestine operation.

Unrolling the plans on the tailgate of his truck, Roger began describing his plans for the basement with obvious pride.

"From the outside, here in the back, we'll put a covered four-car garage. We'll just build it into that knoll on the north side of the dorm and connect it to the old building. The fact that there are only two doors into the original old basement helps us since we don't have to deal with people looking in windows. We'll leave those two doors the size they are, only replacing them with new security doors. When you go in either of those doors, it will appear as if you had just stepped into storage rooms. But you can see from the plans that the corner doors leading out of these two storage rooms actually lead back into the different areas of the renovated part of the basement. This hallway to the north leads to the medical wing of the basement. I've had several of my people investigate and get plans for the most up-to-date plastic surgery operating and recovery rooms in the country. That's exactly what we have here. These three rooms in the north corner will serve as examining room, operating room, and recovery room."

"What about all the equipment?" asked Sterling.

"We've got that covered too. We already have on order all of the best equipment that any plastic surgeon would need to do any kind of operation. This is a facility that any metropolitan hospital would be proud of. And we're installing everything that would be necessary for liposuction."

"You know, it seems like it would be easier to just not eat quite so much," Sterling smirked, "but you're right. The people who come here will want to leave with a totally different physical appearance. Being able to remove twenty to forty pounds from someone and have all the bruises and other evidence of that gone in thirty days or so will be a real advantage."

"Do you have a surgeon lined up already?" asked Roger.

"Oh yes! Dr. Hugh Cordell. I heard of him several years ago. He was practicing in California and was doing everything that we would want available for our guests here. Unfortunately, he ran afoul of a number of ethical regulations in California. It appears that he liked the work he did on some of his female patients so much that he ended up screwing some of them after he got through. There were a lot of upset husbands out in California and they jerked his license.

"I had heard that he could be persuaded to do some slightly off-center surgery anyway, and when I talked to him several months ago he was anxious to get started. Since he's lost his license he needs the money, and the theory behind this operation intrigues him too. He's already working at putting together a staff we can trust and he's ready to go to work as soon as we're done."

"Sounds good to me," said Roger. He pointed at a specific section of the plans. "Over on the other side of the north part of the basement is the room for the makeup artist. You can see this isn't just a powder room. We're pulling together a class facility, not only for makeup but for the production of full and partial masks that are so realistic that a person's own mother wouldn't know them. The makeup artist that you contacted, Scott Bigsby, has already called me and told me exactly what he needs. I have the names and addresses of all the suppliers of the equipment and it's already on order. Where did you find this guy anyway?"

"Well, California again. Seems like anytime I need somebody weird I find them in California. And this guy's really good. He worked for one of the major studios for almost twenty years. He started out doing generic sort of makeup work, but then all of the science-fiction movies started coming back in so he moved over into the really weird monster setups. We won't need any of that here, but the talent that he has for altering a person's appearance by adding to or changing noses, lips, chins, ears, and other features is amazing. He can add or take away scars, tattoos, birthmarks, blemishes, and just about anything."

Sterling went on, "He told me that he needed special temperature and humidity controls for a lot of the plastic work and the wigs that he was going to keep in stock. We're going to keep some of the extra wardrobe supplies in this area also. While we'll have to buy additional clothes for everybody who comes in, depending on who they leave as, we ought to have some basic wardrobe supplies here all the time."

Referring to the plans again, Roger explained, "In the center portion of the basement we're going to put the print shop and a couple of additional rooms that I'm sure you'll find use for later. The print shop has probably been the most difficult to try to set up. Not because it was hard to design, but trying to get the equipment that you need is extremely difficult. The three or four American printing machines you needed weren't hard to get. But the ones that will accurately reproduce the European, Asian, South American, and African documentation are going to be a lot more difficult. Especially after 9/11. Security is just so much tighter with special paper, dyes, and holograms."

"I don't care. We have to be able to provide our people with documents that will get them anywhere in the world they want to go. I've got people in a dozen different countries right now stockpiling blank passports, visas, and everything else we'll need to move people out. If we can't provide that for them, everything we're doing here is a waste of time. Anybody can hideout somewhere for two weeks or a month. We want them to be able to leave here and go anywhere in the world with zero chance of detection."

"I understand that and we're going to be able to do it. All I'm saying is that it's not going to be easy. The photography part of this section is a lot easier. We have a photographer that works for us and he's put together a plan which will allow us to provide any kind of photographic identification necessary and we have the dark room right here. Once somebody's altered their appearance and Bigsby is done with them, we can do all the identification documents right here.

"I've even got people getting original customs stamps to use on the passports. In places where we can't steal originals I'm going into the plants that manufacture the stamps and getting what we need there. When this is all set up we'll have the capability to produce birth certificates, driver's licenses, social security cards, passports—any kind of identification documents that a person would need to cash a check at the grocery store in town or fly to Geneva or Rio. Even the newest I.D.'s with holograms."

Coming around the corner of the building to talk with Mr. Sterling, Sam cocked his head toward the dorm and asked, "What do you think of Sterling's plan? It's kind of like a Wal-Mart for criminals, isn't it?"

Roger laughed. "Well, I hadn't though of it that way but I guess it is. I think we can do what Mr. Sterling wants, but we can't guarantee the lowest price around."

"I'm sure you can do the job. If you couldn't, you wouldn't be here."

"Sam, stick around for a few minutes," Sterling said. "Roger was going to show me the plans for the southern third of the basement. That's where the arsenal and all of the security and observation monitors are going to be. Since that's part of your job, you ought to see this too."

"Yeah," Roger explained, "we've got a real first-class set-up here. We have cameras that cover the entire grounds, all of the public areas and the other outbuildings, including the guest house. Then there are all of the heat and movement sensors along the perimeter of the manor house, plus the video cameras installed near all the roads into the property. We'll be running underground lines to those and putting them up in trees where they won't been seen, but will give us plenty of advance warning if anyone tries to sneak in."

"What about the special surveillance cameras?" Sam asked.

"Well, we know that all of the guests will want to come in and see this part of the security operation. If they don't feel safe they're not going to come here. See this secondary control room back behind the main room? This smaller room will monitor all of the hidden cameras and bugs in the eight suites above us plus those in the guest house. They won't know it, but they wont be able to sneeze or fart without us knowing about it. Anything they say, anything they do, and any plans they make, we'll have on tape."

"But you're sure that no one is going to be able to discover any of these devices, right?" asked Mr. Sterling. "If anybody finds any of those bugs, we're out of business and probably dead!"

"No chance," said Roger. "We're using the latest optics technology there is. The cameras that we're using are so small and unobtrusive that It would be like finding a single thread of hair in a shag carpet. The camera and audio can all be run in on one small wire and if anybody ever finds one you can personally kick my ass."

"If that happens, I won't have to do that. Whoever finds it will do that for me."

"What about the arsenal and target range? With Charles' public gun control position and not wanting firearms in evidence, where are you going to put a place for my guys to play?" Sam asked.

"Got it covered. Look along the front wall of the basement," Roger said, pointing to the basement plans. "You see this twelve-foot wide room running along the entire front wall? That's your indoor rifle and pistol range. Using extra insulation and triple thick walls with acoustical tiles sandwiched in between, you could just about set off an atomic bomb down there and nobody would hear it. And you have access from the central control room so if any of your guests feel the urge to pop a few caps, they can come down there and play too."

"And the arsenal?" Sterling asked.

"It's in this room right next to the range. I know it doesn't look that large but using modern storage techniques, this room will hold five thousand automatic rifles, one thousand machine pistols, one hundred RPG's, dozens of hand-held stinger missiles, and five-hundred-thousand rounds of ammunition. We'll run gun racks up and down the floor and double racks on all four walls. I know you'll have other arsenals in other places and some bigger than this, but this will be a good supply point for at least the mid-Atlantic states."

"Well," said Sam, "I don't know. You gotta remember how close to D.C. we are."

"Oh," said Roger with a wink, "you mean the gun-control laws don't make you quake in your boots?"

Laughing at the thought, Sterling said, "I suppose we may be able to sneak one or two by the D.C. police. That's a tough law and it works so well," he said with another laugh, "but we'll risk it."

"Did you cover communications yet?" Sam asked.

"We'd touched on it. Every suite will have its own separate phone lines, fax lines, cable and satellite hook-ups, and cellular phones. Naturally, we'll have bugs on all of those. There won't be anything that goes on around here that we don't know about," Roger declared.

"Have you been in touch with the building inspector about these plans yet?" Mr. Sterling asked Roger.

"Sure have. That little folder you gave me on him was just what I needed. With what little bit they pay him and the four kids he's got ready to go to college, it wasn't too difficult to get him to agree that he really didn't need to look too closely at the basement renovations. He has the public set of plans in his office. As far as he or anyone else is concerned all of this basement is just storage. He'll have to come out periodically and go through the motions but we don't have to worry about him getting too curious."

"Just make sure he stays in line. What was his name? Simmons?"

"Yeah, Paul Simmons. He doesn't know everything that's going on here. I've satisfied him that everything is going to be structurally sound but he doesn't know what type of equipment or operations are going in."

"Okay, that's good. He doesn't need to know anything else anyway. He just needs to know to keep his nose out of this area," said Sterling, "Let's go around to the front. I want to see the plans for the landscaping, pool, recreation hall, and helipad."

"Yeah, I was wondering about that," Sam said. "A helipad doesn't quite fit in with a pre-Civil War home."

"No," said Roger, "but that's the beauty of this place. There're so many trees around back that we can screen just about anything we want to. We'll put the helipad over behind the guest house, but off to the left a bit so that it's only a short walk to the guest house or main house from where you land."

"Are we going to have any problem from the local airport officials?" asked Sam.

"Not a bit. You remember Bill Arnold? Well, he's going to be running the airport operation. When the sheriff's department found that bag of cocaine we planted in the other guy's car, it didn't take long for the county to get rid of him. Arnold was one of the controllers fired by Regan. When I talked with him about our little arrangement here in Virginia, he couldn't wait to come out of retirement and get back at the system. With my donation to extend the runway another thousand feet, build another hangar, put in a larger fuel storage tank, and base two of my corporate jets here, the county jumped at my recommendation of Arnold. Now we can move people in and out of Virginia anytime we want. If we need to 'lose a flight' or bring in one that's never logged in, we can do that too.

"With the limos here at the farm and our control of the flight schedules," Sterling continued, "we can pick up and take people to the airport whenever we need to and no one will ever get a look at them. It won't make any difference if the locals see limos going back and forth because the beauty of this conference center is that people are going to expect to see important people coming and going on a regular basis. These rednecks are going to get used to seeing long black limos and that's what I want."

"Well," Sam grinned. "I knew you had all of that covered. What about the local police?"

"I've done my homework there too," said Sterling. "While you were in France back in October, I took the liberty of meeting with the candidates for the sheriff's election in November. The old geezer who'd been sheriff here for thirty-two years finally hung up his six-shooter and let the young guys fight it out. You know how I have a sixth sense when I meet somebody that I think I can get to. Well, one of the sheriff's candidates really set off the bells and whistles."

"You mean Sheriff Longley belongs to us?" asked Sam.

"Bought and paid for. You know, people were right when they said it was cheaper to live in the country. That one hundred thousand dollar under-the-table campaign contribution was all it took. Chicken feed. If I had been trying to do the same thing up north, it would have cost me at least a million. There are several deputies who are in our corner too, but most of the deputies are just as ignorant as the rest of the locals. They don't have a clue about what's going on here.

"And we don't need much from the sheriff's department. Basically what we need for them to do is to leave us alone. In return for my contribution all I really asked Sheriff Longley to do is not been too vigilant in this part of the county. I told him that we had our own security and that a lot of my foreign clients were afraid of uniformed police. He doesn't really know what's going on here and he doesn't want to know. If he needs to know more later, fine. But for now, it's enough that he'll keep his people away from here. If we need a favor later, we can count on him."

Sam whistled a low whistle and said, "This is really a lot to keep secret in such a small town. What if people get suspicious?"

"I've got a couple of ideas that we'll use to distract the locals if we need to," Sterling continued.

"What's that?" asked Sam.

"Well, it never hurts to have a little extra diversion when you're getting ready to make some major moves. My people tell me that there are some gun-control advocates in Clarkton. An Andrews woman is one of them. Nobody's really paid that much attention to them yet, but if we could get the locals stirred up about that, they're a lot less likely to worry about what's going on over here."

"What do you mean, 'get 'em stirred up'?"

"Well, what if we gave the anti's a little bit of funding to start an organized drive to prohibit hand guns in the county and maybe even semi-automatic weapons? That would sure stir up a beehive of activity amongst all the country boys down here. They like to get out and shoot up the neighborhood during deer season.

"Christ, you can't even drive down the road without seeing thirty pickup trucks with a rifle and Confederate flag hanging off the back of it. I can't think of anything else that would draw public attention away from Belleview more than a good old-fashioned local gun-control ordinance. And there's something else that might be a good diversion."

"What's that?" Sam said.

"The Confederate flag. All the blacks here are way too docile for their own good. Everywhere you look there's a battlefield marker, monument, or Confederate flag. If you took one of those and drove through some neighborhoods just north of here you probably wouldn't survive the trip. What if we were to donate a little money, anonymously of course, to erect some sort of Confederate monument and at the same time, use a couple of our boys to get the local blacks cranked up about the KKK and all of that?"

"Hmm, that's a pretty damn good idea," Sam said. "Between a little gun-control fight and getting the blacks and whites to look sideways at each other, we can pretty much do anything we want to down here. You know, I love it when these gun-control people have their gun turn-in days. You got all of these folks who think they're safer when they turn in their guns. That's beautiful! If I were a burglar, there's nothing I'd like better than to know which houses and which families have turned in all their guns and no longer have anything but a pocket knife to defend themselves with."

"That's true," said Charles. "If we ever needed to know that, the sheriff could give us access to the computer records about it. And if we ever needed to know what kind of guns people had, we could find that out too.

"We may need to take advantage of this war on terror too. I want to plant some anthrax in some Iraqi homes up in Fairfax and some stinger missals down in Richmond. We'll probably even fire one at an airplane. Not to shoot it down, just to raise the alarm. There's so much focus on terrorism now, the war on drugs is being ignored. Now is the perfect time to import all the drugs we can while the heat's off.

"Sam, I need for you to look into all of these matters. Get the addresses and phone numbers of this Andrews woman and any of her friends who are interested in this gun-control idea. Have some of our people at the national headquarters in Washington get in touch with them and arrange to make an anonymous contribution to fund whatever local gun-control ordinance they think might work. I need for you to get the names, addresses, and phone numbers of the head of the local NAACP and get the address and phone number of Mrs. Hawkins, the president of the local UDC."

"What the hell is the UDC?" asked Sam.

"United Daughters of the Confederacy, I think. Jesus, can you imagine all of the old crones sitting around crying about something that happened 140 years ago? Well, no matter. It's important to them so they'll fight for it. Also, there's some other group here that has something to do with Confederate veterans. Call the Chamber of Commerce and find out who they are. We don't want to be obvious about what we're doing here. We just want to turn the heat up on both of these pots to simmer. Then if we need to, we'll be able to turn them up to boiling anytime we want to."

"You got it," nodded Sam.

Sterling was quite pleased with his work over the last four months. Without raising any eyebrows, without any suspicion whatsoever, he had moved into a community and was well on his way toward the operational organization which would bring world-class criminals to the neighborhood. As far as he knew, no one had taken the time or trouble to really look at his operation or think about what he was doing. That was, he supposed, because he had done such a good job organizing.

Rapidan County, he thought, *you've been bought and paid for. You belong to me now and you don't even know it.*

CHAPTER ELEVEN

THE MONDAY AFTER opening week Allen came home and without speaking to Brenda went straight to his room after school. When John got home Allen came to his door with a confused look on his face and said, "Dad, we need to talk. You know most of my friends thought getting my buck was great. Heck, the school board might as well have closed school for opening week of deer season cause over half the guys took off to hunt anyway. But Mary Sue Andrews just couldn't believe I would kill a deer, or any other animal!

"In front of all my friends, she said, 'How could you kill another living thing when you don't need the meat? When you don't need the skin for clothes? What sport is there in blowing an innocent deer to bits for the fun of it?'

"I tried to answer her. I told her that the meat and hide weren't wasted, that it had been a clean shot and that the deer didn't suffer. I even tried to explain to her about the woods and the special feeling I get being with you and being included in the hunt with the other older men. How I feel more self-reliant, self-confident. But she just wouldn't listen or even try to see my side of the story."

"Son, there've always been some people who don't understand what hunting is about. They've either grown up in the city like Mary Sue's mother or they don't know, or have forgotten, that part of being human is being a hunter. If we weren't, none of us would be alive. There's a natural order in this world that dictates that some species exist to provide for the needs of the others.

"Their usual response to hunters is that either they say you can buy your food at the grocery store so you shouldn't need to go kill it yourself, or you should be a vegetarian. No one, they say, needs to eat meat. All animals, they argue, have a right to live, just as you do.

"Well," John continued, "I guess it's true that we could get all our meat from the store, but we'd sure miss out on a lot if we did that. You remember that hindquarter that we barbecued last year at the cabin? Between that venison, the corn on the cob, and your mom's peach cobbler, I thought we'd died and gone to heaven. Or those bass fillets we fried out on the sand bar last spring. A good wood fire late in the evening with just enough smoke to keep the early mosquitoes away. The fried potatoes and water bread. I don't know about you but I haven't slept that good in a long time. There are some things you just can't buy at a store!"

John knew he was preaching to the choir but said, "Just like anything else you do for yourself, there's a sense of accomplishment when you provide for yourself, when you've gone out and proven that you, just like your grandfather and his father before him, are capable of sustaining yourself without a Food Lion or a 7-11 in your back pocket. I dare say that Mary Sue would probably starve to death if she got more than a mile from the nearest shopping center.

"There's just no way around it. Not one living thing ever got out of this world alive and some animals exist to help sustain others. To reject that is to hide from the reality of life. We all have our time to go and that includes sheep, goats, fish, shrimp, deer, and everything else living on this earth, including us."

"I know, Dad. It was just really hard to hear her say all those things about something we all like to do. And she wouldn't even try to listen. You always told me to try and listen to other people, to understand their side, even if I didn't agree. I guess not everyone has learned to do that, huh?"

"Allen, you've learned quite a lesson. And as much as I hate to admit it, I guess I owe Mary Sue a thank you."

Allen looked puzzled. "Why thank someone who takes pleasure in beating you up?"

John smiled. "Son, you've just had your first experience with a zealot."

"A what?" asked Allen.

"A zealot. Someone who thinks they know more than you, are smarter than you, knows what's better for you and everyone else, and intends to see that everyone else receives the benefit of their wisdom and intelligence, whether they want it or not. It's generally their way or no way."

"Like the Democrats?"

"Well" replied John, laughing at his son's political insight, "like some Democrats. But remember, she's entitled to her opinion. She has a right to live her life the way she wants to. But there's an old saying that unfortunately gets lost in the shuffle today."

"What's that?"

"Your rights end where mine begin. That's an important concept that most zealots forget, and that's why its usually good advice to steer clear of them. However, you can't ignore them either."

"Now I am confused. If I'm going to stay away from them, why can't I ignore them?"

"Have you heard of the phrase 'silent majority' in school yet?"

"Yeah, sorta."

"Well, it means that human nature being what it is, most folks would rather avoid a conflict or an argument if they can. The majority of people are usually just interested in living their lives, paying their bills, having a little fun, and not being disturbed. Unless their own little world is directly threatened, they don't stir up trouble or get involved in controversial issues. But there are always a few who seem to have time to devote to crusades which are, what's the word, out of the mainstream."

"Like Mary Sue's mom?"

"Exactly like Ms. Andrews! Now, she does some real good work for the church and the shut-ins. And the Christmas Basket program would be in real trouble without her. But sometimes even good people with good intentions get way too far out in left field. Her ex-husband called himself a hunter, but his trips were never anything other than an excuse to get drunk. I never hunted with him, but I would usually see him over at Grissom's Store every Saturday evening after shooting light was gone, and he was always pie-eyed.

"About the only thing he ever hunted with any success was a drink. But on the rare occasions when he did happen to kill a deer, he generally made such a mess of it that none of it was fit to eat. I heard some of the venison would stay in his fridge until it molded. I guess if I had had that kind of exposure to hunting I wouldn't like it much either.

"You gotta remember, Mrs. Andrews moved here from Philadelphia. City girls usually don't know what to make of country living. They have this ideal in their mind where everything is pristine and clean and nothing ever dies. They're used to their beef and chicken and fish coming in real neat, clean white styrofoam packs with no blood or anything else to remind them that it used to be an animal. They forget that before that chuck roast got on the shelf, some poor ol' cow had to be raised, fattened on grain, slaughtered, bled, skinned, butchered, and wrapped up, all so she could be spared the trauma of its demise."

"But, Dad, you still haven't explained to me why I just can't ignore her."

"Oh, I guess I did get sidetracked. The reason you can't is because when you get a few folks together like Mrs. Andrews, and they home in on one particular subject, they can cause a whole lot of trouble."

"What kind of trouble?"

"Well, not like criminal trouble, not usually anyway. Trouble like imposing their minority views on a particular issue on the majority, whether most folks want it that way or not. Let's say Mrs. Andrews was successful in prohibiting hunting in Rapidan County. What would happen?"

"The game wardens would lose their jobs."

"Probably. What else?"

"There'd be a lot more deer and game in the woods, wouldn't there?"

"There would. And that's not all bad. But what would happen if there were too many deer?"

"I guess they'd run out of food."

"Eventually, they sure would. Plus, overpopulation tends to lead to disease and sickness. And with all the farming here in the county, crop damage would be a big problem. You know there are places here in Virginia now where farmers can't get in a soybean or peanut crop because of all the deer.

"Now Mrs. Andrews would say fine, if they overpopulate, trap them and transport them somewhere where the deer are not as common. Well, the expense of that notwithstanding, you only transfer the problem, not solve it. Without effective management, and that includes hunting, the deer will overpopulate and overrun any range they're put on.

"So you see, its important not to let people like Mrs. Andrews appear to speak for the majority. If our government believes her view is what the majority wants, they're apt to try to make her happy. And that would be a disaster. So when zealots get cranked up, it's up to us to let everyone know that we disagree. To wake up the silent majority.

"So, what do you think? Are you ready to give up hunting or shall I keep buying you a license?"

"I think I'll keep going. Someone has to go with you to keep you from falling out of the tree stand. Besides, Grandpa might object if he found out that I'd converted his sixteen-gauge to a floor lamp."

"Yeah, I expect he would," John said with a rub on Allen's head. *Quite a boy,* he thought to himself, *I think I'll keep him.*

CHAPTER TWELVE

"GRANDPA!" YELLED ALLEN.

Getting up from his chair, John hurried to the front door. "Hello, Dad," he said. "How was your trip?"

"Not too bad. It does seem like it gets a little longer every year. When are you and the family gonna start spending Thanksgiving with me in South Carolina?"

"Well, you know how it is. You're the one that got us started on this tradition."

"Well, I guess I asked for that one. I really do look forward to coming back every year. How's the crew?"

"They're all doin' fine. We killed a couple of nuce ones last week. Allen and I took the whole week off and he got a big one Friday. Go get the pictures, Allen."

John's father was almost seventy. His wife, John's mother, had passed away four years earlier, only two years after they had sold their home in Charlottesville and retired to South Carolina. John knew his father hadn't truly recovered from the loss yet. Every time they talked, every time he saw him, that emptiness still seemed very real. She had left a void no one could fill and time couldn't erase.

His father had been an avid hunter until an automobile accident when he was sixty-one. The crash, a head-on-collision with a drunk driver near Richmond, had crushed one knee so badly he was no longer able to walk without the assistance of a cane. Even then it took a great deal of time and effort to move any distance, and the injury certainly eliminated the possibility of navigating any rough terrain during hunting season.

Noticing his father's limp seemed worse, John asked, "Dad, why don't you let me take you out on a four-wheeler? There are a lot of good stands that you could get to without a great deal of walking."

His father's response was the same as last year. "Son," he said, "if I went and was lucky enough to take a deer, I wouldn't be able to care for it properly and get it out of the woods myself without a lot of help. Thanks, John, but you know I've always felt that if the time came I couldn't manage to care for my own game, I wouldn't hunt any more. Well, that time's come and I'm okay with it.

"Anyway," he continued, "you know how much I still enjoy the company of all the guys at the judge's cabin. Being with those guys during season keeps me connected. Besides you all are the only family that I have left and it's important to stay close. It really makes me feel better to be here to share all of this with you."

"Let's eat, guys," called Brenda from the kitchen.

"I could tell by the smell it was almost ready," said John's father. "And unless I miss my guess, that's some of the best fried chicken in Virginia. You still serving that lumpy old gravy?" he winked at Brenda.

"You bet. I made it with especially large lumps knowing you'd be here for dinner."

Samuel smiled. That's exactly the remark he had expected, even hoped for. *She's so much like Mary,* he thought. He had to swallow hard not too think too much about her.

"You know, Brenda, Mary and I were married thirty-nine years and my memories of her are strongest when I'm with you and the family. It makes me so glad that the two of you have the same relationship Mary and I had. These times here are a real treasure to me." As they took their places around the kitchen table, Samuel was satisfied his family had formed bonds that would stand the test of time.

"When are we goin' out to the cabin?" Allen asked.

"Well, the single guys are probably already out there. But," John said with a sideways glance toward Brenda, "we'll probably go out about the same time we usually do. We'll be having Thanksgiving dinner here about noon tomorrow and, if we survive the experience, we ought to try to get out to the cabin before dark. That way we'll be able to see who shot what and get settled in so we can hunt Friday and Saturday."

"You'll be back by lunch on Sunday, won't you?" Brenda asked. "You know I promised we would all go over to the fire hall for their covered-dish dinner on Sunday afternoon. I've already got four tickets."

"Oh Lord," sighed Samuel, "I'll probably have to buy a whole new wardrobe by the end of the week. This trip is always good for at least ten pounds. The problem is, I gain ten and only lose five. If I live long enough you'll have to widen the front door."

The local Volunteer Fire Department had a fund-raising covered-dish dinner every Sunday afternoon after Thanksgiving. It was an annual affair where the money raised went for equipment but everyone who bought a ticket had to bring a dish too.

When you bought your ticket you drew from a bowl labeled hors d'oeuvres, salads, vegetables, casseroles, meats, or desserts, and had to bring whatever dish you drew in an amount big enough to feed twenty-five people. There were always three or four hundred people there and it was an event that no one who liked to eat would ever miss. And it gave everyone a chance to clean out their refrigerators and get rid of all the Thanksgiving leftovers.

"I guess the both of you are already packed up?" John's father asked between bites.

"Sure am!" said Allen. "All I had to do was take my dirty stuff out from last week, wash it, and throw it right back in the duffel bag. The guns are all cleaned and ready to go. Are you gonna hunt any this year?"

"No, Son, I think my huntin' days are over. I've spent my share of time in the woods and taken my share of game. I'll leave the actual shooting to you young fellas. I get almost more pleasure than I can stand just by bein' out at the cabin for a couple of days helpin' to cook and cut off shirt tails. Don't worry about me. If I never squeeze another trigger, I've still had the privilege of hunting more than I had a right to expect."

Allen didn't really understand why his grandfather didn't want to hunt anymore, but accepted his explanation at face value. His father had told him a lot about their early years hunting and Allen had always wished that he and his grandfather could have hunted together. Yet, even without those experiences, they were almost like father and son.

Samuel knew how Allen felt and he too felt the special bond between the two of them. Allen had taken his grandmother's loss almost as hard as he had, and the grief they shared at that loss overcame the distance which separated them most of the year.

Though Allen knew his grandfather loved him very much he couldn't suspect that he was the primary reason Samuel still came to visit at Thanksgiving. Certainly, Samuel and John were as close as any father and son could be, but the affection Samuel felt for his only grandson was almost indescribable. When Samuel looked into Allen's face he could see Mary's eyes and her smile. It was often difficult for him to speak with Allen and at the same time remember that Mary was gone.

"Did I tell you that the old Fitzgerald place has been sold?"

"No, who bought it?" Samuel asked.

"Some guy from Georgia who owns a big company up near D.C. Sterling is his name, I think. I've seen him in the bank a few times, but haven't met him and don't know much about him."

"You reckon he's gonna let anybody hunt out there?" Samuel asked.

"I don't think so. They're new posted signs all up and down the road and I understand that he may be using the place for some sort of corporate get-away or convention center," said John.

"That's too bad. I know you've wanted to get on that place for a long time. You've got some stands close to that property line down there near the river, though, don't you?"

"Sure do. We've hunted down along that low ridge that's only about two hundred yards from their western property line. It's been a real good spot. You know, that's where Allen got a shot at a nice buck last year. Didn't get him though," John said, looking at sideways at Allen. "Yep, I had to cut off his shirttail for missing that deer.

Ruined a perfectly good shirt! I told him to make sure that he doesn't get over on Belleview. The last thing I need is to have somebody jerking him into court on a trespassing charge."

"That's true. I never did have a problem with you in that area and I don't expect you'll have one with Allen. Well, I'm going to turn in. It's been a long day. I can get the rest of my stuff together and be loaded before dinner tomorrow."

As Samuel limped toward the stairs he looked back through the kitchen door at John, Brenda, and Allen still seated at the table. *It's good to be here*, he thought. *Everybody should have a home that they can at least visit. A family that they can belong to for at least part of the year. I sure hope I'm never a burden to them. I don't think I could stand that.*

He climbed slowly up the stairs into the darkness. He wasn't looking forward to another night of not being able to sleep, not being able to brush back Mary's hair or touch her hand or talk quietly with her about things they had done or places they had been. He wasn't sure how much longer he could stand the loneliness or how much longer he even wanted to try.

CHAPTER THIRTEEN

THE TIME BETWEEN Thanksgiving and Christmas flew by that year. John and Allen hunted together almost every weekend and it seemed the holiday season came more quickly than usual. No Christmas in the Richter home was ever ordinary. Always trying to do something at least a little unexpected, John had gotten Allen a compound bow, already completely set up for hunting. *The perfect gift*, he thought.

While John had bow-hunted for deer for the last five or six years, he had not thought Allen was big enough or patient enough to go with him until this year. Naturally, Allen had been wanting to take up bow-hunting for several years and was ecstatic when he opened the box.

"Wow, this is terrific!" Allen said, bringing the compound bow easily back to full-draw. "What weight is it set at?"

"Fifty-five pounds, I think. That's on the front of the instruction book. It can be set by moving the pulleys to a higher weight but I thought for practicing, that would be a pretty good weight for you to start with. And it's even strong enough at that weight to do a job on a whitetail, if you hit him in the right place."

"This five-pin sight is perfect. I can set it for five, ten, fifteen, twenty-five, and thirty-five yards. If I can't get closer than that to one, I won't even shoot at him. What's this on the front? It looks like a fishing reel."

"It's a string tracker. I know you've been hunting for a long time, and you've done some deer tracking with me, but you know that usually when a deer's hit with an arrow, it doesn't go down immediately like it does with a rifle. I've had deer that I've hit through the lungs run hundreds of yards before they go down. Until you get some more experience, I want you to use this tracker. You just put the end of the string on to the clip on the nock on the arrow. That way, when you shoot at a deer, if you hit him, you simply follow the string to the animal. It makes it a lot less likely that you'll loose an animal because you lost the trail."

"Oh, okay," Allen said. It seemed like a pretty good idea to him though he was a bit offended that his dad wouldn't trust his tracking skills. *That's okay,* he thought, *it won't be long before I'll be able to take this off.* "Can we set up the hay bales this afternoon?" he asked.

"I set them up this morning before you got up. The target's already there and the bucket is set up exactly twenty yards from the target. Why don't you start there? Make sure you use those target points and not the hunting arrows. If you shoot one of those hunting arrows into that hay bale, you'll never get it out."

"I know that. Jesus, I've shot one of these before, you know."

"I know, just reminding you."

All of the rest of the gear for his first bow-hunting season next fall was under the tree too. The full set of Realtree camouflage, a dozen hunting arrows with broadheads, scent shield, face mask, and safety rope and belt would all be unwrapped after Allen got through with his first practice session.

Some of John's and Brenda's gifts to each other were more intimate. The gown and robe Brenda unwrapped while Allen was outside even made her blush a little. "You expect me to wear this?" She looked at John with a grin that reminded him of the first time they spent a weekend together before they were married, seventeen years ago.

"Well, I'd hoped you would, but I guess you won't wear it for long." Johns words proved accurate.

"You're not hunting today?" Brenda asked with a raised eyebrow. "It's the last day of the season, isn't it?"

"No, I've gotten my deer for the year. I'm just going to ride over and see how everyone is."

"And get some of Rick's apple cake?"

"You bet! It's only time of the year I can get it."

"You're not even taking a gun?"

"No, nobody usually hunts today anyway. Judge Collins kind of set that policy. It's a good time to visit."

Arriving at the cabin about noon, John saw the usual assortment of trucks and pickups outside. The smoke from the chimney assured him the inside of the cabin would be toasty warm. Carrying a bag of holiday leftovers, he walked through the door and into the company of good friends. From the abundance of new chamois cloth hunting shirts and camouflage clothing worn by those in the cabin, John could see that it had been a good Christmas for them too. There were several new rifles in the gunrack and a quiet but spirited conversation going on between two of new owners about which one had the better rifle. John knew that that was an argument neither of them would win.

The conversations that greeted him were spoken in low, almost reverent tones. "Boy, you guys sure are quiet. Who died?" John asked with a laugh. "The first week of the season nobody could shut up, and now it looks like everybody just got their Christmas credit card bill!"

"You should talk," said Rick, "you work at the bank where all the money is."

"Yeah," said John, "but not much of it belongs to me."

Judge Collins nodded, knowing that with the season almost over and Christmas and New Year's another memory, everyone would be subdued.

"You know what this reminds me of?" the judge asked. "It reminds me of one of John Wayne's lines as Davy Crockett in that Alamo movie. I know most of y'all are too young to remember, but the night before the final attack on the Alamo, someone asked Wayne what he was thinking about. His reply was 'Not thinking—just remembering.'"

As he looked at the assembled group he said, "Now that's not a bad thing. We all have a lot to remember and be thankful for."

Everyone recognized a certain finality with the end of another hunting season and the end of another year. The cold, steel-gray day with the sun a barely visible yellow disk behind the clouds and the dying embers of the fire in the fireplace seemed all too appropriate for the mood of the men in the cabin.

"Put your stuff on the table," said Rick. "We'll be ready to eat shortly. Looks like everyone had plenty."

"I know we did! Brenda told me to clean out the refrigerator and bring all of it here. She knows how much all of us enjoy this meal." John set a foil-wrapped package of sliced turkey, a bowl of green bean casserole, and left over yeast rolls on the table. "I can't believe I'm getting ready to eat another huge meal."

"Well," said Rick, "brace yourself, cause it's as ready as it's going to get. The gravy's hot!"

Set in no particular order were the remains of five or six turkeys which, if they had all been resurrected into one bird would have made the only seven-winged, three-drum-sticked, double-breasted turkey in the world. In different quantities there were the remains of holiday butter beans; field peas; two different types of corn pudding; five bowls of cranberry sauce (two with berries, three without); sweet potato casseroles (with and without marshmallows and with and without brown sugar and pecans); mashed potatoes and potato pancakes; three different jars of sweet, homemade pickles and one jar of watermelon-rind pickles; what was left of a whole country ham now holding only the barest scraps of lean meat; and, with John's contribution, three different bowls of string bean cassasrole.

On the counter beside the table was a spot reserved for all of the holiday desserts which had been ordered out of the house. It seemed universal that, at the end of the holiday season, all of the wives, usually with the concurrence of the men in the family, dictated that all of the left-over sweets be banished. The diets started Monday.

The desserts were usually John's favorite and this year wasn't a disappointment. Glancing quickly from one end of the counter to the other he spotted the snow white crown of a left-over four-layer coconut cake; half a German chocolate cake; a whole chocolate pie; two pecan pies; a lemon meringue pie from which someone had eaten all the meringue; two plates full of fudge and brownies; one plate holding three chocolate-covered peanut butter balls; and four boxes of assorted Christmas cookies. *Those cookies,* John thought, *will end up as bird food after the first snow.* With the number of homemade desserts, the store-bought cookies would be shunned until they were long past edible.

Even given this abundance, John was disappointed until he spotted the green bowl set toward the rear of the counter. "Hey Rick, is that what I think it is?"

"Sure is," Rick responded. "I even made extra this year. Grandma would be proud." Grandma's apple cake wasn't actually a cake but a dessert with layers of homemade biscuit crumbs and thick, cinnamony, chunky homemade applesauce. The applesauce always contained enough juice to saturate the biscuit crumbs and was made far enough ahead of time and chilled almost to the point of freezing so that the cake was incredibly sweet and chewy and crunchy, all at the same time. Half-way through his first bowl, John said, "Rick, you've got to give me this recipe! I swear I'll never give it away. This is just too good to only have once a year!"

"Now John, you know she'd disown me if I ever gave away her best recipe. Once she's gone I'll pass it on to a few of my best friends." However Ms. Bannister, a very kindly old lady, had the unmitigated gall to be living well into her ninety-fourth year and was showing no signs of imminent demise. *So,* John thought, adding another spoonful to his bowl, *I'll have to just be content with one or two servings a year.*

Unlike several of the meals the first week of the season, there was no formality or schedule to this meal. Everyone was strictly on their own and the only rule was that whoever drank the last cup of coffee had to fill the pot and no one could go by the stove without stirring the gravy. John settled in, content to sit at the table and listen to the conversations swirling around the room about which camouflage was best in this part of Virginia in any particular season, or which knives held the best edge, or which boot would or wouldn't leak in a heavy wet snow.

"You're awfully quite today," said Judge Collins as he walked by the table, placing his hand on John's shoulder. "Are you all right?"

"I'm fine, Judge, thanks for asking. It's just been a hectic holiday season. We've had a lot of company and lots of parties. I enjoy socializing, but it's always a relief to see the New Year come. I'm just ready for a good dose of solitude."

"I know what you mean, and this is just the place for it," the judge said. After he ate and the conversations and fire in the fireplace all became too heated, John stood quietly and walked out the side door. The thirty-degree moisture-laden air was almost a shock to his system. Like a splash of cold water in the face it seemed he had changed worlds as he walked toward the back of the cabin. Inside he could still hear the voices laughing, arguing, trying to be convincing, and he could still almost feel the heat from the fireplace. For now, he wanted to be away from all of that, away from people, away from the cabin, by himself, with just his thoughts and the woods.

Following a trail behind the cabin he walked slowly up the ridge toward a stand of large oak trees about half a mile away. As he went up the ridge, the trail disappeared under the thick carpet of oak leaves. The acorn crop had been very heavy that year and he could feel them crunching under his feet as he topped the ridge.

Finding himself at a large old oak his subconscious had guided him to, he recognized it as one he had used as a stand years before when he had taken one of the largest deer he had ever killed. Thoughts of that day, that hunt, flashed through his mind as he slid slowly down the trunk and sat quietly on the carpet of leaves at the base of the tree. From there, he could look back down the ridge and see, through the bare limbs, the top of the chimney at the cabin and the pillar of smoke which rose from it. Even if he hadn't been able to feel the cold humidity in the air, he would have known it was there because of the way the column of smoke stayed low above the chimney, the smoke held close to the ground by the moisture in the air. *Yep, snow before too much longer*, he thought with a shiver.

He turned his eyes away from the cabin, not wanting to see any vestige of civilization. He looked out over the far side of the ridge and down toward the fields covered with a thin carpet of green winter wheat. In the distance, he could see four or five deer, their grayish-brown winter coats in stark contrast to the wheat. The sight of them didn't make him want to get his rifle or make any attempt to hunt the animals. *No,* he thought, *you've made it this far through the season. I'm sure not going to disturb you.*

It was times like this that he needed to look back on the year that had passed and judge himself. To try and determine where he had succeeded and where he had failed. Where he had done the best job that he could, been a good parent, a good husband. *I don't know how I got so lucky*, he thought. *Brenda and I seem to be able to understand what's important. I just don't know how I could be any happier.* His love for his son was as strong as his love for Brenda, but it was a different quantity and quality.

He thought of a letter to the editor in a Charlottesville newspaper in the 1970's written by someone over in Culpeper. The letter was a rebuttal to a network TV documentary on hunting. The T.V. show was a shameful display of poor and biased journalism which attempted to portray all hunters and sportsmen as uncouth, bloodthirsty killers with no morals, character, or scruples.

John's father had given him a copy of the letter and he still carried it with him. Taking the faded, yellowed article from his wallet, he slowly unfolded it. In the quiet calm of the afternoon he read again about the author's love of the outdoors and the bond he had developed with his young son who shared his adventures with him. How they had hunted and fished together, taken game and enjoyed the bounty of that harvest. But how those benefits were so much less important than the lessons they had learned and the love that had grown as they shared this timeless tradition.

These experiences, recounted so clearly, were obviously important to the writer and struck so close to home they never failed to cause a tightness in John's chest. John had been fortunate enough to have a father who had taken the same care with him and loved him just as deeply. From the time John had read those words, he had always hoped he would have the same type of relationship with his son. And now he did.

Sitting alone in his world, his back against this familiar old oak, John thought, *I know as Allen grows older his world, his interests, his likes and dislikes will grow and change. I don't know, can't know, whether or not Allen will continue to love the outdoors. But I'm certain the lessons he's learned hunting and fishing over the years will stand him in good stead no matter what. Just like Dad taught me I've tried to teach Allen that it's important to be able to be alone with yourself, to think about life and the directions you take, and to be satisfied with those decisions. I hope I've done as good a job with Allen as Dad did with me.*

When he slowly stood it was nearly dark and the temperature had dropped even further. With his bare hand against the rough bark of the oak, John looked intently toward the distant field again. The deer, though barely visible, were still there. "Godspeed and good luck," he said. "It's going to be a bad winter." But he knew that in the spring fawns would be born and the cycle would begin again.

CHAPTER FOURTEEN

As USUAL, THE really severe winter weather in Virginia waited until January and February. By the time the really heavy snows came, all of the outside construction at Belleview was finished, so the project remained on schedule. As the weather warmed and the first signs of spring became evident, about the only thing left to be done at Belleview was the landscaping. This done, Sterling sent invitations to a party to several hundred of the most prominent local citizens for the unveiling of his handiwork.

"I want everyone to see that the restoration has been done and done in a proper manner," Sterling told his secretary. "They should be impressed and I want them to be impressed. We'll do tours of the mansion, the guest house, conference center, and other buildings, but they'll only see what they are supposed to see."

John, as a vice president at the bank, received an invitation. Though not usually overly enthusiastic about such events, he was anxious to get a look at the grounds of the huge farm.

As he and Brenda drove up the long drive that cool March evening, he couldn't help but admire the transformation of Belleview. "Look at this—a new main entrance, paved driveway, and they even transplanted these trees along the drive to the front door. That cost a fortune!"

"It's breathtaking," Brenda said. "I just can't imagine the amount of money he's spent on the place."

A seemingly limitless supply of valets took the vehicles and quickly drove them away from the front of the building so the "Gone With The Wind" impression was not unduly disturbed.

Walking up the front steps to the spacious porch, John and Brenda lingered outside for a few moments before going in. Gazing across the Rapidan River, across the piedmont of Rapidan and Culpeper counties, and further out toward the setting sun behind the Blue Ridge Mountains some thirty-five miles distant, John said, "It's no wonder the Fitzgeralds chose this site to build their family home. This view is incredible."

Inside, Charles Sterling was the perfect host. He greeted guests at the door, calling each by name. "Mr. and Mrs. Richter, it's a pleasure. John, your bank has been so much help to us, I can't thank you enough. Please, come in, enjoy yourself. And feel free to take the guided tour. I'll look forward to hearing your impressions."

As John and Brenda walked through the home it was clear no expense had been spared in providing food, beverage, and entertainment in a style seldom seen in Rapidan County. Sterling had been careful to select a menu which was not too "uptown" for his rural guests. There was, however, an abundance of filet mignon, shrimp, crab, and other delicate but recognizable hors d'oeuvres.

Waiters carried an endless supply of champagne and mixed drinks which were available from four bars set up in corners of the manor house. Sterling's one concession to upscale entertaining was the string quartet which he had brought down from Washington. Playing music easily recognized by southern society, the strains of soft music seemed as at home here as did Charles Sterling.

Tours of the grounds and buildings were given to all of those interested and the evidence of his commitment to Belleview was appreciated by everyone.

No one, of course, was allowed into those areas which contained the amenities for Sterling's future guests and no one became suspicious at the polite but firm rejections to requests for admission to those restricted areas given by tuxedoed guards placed at the appropriate entrances.

As the valet brought John's Blazer to the front, he said with a sigh, "Well, I guess it's time for us to go back to our little hovel. Do you think you can stand that after you've seen this?"

"Well," Brenda said, "I guess I can but now you're really going to have to paint the shutters and the trim this spring. I love where we're living, but it could be a little nicer."

Damn, John thought, *she's going to hold me to that and that's going to interfere with my spring turkey-hunting. I knew I shouldn't have come to this party*. Driving down the driveway, John couldn't help but wonder what the turkey population was on Belleview. *Oh well*, he thought, *I guess I'll never find out.*

CHAPTER FIFTEEN

"HOW AM I going to tell John? I'm thirty-eight—what are we going to do with a baby?" Brenda muttered as she left the doctor's office. While many women would be ecstatic at the news, she was almost in tears. It turned her world upside down.

She and John had decided years ago that Allen would be their only child. Not that a large family didn't appeal to both of them, but economics dictated that one was all they could comfortably afford to raise and educate. They had both seen too many families with more children than they could handle financially and the harm that could cause to the parents and children. They decided it was better to only have one and to do the job right. But now Allen, at almost seventeen, would have a baby sister or brother.

Oh well, no need to worry about when or how. Where do I go from here? She barely remembered the drive home. Her thoughts were a blur. Fortunately, no one was home when she arrived.

Wandering from room to room, she finally settled in the family room. Sitting at the end of the sofa, she drew her legs up under her and hugged an old, over-stuffed pillow.

"Gees," she said out loud, putting the pillow up under her t-shirt. "This is what I'll look like in six months!" She couldn't decide whether to laugh or cry, so she did both.

Between spells, she held a picture of her and John taken on their honeymoon. It hadn't been an extended or elaborate one, just a long weekend at one of those lodges in the Pennsylvania mountains. But what it had lacked in duration it had made up for in passion.

There was still plenty of passion in her life, but not like on the honeymoon. Sex was still an important part of their marriage, but their jobs, schedules, and every-day responsibilities had made lovemaking something that happened less frequently than she would have liked.

I'm old enough, she thought, *to know that passion and romance don't necessarily have anything to do with sex. John still loves me and cares about me.* She knew that by the way he made love to her; the way he still looked at her when he thought she wasn't looking; the way he would touch her hair just after she washed it; or just by the way he took her hand as they sat and watched tv.

"We still talk to each other," she mused. Not just "Good morning" or "Have a good day," but really talked. Once or twice a week they would sit out on the deck and talk about their dreams, their plans for the future. Not only conversations about monumental questions like what college Allen would go to or when they might be able to afford to retire, but the small intimate things important only to them. Or, even important to only one of them. *It's true,* she thought, *we both know how to listen.*

Brenda lost all track of time that afternoon as she swam through the mental waves created by the doctor's revelation. She decided the best way to handle the situation was to get dressed up, take John out to his favorite restaurant and, after a few drinks, break the news to him.

At least, if we're in a public place, he's not likely to kill me right there. I'll be safe for a little while. She grinned.

They'd had, and still had, disagreements. Some even escalated into arguments. But those differences never became more important than their love and their relationship with each other. They could always talk. And she knew that as long as they could communicate, everything would be okay.

The opening door startled her. She wasn't asleep, but felt as if she had been in a dream world for hours.

"Hi, Hon," said John, passing behind her on his way to the kitchen. "Long day." She didn't know if it was a question or a statement and she didn't trust herself to speak just yet.

Looking down, she realized she still had the pillow under her t-shirt. Quickly pulling it out, she thought, *Not that way—I can't let him know now. I'll tell him this weekend.*

She should have known better. John had a sixth sense about Brenda, especially when she was confused or unsure of herself.

"Are you okay? You haven't spoken since I came in. If it's about painting the shutters, I promise I'll do it . . . ." He paused in mid-sentence. As he came around the front of the sofa and could see her face, he instantly knew that there was a real problem. He hadn't seen that look since Brenda had taken the phone call about Allen's broken arm in school.

"What is it? Is it your mom?" He sat beside her and held her as she began to cry.

"No."

No was the only word she could muster and for a few minutes John had to be satisfied that apparently no one in the family had died. Slowly, Brenda regained control of herself and began trying to tell John what had happened or what was going to happen.

"Pregnant!" John almost looked around to see if she might be talking to someone else. "Pregnant!" For a few minutes that word was his universe. It was the only thought that would fit into his brain.

"Well," he said, as the idea slowly took hold within him, "I'll be kiss my ass!" He smiled first, then grinned and hugged Brenda as they both began to laugh hysterically.

"Well, what'll Allen say?"

"He'll kill us. It'll probably embarrass the hell out of him," said John.

"Well, he'd better get used to it. Gosh, I hope they'll be close. There'll be almost eighteen years difference in their ages."

"He'll be fine. Damn, I gotta go call Dad. He won't believe this."

"Oh, he'll believe it all right. He'll just want to make sure that the baby won't interfere with his Thanksgiving dinner or your hunting season. Don't worry. I've already counted. It's due the first of the year. I'll even try to hold off until after doe season!"

"What did I do to deserve you?" John asked, taking her face in his hands and trying to be serious.

"Nothing—yet!" she said, pushing him back on the couch and going for his ribs. If she got to his ribs, he was helpless. And tonight, he was as helpless as he had ever been.

CHAPTER SIXTEEN

"I DO TREE work, Your Honor," said Lester in response to Judge Sellway's question concerning his employment. What that meant was that Lester Morgan was not employed on a regular basis. His response caused a substantial ripple of laughter through the gallery in the courtroom and Lester looked back over his shoulder grinning, though he was not quite sure what he'd said that was so funny.

Striking his gavel on the bench several times, Judge Sellway restored order in the courtroom and, looking intently at the defendant, asked him in a steady, straight forward manner, "You mean you're a tree surgeon? Is that correct, Mr. Morgan?" Judge Sellway was invariably polite to everyone who appeared before him, even those he was getting ready to sentence to a significant period of incarceration.

"That's right, Judge. And I do good work too."

The judge's apparent interest in his profession gave the defendant some hope that the judge might be lenient with him on the petit larceny charge. There were many men in Rapidan County who did tree work and landscaping for a living. Most of them were hard-working men who performed the tough physical labor demanded by their jobs in an honest and efficient manner. Lester Morgan was not one of those.

"Then this warrant should be amended to read that 'Dr. Lester Morgan did unlawfully take, steal, and carry away a pelonia tree having a value of under two hundred dollars. Is that correct?" asked the judge. Judge Sellway was seldom humorous on the bench, and this levity, while not lost on the gallery, most of whom were now nearly in tears, went completely over the defendant's head. When Lester realized he was the butt of one of the judge's infrequent jokes, he knew nothing good was going to be happening with respect to this charge.

"Naw, Judge, you know I ain't no doctor. But I . . . I do work hard and try to stay out of trouble. I didn't know I was over on Mr. Carter's farm. Once I got back in the woods I kinda got turned around and, see, I didn't never cross a fence, so I thought I was still where I had a right to be." The defendant shifted uncomfortably and began to stammer a further explanation when Judge Sellway held up his hand, cutting off the defendant in mid-sentence.

"Just a minute, sir. You've been through this process enough to know that I first need to know whether or not you want a lawyer and if you do, whether or not you can afford one."

"Aw, come on, Judge, you know I don't never want no lawyer. I had one for two or three other charges and they never did do me no good. Just meant I owed the state a few hundred more dollars. What is it I gotta sign for you to do whatever it is you're gonna do?"

The bailiff handed the defendant a Waiver of Counsel form. Lester could only read about every third or fourth word, but he knew the meaning of the document and signed it readily, if illegibly.

"Now you want me to plead guilty or not guilty, don't ya, Judge?" Lester grinned at the judge again, hoping his familiarity with courtroom procedure would somehow be to his benefit.

"That's correct, Mr. Morgan. To the charge I've just read, how do you plead?"

"Well, Judge, if I plead guilty and promise to pay for the tree, will you give me a suspended sentence?" The defendant, though he had dropped out of school after the fifth grade, had been in court more than most lawyers who had been out of law school for several years. He had seen these promises work before and enable others to escape jail. He hoped the judge would at least think about it.

"Don't try to bargain with me, Mr. Morgan. All I need to know from you right now is whether you plead guilty or not guilty. What happens to you after that will just have to happen."

Knowing the evidence was more than enough to convict him and not wishing to get the judge anymore upset with him than he already was, Morgan entered a plea of guilty. After hearing enough evidence to establish the defendant's guilt and the value of the tree which had been wrongfully cut, Morgan was sentenced to thirty days in jail with fifteen days suspended, restitution to the owner of the tree, and a one-hundred dollar fine. Lester could live with that sentence. He would only serve eight of those days and would be out before next weekend. The bailiff indicated he should sit in an area reserved for other new inmates, so he turned toward his girlfriend Sandy and indicated she should come get the keys to his truck.

He and Sandy weren't married but they had two children together and had lived together for the last four years. A pretty remarkable record for him. They even had matching his and hers tattoos: her name on his right forearm and his name on her right shoulder. She had been particularly impressed when he had had the letters l-o-v-e-u tattooed on the knuckles of his right hand. Yes, theirs was true love. It would last forever, or at least until the truck was paid for.

The eight days passed quickly and, on his release date, Sandy and Lester's brother, Floyd, were waiting in the parking lot outside of the jail. Lester had passed his time uneventfully. He had even enjoyed the visit a little. Rapidan County's jail was new and had some amenities which he wasn't at all used to—air-conditioning, color tv, and three meals a day, none of which he had to fix.

"Hey, Little Brother!" Lester yelled across the parking lot to Floyd. Floyd was two years younger than Lester but half again as large. At thirty-four and thirty-six years of age, their claims to fame were their collective criminal records.

Jumping behind the wheel, Lester drove as he, Sandy, and Floyd quickly made their way to the closest 7-11 for a bag of ice and a couple of six packs. Eight days without a beer was just about more than Lester could stand. Reprovisioned and heading down the gravel road toward their trailer, they talked briefly about some other palonia trees Floyd had spotted while Lester was in jail. These trees were highly sought after in the Oriental carving and furniture markets. All

Lester and Floyd cared about was that they could get over a thousand dollars for one load.

"There's at least eight or ten big ones about three-quarters of a mile north of that ol' Belleview house. Ya know the one down near the river? There's somebody up there doin' a lot of work but these trees are far enough on the back side that we can get in, cut 'em, throw 'em on the truck, and be gone before those city fellas know that we've even been there."

Lester was smart enough to know how much to steal at a time to avoid a more serious charge. "If there are that many of 'em and they're that big, we're gonna need some help. We're gonna have to be real careful too. If we take 'em all at once, they'll sure be worth more than two hundred dollars and I sure as hell don't need to be charged with a felony any time soon."

Floyd didn't care. Not as intelligent as his brother and not possessing anywhere near the same amount of common sense, Floyd only knew where the trees were, how much they were worth, and that he wanted them. What might happen as a result of that didn't concern him because he didn't plan to get caught. Though neither brother had been charged or convicted of any serious crimes, Floyd had no qualms about committing them. He wanted what he wanted, when he wanted it, and if anyone got in his way, he knew what to do about that too. Up to this time, everyone had been smart enough not to confront him in such a way as to provoke the deadly anger he sometimes felt.

"City boys, huh?" Lester said. "That sure oughta be easy pickins'. Why don't ya call Steve and the Dobbs boys and let's pick a time to pay those dumb asses a visit."

Sandy, sandwiched between the two Morgan boys, let a smile curl up either side of her mouth. She took no part in the discussions and certainly would not be expected to actually go on the little expedition they planned. But she knew if it was successful she would reap many of the benefits of the larceny. All she had to do was keep Lester happy and she had learned a long time ago how to do that.

Arriving at the dilapidated trailer in a cloud of dust, Lester grabbed Sandy by the back of her jeans and began dragging her toward the trailer. Cackling in anticipation of the rough sex that was imminent, Lester called to his brother, "Call the boys and don't drink all the beer. We'll be out in about a hour. If we ain't, leave us the fuck alone!"

Floyd smiled because he knew the boys would come. He also knew his brother and Sandy would be in the bedroom for more than an hour. And he knew he'd get to drink all the beer. Walking slowly toward the trailer with the cooler in his hand, he looked across to the south, toward Belleview and the source of his next paycheck.

City boys, he thought. *Fancy suits and big cars. They better stay the hell outa my way.* He smiled as he opened another beer and found a dusty, flat spare tire to sit on under a shade tree next to the trailer. Hearing a squeal from the trailer, he smiled a wet, brown-toothed grin, bounced an empty beer can off the wall, and yelled, "Ride 'em, Lester!"

CHAPTER SEVENTEEN

FOUR DAYS LATER and just at daylight, the two Morgan boys drove slowly by the north boundary of Belleview several times. The theft of the trees that Floyd had found was a larger project than they usually undertook and they decided some additional scouting might keep them out of jail. Their cut, load, and run tactics worked fine for one or two trees, but for a grove of eight large trees, planning would be necessary.

Pulling their truck well out of sight down a logging road, they quickly crossed the state road on foot and began their hike to the grove of trees.

Both Lester and Floyd were hunters and good woodsmen. That's not to say that they were sportsmen in any sense of the word, because most of the game they took, they killed illegally. But their skill in observing what was happening around them in the woods was usually very good. But on this day, they were so distracted by the size and quantity of the pelonia trees in the grove, they hadn't noticed the five men who were approaching them from all directions.

"You boys lose something?" one of the men asked.

Startled by this unexpected interruption, the Morgan boys' first impulse was to run, but their avenues of escape were blocked and, while none of the five men who surrounded them displayed weapons, it was clear all five had more authority than just the voice of their leader.

As usual, Lester was the spokesman for the two. "No, sir. We was just sizing up these trees for cuttin' and sellin' up to the sawmill.

Albert Johnson told us about 'em and said that he would sell 'em to us at a good price. You fellas work for him?"

"I'll ask the questions here, you dumb-ass redneck. This land doesn't belong to Albert Johnson and you'd better tell me what the hell you're doing here!" His movements made it obvious that some straight answers would be appropriate, and while neither of the Morgan boys ever ran from a fight, they were both intelligent enough to know they should have some prospect of winning before they jumped in. The prospects here didn't look very good.

"Well, actually, one of our friends told us these trees were here. We just wanted to look at 'em before we came up to the big house an' made an offer to buy 'em. This was just the easiest way to get to 'em. No point in talkin' dollars and cents if they wasn't big enough to cut." Lester hoped this half-truth would be enough to satisfy whoever these men were and that they could get the hell out of there.

"You boys better come with me until we figure all of this out." With a wave of his hand, the other men herded Lester and Floyd toward the manor house.

Well, thought Lester, *all they can charge us with right now is trespassing. That's not so bad. I could use another vacation.*

Approaching the manor house, they walked near the rear of the dormitory. The renovation of the old dormitory was virtually complete and the construction of the two exit tunnels had already been done. As they walked behind the dormitory and saw the scope of the excavation, Lester asked of no one in particular, "What the hell did you boys build back here?"

The leader of the group replied passively, "Storm drains."

"Holy shit, you guys must be expectin' a flood." He and Floyd looked at each other and started to laugh but quickly realized laughter wasn't in their best interest.

Sterling, still in his robe, was seated at a table on the patio behind the manor house having breakfast. He knew from the radio contact with security that two local men had been found on the property and that they were being brought in. He wasn't quite prepared for the pair standing in front of him.

Looking up over his paper as the group approached the patio he thought, *Christ, I thought all of the Neanderthals had died ages ago.*

Both Lester and Floyd were dressed in work boots, blue jeans, and the tattered remains of faded flannel shirts that should have been converted to dust rags long ago. Floyd was hatless but Lester wore a dirty camouflage baseball-style hat. Lester was real proud of that hat. He had gotten it free for buying three boxes of his favorite brand of chewing tobacco.

Sterling had always been a quick study of a person's character and capabilities. From Lester's size, shape, demeanor, and somewhat quizzical but simple-minded grin, he correctly evaluated him as a strong, moderately intelligent young man who probably would follow orders if well enough compensated.

What he saw in Floyd was a completely different story. Sterling always looked into a person's eyes when they first met and could usually gauge the character of the individual by the light, or lack of it, in their eyes. What he saw in Floyd Morgan was a glare that was close to a glaze, reminding Sterling of the mindless, killing stare of a great white shark he had seen once off the Great Barrier Reef near Australia.

This man is truly dangerous, Sterling thought. *If there's enough intelligence there to work with, I can use him.* Sterling saw in Floyd's eyes the same anger, the same hate, the same blood lust he so often felt but could control and hide from everyone else.

"Good morning, gentlemen," Sterling said, smiling and offering them a seat. "Maria, bring two more coffee cups, please." He paused looking both men in the eyes. "Gentlemen, I understand you were interested in some trees located on my property. I should tell you . . ."

"Honest, Mister we weren't gonna steal the trees," Lester interrupted. "We were just gonna look at 'em and then come up here and offer to buy 'em. I swear we were!"

"Not to worry, gentlemen. We may come to terms on some timber business. You're local, I assume? Tell me about yourselves."

"I'm Lester and this is my brother Floyd. We live about six miles up the road over on 641. We got a trailer over there that used to belong to our dad. We do a lot of tree work up in the country. When we can't find no work up there we cut firewood down here to sell later on. We're the best in the county. Floyd here is the best limb man within a hundred miles. We've been doin' tree work all our lives and he ain't fell out of more than four or five trees. He's been real lucky. He's usually landed on his head. He's only broke his leg once or twice. Boy, you should have seen him bounce the time . . ."

"Pardon me for interrupting, but I take it that your usual employment does not provide a regular paycheck."

At the thought of a regular paycheck, Lester had to stop for a minute and think. "Well, I guess not. When we need money we just go cut some trees or sell some firewood. We do a lot of huntin' and trappin' too. We do okay."

"Oh, I'm sure you do. I didn't mean to insinuate that you were destitute."

Neither Lester nor Floyd were quite sure what this man had just said. They both thought he was trying to apologize for something and, for some reason, was being relatively nice to them. This was an unusual occurrence for them and they found themselves flattered to be taken so seriously by someone who obviously had so much money.

"Have either of you ever considered regular employment?" The thought of regular employment, forty-hour weeks, and the deduction of taxes from a paycheck was a totally foreign concept to the Morgan boys.

"Well, no. Not recently. But if you got a proposition, we'll listen."

"Well, I don't have anything specific right now, but give Sam here you names, address, and phone number and I'll get in touch with you. I think we may be able to find something for both of you."

"Ain't got no phone." Floyd scowled, still trying to figure out what was happening. That was his contribution to the morning's conversation. He could tell his brother was impressed with this man from the city, but he wasn't sure yet whether or not he was being insulted.

CHAPTER EIGHTEEN

THERE'S SOMETHING VERY special about early spring along the Rapidan and Rappahannock Rivers. The first rains and the rays of the first few warm days revitalize the piedmont region of Virginia. The rivers, coursing their way as they have for thousands of years toward the Chesapeake, tumble gracefully out of the Blue Ridge across the foothills and join at the eastern end of Culpeper County, just northwest of Clarkton.

John had always been partial to this season in Rapidan County. The lunker smallmouth bass in both rivers began to be receptive to lures fished deep and slow through the pools. In late March, the white perch would begin to nose their way up the Rappahannock River from Port Royal to spawn. Their arrival meant the imminent return of the annual run of hickory shad up the Rappahannock to Fredericksburg and beyond. John and Allen never missed at least two or three trips down Route 3 to Fredericksburg to sample what, with good luck, could be some of the fastest and most exciting fishing on the East Coast.

When the shad were thick in the pools below the Route 1 bridge at Falmouth, a fish on almost every cast was a reality, not a dream. Arriving before daylight and wading out to their favorite spot to await sunrise gave them time to talk, time to enjoy the peace and serenity of an early morning along one of the East Coast's most scenic rivers. Whether their luck was good or bad, they invariably enjoyed their time on the river. The rush of the water over the mist-shrouded rapids just upstream from the bridge, the swirling flight of the ospreys and seagulls, and the outline of the ancient buildings on the heights across the river were all part of this annual experience. Any line-stretching, high-jumping, roe-laden hickory shad on the stringer were a bonus to be enjoyed, both in the catching and in the eating.

April in Virginia also meant the opening of spring gobbler season. Though this was a type of hunting Allen had not come to enjoy, John had always been challenged by it. But he wasn't very good at it and hadn't been very successful.

A gobbler in the spring is one of the most difficult hunts in North America. Though his hormones are in an uproar, he remains one of the smartest of all wild creatures. His eyesight and hearing are unequaled and his native intelligence is a challenge to even the most expert woodsman.

The only two spring gobblers John had ever killed had been called up for him by Roy. As usual, Roy was much more proficient in finding, calling, and fooling these birds. Successful spring gobbler hunting requires the ability to not only blend into the surroundings, but an inordinate amount of patience to remain still while calling to the male bird. Being able to imitate a love-starved hen on any one of a number of different types of turkey calls and doing it in a manner which would fool a spring gobbler is a difficult task at best.

While Roy was certainly one of the best turkey hunters in Rapidan County, even his skill couldn't match that of the men in the Porter family. All of the Porters were decendents of three brothers sold into slavery on the Fitzgerald plantation in the 1840's. Remaining in Rapidan County after the War Between the States, all three brothers married and raised large families within the county. In those most difficult days of Reconstuction, they were able, through strength of character and an abiding faith in their church, not only to survive but to prosper.

During the latter part of the nineteenth century and through the first half of the twentieth century, the Porter family, together with their neighbors, concentrated on raising and providing for their families. Almost without exception, the Porters and their children and their children's children continued to be productive members of society. As times changed and the civil rights movement advanced, many of the Porter children went off to college, some to return to Clarkton as teachers and professionals in other fields.

Through the decades, one thing remained constant with the Porters: they were always some of the best hunters, fishermen, and woodsmen in the county. From the early days after the war through the turn of the century and the Depression, they had always been able to provide for their families, not only through money earned but through their skills and abilities in the woods. Drawing on these well-developed skills, they were consistently able to provide fish and game for their families.

This was especially true of Issac and Rodney Porter and their cousins, William, Scott, and George. All of these men, each in his early-to mid-thirties except Issac, the oldest at fifty-two, had been born in Rapidan County, graduated from high school there, and, with the exception of William who remained single, had married local girls. Issac and Rodney had taken over their father's hardware business in downtown Clarkton, and with modern innovations, had made it even more prosperous than before. Scott, after graduating from Howard University, had returned to Clarkton as a pharmacist and was employed at the local Revco. George drove tractor-trailers for a local manufacturer, and William, who was the most footloose and mechanically inclined of the five, operated a garage out in the county. William had found that running his own small business allowed him the freedom to pick and choose his work hours. He primarily chose to be in the woods until it was absolutely necessary to return to work to generate some income to pay the necessary bills.

When the five Porters teamed up against a smart old tom turkey or big buck, the animal had little chance of survival. The five men had hunted together all of their lives and not only knew Rapidan County intimately, but also had a sense of where each of the others were in the woods, what they were doing, and how the game they sought would be affected by the movements of the hunters.

John had had another unsuccessful early morning turkey hunt in late April when he stopped by the Oak Run Country Store for a Coke before heading home. The store had been in operation continuously since it was first opened in the early 1900's by Frank Gibson's grandfather, Thomas. It was a state-designated big game checking station and John was not surprised to see a number of other trucks and four-wheel drive vehicles in the parking lot when he arrived. He recognized Issac Porter's Dodge pickup and knew there had to be at least one less gobbler in the woods for him to hunt.

Walking across the parking lot he met Issac and Rodney coming out of the store. Issac was carrying a huge gobbler in his left hand, grinning like the proverbial possum.

"Jesus, Issac, how big is he?"

"The beard or the number of pounds?"

"Both!" John said incredulously.

"The beard is fourteen and three quarter inches long and he weighs twenty-four and a half pounds. It's sure the biggest one I've ever killed!"

"Did you get him down by the river?" John asked, not really expecting a detailed answer.

"Naw, I got him over at my granddaddy's place next to Billy Lofton's house. I been huntin' him for two years. He probably was the smartest ol' gobbler I ever came across, but we got him, didn't we, Rodney?"

Rodney just smiled and nodded.

Looking more closely at the gobbler's beard, John said, "You know he's probably going to be as tough as white leather, don't you?"

"Yeah, I expect he will. But Rachael knows how to cook these things so that by the time she gets done, he'll taste like a ten-pound hen."

"I know she does. Say, Issac, you know I gave Allen one of the Hoyt compound bows for Christmas. I've tried to teach him the best I can, but I'm not the world's greatest bow hunter. I wonder if you might have some time to shoot with Allen and give him some pointers. I know you aren't part Indian, but you sure act like you are during bow season."

Issac smiled broadly. He was one of the best bow hunters in the county, and his son James played baseball with Allen Ritchter on the high school baseball team. "Sure, John, I'd be glad to. I'll do the best I can. I just hope you haven't already taught him too many bad habits."

Laughing, John smiled and said, "I'll give you a call after turkey season's over. I know Allen will look forward to that. Has James taken up bow-hunting yet?"

"No, he does a little gun-hunting with me in the fall, but he's too busy chasing girls most of the time to think about spending fall afternoons up in a tree. I expect he'll get into it a little later on, at least I hope so."

"I can understand that. Allen's the same way. Save me a drumstick, will you?" John said, smiling as he pulled open the store's screen door.

"You bet!" Issac said, throwing the old tom into the bed of the pickup and climbing into the driver's side.

As John went into the store he thought, *Christ, those guys are unnatural in the woods. I'd hate to have either one of them after me.*

"Hey, Frank, how ya' doing?" John said as he reached for a knife to cut a wedge of cheese off the block sitting on the counter.

"Just fine, John. If I was any better, I couldn't stand it." Frank was always the same. Always glad to see people. Always hospitable and always had time to talk. His was one of the few remaining old-timey country stores left in the county. John envied Frank a little bit. He never seemed concerned about how much he made or when he made it. He was just always there, always smiling and, even on the opening day of deer season, always open.

CHAPTER NINETEEN

CHARLES STERLING COULD not have expected his enterprise to have been so successful. He had established himself as a respected member of the community and no one suspected the true purpose of his presence. The conference center was complete and he had already accommodated a number of guests. His connections within the criminal community were such that, when they learned of the existence of his facility, he could name his own price for the services he provided.

His own man running the local airport made it possible for guests to arrive in Rapidan County, be transported quietly and without notice to Belleview, and set up there for the transition to wherever they chose as their final destination.

The technique he established to create new identities and backgrounds for these fugitives worked flawlessly. Not only was he able to lay down a new paper trail for these individuals, he was able to make either subtle or substantial changes in their physical appearance. After the changes were made, he provided the appropriate documentation to allow the individual to travel freely in or out of the country.

Early that summer, after having been in operation only three months, Sterling's facility and staff faced an extremely difficult task. His contact in San Francisco had called with an inquiry from a man who had made it on to the F.B.I.'s Ten Most Wanted list. Even worse, the man had found out he was to be profiled the following week on *America's Most Wanted.*

The man, Carl Groves, was the perfect Sterling client, an imminently successful thief made wealthy by his criminal skills—desperate and non-violent. After a briefing from his man in California, Sterling agreed to the deal. The one-hundred-thousand-dollar deposit arrived in one of Sterling's offshore accounts four days before Groves landed at the airport in Culpeper. Taken quickly by limousine to Belleview, he was greeted warmly by his host.

"Mr. Groves, I'm Charles Sterling. Welcome to Virginia," he said, extending his hand to the slightly built, forty-six year old man.

"Thank you, sir. I'm glad to be anywhere that isn't California!"

"I'm sure. Your reputation precedes you. I understand you've been extraordinarily successful in the diamond and jewelry trade?"

"Well, yes. My profession has been very good to me. But that same success can bring a notoriety that can be—how can I put it? Unhealthy?"

As Grove's luggage was taken to his assigned suite, they adjourned to the library in the manor house. Sterling said, "I don't want to tire you and I'm sure you're exhausted from your flight. If you'll tell me when you'd like to have breakfast tomorrow, I'll schedule a meeting with our staff for an hour or two afterward and we can begin your metamorphosis."

"An interesting analogy, Mr. Sterling. I think I like it. I'm a late sleeper. Actually brunch at 11:00 or so would be wonderful. Will that upset your schedule?"

"Not at all. Melinda, will you see to those arrangements? I believe we'll need Dr. Cordell, Mr. Bigsby, the photographer, and the seamstress."

"Yes, sir. I'll contact them right now," she said, leaving the two men alone.

"You told me of Dr. Cordell. Even though I don't want any reconstructive surgery, he'll be involved?"

"Yes. I ask him to sit in on all of these initial sessions. While you may not want any major permanent changes, there may be small things here and there that will make a difference. He may merely suggest a few things. You are free to reject any of those suggestions, of course."

"I understand. And Mr. Bigsby?"

"The make-up artist. He's a master at disguise. The masks he does are phenomenal. I think that's what will work best for you. But let's not prejudge the possibilities. Tomorrow will just be for initial examinations, measurements, handwriting samples, and pictures. With all of those in hand, we can have a proposal to you with all of the options in a matter of days."

"Amazing. I'm really anxious to see the process in operation. What about the financial aspects?"

"We can start that tomorrow too. We can set up accounts from here and I'll begin the wire transfer process so that, in a month or so, all of your assets will be consolidated in Brazil."

The two men talked quietly for a few more minutes and then with cordial goodnights, each retired for the evening—Groves to anxiously await the process of starting a new life with the fortune his criminal prowess provided and Sterling to enjoy and fantasize over the delicious pleasure he felt at tempting fate in such an outrageous fashion.

At one-thirty the next afternoon, Groves met with the staff into whose hands he was placing his future. As they discussed his desires, each evaluated him to determine how they could transform him into someone who could travel undisturbed, despite his well-deserved but unwanted public recognition.

Mr. Bigsby, knowing that his client was bi-sexual and a cross-dresser, said, "Mr. Groves, you're a perfect candidate for dual-sex identities. We'll provide you with a new male identity that will make you look sixty. You'll be bald and have completely different dental work. We also ought to use a padded wardrobe and special shoes, so you will appear to be over twenty pounds heavier and walk with a limp. All of this will be with complete paper work, identifying you as a retired banker from Duluth, Minnesota. I have some great ideas for the female disguise but I don't want to spoil the surprise. Just trust me on that one."

The female identity was to be a striking example of what Sterling's staff could accomplish. After weeks of hard work, trial and error, using partial masks, the highest quality wigs, and the latest in make-up technology, the transformation was complete. Sterling and his client were both speechless at the final product.

Groves emerged as a not-to-unattractive brunette in her mid-thirties. The make-up and fair skin combined to insure that this identity would suit him well. Looking at Sterling and fluttering his new eyelashes, he put his hands under his newly-minted breasts and said, "Well, how do you like my tits? I don't believe I've ever looked better!"

"My goodness," said Sterling, "this is really remarkable. Come with me. We've got to try something."

"O.K." said Groves. "Where are we going?"

"To the manor house. I have a few local guests and this is a great time to see how this works."

"Sure! They won't suspect anything! Especially not with this cleavage," lauged Groves.

"I'll introduce you to them as one of my executives from New York. Just smile and be sweet," Sterling said with a grin.

Walking into the living room, two local men who were interested in doing some computer work for Mr. Sterling rose when they saw the lady enter.

"Gentlemen, I'm sorry to keep you waiting. One of my executives from New York is here for a few days to visit. May I present Miss Alton? Mr. Toms and Mr. Rogers."

"A pleasure to meet you ma'am. I hope you enjoy your visit to my part of the country," said Mr. Toms.

"Well," said Groves in his softest, most feminine voice, "it's been a real eye-opener so far. I'm sure it will continue to be very eventful."

"Yes, I'm sure. If you'd like to see some of our local battlefields and other historical sites, I'd be glad to show you," injected Rogers, his interest in her obvious.

"I'd love to," Groves said, batting his eyes and bending over to pick up a drink in such a way that exposed more of his clevage to the man, "but I'm afraid Mr. Sterling has my remaining time here too well planned. Maybe next time?"

Taking her hand, the man smiled his best smile. "I'll hold you to that."

"I'll be going back to the conference center now, Charles. I'll see you there in a few minutes?"

"Yes. I'll help Sam entertain my guests for a few more minutes and then meet you there."

By the time Sterling found him, Groves had already filled everyone in on his success.

"Yes," he said, "I thought that guy was going to try and jump my bones right there! I can't wait to try this on a customs agent!"

His confidence firmly in place, Groves left Belleview ten days later. Using the female identity he easily passed through all the security which should have prevented his escape. A week after his departure, Sterling received a postcard from Rio which read:

> "Arrived safely. Thanks to you and staff. Hugs and kisses to my two local friends.
>
> Love,
> Judy

What a trip, Sterling thought. *He'll send us some good referrals too. It's working like a charm!*

Sterling had a very carefully chosen set of referring agents across the country who were all well known to him. Potential clients were never told in advance the exact location of the facility nor who its true owner was. In that way the appropriate level of anonymity was maintained. At fifty-thousand dollars per week, he was assured that the guests who arrived at Belleview were so grateful to be there that they wouldn't jeopardize his operation.

While Sterling's security precautions were state of the art, he was nonetheless continually concerned by the local traffic and the number of individuals who were in the woods hunting or fishing on a constant basis. He hadn't realized the extent to which these outdoor activities were still prevalent in rural areas such as Rapidan County. Though he had around-the-clock security at the front gate and regular patrols around the perimeter of Belleview, along with countless posted signs, there was an endless parade of local people who sought permission to hunt on the property. These requests were invariably refused with the polite explanation that the owner did not approve of hunting or firearms. In addition, Sterling had established a small herd of beef cattle, not only to supply the dinner table but to give additional legitimacy to what he would claim to be a farming operation.

Not one to rely on posted signs or the willingness of all the local hunters to abide by his refusal to allow hunting, he had ultimately decided to hire Lester and Floyd Morgan as his private game wardens.

"Sam," Mr. Sterling said, "that background check tells me that the Morgan boys are exactly what they appear to be. They both have criminal records and they'll bend the law as far as they need to and break it when it suits them. If I pay them enough, they'll do whatever I want them to, especially Floyd. I think he'll take whatever steps necessary to enforce my rules at Belleview."

"I don't know," said Sam, shaking his head. "I expect they'll be reluctant to take any form of employment that will compromise their freedom. These are not nine-to-five people. They aren't going to want to punch a time clock or be obligated to be at any particular place at any particular time. And they aren't going to agree to be sober if they don't want to be."

"I understand your concerns and we'll keep a close eye on them. If they turn out to be too much of a liability, they'll just disappear. And no one around here will miss them either!"

Sam smiled at the comment and knew Sterling wouldn't hesitate to eliminate anyone who threatened his enterprise. Contacting the Morgans, he had them meet with Sterling a few days later.

"Gentlemen," Mr. Sterling said, "I need for you to keep a watchful eye on Belleview for me. Be my game wardens, if you will. You may do all of the hunting and fishing on the property that you want. In fact, you will be the only people in Rapidan County who have the right to hunt on the property. You may completely disregard any game laws and, no matter what the season or regulation, take whatever animal you wish. Just don't advertise that around the county. I will also pay you fifty-thousand dollars a year, each, for this service.

"Your obligation to me will be to patrol the farm on a daily basis at the times which you chose. As opposed to the other security personnel in my employ, you are to go deep into the property and circulate through all of the wooded areas to prevent poaching or to catch anyone you find on the property. I know you're woodsmen and I don't want anyone on the property for any reason without my knowing it. My other security personnel are not woods-wise, but I sense that you'll know instinctively when someone is on the property who shouldn't be. When someone is found, they are to be escorted to the property line and told, in no uncertain terms, not to return."

Lester and Floyd couldn't believe their luck. They would get almost unfettered access to all the hunting and fishing they wanted, get to run others off, and get paid more money than they had ever dreamed of.

"We'd be proud to work for you, Mr. Sterling," said Lester.

"Yeah," Floyd said, "what's not to like?"

"I know I can count on you boys," Sterling replied. And count on them he could.

The fact that Sterling had hired two such well known outlaws raised the eyebrows of many of the Rapidan County locals. Soon, the rumors of rough treatment and threats of physical violence by the Morgans on Mr. Sterling's behalf caused some suspicion.

These suspicions were heightend one day that fall when four of the Porter brothers' best deer dogs all disappeared while on Sterling's property. They had gotten out a kennel door that was left unlocked. Striking the trail of a deer, they ran the animal onto the old plantation. Finding the dogs gone, Issac and Rodney were out looking for them when a mail carrier told them he had seen them just minutes before, crossing the road in front of him and going onto Belleview. As Issac and Rodney approached the front gate to request permission to go onto the property to try to catch the dogs, they heard four quick shots about half a mile away.

Denied permission to come on the property, Issac said, "Let's ride to the other side of the property to try and head the dogs off. Maybe we can get 'em before they cross the river." But after hearing the shots fired, they never again heard the dogs running nor were they ever able to locate them. An hour later, still riding up and down the road trying to find the dogs, they saw the Morgan's coming out of one of the logging roads that crossed Belleview.

There was no love lost between the Morgans and any members of the black community. Issac and Rodney knew how the woodcutters felt, and credited the animal-like grins of the Morgan brothers to their known dislike and prejudice against blacks. Had they seen the bloody dog collars on the floorboard of the Morgans' truck or known that the bodies of their four dogs were under the tarp in the back of the pickup as they passed each other, the confrontation would have been a violent one.

"What are you lookin' at?" Floyd yelled at the Porters as they drove by, slamming his left hand against the side of the truck and spitting a stream of tobacco juice at them.

Issac and Rodney knew there was no point in responding and continued down the road in hopes of finding the dogs.

"Floyd," said Lester, "we need to go ahead and get rid of these dogs. They won't be runnin' any more deer on Belleview."

"Goddamn right. Let's go down and throw 'em in the river. They'll float all the way to Fredericksburg. If that son of a bitch looks at me like that again we'll do the same thing to him we did to those dogs and throw him into the river."

"Naw," said Lester, "we need to dump the dogs somewhere they'll be found. If they ain't found, people won't get the message. Let's dump 'em down by the bridge. Someone's bound to find them and call the sheriff. Won't nobody be able to link 'em to us."

"O.K.," said Floyd, "I like that better anyway. Man, would I love to be there when those Porter boys see what we done to their dogs. That'll teach 'em."

Floyd didn't know why he hated blacks so much. He only knew that he did. There was a smoldering sense of resentment inside of him, instilled by his father and grandfather who never ceased to talk disparagingly about blacks. He had grown up being taught that any black was his enemy, especially one who had done better in life than he had. The problem was that almost all of the local blacks had done better than he had, and, in his primitive fashion, he sensed his failure compared to their success.

"Son of a bitch looks at me like that again, I'll kill his ass!"

"Take it easy, Floyd. You ever go up against those boys you better have both barrels loaded. I seen both them guys shoot."

"Bullshit. I ever decide to do anything about him, he'll never see it comin'. I got his dogs and I'll get him too." Floyd was like that. When he hated somebody he hated them all the time and he never stopped.

Sooner or later. Sooner or later, his ass is mine, thought Floyd.

It was early the next morning when a fisherman discovered the torn and bloody remains of Issac's four deer dogs. The deputy who responded recognized the dogs and had the dispatcher call the Porters to meet him at the Germanna Ford Bridge over the Rapidan.

When Issac and Rodney arrived, the deputy led them over to a corner of the small parking lot used by the public as access to the river. There, heaped in a pile, alive with maggots and green-bottle flies, lay his dogs. They had not only been shot but for all intents and purposes, butchered.

"Man," said Issac, "who'd do this to my dogs? They're just running deer, just doing what they were trained to do. I'd have taken the blame for 'em getting out. Paid damages, whatever. But this! These are some sick bastards. I ain't seen anything like this since Nam."

Turning from the putrid remains, it took him several minutes to regain his composure. They then spread a tarp over the bed of the pickup and loaded the dogs' remains, covering them and beginning the trip home to bury them.

Silent for a long time, Issac finally said, "You know who did this, don't you?" Not waiting for the answer, he continued, "The Morgans. They're the only ones who could have, who are violent and dangerous enough. We're not going to let this go. I'm calling the sheriff as soon as we get home."

He did and Sheriff Longley was sympathetic and promised a full investigation. And, though he went through the motions, the result was that no arrests were made.

"Not enough evidence," the sheriff said.

And the hate between the Morgans and the Porters escalated.

The disappearance of the Porters' dogs and the subsequent discovery of their mutilated bodies also fueled more local concern and suspicion about the activities at Belleview, as did the increased frequency of late night flights in and out of the airport.

As spring turned to summer, Sterling felt some additional diversion would be beneficial. Being aware of the seeds of racial tension in the county, he had already identified some local organizations he could turn to his own advantage. He knew exactly what kind of diversion would work.

CHAPTER TWENTY

"SAM, WHAT KIND of drug problem do they have in Rapidan County?" Sterling asked.

"Well, there isn't really a bad drug problem. There are a few small-time dealers and enough addicts to keep them busy. But, all in all, it's not bad."

"Well, why should the folks in the inner-city have all the fun? Why don't you get some of our friends up in D.C. to realize what a market they're overlooking here in the sticks. Call Tyrone. Tell him we need two or three of his boys to come down here and stir the pot a little bit. They'll need to bring a good supply of crack with them. Tell them I'll underwrite it, but I want the supply to be cheap and easy to get. Make sure they bring some semi-automatics with them to distribute. I'll pay for those too. It's time Rapidan County developed a serious drug habit. Tell him to get this together and get down here in the next week or so. I want to meet these guys and talk with them before they get started."

"You got it. This oughta be fun."

Sterling's plan was as diabolical as it was simple. Rapidan County's proximity to the Northern Virginia and the Washington, D.C. metropolitan area meant that a certain number of urban families, both black and white, had moved into the county. With them came many of the problems which had plagued the urban areas for years. In the last five years or so there had been increased drug traffic and it was not unusual to see the arrest and conviction of locals for offenses related to cocaine traffic on the court docket. However, until now, there had been no really significant amount of drugs in the area. Neither had there been any violent confrontations between drug dealers or between the dealers and the police.

"Tyrone! You're as ugly as ever!" Sterling could say that to this large black man and get away with it because of his position and because of the resources available to him. Tyrone would permit this joke only from Sterling because he knew what the man could do for him. Had anyone else attempted such familiarity, he probably wouldn't have survived the experience. Tyrone had grown up on the mean streets of South Washington and had received a graduate degree in survival and life on the streets. The primary rule of that education was to be the strongest, the best-armed, and best-equipped dealer on the streets. If you were crossed, if someone didn't pay you, if someone ripped you off, they died—a simple rule he lived by.

After receiving Sterling's call, Tyrone had gotten several of his associates together and driven the sixty or so miles from Washington to Belleview. Curious about what his role might be in such a small community, he got straight to the point. "What the hell am I doin' down here in this little redneck haven? I can't see no advantage to my operating in this hick town. What do I get out of this?"

"Calm down, Tyrone. There's more here than meets the eye, but you don't need to know everything that's going on. What I need for you to understand and to help with is a diversion for these locals. I have my own reasons for being here and my own reasons for not wanting anyone to worry about what goes on here. Some folks are getting a little too curious and I want something that will take their minds off Belleview and make them look elsewhere."

"What kinda diversion?"

"Well, the blacks and whites get along a little bit too well down here in the country. I don't know how they've managed to do it, but they're mostly civil to each other. That needs to change."

"What do ya want me to do? Just shoot a few of 'em?" Tyrone could be pretty direct.

"No, I don't want to be that obvious. What I need for you to do is give a little incentive to the two or three small-time drug dealers that we have here. Sam has their names. Just make connections with them. Make sure they have plenty of crack and make sure that it's inexpensive enough for these folks down here to sample. I'll underwrite the cost of all of it. I want to make sure that they're well-armed too. As part of becoming associated with your organization, you can loan them a couple of nine-millimeters each-maybe a street-sweeper or two, whatever else you think they might need. This doesn't all need to be done at one time. Maybe over the next month or so you can filter all of this in. I really don't care whether they make any money at it, though I expect they will. Hell, let them give it away for a while. We just need to generate some consumer appreciation of our little tannish rock-like friends."

"That's all? You just want me to dump some crack on the market?" Tyrone asked. "You don't need me to do that!"

"No, its more that that. I need a couple of your guys to move to Clarkton for a little while." At that comment, several of Tyrone's friends looked at each other and at Tyrone indicating none of them were very interested in giving up their city lifestyle for the fresh air and clean living of the country. Sterling saw their skeptical glances and continued.

"I'm not talking about moving here permanently. I just need a couple of your guys to stir up some discontent among some of their younger, less sophisticated brothers. There are a group of younger blacks here in the county who seem to want to enjoy a bit more of the modern lifestyle than they can find. Sam tells me that there's a group at the high school and a number of others who are out of school who can probably be stirred up without much trouble. A couple of your boys just need to point out to them the inequality of their situation versus the white folks around here.

"Understand, I don't want riots. I don't want the town burned down. I just want people to get a little more concerned about whether or not they can trust each other. You know, burn a cross here and there. Spray paint a few well-chosen words on several black churches. Point out to the black kids with no jobs that all the white kids are getting the breaks. You know, fan the flames a bit."

"No problem but this'll cost you, you know. Twenty thousand to start oughta get you a little fire." *I'm not stupid,* he thought. *There's something bigger behind all of this and I don't care what it is, I just want to make sure that I get a piece of it.*

"No problem. Sam, take care of that for Tyrone, will you? When can we expect some results?"

"By the weekend," said Tyrone.

True to his word, there were several new tenants in local apartment buildings by the weekend. These young black men paid rent in cash, drove nice vehicles, dressed well, but had no visible means of support. They were seen all around town and frequented some of the fast-food restaurants where the younger blacks hung out. At the same time, the two primary local drug dealers who hadn't been caught found themselves approached by unknown but obviously well-connected individuals who offered them a quality product at an extremely reasonable price. Neither of these young men were inclined to turn down an opportunity to increase their market, and, within two weeks, the supply of crack cocaine in Rapidan County rose considerably.

This increased drug traffic did not escape the notice of local law enforcement. Late night patrols in certain sections of town reported increased sidewalk traffic. There were more complaints by local citizens about knots of young men and women out on the streets late and there were more disturbances and fights. There was also an increase in the number of weapons found during routine stops, especially late at night. There was, over the following months, an increase in property crimes resulting in the theft of easily disposable items like jewelry, guns, and electronic equipment. This increase in drug activity and associated crime was attributed by the local population to their proximity to the metro area. Sterling had again successfully initiated a well conceived plan and no suspicion was cast on him or his organization.

The second part of his plan also went into effect. In addition to increasing the supply of drugs and guns on the street, Tyrone's friends infiltrated the local black community, especially that group of young blacks who already tended to be dissatisfied with their lives. These were primarily the young men and women who had been unsuccessful in school and unsuccessful in finding any job they considered to be appropriate and financially rewarding. Concentrating on those individuals, it wasn't difficult to stir up in them a heightened dislike and distrust for the local whites.

At the same time these passions were heating up, Tyrone's men took steps to see that the blacks had visible evidence of white discrimination against them. Taking hints from the action of the Klan in the deep south during the 1960's, Tyrone's men spray-painted racial slurs on several local black churches and even burned a cross in the front yard of the President of the local N.A.A.C.P. chapter. Leaving evidence pointing toward local whites, this ruse had its desired effect.

Sterling's plan to create distrust between the races exploded across the county newspaper's headlines after a brawl at Rapidan County High School's last home baseball game of the season, a night game that was particularly well attended. This disturbance was the result of an argument over some spectators standing in front of the fence along the first-base line.

Some of the younger blacks infected by Sterling's resourceful efforts participated in blocking the view of the fans sititng in the lower bleachers. Though asked politely to move several times, their response was as vulgar as it was negative. Several of the spectators took exception to their language and gestures and came out of the stands to respond.

The shouting, bumping, and shoving deteriorated quickly into a free-for-all involving over twenty teenagers. For several minutes the bedlam created stopped the game and caused most of the fans not involved to run from the area. The players, including Allen and James, moved away from the fight, staring in disbelief as they watched the brawl.

Though there were several deputies present for traffic control, the fight couldn't be stopped until five other deputies and the sheriff arrived. Even then it took several more minutes to separate the combatants. There were a number of arrests and, though several knives were found, none had been used.

The game was cancelled because of the fight and Allen was still shaken when he got home. It was the only game that either John or Brenda had not been able to attend. They shook their heads in disbelief as Allen recounted the events as he had seen them.

"I couldn't believe it, Dad. I've read about this stuff, but I've never seen it. I've known some of those kids for years and it was like all of them, black and white, just turned into animals. I don't know what's happened. What's going on? It's like they hate each other and no one knows why."

Later, several shotgun blasts fired at black homes by Tyrone's men fueled the flames of discontent. The perception that there was still a strong element of discrimination in the white community strained relations between the races in Rapidan County as they had not been in decades and confrontations on the streets and in the schools increased.

As Sterling learned of these events a smile crossed his face.

Yes, he thought, *a little discrimination can go a long way. These folks are so wound up about who's discriminating against whom, they've forgotten all about me. Perfect!*

CHAPTER TWENTY-ONE

"JUDGE COLLINS, WE really would love for you to speak at the dedication of our monument on the ninth. That's the national Confederate Memorial Day, you know." Miss Rollins smiled her most persuasive smile. At a very prim and proper eighty-seven years of age, she knew she could impose on the judge for this favor. The other members of the committee seated in Judge Collins' office nodded their agreement to her request.

"You simply must be the key-note speaker. You're the only one who can put into words why the monument and this dedication ceremony is so important! It's been an embarrassment to us for decades that we're nearly the only county in the state with no monument to our Confederate veterans!"

The Judge nodded and smiled. He had known in advance why the members of the committee had wanted to see him. And he knew he would accept the invitation to be one of the speakers at the ceremony.

"Miss Rollins," the Judge replied, "I'll be honored to be one of the speakers. All of you in the United Daughters of the Confederacy and the Sons of Confederate Veterans have done a wonderful job of pulling this service together and it will be a privilege to participate.

"Although," the Judge hesitated, "I think Isaiah Thompson should be billed as the key-note speaker. He's the last real son of a veteran anywhere around here, isn't he?"

"You're right, Judge. He is and he's agreed to come and speak too," replied Miss Rollins. "He said he had a special surprise for us.

Something he wrote back in the twenties about why it's important for us to remember the veterans. He won't tell us what it is, but assures us it is a fitting tribute."

"Well," said Judge Collins, "it's settled then. I'll speak after Mr. Thompson and do the best I can. I'm sure his remarks will be a tough act to follow!" Leaning forward, his eyebrows furrowed with obvious concern, the judge continued, "I don't mean to bring up a subject that might dampen your collective enthusiasm, but have you spoken with Sheriff Longley about security for the ceremony?"

Judge Collins concern was founded on rumors and bits of information he had heard ever since the anonymous donor had sent the six-figure check to cover the cost of the Confederate monument. After the first wave of articles in the local paper about the donation and the erection of the monument on the lot across from the courthouse, there had been an undercurrent of dissatisfaction, even indignation, in parts of the local black community.

Unknown to those gathered in Judge Collins' office, this was precisely what Sterling had envisioned when he gave the money for the monument. He had several of his contacts in the community begin talking openly about the monument and the insult it was to the local African-American population. A number of letters to the local paper had crystallized opinions for and against the monument and the planned celebration.

Responding to the judge's question about security, Miss Rollins said, "Well, yes, we've spoken to the sheriff and he assures us that he'll have plenty of officers on duty that day. We all want this to be a quiet and dignified service to honor those from our county who fought in the War. We don't intend to offend anyone, but we have the right to honor the memories of our ancestors and the courage they displayed on the battlefield."

"You're preaching to the choir, Miss Rollins. I agree with everything you've said. I just wanted to make sure the ceremony would be just that—a memorial to the men who served."

And what a ceremony it would be. Despite the expressed and implied objections of some of the black community, plans for the service included the attendance of local and state officials in both the U.D.C. and S.C.V., local politicians, authentically uniformed Confederate reenactment units, and even a properly outfitted band which would provide period music during the ceremony. The local high-school band had declined the invitation to participate, citing a busy practice schedule. Miss Rollin's felt there were other reasons for their refusal but didn't press the issue.

Reverend Joshua Robinson, one of the most active and respected black preachers in the county, had heard complaints and felt the real dissatisfaction and disaffection of many of those in his congregation. Several weeks before the planned ceremony, in an effort to calm the fear and anger he had seen, he spoke of the issue in his sermon.

In a bass voice that could resonate like a distant clap of thunder, he launched into the subject with the same zeal he had for all issues he addressed from his pulpit. "Brothers and Sisters, God knows there are many of you who carry a great weight in your heart. A weight put there by the realization, by the certainty that many of your ancestors came to this great land in bondage!"

A loud chorus of "Amens" came from the congregation for, with that opening remark, most in attendance knew what subject was to be addressed. Even those who hadn't paid much attention to the reverend's earlier message sat up a little straighter and listened more closely.

"Came to this great land as slaves!"

"Amen," was the response, only louder.

"Came to this great land against their will, on filthy slave ships, to work in the fields and homes of the plantation owners in the north and the south!"

Again, a loud "Amen" followed the reverend's words.

"And now, many of you have heavy hearts, because here, in our home, in our county, there is a monument built and soon to be dedicated to a cause that would have kept slavery!"

To that statement, many of the amens turned to shouts of "No! That's not going to happen!"

Raising his hands, Reverend Robinson continued, "And God knows you feel this is a slap in the face! Is disrespectful to you, to your ancestors who toiled as slaves. Many of whom never drank from the cup of freedom!"

Again, loud shouts of "Amen" rang through the assembly.

Lowering his voice and looking intently at his audience, Reverend Robinson said. "All of you know me. I've lived my life right here in this county. My parents, my grandparents, my roots are here in this soil, just like many of you. And I love this place, this part of Virginia we call home.

"And all of you know what a struggle we had in the fifties and sixties to end segregation, to gain those freedoms the Constitution of this great land guarantees to all citizens, black and white! I was part of the struggle, many of you were part of that struggle. And that struggle goes on!"

As he warmed to his subject, another wave of "Amens" swept the congregation.

"But, Brothers and Sisters, I don't want this monument, this service that's planned, to distract us from the truly important aspects of the struggle that continues. I am blessed to teach the history of this country to our teenagers at the high school. And I know, and many of you know, that the Civil War was caused by many issues, not just slavery. Yes, to us, that was and is the most important cause. We will always honor those Union soldiers, black and white, who fought and died to free our people. And God bless their immortal souls for their sacrifice!"

And with that statement, the entire congregation came their feet with the loudest "Amen" of the day.

"But we have to do what we ask our white brothers and sisters to do. And that is to see both sides. To try and understand both points of view. I believe in my heart that this monument, this service, is not about hate, is not about glorifying slavery, but is about those folks honoring their ancestors. Just as we have the right to remember and honor ours, they have the same right."

The congregation, somewhat surprised at the reverend's last comment, became more subdued.

"I see some of you here today wearing scarves with colors and designs that show your pride in your African heritage. I look back with pride at all those programs we had just last February for Black History Month. And I look into the eyes of all our children and see the strength and intelligence of the future of our community.

"But I remember too that slavery existed in Africa long before there was a United States, and I am ashamed. And more recently that awful time in Rwanda when nearly a million of our brothers were murdered by their countrymen in about one hundred days. And I am ashamed. And even now, in parts of our homeland, our brothers starve and kill each other. And I am ashamed. And I look at what happens today on the mean streets of Washington, D.C. and other metropolitan areas where some of our brothers have lost their way, and they kill each other over a pair of shoes or a leather jacket. And I am ashamed.

"But I don't bring these painful facts to you here in the church without purpose. And that is to remind all of us that every civilization, every country, every ethnic group has in its past and its present both good and evil. That every nation can point with pride to its accomplishments but must also deal with its failures, with those things of which it is not proud. The failings and atrocities committed by our brothers against each other do not and should not keep us from celebrating what is good and noble about our great African heritage.

"And so to do our white brothers and sisters who know that slavery was wrong have the right to commemorate the valor of their ancestors during the Civil War. In doing so, they are not celebrating slavery, but remembering the sacrifices of their ancestors on the battlefields of that war. A war that was fought for many reasons.

"I ask all of you, in the next two weeks, to look into your hearts, examine what and how you feel, and why you feel that way. And ask yourself, is it more important to focus on hate and distrust or is it more important, more Christian, to give them their afternoon of remembrance and move on with our lives, our struggle? I ask you, what does the Bible tell us to do?"

And with that closing, and a smaller chorus of amens than he had hoped for, the service ended.

CHAPTER TWENTY-TWO

THE DATE OF the ceremony dawned clear and unusually cool for early June in the piedmont of Virginia. A bright blue sky encouraged attendance and almost all the members of the sponsoring groups and their families were there. There were also many interested out-of-town visitors present who had ancestors who fought in the company from Rapidan County.

The monument itself was not tremendously imposing. Like many others, Rapidan County's monument was a simple four-sided granite obelisk. The base of the monument was five feet on each side and tapered to a height of twenty-two feet. The granite for the monument had been quarried in nearby Culpeper County and had been provided at a discounted price to the sponsoring organizations. Brass plaques were installed on each side of the monument. On the north face of the monument, the plaque named the local unit whose official designation had been company H, 13th Regiment, Virginia Volunteers, nicknamed the Rapidan County Rangers. On the east and west faces of the monument were a list of names of all those who had served in the company during the war, along with a notation regarding the fate of each soldier. On the south face of the monument was a long and distinguished list of the battles in which Company H had participated. Fighting under Stonewall Jackson's command, it had participated in the Shenandoah Valley Campaign; the Seven Days Campaign on the Virginia peninsula in the spring of 1862; the Battle of Cedar Mountain in neighboring Culpeper County in August, 1862; as well as Second Manassas, Antietam, Gettysburg, and most of the other major engagements in Virginia until the surrender at Appomattox.

The UDC and SCV had spent a great deal of time placing Confederate, Virginia, and United States flags in and around the area. They had also obtained permission for the Confederate reenactment groups to camp for the weekend on the courthouse lawn. These groups had taken part in filming the movie *Gettysburg* and their presence lent an authentic air to the day. Everyone enjoyed the living history demonstration of those modern-day Confederate soldiers.

While he had been invited, Sterling had decided not to attend, citing a pressing business appointment. However, he couldn't resist riding through town to see what his two-sided plan had accomplished. Passing near the monument, now covered with a large replica of a Confederate battle flag, Sterling asked, "Sam, what's going to happen here today? Do we know?"

Smiling, Sam replied, "Well, our friends from the District have been very successful in raising the hackles on the necks of a lot of the locals. You know this is a sore subject with lots of folks and it didn't take too much stirring to get the pot near boiling!

"There's a pretty good size group," he continued as they passed the Confederate camp at the courthouse, "that's going to march on the ceremony. Some have signs with "No KKK" on 'em. Others may have more planned than just marching. I'm kind of glad we're not going to be here."

"God, I love it when a plan comes together," Sterling said as they turned toward Belleview, the Virginia and Confederate flags blowing in the wind behind them.

Rumors of the pending confrontation had not only reached Reverend Robinson's ears, but also Sheriff Longley's. No amount of discussion would convince the organizers to cancel the ceremony and Sheriff Longley reluctantly realized his job was gong to be more difficult than he had first thought. All of the county's deputy sheriffs were on duty and had special instructions to encircle the site of the ceremony. They were to keep any protestors as widely separated as possible from those actively participating in the ceremony. But, recognizing everyone's right to free speech and to protest, he was obligated to provide protection for all those in attendance.

Promptly at 11:00 a.m., all of the guests and dignitaries took their places. The Confederate reenactors, dressed in authentic reproduction uniforms, marched from the courthouse lawn to the site of the monument and there presented the Confederate, Virginia, and United States flags to the tunes of "Dixie" and "The Star-Spangled Banner."

After retiring the colors, and with the monument still draped in the large Confederate flag, Miss Rollins introduced Isaiah Thompson as the ceremony's first speaker.

Rising slowly from his chair on the grandstand and assisted by one of the uniformed reenactors, Mr. Thompson slowly approached the podium. He was dressed in an old black wool suit with a vest, white shirt, and string tie. His bare head showed an abundance of white hair substantially displaced by the morning breeze. On his left breast pocket he wore the Confederate Veterans Reunion medals which his father had received for attending veterans meetings held across the south in the late 1800's through the 1920's.

Now assisted by a reenactor on one hand and his father's gnarled old hickory cane in the other, Mr. Thompson approached the microphone with a sense of purpose. A former school teacher, he began in a firm voice, his pride in his father evident by the words he spoke.

"I sure do you thank you, Miss Rollins, for asking me to speak a few words about my pa today. He'd be real proud to see his name on that marker over there. Some of y'all remember my daddy, I expect. He joined what was left of Company H in the winter of '64 when Lee moved the army south of the Rapidan after Gettysburg. He was only fifteen when he joined up, but was old enough to fight with the company in the Wilderness and at Spotsylvania Courthouse. Those of you that knew him remember his left arm hung useless by his side. That's because a Yankee miniball hit him in the elbow at the Bloody Angle over in Spotsylvania County.

"I remember him telling me about it plenty of times. They took him back to an aid station and were getting ready to cut his arm off above the elbow and he told them to leave him be! He must have been pretty short with the doctors. He told me that they told him if he was that dead set on dying that they would let him die. Well, he fooled them. The elbow healed but the nerves never got to the point where he could do much with that hand anymore. I guess he was probably the best one-armed farmer in the county after the war.

"Pa married his third wife, Liza, in 1901. She was my mother. He outlived all three of them. Liza died pretty shortly after I was born and he never did find another woman that he could live with.

"I remember going with him to a lot of these veterans meetings in the early 20's and how much it meant to him to be with the other soldiers. By then, there weren't any left that he had actually fought with. But being with those men who had shared the same camps and fights is what kept him going as long as he did.

"What all those men went through was the hardest thing they ever did. Pa always tried to make sure I understood that it was important for me to remember what they did and how they did it. I'm sure he's looking down right now and grinning to see that we've finally put up a stone to him and his company.

"Now understand I'm not any kind of poet. But what was important to my pa is important to me. I hope you'll forgive the sentiment, but it's hard to talk about what all they did without getting a little choked up. I wrote this a year or so after he died in 1928 and I've never read it to nobody before. I hope you'll think it's worth listening to. I titled it 'Reflections' and I think you'll know why in a minute."

Thompson removed a faded, yellowed sheet of paper from his pocket. The paper was folded over in thirds, and, as he unfolded it, it looked as if it might disintegrate in his hands. He held it tenderly between his fingers and slowly, hesitantly, began to read:

We are their eyes
For we see the trails over which they marched,
The hills they climbed,
The fields where they camped,
The ground they fought for,
The flags for which they died, and
The graves in which they lie.

We are their ears
For we hear the fond farewells,
The call of the bugle and rattle of the drum,
The shuffle and tramp of soldiers on the move,
The thunder of the guns, the prayers of the dying,
The silent sounds of those long past who whisper,
"Remember! Remember us for we fought for what we believed."

We are their voices
For we say the sad good-byes,
Sing the honored songs,
Tell the stories of deeds bravely done, and
Pledge our efforts to the memory of their sacrifice.

We are their hands
For we feel the old woolen garments,
Hold the thin and fragile tintypes of youth gone off to war,
Carry the ancient banners, and
Touch one another as compatriots,
Sharing a heritage that cannot be denied.

We are their hearts
For within us lives the soul and spirit of our forefathers,
Courses through us their life's blood.
Hearts which proud and strongly beat
When we remember the heroism
On the battlefields of yesterday.

And we are their minds
For when we think, we remember;
When we remember, we love; and
When we share these feelings, we teach.
Teach others of the importance of this magnificent heritage.
And when we teach,
We insure that they shall live forever.

Mr. Thompson's comments and poem were so obviously heartfelt and generated by such a deep love for his father, there were few dry eyes in the crowd when he stopped speaking.

As the applause died down and he was being helped back to his seat on the grandstand, there was a disturbance several blocks down the street. Turning curiously, those seated furthest back in the crowd could see a group of twenty or so young black men and women approaching the site of the ceremony carrying posters and shouting. As they got closer to the monument the language on the posters became legible.

"KKK GO HOME"—"NEVER AGAIN!"—"THE CONFEDERACY IS DEAD"—and a concerned and fearful murmur went through the crowd around the monument.

One of the young men carried a six-foot wooden pole with a Confederate flag hanging upside down at the end of it. As the marchers neared the monument another young man lit a match and set the flag on fire. As the deputies moved in to keep the groups apart, the marchers began to chant, "Tear it down! Tear it down!" Before the deputies could get the protesting group back, one of the young men took a rock from his pocket which he threw at the monument. When the rock struck a corner of the monument, a small piece of granite broke away and fell to the grass in front of the monument.

Many of the people in the audience were standing up by this time and some were beginning to move fearfully away. Several of the uniformed reenactors began to help Mr. Thompson off the grandstand while several others confronted the crowd of protesters. While their .58 caliber muskets were unloaded, the bayonets were fixed and menacing even though they would not have been dangerous except in close contact. With a few well chosen commands, the commander of the reenactment unit prevented any advance on the protesters by his men.

As the confrontation verged on somthing more violent, Reverend Robinson hurried down the street with six or eight members of his congregation, some of whose children were in the ranks of the protesters.

"Wait a minute! Wait a minute! Calm down! Listen to me!" he said directing his comments to the protesters. "You can't do this. They have just as much right to be here and to say what they want as we do. You don't have to agree with them. You don't have to stay here and listen to them, but they have a right to express themselves by meeting here. You know me-you know what I, what we have been trying to accomplish. Violence won't help. If you want to stay, stay and protest. You can do that.

"These people live here and you know them. You may not like what they're doing but they have a right to do it. Either stay here and protest peacefully or leave. Remember Dr. King and how he taught us to act. How to protest. How to progress. He was right and this is wrong."

Though there were initial shouts directed at the reverend from the protesters of "Uncle Tom—Go Home!" those comments came from a few of the newly transplanted blacks who had not grown up in Reverend Robinson's church. The vast majority of these young men and women had been in his church all of their lives. They had heard him talk about the sacrifices of his younger days during desegregation. Although they did not agree that the ceremony should continue, they did know that Reverend Robinson had always been truthful with them. He had always given them advice which helped them tell right from wrong.

Those few in the crowd who did not give Reverend Robinson the respect which he deserved were quickly silenced. For the time being they would heed his advice. Retiring reluctantly to the sidewalk across the street from the monument, they continued to display the posters and gaze angrily at the monument. As the remains of the Confederate flag smoldered in the middle of the street, Reverend Robinson and the other, older members of the congregation joined the young protesters and looked back toward the grandstand.

CHAPTER TWENTY-THREE

DURING THE CONFRONTATION, Judge Collins had remained on the grandstand and had closely observed not only the activities of the protesters and the sheriff's department but the effect of Reverend Robinson's words on the crowd.

Approaching the podium, Judge Collins began speaking.

"Ladies and gentlemen, ladies and gentlemen," he said, trying to get everyone's attention. "Please return to your seats. The excitement is over. There is no danger. We all recognize each other's right to speak freely about what concerns us. The War Between the States ended almost a hundred and forty years ago, yet it still generates powerful feelings in many of us. If it didn't, none of us would be here. Let's return to our program. If I'm not mistaken, it was my turn."

As he said this, he looked over at Mrs. Rollins. Still wide-eyed from the excitement, she only nodded. She intended a rather lengthy introduction of Judge Collins, but was too disconcerted by the near riot to do anything other than smile weakly.

Judge Collins had a written speech which he laid before him. His long experience at the bar and on the bench had prepared him well for making adjustments based on the unexpected events. He began in strong, slow, well-measured sentences.

"Our nation has been forged on the anvil of time, tempered by fire, tested by many great and terrible events, and led by many men and women, great and small. Through their trials, we have evolved into the greatest nation on earth.

"Our history is the saga of a civilization coming to grips with its own greatness, its own shortcomings, and its own destiny. Indeed our journey is not complete.

"The constellation of events which form our past are replete with these great events, some proud and wonderful accomplishments, and yes, some terrible and tragic occurrences.

"The existence of slavery on this continent, in these United States, is as dark a stain on the tapestry of our nation's history as can be found. Its presence here can never be reconciled with our Constitution, our Bill of Rights, or any other principle upon which our democracy was founded."

These few initial conciliatory remarks, in addition to Revered Robinson's continued presence, had the effect of drawing everyone's attention to Judge Collins and away from the protesters, the flags, and the monument.

"Yet, it did exist. It is a part of our country's past, though I know of no one who is proud of that fact. We are here today at the behest of many of our citizens whose ancestors fought for the Confederate States of America. Their sacrifices on the battlefield, on the march, and in camp have been too long ignored and it is entirely proper that we commemorate their service by the dedication of this monument.

"The War between the States was caused by many factors, all combining at that time to cause the conflict. It was one of the most critical events in our history and was a defining period in the foundation and continuation of this democracy.

"Many of my ancestors, including my grandfather and four of his brothers, all fought for the Confederacy. Like most confederate soldiers, none of them owned slaves. My ancestors were all small farmers who made a modest living up and down the Rapidan. From letters and diaries they left, I know they joined the Confederate Army, not to protect anyone's slaves, but to preserve what they perceived to be Virginia's right to choose the direction this state would follow. To oppose what they felt was the impending domination of Virginia by the federal government in many areas where they felt the federal government had no right to interfere. Theirs was a fight to preserve states rights rather than to preserve any particular institution.

"We can argue at length as many scholars have done continuously over the past hundred and forty years about what the most important cause of the war was, what the purposes of the war were. But what deserves recognition, reverence, and remembrance is how these men and women discharged their duty to their state and to the ideals to which they pledged their support.

"Anyone who has examined the great battlefields of this war cannot help but be struck by the manner in which these battles were fought, the courage displayed by the soldiers of both armies, and the huge and terrible sacrifices they willingly endured.

"The flags and monuments of both armies signify the devotion of these soldiers, northern and southern, black and white, foreign and American, who participated in this long and bloody struggle. All of these men and women were heroes. Not because one side was right and one side was wrong. These soldiers, these Americans, deserve our respect and admiration because of how they fulfilled their duty as they perceived it to be. The dedication of the individual soldier to the ideals he was willing to die for stand as testament to the principles which are the foundation of this country. This then is the tribute embodied in this monument which we dedicate here today."

Directing additional comments to Reverend Robinson and the crowd who stood across the street, Judge Collins continued, "Your ancestors deserve to be remembered, to be honored, and to be respected. They endured the trials, the indignities, yes, the horrors of slavery. They were, and you are, ancestors of a strong and noble people who are not to be ashamed of their past, but proud of the manner in which they, and you, have survived it and have helped make this nation the great country that it is. No one would ask you to forget your heritage. We are all proud of the sacrifices and contributions of African Americans. Anyone who is not is truly ignorant.

"It is unfortunate that some few radicals and extremists use our Confederate ancestry in a manner which is repugnant to all of us. Everyone here denounces the misuse of our Confederate heritage and the Confederate flag and encourages its use for proper historic purposes only. Destroying this monument or any other monument of the War would not change the wrong-thinking of those people who do not truly understand the importance of the preservation of our history.

"Other nations, other leaders, other governments have tried to erase portions of their past, have sought to deny the happening of some events, to eliminate symbols which may be offensive to some. But those efforts ultimately fail. We cannot undo the past nor rewrite history because some of it was cruel. We can and must remember all parts of our background and take from it what we can learn and use today. Even out of the most terrible tragedy we can glean some good. We are, we must be, capable of living together under one flag, yet still respect the different aspects of our history, heritage, and cultures."

Signaling for the honor guard to remove the Confederate flag from the granite monument, Judge Collins concluded, "We dedicate this monument today not to perpetuate the painful memories of the past, but to honor the devotion to duty and the sacrifices endured by that portion of our citizenry who served in the army of the Confederate States of America. While that cause was lost, the strength of character and principles on which they based their devotion to their duty are integral and important parts of our history and our lives.

"I want to close with a quote from General Joshua Lawrence Chamberlain. He was the Commander of the Union left flank during the battle of Little Round Top at Gettysburg and went on to become one of the most distinguished Union generals in the war. So impressive was his war record that General Grant chose Chamberlain to accept the formal surrender of the Confederate Armies at Appomattox in 1865. Chamberlain, seeing the beaten enemy approaching him in defeat and submission, determined to mark that occasion with a display of admiration. Chamberlain, as the first Confederate soldiers marched through his double line of Union troops, gave the order, 'Carry arms.' This was a marching salute and was used to show respect for the person or unit to which the salute was given. In justifying his salute to the surrendering Confederate Army, General Chamberlain later wrote in his book, *The Passing of the Armies*:

> 'Before us in proud humiliation stood the embodiment of manhood: men whom neither toils and sufferings, nor fact of death, nor disaster, nor hopelessness could bend from their resolve; standing before us now, thin, worn, and famished, but erect, and with eyes looking level into ours, waking memories that bound us together as no other bond;-was not such manhood to be welcomed back into a Union so tested and assured?'

"It was possible for Union soldiers to forgive those men who just the day before had been their mortal enemies. They honored them with a formal salute and were ready as General Chamberlain said, 'to welcome them back into the Union.' Surely, then, it is incumbent on us now to remember their sacrifices, and to honor their valor and their devotion to their duty as they perceived it. This is the reason for this monument. This is the reason for our presence here."

With those words, the Confederate flag cleared the monument and a slow wave of applause ran through the spectators. At the same time Reverend Robinson spoke quietly to the crowd across the street.

"Let it go, let it go. Judge Collins is right. You don't want to ruin your life because of something that happened a hundred and forty years ago. You got to build on the freedom you have today. You got to make it better and you can do that by remembering what all of your ancestors went through to get you where you are today."

True to these words, Reverend Robinson's sermon the following Sunday was on the importance of each of his church's families remembering their ancestors, their backgrounds, and the importance of using the strengths of their ancestors and their sacrifices as building blocks for the future.

The following Monday, Judge Collins was glad to see that the monument stood undisturbed save for the small chip knocked loose by the rock. The monument would remain, an accepted part of the history of this small Virginia community.

Sterling, however, wanted to keep feelings running hot. "I'm surprised that Judge Collins and Reverend Robinson could calm those folks down so easily, but it worked well enough for the time being. No one suspects us here and the local media attention to the monument will distract people for a while. But we need additional diversions. You know we have a very important client coming early in the fall for what will be a lengthy stay. It's important that the locals continue to be otherwise occupied and that our activities not be observed."

Nodding in agreement, Sam asked, "Is it time for the second phase of your campaign to keep the locals preoccupied?"

"Indeed it is," said Sterling. "What's the name of that woman we found out was sort of active in the gun-control groups and the anti-hunting activists group?"

"Andrews, I think," Sam responded. "I've got her name, address, and phone number written down somewhere. You want that?"

"Yes. I think it's time that we began looking at what we can do to make Rapidan County safer. Anything we can do to stimulate gun control and registration of firearms, limit hunting, and keep guns out of the hands of these local folks will keep them busy and keep us a lot safer!"

Sam smiled broadly. Both of them knew no amount of gun control would ever keep them from obtaining and possessing the firearms they wanted. They had about the same amount of respect for those particular laws as they did for any other law which pretended to direct or control their activities. Sterling did see, however, how the gun control and anti-hunting issues could accomplish several worthwhile goals for him.

"Sam, get that information for me. Also, I need to know what organizations she belongs to, how active she is in them, what kind of local support there is for those groups right now, and who our contacts in those groups are. We need to start turning those activities to our advantage."

CHAPTER TWENTY-FOUR

SUMMERS ARE WARM and inviting along the Rapidan. Though the temperature could rise above one hundred degrees, even the hottest of days would ordinarily reach only the low nineties. Much of the county was still wooded; indeed, many of its huge, old oak and sycamore trees still lined Main Street and many of the side streets. The presence of these ancient trees provided an insulating layer of shade on extremely hot days. The Rapidan River and Clarkton's proximity to the Blue Ridge Mountains also kept tempretures cooler when the mercury rose.

While John, Brenda, and Allen took a summer vacation together, usually a week in Nags Head or Myrtle Beach, float trips down the river were for John and Allen alone. Brenda had been on one of them several years before and had decided that the snakes, brush, bugs, and lack of toilet facilities were good reasons for her to stay at home on these weekends. Besides, now she was five months pregnant.

"No, thank you very much. I have two new books to read, a car to wash, some ironing to do, and a baby to nurture. You kids go play in the river."

"Gosh, Allen, sounds like we're being thrown out of the house." John smiled at Allen, all three of them recognizing river fishing was something only the two of them would truly enjoy. Brenda was smart enough to know that there were times when John and Allen needed to be alone. She wasn't insulted or offended nor did she feel left out. She and John did many things together which didn't involve Allen. And she and Allen had done many things together which didn't involve John. This family's ability to recognize what was important to share with each other, individually, and as a family, was one of the reasons they were all as happy as they were.

"And besides," John said to Brenda, "you'll be visiting your parents in Richmond and I know you and your mom will be shopping for two days. We'll be much better off on the river."

Allen was working part-time that summer at a local gas station but had gotten the weekend off. On Thursday afternoon, he and his father began stacking gear in the garage.

"Let's try to get everything out here together, Allen, so we can make sure we don't forget anything. Once we leave the bridge on Route 29 there won't be any place for us to stop and get anything we need until we get to the pick up point down at Ely's Ford."

"Dad, when are we going to get a canoe to do these trips? This flat bottom aluminum boat is a real pain to get though some of the rapids. I know the water is up a little bit right now because of those last thunder storms, but we're still going to have to get out and do a lot of pushing and pulling. An honest-to-God canoe sure would be a lot easier."

"I know it would, son. But you have to remember that one of our concessions to Mom so that she doesn't get upset about us going on these trips is that she believes this boat is a lot more stable than a canoe. She was really worried when you were younger about a canoe tipping over and me not being able to find you until you floated down to Fredericksburg."

"I know that, but I'm a lot older now and I can swim circles around Mom."

"True enough. But this is the only boat we've got for right now, so we'll just have to make do with it. Look at the bright side—we'll be able to take some extra gear with us in this boat that we wouldn't be able to get into a canoe. At least we'll be a bit more comfortable that way."

"Okay." Allen knew that it wouldn't do any good to argue further. They would be taking the little twelve-foot aluminum boat this weekend and he knew he would do a lot of pushing and pulling. *But,* he thought, *the trip was worth the extra effort.* Over the years, he had developed as much of an affection for the river as his father had. He never really cared whether they caught much or not. All they ever really wanted to keep was enough to cook for dinner at night. The real fun for him was sitting in the front of the boat, heading downstream, not being able to see anything or anyone else. When he was younger, he had pretended he was an explorer seeing the river for the first time.

Peace and quiet can be awfully nice, but I'll stick my Walkman and earphones in my pack just the same. A little music on the sandbar tomorrow night won't be bad either. He didn't ask if he could take it along. He knew that wasn't something his dad would appreciate, but he would tolerate it as long as it wasn't played too loud or too long.

"Well, let's see if we've got everything," John said. Stacked in front of them was enough equipment to last more than just the two days they'd be on the river, but they did like to be comfortable.

"Allen, while I load the cooler, lantern, tarp, and fishing gear, put those sleeping bags and the extra clothes in those three water-proof packs I got last year. I don't know about you, but I'm not interested in sleeping in a wet sleeping bag tonight."

"Yeah," Allen said, "I remember that sharp turn last year and how the boat got sideways and turned over. What an mess! Everything got soaked."

John wanted to make sure that wouldn't happen again and well-placed check marks in that year's spring and summer Cabela's sportsman's catalogue had insured that water-proof bags were under the Christmas tree. For Christmas shopping, Brenda merely had to go though the hunting, fishing, and camping catalogues that came to their house regularly to determine exactly what gifts were needed.

Checking the gear stowed in the back of the station wagon, John asked Allen, "Did you get the bag of extra lures and line off the kitchen cabinet?"

"Sure did. I saw you got a couple of extra Tiny Torpedoes. Those smallmouths really like that perch color, especially early in the morning."

"They always have. I've been fishing with that surface lure ever since I was a kid. It's been just as good on the Rapidan as it was on the James River, the Shenandoah, and that one time your mom and I went to New Hampshire and I had a chance to do some fishing up there. They just can't seem to resist that plug sputtering across the top of the water."

He watched Allen for a moment as he continued to load the back of the wagon. *He's getting much bigger and older so quickly. I never knew that time could go by as fast as it has.* John was very proud of his son. Not because he was a gifted student or athlete, but because he tried as hard as he could at everything he did. He was successful enough academically and they didn't have to force him to study. And he hadn't been, other than a few incidences of impetuous behavior, a disciplinary problem. His friends seemed to be normal kids and, John thought, *in this day and time, normal is nice.*

"Who's taking the car down to Ely's Ford, Dad?"

"Roy's going to take us down to the bridge on Route 29. We'll unload everything there and then I'll take the car on down to Ely's Ford. You can stay with the boat and stuff until Roy brings me back up. You only have to promise not to catch anything while I'm gone!"

"No way. You know there's a good hole just downstream from the bridge, and since you won't let me drive yet, I guess I'll just have to go down there and catch one!" He enjoyed the good-natured competition on these trips and, every once in a while, would catch a smallmouth bigger than John.

Roy arrived a few minutes early and began helping load the station wagon. Picking up a relatively small cardboard box he was surprised by its weight.

"Christ, John, what the hell have you got in here?" Very strong but on the smallish side, Roy had not really had any trouble picking up the box but was just giving John the hard time he deserved. Roy and John had spent a lot of time on the river and Roy was sorry he couldn't go along this weekend.

"Well, Roy, you know how partial I am to fried bass fillets and you know that you can't cook a proper bass fillet in anything other than a twelve inch Griswold skillet."

"No wonder this box feels heavy. You got a ten-pound cast iron skillet in here. I guess if you ever went on a backpackin' trip you'd have this skillet strapped on your back."

"You just be careful with that box. That's my dinner you're messin' with."

"And we all know how important that is to you," Roy said, poking John with his index finger near John's beltline. "Puttin' on a little weight, are we?"

"Well, I don't have your metabolism, you little runt." John had always been envious of Roy's ability to eat everything he wanted and as much as he wanted without gaining an ounce. Roy was one of those lucky individuals who burned up every calorie he ingested whether he was active or not. John, on the other hand, tended to put on a few pounds if he even looked at good food. It took a conscious effort on his part to stay in reasonably good shape.

"That's all right, Buddy. Allen and I'll think about you tonight on the sandbar above Germanna Ford, about the time the bass fillets and waterbread come out of the skillet and the cole slaw hits the plate. I'll eat some for you."

Roy just smiled. He enjoyed the ribbing and envied them a great deal. Not only their trip down the Rapidan that weekend but the relationship which he had seen grow and develop between John and Allen. He didn't have any children, and, at this stage in his life, it didn't appear that he would. Inwardly, he would always regret not having a son and experiencing the kind of relationship that John and Allen had.

As they unloaded the gear near the bridge on Route 29, Roy said, "Take care of your dad, Allen. He needs all the help he can get. Here's some extra rope. If you lose the anchor just tie this on to your old man and roll him out the back of the boat. Brenda's been saying for years what a fine anchor he makes."

"I'll be back in about an hour, Son," John said. "Go ahead and fish some if you want to. Just keep an eye on the gear."

Allen watched Roy and John drive off and shook his head. As his first cast sailed out over the pool and the lure splashed softly next to the rocks on the far shore Allen thought, *Christ, what a pair. They deserve each other.* He smiled at the thought. Even at his age he appreciated the value of the friendship that his dad had with Roy. *Somebody you can count on. That's good. Maybe someday I'll be that lucky.* His thoughts of the future were interrupted by the splashing strike of a two-pound smallmouth bass. Setting the hook reflexively, the light rod bent nearly double as the fish headed downstream. For nearly five minutes, Allen tried to coax the fish into the slack water near the boat. Playing the bass through three tail-walking jumps, he finally slid it into the shallow water at his feet and, grabbing the fish's lower jaw, held him up. The bass, a glittering bronze and black specimen, had given an excellent account of himself, Allen thought as he lowered the fish back into the water. *You've earned your freedom. Dad'll never believe I caught one that size right here. But that's all right. I know. And I know I can come back and try for him again.*

CHAPTER TWENTY-FIVE

JUST AS ALLEN had thought, his dad didn't believe the fish story he had to tell.

"Right! And I caught a five pounder downstream before I came back here!" John said.

"I did! Here, smell my hand," Allen said as he struck his left hand under John's nose. Sure enough, his hand did smell of fish.

"Yeah, but you could've just rubbed a little blue gill all over your hand. That's probably just what you did!"

"But . . ." Allen started to say.

John held up his hand. "Listen, we can stand here for an hour and argue about this phantom smallmouth, or we can get the boat in the water and actually go catch some. What do you say?"

"O.K., O.K, but I'll show you. I'm going to skunk you bad this trip!" he said as he got in the boat, sitting on the middle seat.

John pushed the boat out into the current. The water, only two feet deep, swirled warmly around his feet and legs. Both he and Allen were wearing t-shirts, shorts, and tennis shoes. As they floated downstream they would stop periodically along the deeper holes and would either fish from the boat or, stepping out onto the sand and gravel bottom, wade up and down, fishing the more remote portions of the river.

Each would take turns sitting in the back of the boat and letting the other have first choice of the spots as they floated downstream. Moving slowly, they cast small top-water lures or spinners back up under the overhanging brush and into small pools and pockets formed by rocks, trees, and limbs which had fallen into the water.

This stretch of the Rapidan, while not wide, provided a variety of water to fish. There were some long, flat, sandy stretches where paddling was required and these usually held only a few fish. However, most of the river provided at least some moving water and many rocky rapids with pools at the end. Most were small enough so John and Allen could anchor upstream, wade a few yards downstream on the shallow edge of the pool, and fish the headwaters while the fish were undisturbed by the boat having come through.

On the larger holes, John and Allen would run the rapids and floating down through the deeper water, anchor briefly and fish back upstream. Both knew the fish generally faced upstream, the direction the fish's food usually came from, and their luck would be better fishing from the bottom of the pools.

"You know," John said, "it never ceases to amaze me exactly how much life there is along the river. From the smallest aquatic life to the minnows, crayfish, fresh water clams, snails, bream, catfish, and bass to the deer and turkeys we see on these trips, the Rapidan is a world in and of itself. It's remained relatively unchanged over the last two or three hundred years."

Nodding, Allen knew not to interrupt when his dad got philosophic. It was on these trips that John was able to reinforce his belief in what was real, what was natural, what was worth seeing and preserving. As he sat in the back of the boat watching Allen fish, he thought, *There's a natural order to things, a reason for all of this. I don't know what it is and I can't explain how it came to be, but I know it's here and I know it's real. I know that Allen and I enjoy being here and that we are better people because we're able to spend time together on the river.*

Allen had removed his t-shirt and seemed to be more interested in working on his tan than catching dinner. Swinging the tip of the four-and-a-half foot spinning rod back and arching the small chartreuse spinner-bait toward a pocket on the far bank, the lure wrapped itself around a tree limb about four feet above the water's surface.

"Damn!" Allen said under his breath.

"I heard that. You know you're going to have to fish a little deeper than that."

That was his dad's standard comment when one of his casts went astray. Twitching several times on the end of the rod, Allen was able to make the lure flip backwards off the limb. It even landed only a few feet from where he had originally intended the cast to go. The bass that hit the spinner the instant it touched the water must have been watching it as it hung from limb. John could see Allen's grin as he fought the smallmouth and as the bass cleared the water a fourth time, Allen glanced over his shoulder at his father and stated matter-of-factly, "Well, when you've got it, you've got it."

"You'd better hold off on the bragging until you get that bass in the boat. That's dinner. If you don't land that bass, all we'll have for supper is a cornmeal sandwich." John had watched closely and the bass seemed well hooked. A minute or so later, Allen leaned over the side of the boat and got a firm grip on the sixteen-inch smallmouth's lower jaw. Lifting the tiger-striped fish into the boat, he held it up briefly while John took a picture with the camera he carried on all of these trips. A snapshot of a boy, a bass, a boat, and a sunburn. The grin was what made the picture special.

"A trophy for the skillet!" Allen said. "With these three bream and maybe one more bass we'll eat good tonight." Clipping the bass onto the stringer and letting it settle back into the water, they both began to anticipate the meal that was waiting for them downstream.

As they rounded a bend in the river where the Belleview boundary line began, John and Allen saw two men standing in the shadows of the trees lining the east bank. As they floated nearer, John recognized Lester and Floyd Morgan. Though John and Allen both waved to the two men as their boat passed, neither of the Morgans returned the greeting.

"Who are they, Dad?"

"The Morgan brothers. Bad guys. I haven't had anything to do with either of them. I just know they're trouble."

"They were both carrying rifles, weren't they? What's in season now?"

"Nothing, son, that's just what I mean. They're either hunting out of season or worse. Let's paddle for a while. I'd just as soon put some distance between them and us."

With that, they put down their rods and paddled hard for about ten minutes. Even though they passed over several nice spots to fish, John wanted to leave the Morgans well behind.

This time of year it didn't get dark on the river until almost nine, but there was a particular sandbar in the middle of the river a mile or so upstream from Germanna Ford where they were fond of camping. The river at that point widened significantly and there was usually a decent breeze to help keep the mosquitoes at bay. The island was wide enough to almost always have a good supply of driftwood for a fire. Though John had checked the weather forecast and no more rain was called for, the island was also high enough out of the water so that if there should be an unexpected storm upstream, they could survive a foot or so rise in the water without having to move.

Their camp was very simple, consisting of a large tarp, half of which was laid across the ground and the other half pulled into a V and secured on forked sticks they had carried with them and driven into the sandy soil of the island. A limb wedged across the back of the V would hold the bottom of the tarp securely to the ground. The foam pads and sleeping bags laid out under this would provide all the shelter and comfort they needed for the night. The fire was built a few feet in front of the lean-to and would provide not only light but heat as it reflected off the lean-to and down onto the sleeping bags.

The campfire they built wasn't large. That would take too much wood and also tended to burn dinner. As John finished up the lean-to, Allen came back from the downstream side of the island with an armload of wood.

"Grab six or eight of those larger rocks and make us a little fire pit. We've still got a couple of hours before dark, but I'd like to get these fish cleaned soon so we can get dinner on before it gets much later. It'll probably take half an hour to forty-five minutes for the coals to burn down so we can cook."

Allen had anticipated building the fire pit and finished it quickly. "You want me to clean the fish?" he asked.

"Naw, you caught most of them. I guess the least I can do is clean and cook them. Why don't you go ahead and get the fire started and bring the cooler over? There's a Tupperware dish in there with some egg and milk already beaten together and a zip-lock bag with the flour, cornmeal, salt, and pepper already mixed up. If you'll get that out I'll be ready to commence cooking in about half an hour."

By the time John had finished cleaning and filleting the two smallmouths and three of the larger river bream they had kept, the fire had burned down nicely. In the meantime Allen had gotten all of the fixin's out of the cooler and had set them near the fire. He found the two flat rocks they had used in the past to hold the skillet and positioned them so some of the coals could be raked in between the two with the skillet placed on the rocks to heat.

Pouring about a quarter of an inch of oil into the skillet and setting it between the rocks, John began the process of battering the fillets. He first dipped each in the milk-and-egg mixture, then the flour and cornmeal batter, and set each as it was finished on a paper plate next to the fire. As the skillet absorbed the heat from the coals underneath it, John could see the oil begin to move. Putting a little river water on his index finger and dripping that into the oil, he was satisfied it had reached the proper temperature when the water began to pop and skitter across the surface of the oil. The four bass fillets came close to covering the bottom of the skillet and began to sizzle immediately, their edges turning a bubbly, golden brown. The smell of woodsmoke and frying fillets was so strong they could almost taste them already.

"There's no better way," John said aloud though not speaking directly to Allen, "to enjoy fish than what we have right here. Nothing I've ever had in a restaurant anywhere even comes close! The company's not bad either."

When the fillets were done on the bottom John turned them over with a fork and got the container of waterbread mix out of the cooler. A recipe from another hunting buddy who lived in Fluvanna County, this was a simple mix of cornbread, water, and salt. John formed this stiff mush into small patties and put them into the skillet along with the bream fillets. It was a kind of poor man's cornbread but was an excellent accompaniment to the fresh fish. John did cheat a bit with the rest of dinner. As the bass fillets cooled and the bream fillets and waterbread cooked, he retrieved a container of coleslaw from the cooler that Brenda had made the day before. "I heartily approve of cooking outdoors on a camping trip, but I'll be damned if I'm going to haul along everything it takes to make coleslaw when all I have to do is open the container."

"Aren't they done yet? I'm so darn hungry I could eat an oar," Allen said.

"Hold your horses, I think these'll be ready in a couple of minutes. Why don't you grab a couple more plates and the ketchup out of the food box and we'll be about ready. Grab the jug of tea out of cooler too."

Dinner was what it was supposed to be: simple, delicious, and filling. After the long day on the river there weren't any leftovers and the clean up was easy. All of the trash and containers went back in the cooler; the left-over grease was poured out of the skillet back into its original container and the skillet itself wiped clean with paper towels.

It was just dark when dinner was finished and Allen asked, "Do you want to me to get the lantern out and light it?"

"Not for me. If you want to, that's fine. The fire gives me light to see everything I need to see."

"Yeah, you're right. No point in wasting the propane."

As John and Allen sat near the front of the lean-to with the fire burning slowly down to embers, they had the opportunity to appreciate the river and their solitude. From the tip of the island they could look upstream and across an open field. Through the thin screen of trees bordering the river they could see the Blue Ridge in the distance. The mountains were a deep lavender-purple in front of the already setting sun and the first stars were barely visible through the canopy of trees above them. The sharp outline of the mountains with the faded glow of the sunset behind them and the encroaching darkness to the east made the river, the sandbar, the fire, and the two of them feel like they were the center of the universe.

Into the silence came the slow drone of a few mosquitoes, the downstream slap of a beaver's tail at the base of the next pool, and the nearby splash of two mallards settling in for the night. There was no philosophy here. No in-depth discussions about the meaning of life or death, just simple appreciation.

Allen climbed into his sleeping bag and zipped it up around his shoulders. His head rested on the life jacket and wool shirt he had been wearing. He was asleep in a matter of minutes, but John kept the fire going a little while longer. He hated to give up the day. It had been very special and he knew as soon as he lay down he too would be asleep. Finally giving in, he crawled into his sleeping bag. In the last light of the fire, he could see its reflection off his son's sandy-blond hair. He could see the soft rise and fall of the sleeping bag as Allen breathed quietly and it was all he could do to keep from reaching over to touch Allen's shoulder. He almost wished he could hold Allen again as he had when the boy was a child. *No,* John thought, *those times are gone. But no matter how big you get, you'll always be my son.* With that thought to comfort him, he closed his eyes and let the water rushing over the rapids at the end of the sandbar sing him to sleep.

CHAPTER TWENTY-SIX

"SAM, WHAT WAS that light down on the river last night?" Mr. Sterling asked.

"I noticed that, too. I sent Lester and Floyd down there to check. It was just a couple of locals camping on the river. They're harmless."

"You know better than that, Sam." Mr. Sterling frowned and looked at his long-time employee. "Nobody is harmless. With what we've invested in the operation here, we have to suspect everyone. We can't afford to lose that edge. You know what to do with anybody we find on the property, especially if they get too close to the old dorm."

"We've got it covered. I just mean . . ."

"I know what you meant and you know what I mean. You just make sure that everyone knows what I expect. Things have been going well and I want to make sure it stays that way. The sheriff is being real cooperative and a number of his people know that we're entitled to a little extra service. When's D'Angelo supposed to arrive? I know we got his deposit several weeks ago and that his plane is due in today, but no one's told me what time."

"I've got all that taken care of, Charles. His plane arrives at nine tonight. We have three of the limousines ready to go and have alerted the sheriff that his night patrol should be somewhere other than the airport tonight between nine and ten o'clock. I can't believe D'Angelo and his crew are coming here. He's one of the real big shots, isn't he?"

"That's a polite way of putting it. I've known him for years. He's one of the top three or four drug suppliers in this country. His organization brings in more cocaine in a week than most dealers see in a year. He's been operating in the southwest and northeast for the last four years, but the DEA is getting too close. He's got more money socked away than he could spend in ten lifetimes and has decided it's time to get the hell out of here."

"How many people is he bringing with him?" Sam asked.

"Well, he's reserved all four suites on the second floor. I think he has four in each of three suites on the second floor and he and a friend in the other.

"We haven't talked in any great detail," Sterling continued, "but I think he's going to want some major personal renovations. He's made a huge amount of money but he's also made a lot of enemies along the way. He's the kind of person who won't accept mistakes or interference. There's a trail of bodies all across this country to attest to that. The men he's bringing with him are the ones he's had the longest and trusts the most. I expect any one of them would kill you in a heartbeat if D'Angelo crooked his little finger.

"This will certainly be the greatest test of the system since we set up. He and his party will be staying through November, I expect. Not only does he need some time for the heat to die down, but if he wants the kind of reconstructive surgery that I think he does, it will take a number of months for that to be done and for him to heal."

"He wants to leave a new man, huh?" Sam asked, grinning.

"He sure does. He's got more enemies outside law enforcement than he does inside. There are probably a dozen people in every state who would love to put a bullet in his head. When he leaves here he doesn't even want his mother to be able to recognize him. He's got the resources to make these changes and then go anywhere in the world he wants and do anything that he wants. And besides, he wants in on the gun-running operation. He's got good contacts in places that'll supply us with enough automatic and semi-automatic weapons to fill three or four extra armories around the country."

A woman entered to room quietly. "Ah, Melinda, just the person I needed to see," Sterling said. "I want to get everyone together this afternoon after lunch, just to brief them again on D'Angelo's arrival, what he'll expect, and what I'll expect from everyone. Make sure that the chef, housekeeping, Dr. Cordell, security, and the drivers are all there."

"Even Lester and Floyd?" Melinda asked. The questioning look in her eyes reflected the concern that both Sterling and Sam had about their two local employees. While both of them had been reasonably reliable, they were still considered loose cannons.

"Especially Lester and Floyd. Lester has a few grains of sense, but I'm not at all sure about Floyd. We need to let these guys know what the situation is and what's at stake. We can't afford for anybody to screw this up. By the way, is everything ready for our little party tonight?"

"Absolutely, Mr. Sterling. I just double-checked everything and it should be quite an introduction to Belleview. Even the extra ladies. That's all being handled very discretely out of Washington. One of the cars is on its way now. They'll be brought in the back way and won't have any idea where they are even after they get here."

"Good, I don't like bringing in people for one-night stands, but I don't think our usual staff would be up to the kind of party that I expect we'll have tonight. Make sure they're well paid and make sure they're out of here by noon tomorrow. "Sam, I also need for you to double check with Bill Summers at the airport and make sure everything is cleared there. We don't want any other flights coming in or going out an hour either side of D'Angelo's arrival."

"I've already done that, but I'll call them again. He's let everyone else know that the airport runway will be closed for repairs this evening and can re-route any emergency calls that might come in to Charlottesville, Fredericksburg, or Manassas."

"Great! Sounds like its coming together."

The meeting Mr. Sterling had called for two o'clock was well attended. Everyone knew something special was happening and even Lester and Floyd were especially attentive. Sterling, while not disclosing too many details, easily impressed on everyone the nature of the group that was coming, what they would expect, and what might happen should there be any problems. By now, the organization was running smoothly. Since their first "guest" that spring, nearly a dozen individuals had been through Belleview successfully. While those people were some of the country's worst criminals, Belleview had seen nothing like Rafael D'Angelo and his entourage. The size and scope of the project would tax the facility to its maximum and Sterling was especially conscious of the need for the tightest security possible.

During the afternoon meeting he was emphatic about that point. While the details of the project and the importance of the visitors was generally more than Lester and Floyd could comprehend, they knew they were being given special instructions. They were also cautioned about what failure might mean to them. Floyd never responded well to anything he perceived as a threat and, while he was not capable of verbalizing an objection to possible criticism, several primal thoughts did occur to him.

Why does the son of a bitch think I can't do my job? he thought, holding his head slightly down and looking out from under the bill of the filthy baseball cap he always wore. *You want me to keep people off, goddamn it, I'll keep 'em off. That's pretty fuckin' simple. Most people have gotten the idea around here anyway. Between a few hunters that we've scared along the roads, a couple of dogs we killed and left layin' by the river, and a few flat tires, most folks know to stay the hell away from here. Why the fuck does he think that's gonna change?*

Lester could sense Floyd's anger and, hearing Floyd mutter under his breath, grabbed his brother's arm and whispered coarsely in his ear, "Shut the fuck up! He's just tryin' to make sure we understand that this is really important. We get paid good money just for keepin' an eye on this place and you don't need to be screwin' that up!"

Pulling his arm away from his brother's grasp, Floyd glared at Sterling. They operated at such extreme opposites of mental abilities that Sterling could scarcely have understood Floyd's thoughts. Floyd was only motivated by a few primitive instincts, and the hardest one for him to control was his anger. *I've never liked that son of a bitch. Treats me like shit. I may be stupid but I'll kill his ass in a heartbeat. He wants security, goddamn it, I'll give him security.*

TWENTY-SEVEN

THE SLIVER AND blue twin-engine corporate jet had barely enough room to land at the small airport at Brandy Station in Culpeper County. As promised, Summers had cleared out all of the other employees except two who were on Sterling's payroll. As far as the public knew, the airport had been closed for over an hour and would remain closed until later that evening.

As the plane taxied up to the hangar, Summers and Sam walked out onto the tarmac. As the engines slowed, the handle on the passenger side of the airplane turned and the door opened, the steps falling into place. The first four individuals off the plane were obviously part of Mr. D'Angelo's security. While a fifth man stood at the door, a Glock semi-automatic pistol in his hand, the other four men spread out and searched the hangars and small terminal building. Sam could see all four were carrying fully automatic Heckler and Koch machine pistols. *Christ, what an army!* While almost all of their other guests in the past had been armed to some degree, this was extreme.

Bill Summers and Sam stood silently as the search was completed. As the leader of the security team passed them on the tarmac, Sam asked, "Everything okay?"

The man Sam would come to know as Michael glared back and said, "It better be."

When Michael disappeared into the plane, Sam waved the three limousines through and onto the tarmac. As they pulled up, Sam looked up toward the plane in time to see one of the most strikingly beautiful women he had ever laid eyes on emerge from the plane. *Well, maybe this won't be so bad.* Smiling, Sam extended his hand to help her down the steps. Before that contact could be made, one of Mr. D'Angelo's security men quickly stepped between Sam and the young woman, pulling Sam's arm behind him in a fashion that quickly brought him to his knees.

"That won't be necessary, Richard. I'm sure he meant no harm," D'Angelo said. "Go ahead, Lynn," he said as he followed the young woman down the steps.

Sam got back to his feet, and, messaging his arm, extended his hand. "Mr. D'Angelo, my name is Sam Cross. Mr. Sterling extends his best wishes to you and wants to welcome you to Virginia."

D'Angelo, a short, slight, dark-haired man in his early forties, smiled and took Sam's hand. "I hope you will forgive Richard. He's sometimes over protective of me. They forget that I took care of myself for a long time before they came into my employ."

That comment was made with a slight smile and a quick glance toward Michael and Richard. The comment brought grins; they knew D'Angelo was one of the most vicious and uncompromising men they had ever known. Though slightly built, he had ascended to his position on the bodies of his competitors, many of them personally dispatched and often in a manner calculated to exact the greatest amount of pain prior to death. The men surrounding him knew what their fate would be if they disappointed him. That exacting standard was what attracted them to him. They knew with his patronage, there was little they could not have and do as long as they protected him.

Lynn Myers was a study in beauty and grace. Several inches taller than D'Angelo, she was indeed striking. She was feminine yet athletically powerful. With a college degree in business administration, she spoke four different languages, had a small craft pilot's license, and was an excellent pistol shot. She had been attracted to D'Angelo from the first time they met and, though she had ultimately learned about his true character and nature, she was too attracted to his personality, power, and money to sever the relationship. Her education and native intelligence notwithstanding, she was as deeply involved in his criminal enterprises as any of his other associates and would do anything for him.

"Shall we go, Sam?" D'Angelo said, more a command than a question. "I'm indeed anxious to see Belleview. I was assured it will meet the highest standards and I look forward to my small vacation. It's been a long time since I spent four months in any one place."

The entourage of limousines made an uneventful trip from the airport to Belleview in half an hour. As they drove up the long entrance road to the front of the manor house, Sterling walked down the steps to greet his friend and most infamous guest.

"Rafael, welcome to Belleview." Sterling shook his hand and extended an invitation to enter the manor house.

"It's my pleasure to be here, Charles. Please allow me to introduce Lynn Myers. Ms. Myers is a very close personal friend and an invaluable part of my operation."

Taking Lynn's hand and smiling, Sterling said, "Now I can understand why he's been so successful. Sam, see that all of the luggage is delivered to the proper suites and that these gentlemen are given a full tour. I understand Mr. D'Angelo wishes to supplement our security with some of his own men on regular shifts."

"That's correct, Charles, and I appreciate your willingness to allow us that courtesy. Michael, see that the men are thoroughly briefed and set up a schedule."

"You wish those schedules to begin immediately?" Michael asked.

"Yes, certainly!" D'Angelo said. "You know the routine."

"If I may be so bold," Sterling said, "I have our full staff of security on duty tonight so that all of your men can enjoy the welcoming festivities. If your men would like to inspect the grounds and buildings and then join us, I think you'll find security more than adequate this evening."

"Very considerate. Michael, get everyone settled in, see to the arrangements, and, if you're comfortable, have everyone join us here."

"Yes, sir," Michael said. The thought of an evening off with the ladies he could see through the front windows of the manor house made him more than appreciative of the possibilities. Finding that Sterling had made every preparation, he and the other members of Mr. D'Angelo's group returned to the manor house in a little under an hour to join the party already in progress.

Neither they nor D'Angelo were disappointed in the preparations for their welcome. While Mr. D'Angelo was used to the finest money could buy, it was seldom he had an opportunity to relax and enjoy a setting such as Sterling provided. The hospitality of the traditional southern manor house was carefully orchestrated.

The food was abundant and the finest that could be had: crab, shrimp, and oysters from the Chesapeake Bay; carefully smoked and cured country ham; roast filet mignon; and pastries made especially for the occasion, were available in unlimited quantities.

The staff, impeccably trained and dressed, were present to provide whatever the guests requested. While their service was not intrusive, they seemed to anticipate the desires of every guest.

Sterling had made certain there was also abundant female companionship for all of the members of D'Angelo's party. A few of the young ladies were on the staff of Belleview. But, due to the size of the party, additional women had been brought down from Washington. These ladies were not the typical off-the-street hookers but were of the highest caliber, many with advanced educations. All were beautiful, well-mannered, and articulate and, while their gifts of intelligence and education were wasted on some of D'Angelo's staff, their physical attributes were appreciated by all. The choice of females was as varied as the buffet in the dining room and D'Angelo's staff did not hesitate to make their selections. The girls were all well aware of their roles at this gathering. Some lingered in the manor house, engaged in different levels of conversation. Some went more quickly to the different suites to perform more sexually-oriented favors for Sterling's guests.

Sterling, D'Angelo, and Lynn quietly observed the party in progress. D'Angelo, amused at some of the pairings, said, "My friends really appreciate their introduction to southern hospitality. Some of them are obviously a little more used to the slam, bam, thank-you-ma'am approach. We may make gentlemen out of them yet." He knew that was not likely but they continued to be amused by the behavior they observed.

Dr. Cordell, the resident plastic surgeon, passed the living room and Mr. Sterling called to him, "Dr. Cordell, could I have a moment of your time, please?"

"Certainly," Dr. Cordell had not met Mr. D'Angelo, and, as he entered the room, both Sterling and D'Angelo rose.

As he shook Dr. Cordell's hand, D'Angelo said, "I suppose I shouldn't grasp so firmly the hand that will hold the scalpel. I wouldn't want your hand to be unsteady, would I?"

Dr. Cordell had been looking at Lynn when that remark was made and when he looked back at D'Angelo he began to smile, sensing he had been attempting some humor. Any thought that the remark was a joke disappeared when Dr. Cordell looked into D'Angelo's eyes. The intensity of his glare sent a clear and convincing message to the doctor. Still smiling, he thought to himself, *Truly the eyes of a killer.*

"Rest assured, you will be more than pleased with the results," Sterling said. "Dr. Cordell is a real artist."

"We'll get together in a few days for an initial examination. I'm sure you have some idea about what you'd like to have done. I'll need to take some tissue samples, blood samples, have some x-rays made, and do some computer work to see what different options are available. But we can talk about all of that in the next few days. No need to talk shop now."

"I look forward to it too, Doctor. My future is in your hands."

The festivities at Belleview lasted well into the morning hours. At nearly three a.m., Sterling, D'Angelo, and Lynn left the manor house and walked toward the dormitory. The moon was near setting behind the Blue Ridge and the vast expanse of piedmont between Belleview and the mountains lay peaceful and dark below them. Stopping on the lawn between the manor house and the old dormitory, D'Angelo said, "You've picked a wonderful spot for your little enterprise—so quite, so peaceful. Such a wonderful place for such desperate people. A true refuge."

"It's become all I hoped it would be," Sterling said. "There have been very few problems and we've been able to deflect public curiosity from us in a number of ways. These rural people are a simple, trusting lot. They do, in general, believe what you tell them."

"I trust you'll be able to maintain them at this level of naiveté."

"I have no doubt we'll be able to do so."

D'Angelo was beginning to believe Sterling would be able to fulfill his promise but, on the off chance he could not, D'Angelo had his own ideas about how he might leave Belleview—if it became necessary.

CHAPTER TWENTY-EIGHT

"HEY, DAD, COME here and look at this," Allen yelled. He had been practicing regularly with the bow they had given him for Christmas the previous year. While John still hunted with a more traditional fiberglass recurve bow, Allen had wanted to begin bow-hunting with this more modern style.

Stepping out onto the back deck of the house, John could see the group of six arrows clustered closely together behind the front foreleg of the molded plastic deer target. He and Allen had taken part of the backyard for a target range and had both been using it regularly.

"How far?" John asked. "You must have been right on top of him to get that good a group!"

"Was not! All six of these arrows were from thirty-five yards. I bet you can't do that." Allen was a bit defensive until he realized his father was just trying to aggravate him. He knew his dad wouldn't let him hunt with the bow this year unless he proved he was proficient enough to shoot accurately at targets at least thirty-five yards away.

Modern equipment had advanced to where the razor-sharp broad heads, when shot accurately, would usually cause the death of the animal within sixty seconds. Allen knew that arrows kill primarily by causing hemorrhaging and they both wanted to make certain no deer would be wounded or left to die in the woods because he had made a bad shot.

Pulling the arrows from the target he yelled back, “You just wait right there. I'll show you!”

“I'm sure you will.”

The compound bow Allen had gotten for Christmas had a system of pulleys on it that made it much easier to shoot than the more traditional longbows and recurve bows. Even though the arrow was thrust forward at the same high velocity of standard bows, the system of pulleys made the string much easier to pull back and hold at full draw. While he was still not very accurate at forty-five yards, at a distance of thirty-five yards or less he was more than accurate enough to hunt deer.

Stepping back to the thirty-five yard line he had marked off in the yard, Allen proceeded to place six more arrows within the pie-sized area directly behind the deer's foreleg. Any of these shots would have inflicted a mortal wound to a deer of that size.

“O.K., smart ass, get up in the tree stand and let's see you shoot that well. And make sure you put that safety belt on while you're up there.”

Since deer generally don't expect danger from above, most bow-hunting is done from tree stands and John had gotten two portable tree stands for them to use. By using the seat and straps alternately, they could climb up to any height they needed.

John had been very careful to teach Allen to always use a safety belt once up in the tree stand and to always use a rope to pull the bow up into the stand after he climbed up into it. That way, should he ever fall, he wouldn't be in danger of landing on the arrows in the quiver built onto the side of the bow.

Climbing quickly to a height of eighteen feet, Allen secured himself to the tree with the safety harness and pulled the bow up. Untying the rope from the top limb of the bow, he proceeded to place six more arrows in the designated target area in about two minutes. After the sixth arrow hit, Allen looked over at his father with a grin that was a statement and a question all at the same time. “Well?”

“Well, I guess you'll be going bow-hunting this year.”

“Hot damn!” Remembering to whom he was talking, he glanced back over at his dad and said, “Whoops! Sorry about that.”

John just laughed. Allen was getting old enough to cuss a little bit and under the circumstances it did seem forgivable.

Climbing down out of the tree stand, Allen said, "I'm not sure that the bow is shooting as well as it can. I really need to get somebody to help me fine-tune it."

"Well, that's not me. You know I'm kind of a dinosaur when it comes to bow-hunting with a compound bow. I still use that old Bear recurve bow that I've had since before you were born. While I finally did put a sight on it, there's no fine-tuning in it. I just bring it up and shoot it. I'll tell you what, though. Issac Porter is the best bow hunter I know. You know him, don't you?"

"Sure, I play baseball with his son James. But I didn't know he was that much of a bow hunter."

"Yeah, he and his brother and his cousins all got into primitive weapons before I did. They all shoot top-of-the-line compound bows and can shoot circles around you and me both. I've done some work for him down at the bank and I think if we call him, he'll be glad to help you tune the bow. With the opening of bow season coming up in just a couple of months, I'm sure he and his brother and cousins are all shooting about every day anyway. Come on in the house and I'll give him a call."

Sitting at the kitchen table, John dialed Isaac's number and when his wife answered, John said, "Rachael, this is John Richter. Is Issac home?"

"He sure is. He's out in the yard. Can you hold on a minute?"

"Sure. Thanks."

John could hear the screen door open and close as Rachael went out to call her husband. "Issac, John Richter from the bank is on the phone. Did we miss a payment?"

"No, not that I know about," he said, taking the phone. "Hello?"

"Issac, this is John Richter. How are you?"

"I'm fine. What can I do for you?"

"Well, remember I asked you to help Allen with his bow?"

"Sure, when does he want to come over?"

"Well, if you're not too busy I can bring him over right now. With the season only a couple of months away he wants to get things sorted out as quick as he can."

"That's fine. It gets me away from the damn lawn mower. Pack all of his stuff and bring it over. Bring that old recurve of yours too and we can have a little contest."

"Well, the way I shoot it won't be much of a contest, but I'll throw mine in the truck too. We'll be over in about fifteen minutes."

Arriving at Issac's house, John and Allen saw his range was very similar to theirs. There were several hay bales set up with traditional archery targets on them, together with several molded-fiberglass deer targets next to them. The range was on the edge of a woodline so treestands could be set at several different distances and heights. All of these spots were positioned so that, should an arrow miss its target, it would hit a tall dirt bank behind the targets.

By the time John and Allen arrived, Issac's brother Rodney was already there. Rodney was not quite as good a shot or tracker as Issac, but always seemed to have a sixth sense about where the deer were likely to be on any given day. As John and Allen walked around behind the house, Rachael stuck her head out the back door and called to them, "Ya'll be careful. Damn silly business, all of you actin' like a bunch of Indians. Have fun and don't shoot each other."

"Hey, John. Hi Allen. Nice to see you again." Shaking hands all around, Issac said, "Let's take a look at what you got there. Has it been shooting all right?"

"Well, it shoots pretty good but there seems to be a little vibration in the upper limb. I don't know if I ought to put a stabilizer on it or maybe adjust the draw weight up or down a little bit. What do you think?"

"Well, let me take a look at it first. You know, you don't really have anything weird or unusual on the bow. Let's just make sure everything's tight first. How long have you had this string-tracker on the bow?"

"I just put it back on last week. Come to think of it, that's when I first noticed the vibration. You think that might be it?"

"Could be. This has an adjustment on it and if we reposition it a little bit that might take care of the vibration. How much string will this thing hold anyway?"

"Well," John said, "I got it from the Bass Pro Shop and I think it was advertised at holding three hundred yards of string. I thought it would be a good idea to use this. If he does get an arrow into one it'll make it a lot easier for him to find it."

"You don't have to be a beginner to need one of these. They add very little weight to the bow and even somebody who's hunted as long as we have can always use a little extra help. The string attached to the arrow weighs so little and comes off so easily it doesn't affect the flight of the arrow at all."

Allen seemed relieved to know one of the best bow hunters in the county approved of what he had considered up until then a beginner's piece of equipment.

Issac could see Allen's concern. "Son, one thing you need to learn is don't ever turn down some kind of help. Especially where it lets you retrieve an animal you might otherwise lose. If you're going to hunt with any primitive weapons, you owe it to the animal you're hunting to be as accurate as you can. You do everything you can not to wound it and let it get away and die needlessly."

"Allen and I've talked a lot about that. He understands the great responsibility that hunting with a primitive weapon imposes on the hunter. That's why I made him practice to the point where he's pretty good up to thirty-five yards. He's promised me that he won't take a longer shot than that until he gets more experience."

"Allen, that's real important," Issac continued. "With a bow you have to be more certain of your shot and more certain that there aren't any obstructions in the way. If there's any doubt in your mind about whether or not you can put the arrow in a killing zone, you're just better off not shooting. You have enough respect for the animal you're hunting not to take a chance on only injuring it. A deer gut-shot with a bow dies a long, slow, painful death. You need to think about that before you release an arrow at an animal."

"Well," Issac said, "I think we've got this fixed up. Let's see what it'll do. Rodney, go into the house and get an apple, put it on your head, and stand over by that tree. We'll see how good a shot the boy is."

"Bullshit!" Rodney said as all four laughed. While the adjustment to Allen's bow proved to be the right medicine to correct the vibration, there was never any doubt about who the best shot was when the practice was over. Issac's eye-hand coordination and years of practice enabled him to consistently place arrows in a three to four inch circle at sixty yards.

On their way home Allen asked his father, "Do you really think I'll be able to go this year?"

"No doubt about it. You've put in your time and I don't have any problem at all with your ability to take a deer with that bow. I'm really proud of the patience you've shown developing your ability with it."

"Where do you think would be a good place for me to hunt?"

"Well, you'll have your driver's license before the season opens and I expect that hardwood ridge near the river or that pasture land over on the Hughes place would be a good spot."

"That's right down from Belleview, isn't it?"

"Yep, sure is. But remember you need to stay away from there. The guy that bought that place won't give anybody permission to hunt and he's real particular about trespassers."

"Okay, I can remember that," Allen said as he leaned back. *Man,* he thought, *I cant wait to get into the woods this fall.*

CHAPTER TWENTY-NINE

THE OPENING DAY of dove season in Virginia is a harbinger of many things. It is traditionally the Saturday before Labor Day, and, even if the weather doesn't cooperate, it technically signals the end of summer and beginning of school. And for most everyone it signals that downhill slide to the end of the year. For most of the male population of Rapidan County, it also means that Virginia's general hunting season is nearly at hand.

Stepping out on the deck that morning, John said, "This weather is perfect. It's usually so hot, but in the grand scheme of things this is almost crisp. Heck, it's only supposed to be erighty-two degrees with light winds and no chance of rain. What a day!"

Allen, equally excited by the prospects of the day, could only nod in agreement. The relatively dry summer had matured the corn, wheat, and milo crops a little ahead of schedule and a great many of the county's numerous cornfields had already been cut and chopped for silage. John and Allen knew one of the great benefits of the age of modern farming was that the machinery used to harvest these crops was not tremendously efficient. Up and down each path a corn-picker or combine made, bits of the grain would be strewn over the ground. In addition, the equipment could not harvest every stalk and much of the corn, with the ears still attached, were crushed under the wheels of the different vehicles.

This method of harvesting, while somewhat wasteful, was the most practical for the county's farmers and was a boon to the dove population and the dove hunters. And because the grain was scattered inadvertently through normal farming operations, it was not illegal or improper to hunt over these harvested fields.

Having scouted a number of these fields for several weeks prior to the opening of the season, John and Allen knew their hunt would be a good one. They, together with Judge Collins and a dozen or so of the other regulars in their hunting group, would take their stands on the edges of one of the larger cut cornfields on the Hughes property along the Rapidan River a little before noon.

"Why do we have to be there so early?" Allen asked. "Everyone knows doves don't usually begin to fly until later in the afternoon."

"Well," said John, "it's just a magical time of the year. The first hunt of the fall. Besides, we can get out in the field, set up blinds, have a relaxed lunch, and just visit with everybody."

The trucks and cars began to gather around eleven o'clock that morning and everyone parked under the shade of several large oaks just off the hard-surface road on the edge of the cornfield. This field had only been harvested about a week before, so there was still plenty of grain on the ground. As John and Allen pulled in beside the others, John said, "Why don't you grab the cooler and we'll go ahead and eat with everyone else."

"Sounds good to me," Allen replied as he got the cooler from the back of the truck and went to Rick's pick-up. The tailgate of his truck had become an impromptu buffet table and everyone else had already begun to eat.

Since hunting could not begin until noon, guns were left in cases and stored in vehicles. For safety reasons, there was no alcohol consumed at lunch, nor would there be any drunk during the hunt. While most everyone had some cold beer in their cooler, everyone agreed that was for after the hunting was over when the guns were put away. While some hunters weren't smart enough to remember that important rule, everyone who wanted to hunt with this group would.

The lunches were as varied as the individuals who ate them. Many came with bologna or ham and cheese sandwiches; some fried chicken and potato salad was in evidence; a few had store-bought subs; and there was a wide selection of chips, cookies, and a couple of slices of homemade chocolate cake. Tins of sardines in mustard sauce, Vienna sausages, cartons of chocolate milk, and several bags of Double Stuff Oreo cookies rounded out the menu.

John and Allen sat with Rick, the camp cook, under one of the larger oaks. After eating, Allen was soon asleep. "Geez, look at the kid. Dead to the world," said Rick.

"Yeah, but these doves will wake him up in a hurry," replied John.

With lunch over and noon approaching, the coolers were closed up and the gun cases, shells, and shell vests were brought out.

"Hey, Sleepyhead—have I got to do all the shooting today?" John said as he nudged Allen in the ribs with the toe of his boot.

Peeking out from under the baseball cap he had pulled low down over his eyes, Allen replied, "I'll shoot circles around you today, old man!"

"Old man?! You little punk. Grab your twenty gauge and get ready to defend yourself!"

Each man had his own preference and opinion with respect to the best gun for the fast flying, difficult-to-hit mourning doves. Most of the hunters opted for the larger twelve-gauge shotguns with relatively short, open chokes. These guns threw a wider pattern of pellets and made it more likely the dove would be brought down. A few of the hunters, John and Allen included, hunted with older, more traditional double-barrel shotguns. John's was a sixteen gauge L.C. Smith while Allen hunted with his grandfather's twenty-gauge Sterlingworth Fox. When Allen pulled his little double out of the gun case he knew what the general reaction would be. As he opened the little twenty-gauge to be sure it was unloaded, several of the other hunters noticed the tell-tale design of the shotgun and an admiring group gathered to look at it.

"Christ, I could buy a pretty good used car for what that shotgun is worth," Rick said.

"John," Judge Collins said, "why do you make that boy hunt with an antique like that? Allen, you better hunt from the car so you don't get any scratches on that thing!"

"That's okay," Allen said, "I've hunted with this shotgun before. You guys see if you can give me all this grief when the day's over."

John stood back and let his son defend himself from the good-natured jabs. Most of the men here had bird hunted with Allen before and knew that, despite his age, he was already a good wing-shot and would certainly get better as time went on. However, that didn't stop the ribbing. And there were none in the group who wouldn't have liked to own the little twenty-gauge.

"Well," Judge Collins said, "I've got about a quarter of twelve and I think I see a walnut tree that's got my name on it. You guys spread out good, call your shots, and remember not to shoot at any low birds. The limit's still twelve this year, isn't it?"

"Yep," said Rick, "Why, Judge? Do you need somebody to help you fill your limit?"

At that remark a great whoop of laughter erupted from the group. If there was anyone who didn't need any help shooting doves, it was Judge Collins. Although well past sixty, his aim was still deadly with a shotgun or rifle.

Looking back at Rick, Judge Collins said, "Rick, I'll tell you what. I'll take one box of twenty-five shells out into the field and you take one box of twenty-five shells. At the end of the day we'll see who has the limit and who doesn't. Deal?"

"No way, Judge. I've seen you shoot and I know how I shoot. I'm taking two boxes with me and I've got two more boxes in the truck."

"And you'll probably need all four boxes," said the judge. With that matter settled, everyone separated and walked to different spots in the field. True to form, while a few doves sailed in and out the first several hours, the large flights didn't start arriving until nearly three o'clock in the afternoon. From three until almost five, there were so many doves flying in and out of the field that is was sometimes difficult to pick a single one to shoot at.

John and Allen, standing about a hundred yards apart near two gaps in a fence row made up of tall cedar trees, collected their limits after several hours of shooting. Neither was able to get their twelve-bird limit with only one box of shells. Only Judge Collins was able to accomplish that feat and even then he got his twelfth bird with his twenty-third shot.

After everyone had collected their limits, they met back at the grove of oaks and, while rehashing the hunt, quickly cleaned all the birds, bagged them, and put them in their coolers. Each had their own favorite recipe for doves and there was no one who didn't like their delicate flavor. Some of the dove breasts would be marinated overnight in soy sauce, wrapped in bacon, combined with potatoes and onions, and wrapped in foil. Others would be poached until almost done, de-boned, and baked in barbecue sauce and served with wild rice. Some would be simply grilled over the coals. No matter how they were fixed, everyone always enjoyed this first meal of wild game as an entrée into the fall season.

On the way back home, John and Allen stopped by the Oak Run Store for a drink and to say "Hi" to Frank. As they stepped into the familiar cool darkness of the store, the spring in the old screen door announced their arrival. Adjusting their eyes to the light, they were passed by several men they didn't know. One had his hair pulled back in a ponytail, a rare sight in this part of rural Virginia. Despite the heat, both wore dark linen sports jackets. As they walked past John he thought he saw a pistol butt sticking out of one man's waistband. Carrying several grocery bags and not speaking as they left, the screen door swung open and slammed shut behind them.

Waiting until they were well across the parking lot, John said, "Frank, when did the Mafia start shopping here?"

"Oh, those guys? They started showing up a couple of months ago. I think they're staying up at Belleview. You know, those folks stay mostly to themselves, but from what I've seen, the people that Sterling character has in there aren't the kind of folks you want to mess with."

"I've wondered about that. It was supposed to be a retreat for his business associates and something to do with seminars and stuff like that. If those are the kind of guys he's got working for him, I'm sure I wouldn't want to be involved in that business."

"Well, they've never been any trouble and they do spend a little money here, but I'm always a little uncomfortable when I'm alone and some of these fellas come in. I guess they're okay. What can I do for you?"

"We ran out of drinks about an hour ago and I haven't had a good pickled egg in about a month."

"We got plenty of both. You know where they are. Just help yourself. How was the hunting?"

"Great! I shot as badly as I ever do, but I still had a lot of fun."

"Well," said Frank, "that's the point. There've been a lot of guys in and out all afternoon and it seems like there were plenty of birds. I know I haven't been able to keep shells on the shelf today. That's always a good indication of the number of birds, ain't it?"

"Sure is. But I tell you, if Allen gets to be any better shot, I'll only have to start buying him a box of shells a year," John said, pulling the bill of Allen's cap down over his eyes.

At Belleview, D'Angelo's men returning from the store were approached by Sterling. "What took you men so long? You know I don't like for you to be out and about, especially in the daytime."

"We couldn't help it. This must be some kind of special hunting day. The store was crowded with guys and it seems like every pickup truck in the world has two or three guns hanging up in the back of it. They've got enough guns and ammo around here to start a small war."

The man who made the comment didn't fully appreciate what he had said, but he had touched on a subject that was of great concern to Sterling.

"Opening day, huh? I think it's time the reality of gun control came to this little piece of rural America. Sam!" Sterling yelled, "Get hold of that Mrs. Andrews. The one who's all tied up in the anti-gun movement. It's time to give her the wherewithall to stir the pot a little bit."

CHAPTER THIRTY

"HELLO, NATIONAL COMMITTEE Against Firearm Violence. May I help you?"

"Yes, this is Charles Sterling. Is Robert Carter in, please?"

"Yes, just a moment. I'll connect you."

"Hello?"

"Robert?"

"Yes."

"This is Charles Sterling. How are you?"

"Fine, Charles. How are things out in the country?"

"Doing very well. I need to see you as soon as possible. Have you got an afternoon free anytime this week?"

"For you, sure. How about tomorrow afternoon around two?"

"That's fine. Do you know how to get here?"

"Sure, I came down for a little unveiling party you had back in the early spring. Anything special going on I need to know about?"

"Not anything we can talk about on the phone. I've got a peculiar sort of situation here and I think your organization may be able to be of substantial help."

"Okay, I'll see you tomorrow afternoon at two o'clock."

Sam had come into Mr. Sterling's office at the tail end of that conversation, catching only the portion about a meeting the next day.

"Who was that?"

"Bob Carter up at the NCAFV."

A slight smile crossed Sam's lips. "Bringing in the gun control folks, huh?"

"Absolutely. We've had several trespassers recently and my people in town tell me that there's more gossip about our operation here. A little gun control activity ought to deflect any interest in what we're doing here. You think people got excited about that Confederate monument crap? Just wait."

"Boy, you aren't kidding. I think everybody in the county has a couple of guns stuck away somewhere. If there's anything that'll make people stop worrying about what's going on here, it's worrying over their guns."

"You know," said Mr. Sterling, leaning back in his chair and gazing out the window, "you would think that most people would be smart enough to figure out what's going on."

"You mean at Belleview?"

"No, with the gun-control fanatics. Sure, there are lots of well-meaning people who actually believe that taking guns from all of the people would stop the violence and the crime. And I'm sure some of the gun-control legislation might prevent a crime or two here and there. But who really benefits most? The criminals do.

"Why in the world the gun-control zealots think that strict gun control legislation will prevent criminals from getting guns is beyond me. Look at the cities in this country with the strongest gun control laws. Hell, they have the worst records for violent crime. The most stringent gun-control legislation removes the guns from the law-abiding citizens and leaves the criminals the only ones who are armed. And just look at the mess the anti-gun legislation has caused in England and Canada. Crime is just as bad there and now the Canadians won't even try to enforce their own legislation because it just doesn't work. And in D.C. they have the strongest gun control laws around and the worst problem with guns on the East Coast. Sure makes my day!

"Think about it," he continued. "All of the bad guys we've had come through here are unanimous in their support of the strongest gun-control bills that can be passed. I don't think we've had anybody here who isn't a strong contributor to the NCAFV and any other gun-control group that pops up. It's to their ultimate advantage that there be as few guns in public hands as possible. Our clients are never gonna give up their guns. Why in the world should they? If they were all going to be law-abiding citizens there wouldn't be any need for the police, the courts, or jails."

"Does anybody other than Mr. Carter know that you're the primary support for the NCAFV?"

"Hell no! I filter my contribution to them through several dozen different businesses and corporations. No one could ever trace the money that supports that group back to me. Having that organization available to direct into specific areas has been a real advantage. Anytime I need a diversion, they can create it.

"Besides, even with the Brady Bill and Clinton's ban on assault weapons, we still got all of them we wanted. Hell, the government can't stop us from bringing in boatloads of marijuana and tons of cocaine. We can get anything we want and have it whenever we want. That's why our firearms operation is going to be so successful. We're stockpiling now in a half-dozen areas all over the country. Before long we'll have tens of thousands in reserve. Let 'em pass all of the gun laws they want. We've got a hundred years' supply and that will be big money if the gun-control boys get their way. And you know laws only work if you're inclined to abide by them," Sterling said. Smiling again and looking at Sam out of the corner of his eyes he said, "I don't particularly feel like being law-abiding today, do you?"

Laughing, Sam said, "Not really. Things would get pretty dull if we decided to do that. Yep, I think we've gotten the crime rate up enough around here so that people will take a strong anti-gun effort pretty seriously."

The next afternoon Robert Carter arrived at Belleview promptly at two o'clock. He had learned it was important to him, his position, and his bank account to be punctual where Charles Sterling was concerned. Sterling and Sam were having a late lunch on the patio when he arrived.

"Hello, Bob, how are you?" said Sterling, rising to shake his hand warmly.

"Fine. It's a great day for a drive. This part of Virginia in the early fall has always been a favorite of mine. Life in D.C. really sucks, and it's nice to be able to get away."

"Join Sam and me for lunch? The crab salad is terrific."

"Charles, you talked me into it. Some extra cocktail sauce would be good too."

"I'll see to that, Mr. Sterling. Excuse me, I'll be back in just a minute. Something to drink too?" Sam asked.

"A cold beer would be great."

"Well," Sterling asked, "how's the organization doing?"

"Terrific! With the funding you've provided we've been able to advertise our organization nationally. We've been able to put the right kind of spin on the issues that you've picked out and people can't seem to send us money quick enough. Gun control is really a hot issue. It's amazing how many people think that outlawing some or all firearms will make crime go away. If they only knew who was behind some of it."

Nodding in agreement, Sterling said, "I've given this a great deal of thought. I have a huge investment in Belleview and there's certainly no question in my mind that promoting gun control is one of the best ways to protect my operation. You have to look back at the history of this country and the way it's developed over the last fifty years to understand why so many people misunderstand the gun control issue."

Carter had never thought that much about how the sociological development and demographics of the last fifty years had contributed to the misunderstanding of the gun-control issue. His failure to grasp Mr. Sterling's point was obvious from the look on his face.

"I'm not sure I understand what you mean."

"Look at it this way. In the last fifty years urban areas have grown by leaps and bounds. There's a lot less of rural America than there used to be and country folks aren't the majority they used to be. You've got generations of people who have grown up in urban areas. And I include the suburbs in that category. Instead of growing up in rural areas where firearms, hunting, fishing, and outdoor activities are everyday occurrences, most of these folks don't even know which end of a gun to pick up. The traditional experiences and education that most people had growing up in rural America have drastically changed in this urban sprawl. People are naturally afraid of things they don't understand and there are millions and millions of people in this country who've never handled a gun. They only know what they see on the daily news and we all know how distorted that usually is."

"I see what you mean," Bob said.

"When you couple all of that ignorance with the image that the non-hunting public has of today's modern gun owner, it's not hard to understand why a lot of people would say, 'Hell, let's just get rid of the guns and all the crime will disappear with it.' It's to our advantage to promote this misguided effort in the right direction since it can't do anything but help us."

As Senior Executive Vice President of the NCAFV, Carter was responsible for setting the policy of the group and initiating different drives in whatever areas seemed most likely to present a possibility of success. Only a few people knew Carter reported directly to Charles Sterling. The president of the NCAFV was merely a figurehead appointed to that position because of his national reputation. While the NCAFV had grown tremendously in the last three years and had been instrumental in lobbying for several successful minor gun-control bills, it was still small enough to need to direct its attention to a single geographical area in the hopes of generating a test case for litigation and publicity.

"What is it we want to do here, Charles?" Bob asked. He had a general idea of what Sterling probably would want to have done but needed specifics to get things started.

"Here's your salad, Bob. Extra cocktail sauce, horseradish, and lemon. Right?" said Sam.

"Absolutely. This looks great."

"Well," Sterling said, "you know what the deal is here. You know you're one of the few people outside the immediate operation who knows what's going on and what my investment is. What you don't know is that my guest right now is Rafael D'Angelo."

At the mention of Mr. D'Angelo's name, a worried frown crossed Bob's face and his lips came together in a low whistle.

"Jesus, you're playing with one of the really big boys."

"I am one of the really big boys," Charles said, laughing at Bob's choice of words.

"I know, I know. I didn't meant that-"

"No offense taken, Bob. I know what you meant. But this is a big deal. D'Angelo's not just here for some slight modifications. We're also making arrangements to take a great many of his resources out of the country."

"You mean . . ."

"That's right. He's been quite successful but, at the same time, the heat has gotten intense. He's decided that it's time for him to retire. The only way he can do that in comfort is to get himself out of the country and take his profit at the same time. He's done as much of that as he can through wire transfers to Swiss bank accounts and to off-shore banks. But he has a great deal of cash and can't move it by ordinary methods. And he wants in on the gun-running and underground arsenals we're developing. With his contacts outside the country, he's a real source of supply and customers for us."

"When do you think he'll be ready to leave?"

"Hopefully it will happen by the first of the year."

"Well, that ought to give us time to get things stirred up around here," Bob said.

"Oh," Sterling said smiling broadly, "I'm sure it will!"

"Do you have any details?" Bob asked.

"Sure. Sam, tell Bob about our Mrs. Andrews."

"Stacy Andrews," Sam said, smiling. "Do you want the file?"

"Well, not now. Just give Bob a general idea about her and what we want to do, and let him take the file with him."

"Well, Ms. Andrews is a transplant to Clarkton. She's lived here about ten years. She's divorced, has a sixteen-year-old daughter, and is in all kinds of organizations. Our printouts show that she's an active member of several radical conservation and criminal-rights groups. She's been on the fringes of some gun control activities and we think, with a little encouragement from such a reputable organization as ours, she could be very useful to us."

"I get the idea," Bob said. "Did you have any specific agenda in mind for Rapidan County?"

At that question, Mr. Sterling leaned forward, looking intently at his guest. "I want a major effort here in Rapidan County. We don't just want to stir up the pot. We want it at a full boil. I have three members of the Board of Supervisors in my pocket. I want a local ordinance proposed that would ban all semi-automatic weapons."

"You mean semi-automatic pistols?" Bob asked.

"No, semi-automatic pistols, rifles, and shotguns."

"Wow! That'll sure bring them out of the woodwork," Bob said.

Laughing heartily, both Sterling and Sam looked at each other.

"Yeah," Sterling said, "I can hear those NRA guys choking on that one right now."

"Do you expect a successful effort?" Bob asked.

"Certainly not. My attorney tells me there's a state law prohibiting local ordinances like this. But you can claim you're making this a test case to challenge that law in court. And, that type of ordinance would be found to be unconstitutional even if it was passed. However, with three Board members to move it along, we can sure get everybody fired up. If it passes, so much the better, but I don't expect it to. You ought to also plant the seed for a local gun-buy-out effort. That's always great for a lot of publicity and it does get a lot of folks to disarm themselves. You know, the bottom line is to create a distraction and to get as many guns out of the public's hands as possible. The fewer guns they've got, the easier it is for us to operate."

"Okay, I just wanted to get a feel for how strong an effort you wanted," Bob said.

"Don't misunderstand me," Sterling said. "I want the strongest effort this organization has ever made. While I don't expect it to succeed, I do expect it to make one hell of a lot of headlines, create a lot of bad feelings, keep public attention away from Belleview, and disarm as many citizens as possible. We don't have to pass an ordinance to be really successful. Do you understand me?"

"Absolutely. Let me get a copy of that file and I'll make contact with Ms. Andrews in the next day or so."

"Do you know how you're going to approach her?"

"Not just yet, Charles. Let me look at the file first. I have some good ideas. These get-involved-do-gooders usually respond well to praise, funding for their pet projects, and a lot of stroking. From what you've told me, it shouldn't take much to get this Andrews lady and all her cronies cranked up on a gun-control ordinance. Having three of the nine members of the Board of Supervisors in hand will speed the process along. It wouldn't surprise me to get something on the agenda for a vote within the next couple of months."

Though Sterling was not a hunter, he had done his homework. He was aware of the different hunting seasons in the piedmont area of Virginia and couldn't help but note the irony of when such an ordinance might go to a vote.

"That would be terrific. The opening day of deer season in this part of the state is the third Monday in November. Can you imagine the uproar that a vote on banning semi-automatic shotguns and deer rifles would cause a week or two before the season was supposed to open? This whole county would shut down."

The men laughed heartily at the problems they were about to create.

CHAPTER THIRTY-ONE

"MS. ANDREWS, THIS is Robert Carter. I'm the senior vice president for the National Committee Against Firearm Violence headquartered here in Washington. How are you this morning?"

"I'm fine," Ms. Andrews said in a questioning tone. She didn't know Mr. Carter and had only heard recently of his committee.

"What can I do for you?" she asked.

"Ms. Andrews, I know you don't know me, but some of our mutual friends in the animal rights movement gave me your name and phone number as someone I should talk to in Clarkton, someone I could rely on. Do you have a few minutes?"

At the mention of her friends in these other organizations, her interest was piqued. After her divorce, she had found a sense of accomplishment in her involvement with these groups. Her poor experience with her ex-husband's hunting exploits had soured her on both hunting and gun ownership, though she had yet to get rid of a small thirty-eight-caliber revolver her husband had given her.

"Well, I do have a few minutes before I need to leave for the office," she said.

"I don't want to take up too much of your time this morning, but I did want to introduce myself and let you know what our committee is planning. As you may know, the NCAFV is actively involved in trying to reduce violence and crime in the United States through an aggressive policy of gun control. We are not an extremist group, though we do believe that all semi-automatic weapons—rifles, shotguns, and pistols—should be banned. These are the weapons that are used most frequently in criminal enterprises and we feel strongly that, if those types of weapons were no longer available, many of our present problems would be less severe, if not solved. We recognize that merely banning those weapons wouldn't end crime and violence altogether, but at least it would be a start. We're a very well-funded and well-organized group and have already rented a small storefront in downtown Clarkton for a local headquarters for this effort."

Warming to his subject, Carter continued, "We've chosen several areas throughout the country to propose ordinances which would accomplish the banning of semi-automatic weapons. We've chosen Rapidan County because of its proximity to the Northern Virginia/ Washington metropolitan area and because of the increase in drug traffic and crimes of violence that we noted in the statistics out of your court system. We were informed that you've been very actively involved in some other related areas and that you might well be interested in joining our effort in Rapidan County. If you're interested, I'd like to come by and talk more with you. Since this particular effort is so close to the headquarters here in Washington, I'm going to personally supervise the Rapidan County effort."

Ms. Andrews had listened carefully and didn't need any more encouragement than he had already given her. His recognition of her efforts in other groups coupled with her concern over local crime and violence naturally inclined her toward accepting Carter's offer.

"I would love to know more about your effort. It sounds like something I would really like to get my teeth into. You know I have a sixteen-year-old daughter. One of the reasons I stayed in Clarkton after my divorce was because of the lack of crime, violence, and drug activity. It seems now that that's on the front page every day. Anything I can do to help eliminate any of this kind of activity I would be glad to do."

"That's what I was hoping you would say. I will be at the office on 210 West Main Street tomorrow around two o'clock. Can you meet me there?"

"Let me check my calendar. Let's see, I have to show a house at three, but I could meet you there at two for about an hour. It that okay?" she asked.

"That's fine. I might ask that, between now and then, you make a list of other local citizens who you think might be interested in helping with our effort. We want all of the local involvement we can get. We're a national organization but, being from out of town, we don't want to seem like we're trying to ram this down anyone's throat. The more local support we get the more seriously everyone will take this effort. It's not going to be easy. I'm sure there are a lot of folks there who like to hunt and are going to be very protective of their rights."

"You're sure right there. Around here in the fall there are guns and hunters all over the place. You can't even go to the grocery store without seeing somebody haul a dead animal through town on the hood of his car. It's disgusting!"

"I understand exactly what you mean. While we're not specifically an anti-hunting group, there's no love lost between most of our members and these so-called sportsmen."

"Well, then, I'll see you tomorrow at two o'clock. Thanks so much for calling."

"You're welcome. I'm sure our meeting and our efforts will be beneficial to everyone."

With the involvement of Ms. Andrews, Carter's efforts in Clarkton were assured of finding a public forum. While her business and her daughter's after-school activities kept her busy, she still had plenty of time to devote to pet projects.

As Carter had requested, Ms. Andrews brought with her a list of nine local individuals who, she assured him, would take up the committee's banner and who would give their effort local credibility. Indeed, at their initial meeting it was obvious to him that this effort would be substantial and its real purpose not at all apparent.

Through all of the avenues and resources available to the committee, the drive for a local semi-automatic weapon ban hit the ground running. The local office for the NCAFV opened and, almost instantly, a mass of information was being distributed on a daily basis touting the benefits of the proposed ban.

The three members of the county Board of Supervisors who were under Sterling's influence got on the bandwagon early by agreeing to sponsor the proposed ban as drafted by the committee.

The language of the ordinance itself was very brief. A copy of it was posted prominently on both windows of the committee's storefront and could be read in just a few minutes.

John Richter had heard about the leasing of the store to a national gun control group and had heard early rumors of the proposed ban on semi-automatic weapons. Learning that a copy of the proposed ordinance was displayed in the office windows of the NCAFV just down from the bank, he went to see for himself. Turning the corner he had no trouble spotting the NCAFV headquarters. With red, white, and blue bunting hung all across the front of the building and large signs in the front windows showing a semi-automatic assault rifle in the middle of a red circle with a slash across it, there could be no question about the purpose of the group. There was a small cluster of people in front of the store reading the proposed ordinance as John approached.

"Have you seen this thing?" Roy asked incredulously.

"No, I haven't had a chance to read it yet. Let me see."

"Well, let me tell you something," Roy said, "it's all bullshit! I don't know where these people are coming from. I don't even know who they are."

"Well, I think the NCAFV is headquartered in Washington, but I understand that Stacy Andrews is one of the locals who's really involved," John said.

"Hm-m," Roy said, "that explains a lot. Now I know they're a bunch of fruitcakes!"

Walking up to the storefront, John looked at the proposed ordinance.

"IT SHALL BE UNLAWFUL FOR ANYONE TO BUY, SELL, OWN, OR OTHERWISE POSSESS ANY FIREARM (RIFLE, PISTOL, OR SHOTGUN) CAPABLE OF PROPELLING A PROJECTILE, BULLET, OR MISSILE IN A SEMI-AUTOMATIC FASHION THROUGH SUCCESSIVE TRIGGER PULLS WITHOUT THE MANUAL OPERATION OF A BOLT

OR LEVER BETWEEN SHOTS. THIS BAN SHALL NOT INCLUDE SINGLE-SHOT WEAPONS OR WEAPONS WHICH, AFTER EACH SHOT, MUST BE MANUALLY RE-LOADED THROUGH THE OPERATION OF A LEVER OR BOLT. ALSO SPECIFICALLY EXCLUDED FROM THIS BAN ARE SINGLE-SHOT PISTOLS AND PISTOLS UTILIZING ROTARY CYLINDERS. A VIOLATION OF THIS ORDINANCE SHALL BE A CLASS ONE MISDEMEANOR AND PUNISHABLE BY UP TO A $2,500.00 FINE AND/OR UP TO TWELVE MONTHS IN JAIL."

"My God, they're serious. Do they really expect to be able to pass this?" John wasn't talking to anyone in particular, but seemed to be summarizing the general disbelief that such an ordinance could legitimately be considered by their local government.

"That can't be legal. It's gotta be unconstitutional, even if they pass it," Roy said. "The problem is that if they pass it, it could take several years to make its way through the court system to see whether it is or isn't constitutional. And look at the three bozos who are sponsoring it on the Board of Supervisors. All three of them moved here from somewhere else. I don't think any of those three have lived here more than ten years."

"Well," said John, "none of the three are from my district but if I know the citizens of this county at all, all three of them have just cut their political throats. What's the time frame for this ordinance?"

"There are already public hearings scheduled for next month. October 5 and 6, I think. The'yd better get ready for a real flight if they think this thing is going to go through uncontested. There're a lot of people here in the county who just flat wouldn't obey this law. And none of them are criminals either."

"Roy, you're right. I can't believe that this ordinance has a snowball's chance in hell of passing, but it's sure gonna cause a lot of hard feelings. I've seen some of the letters to the editor and a lot of local people out passing flyers in support of this ordinance. It's going to be really important for everyone to make their views known."

"Well, you can be sure I'm going to be at the public hearing and put in my two-cents worth. If they think they're taking any of my guns they've got another think coming. The supervisors know they've got a real hot potato and have already put up sign-up sheets for people who want to speak at the public hearing. They're limiting everybody to five minutes each. If they didn't, the hearings would probably take a year. I'm going to go sign up for my five minutes. Do you want me to put your name on the list too?"

John had been active in many civic organizations, coached the little league baseball team when Allen was a player, and had spoken to several different civic groups on bank-related issues. While he and Brenda both were conscientious about voting, he had never taken an active role in opposing or supporting local legislation. Until now, nothing had provoked him that much.

"Sure, put me down. My conscience wouldn't let me rest if I didn't tell the board how I feel about this."

"Okay, I'm going over to the courthouse now. I'll sign us up. By the way, you about ready for opening day of bow season?"

"Absolutely. Allen and I have been practicing a lot and he's getting real good. That new bow is terrific, especially after Issac fine-tuned it for him. I'm really glad that he's gotten into bow-hunting. It gives us something else that we can do together."

"I know what you mean. I really enjoy getting out early in the year when there aren't so many people in the woods. If this damn ordinance passes, it looks like bows might be all we have left to hunt with."

Neither John nor Roy could actually believe that the Board of Supervisors would pass this ordinance. However, the mere effort was chilling, not only to them, but to the hundreds of hunters and other gun owners in the county. This direct, immediate, frontal assault on that basic constitutional right brought a huge and overwhelming reaction from local citizens. When Roy went to the court-house to sign up to speak he found, even though hearings were over a month away, half the number of the speakers to be allowed on the first night of the hearings had already signed up. Reviewing the names on the list, Roy noted with disdain that other gun-control advocates were already on the list. He did, however, note with satisfaction that a number of hunters whom he knew well were on the list too. Turning to walk away after adding John's and his names to the list, he saw Judge Collins coming down the hall.

"Good morning, Judge. How are you?" Roy asked.

"I'm fine, Roy. I guess I'm here to do the same thing you are. While I usually like to keep my opinions to myself since I retired from the bench, this is something I can't let go by. This is such a flagrant infringement on the Constitution that I can't even believe the Board is going to consider it. If I didn't offer my opinion and it passed, I don't think I could live with myself."

As they talked, Stacy Andrews walked up behind them. Unseen at first, she said quietly, "Excuse me, gentlemen."

"Certainly," said Judge Collins, stepping aside, "after you."

As she added her name to the list of speakers just after John's, Roy could only glare at this woman who so openly supported the gun ban. When she spoke directly to him, he could only nod in recognition.

As Judge Collins put his name on the growing list, Roy said, "Judge, beats me how you can be so civil to that woman, but I'm sure glad to see you're going to show up. What you say means an awful lot to many of the people around here. And you know more about the legal aspects of this than anybody else who's speaking. I guess the county attorney is telling the Board members what kind of mess they're jumping into."

"Don't assume that this is going to pass. I have a lot of confidence in the overall wisdom of the Board. The three members who are sponsoring this have never impressed me too much anyway. While they might pick up an extra vote, I don't think they'll get the five that they need for a majority. I hope our Board is too smart to fall for this kind of sensational legislation. Even Congress had the good sense not to renew Clinton's assault weapon ban."

"Speaking of local officers, what does Sheriff Longley have to say about this?" Roy asked.

"I haven't talked to him about it. He's been strangely quiet. I heard somebody say he'd indicated that he would enforce whatever laws and ordinances were passed by the Board and by the Legislature."

"Christ," Roy said, "what's he going to do? Come look in my closet to see if I've still got my Browning semi-automatic?"

"I hope it won't come to that, though that happened in England and parts of Canada. I guess if enough of us show up and voice our objections, the Board won't pass it. But we certainly have to show them that the majority of the citizens in this county don't agree with this type of legislation. The last time I looked, this was still a democracy, we still had the Bill of Rights, and the majority was supposed to rule."

"Yeah, that's the way it's suppose to work. Well, we'll see you there, Judge."

As Roy walked away, Judge Collins looked back at the list of speakers and thought, *Majority rule—the foundation of our government, our democracy, our society. We can't let this minority take something this important away from the majority simply because they were louder or better organized. Well, not this time. Not here, not now.*

CHAPTER THIRTY-TWO

"LADIES AND GENTLEMEN, this meeting is called to order!" Even banging his gavel on the table in front of him as loudly as he could, it was almost impossible for Larry Monroe, the board chairman, to be heard over the crowd before him. The sign-up sheets for the two nights of public hearings on this proposal had filled up in three days. The controversy had grown to such proportions that the normal hearing room for the Board of Supervisors in the courthouse had long since been deemed too small. The hearings had been moved to the local high school auditorium which could seat four hundred and fifty people. All these seats were full and there were another hundred people standing along the aisles and in the back of the auditorium. The nine Board members were seated at tables joined end-to-end on the auditorium stage and there was a podium with a microphone at the front of the auditorium, facing the Board.

Tapping the microphone in front of him, Monroe again called for order. After several minutes the crowd became silent and he began the hearings.

"Ladies and gentlemen, we are in session here this evening to take public comments concerning the proposed ordinance number 4218-b, an ordinance banning the sale, ownership, or possession of semi-automatic weapons in Rapidan County. These public hearings are for individual citizens to express their support or opposition to this ordinance. Because of the number of speakers who are signed up, comments will be limited to five minutes."

Looking around the auditorium, Mr. Monroe could identify many of those present for the hearing. Born and raised in Rapidan County, he saw many with whom he had gone to school and had worked with over the years. The audience was composed of about seventy-five percent men and twenty-five percent women including a number of teenagers. He could pick out many of those who would oppose the ban by their clothing. There were many dressed in different types of camouflage jackets, red-and-black plaid wool hunting shirts, and wearing or carrying blaze-orange caps ordinarily worn by sportsmen.

There were also a sprinkling of suits in the crowd, several uniformed game wardens, a number of deputies, and Sheriff Longley.

But there were a large number of individuals in the crowd Monroe didn't recognize. He wouldn't recognize these people because they were from outside the area and were here to support the legislation. A number of them were signed up to speak and, though they had a right to express their opinion, he wondered what ulterior motive they may have had to come to this small county to support legislation which would impact how he and his fellow citizens would live their lives.

"I think all of us are aware of how controversial this ordinance is. I don't think in my lifetime I have ever encountered anything which has generated so much comment. It's clear there are very well divided lines of thought on this issue and both the supporters of the ordinance and those who object to its passage feel very strongly about their views. I will ask each of you to respect the other's right to express his or her opinions and that you neither applaud nor make negative comments about a particular individual's view. Each of you who have signed up to speak will have an opportunity to tell us what you think and what you would like us to do. We are here to listen to your views. We do not expect to ask questions of you. We want you to tell us how you feel about this ordinance and why. With that I call the first speaker, Mr. William Butler."

William Butler stood up from the front row of the auditorium. A short, heavyset man, he approached the podium slowly. From the camouflage baseball hat that he carried down to his leather hunting boots, he gave the appearance of one who was used to being outside and was comfortable in the woods and with firearms.

"Thank you, Mr. Monroe. All of y'all who live here know me and my daddy and my granddaddy. As far as I know my family's always lived right here in Rapidan County. My granddaddy doesn't get around much but when he heard about this new law y'all are thinkin' about, he made me promise to bring him. He can't hear very well anymore and ain't well enough to get up and tell you how he feels himself, but I promised him that I'd do it for him.

"My granddaddy's rabbit hunted all of his life. He says it's what's kept him young. He taught my daddy how to hunt and Daddy taught me. He's going to be ninety-three this spring and he still goes with us huntin' every fall. He can't actually get out and hunt no more. He can't even get out of the truck. But he can still hear the dogs run if they're close and he turns his hearin' aid all the way up. It's one of the few pleasures left to him.

"Since longer than I've been alive he's hunted with his old Remington semi-automatic twelve-gauge. He and that old shotgun have seen a lot of days in the woods and have put a lot of meat on the table. While he can't actually shoot it anymore, he takes it along with him in the truck and just sits there with it cradled in his arm. I can tell by how he holds it how much it means to him and all of the good memories that it brings back for him. When you get old, you need those things. You need the things around you that help you remember when you were young.

"I'm young and I can hunt with whatever I want to. But I don't like this law and I'm not sure I would obey it if you passed it. But to take Granddaddy's gun away from him would be just plain cruel. It's too much a part of him and he ain't going to be with us that much longer. Thank you for listenin'."

William's grandfather had only been able to hear a little of what he said, but as his grandson sat down next to him, he put his hand on William's arm and asked loudly, "Can I keep my shotgun?"

"I don't know yet, Granddaddy. We'll have to wait and see."

As the first hour of the hearings wore on, many other people spoke. Some were in favor of some form of gun control, but the majority were opposed. As the end of the first hour approached, Chairman Monroe said, "Ladies and gentlemen, after this next speaker we will take a ten-minute recess. According the the sign-up sheets that I have, our first speakers after the end of the recess will be John Richter, Stacy Andrews, Judge Collins, and Issac Porter. Please make sure you're back promptly so we'll be able to get started in ten minutes."

Well, thought John, *I guess I get to kick off the second half.* Though he had done some public speaking in the past, his throat felt unnusually dry. Stepping out into the hall he finally made it through the crowded corridor to a water fountain. The debates and arguments concerning a proposed law swirled through the crowd. As John bent to drink he thought, *Will it make a difference? Hard to tell, but it's too important not to speak.*

CHAPTER THIRTY-THREE

"ORDER! ORDER! LADIES and gentlemen, please find your seats again. There are still a lot of speakers and unless you're prepared to spend the night, we need to move along. John Richter is the next scheduled speaker. John, are you in the auditorium?"

Rising from his seat near the middle of the auditorium and stepping in front of Roy he felt a pat on his back and looked back at his friend. "Give 'em hell, John," Roy said with a grin.

"Mr. Monroe, Board Members, ladies and gentlemen, my comments this evening on the proposed ordinance are brief. All of you know that I'm a hunter, and I consider myself a sportsman too. My father was raised to respect firearms and to know how to use them and he raised me the same way. My son, Allen, is getting the same education.

"Among other things, I was raised to believe that an adult has an obligation to provide for and to protect his family and his home. My father taught me that I have a responsibility to keep my children out of harm's way and not to expose them to loaded guns and other things that could hurt them. But when they were old enough to learn, he also taught me that I had a responsibility to teach them to appreciate and respect firearms.

"Life is full of many dangers and guns are a part of our world, a part of our life. Just like automobiles and medicines, many things are dangerous if used the wrong way. But if we teach our children how to respect firearms, how to use them safely, then they become responsible citizens and responsible gun owners. In my opinion, everyone should learn how to use firearms. If a person is not ready and able to defend his or her own home, his or her own family, then he or she must expect, sooner of later, to pay for that inability to provide that protection. We should be encouraging firearms education, training, and practice, not try to eliminate the means to protect ourselves from those in our society who would, without remorse or hesitation, take whatever we have by force.

"There isn't one of us here who doesn't know that this proposed ordinance is merely a first step in the attempted removal of firearms from the possession of all law-abiding citizens. Who here doubts that if this ordinance is passed and it proved itself to have no impact on crime, that these people," he said, glancing to his right, "will still go after your revolvers, bolt-action rifles, and pump shotguns? I don't think that this law, if passed, would take any guns away from criminals. It would, though, make those of us who rely on semi-automatic weapons for hunting or protection less able to accomplish those purposes. I ask you not to adopt this ordinance. Thank you for listening."

As John turned from the podium and walked back to his seat there was polite applause from the pro-gun ownership faction and silence from that small group supporting the ordinance.

"Thank you for your comments, John. Ms. Andrews, I believe you're next," Monroe said, searching the auditorium for her.

As she rose and walked toward the podium the small group of people supporting the ordinance cheered and clapped heartily while the majority of those in attendance booed loudly, hurled catcalls, and waved pro-gun banners. One even used a turkey call. The loud gobbling noise which resounded through the auditorium brought gales of laughter from the majority of those in attendance as well as a loud shout from one of the hunters in the audience. "That's what this ordinance is, lady, a real turkey!"

Andrews, while embarrassed at the reception she had received, had expected it and strode firmly and resolutely to the podium.

"Order! Order! Let's have some quiet! She's entitled to her opinion just as you are," cautioned the chairman. Though he would not be one that would vote in favor of the ordinance, he was going to make certain all sides had an equal opportunity to be heard. Despite his opposition to the ordinance, he apologized to Ms. Andrews and indicated that she should proceed.

"Mr. Chairman, ladies and gentlemen of the Board, ladies and gentlemen," said Ms. Andrews, giving special emphasis to the word "gentlemen" and cutting her eyes back over her left shoulder toward where the majority of those who had ridiculed her were sitting. While she wanted to finish that sentence with "and I use the term gentlemen loosely," she knew she had few friends in the auditorium and didn't want to lose those she did have. Fixing her eyes on the members of the Board, she continued.

"Thank you, Mr. Monroe. All of you know my position on this ordinance. While I am not a native of Rapidan County, as are many of those who have spoken before me, I have lived here for a number of years. After my divorce, I could have left Clarkton and moved back to Philadelphia with my daughter. I didn't do that because I consider Clarkton and Rapidan County my home. There is a quality of life here that you cannot find in large cities. I grew up in a metropolitan area and I have seen the crime and violence of the big city. I don't want to see that happen here in Clarkton.

"In my opinion, this new ordinance should be passed. It will eliminate the most dangerous weapons that are out on the street. My ex-husband was a hunter and did not own one single semi-automatic weapon. I know from personal experience that there are many different types of rifles and shotguns other than semi-automatics. Just because one type of weapon is no longer available should not stop any true sportsman from becoming proficient with those other types still available. If a hunter can't adapt to that extent, he shouldn't even be in the woods.

"With the exception of law enforcement personnel, I see no reason why any individual should need to own a semi-automatic pistol. From what I understand, they are less accurate than revolvers and are involved in violent crimes more often then any other type of firearm. I see no legitimate excuse for a private citizen to have a handgun that will shoot fifteen bullets in three of four seconds. There is no way that such a weapon fired at such a pace can be accurate, and you certainly can't hunt with such a pistol. In fact, the only reason for the existence of semi-automatic pistols is to increase the level of firepower available to the individual. Obviously, this level of firepower only appeals to those who have some lawless purpose in mind, and it's important for the safety of our children that we get these firearms off the street.

"If it were up to me . . . ." she began to say. However, the shouts from the audience interrupted her temporarily.

"Well it ain't up to you lady!" came a voice from the crowd.

Chairman Monroe, banging his gavel on the table repeatedly, restored order. "Please proceed, Ms. Andrews."

"Thank you, Mr. Chairman. If it were up to me, handguns would be illegal to own privately. While there is apparently a small percentage of hunters who hunt with handguns, the right to hunt with a handgun does not make up for all of the damage that handguns do in our society. In my personal opinion, only the police should own handguns. However, that is not what is at issue here. We are only talking about a ban on semi-automatic weapons. I submit to you that a ban on the possession, sale, or ownership of semi-automatic weapons would decrease the crime in our county and would make Rapidan County a safer place to live, to work, and to raise our children. True sportsmen should not take exception. If they would adapt to the other types of weapons available, they wouldn't even know the difference. I urge passage of this ordinance. Thank you for your consideration."

The pro-gun majority in the audience gave Ms. Andrews the same treatment as she made her way back to her seat as they had when she first approached the podium. While her comments had been measured and well-presented, clearly she had failed to change any of their minds.

"Thank you, Ms. Andrews. Judge Collins, you're next, on the list," Mr. Monroe said.

Judge Collins had been seated near the rear of the auditorium and had not participated in any of the previous demonstrations of either support or objection to the proposed ordinance. Dressed conservatively, he strode toward the podium with an air of one who expected everyone to pay attention to what he had to say and to take him seriously. The pro-gun faction applauded heartily, anticipating a strong voice for their side. Even the gun control proponents gave polite applause to the retired judge. They knew in advance he wouldn't support them, but they recognized his position and influence in the community and knew it would do no good to be disrespectful.

Standing erect behind the podium and squaring his shoulders toward the members of the board, Judge Collins waited for the applause to die down, for the precise moment to begin speaking for maximum affect. His voice was clear and firm.

"Mr. Chaiman, ladies and gentlemen of the Board, distinguished guests, thank you for this opportunity to express my opinion concerning your upcoming vote on the proposed ban on semi-automatic weapons in Rapidan County. I am, as are the majority of those in attendance here, opposed to your passage of this ordinance."

Upon finishing that sentence, the crowd of pro-gun supporters erupted in loud cheers and applause. Before Mr. Monroe could use his gavel, Judge Collins turned to the crowd and, motioning with his hands, indicated that he would appreciate their silence. His control over the spectators in the audience was as firm as his control over his courtroom had been when he was on the bench.

"We have heard and listened to all of the speakers tonight. Everyone who's taken the time and trouble to come here has done so because the proposed ordinance involves an issue which is fraught with emotion and one which touches the very essence of our society. The emotions surrounding gun ownership and the protection of one's life, family, and home versus the death and destruction that the misuse of firearms causes is understandable, but these conflicts must be resolved.

"In my remarks tonight I am addressing both the language and validity of the Second Amendment to the United States Constitution as well as Article One, Section 13 of the Virginia Constitution. While the language of these is somewhat different, the meaning and effect of each is the same, so to avoid confusion, I will refer only to the Second Amendment.

"The first and most important consideration is this. Is the Second Amendment still valid in our world today? This Amendment, one of the corner-stones of our Bill of Rights, reads as follows:

> A well regulated militia, being necessary to the security of a free state, the right of the people to keep and bear arms, shall not be infringed.

"Such a simple, straightforward, and unimposing sentence. And yet look at the furor it generates." Judge Collins paused for a moment and looked into the eyes of each of the members of the Board of Supervisors.

"It is important initially for us to recognize what this Amendment, indeed, the entire Bill of Rights, is. This document was never intended to be, nor is it, a granting of rights by our government to the people. The Bill of Rights was a recognition by our government of those rights which were and are so vital to individual freedom that they are considered to be those with which we are born. Those personal rights of each citizen—the freedom of speech, the freedom of religion, the freedom from warrantless search and seizure, the right to keep and bear arms, and all the others—are rights which we enjoy as human beings and citizens of a free country. We do not have those rights because the government gave them to us nor do we enjoy these rights at the whim of the government. The Bill of Rights is the promise by our government that we, as citizens, would always retain our most basic human freedoms.

"All of that being said, there are still many who argue that the Second Amendment is no longer important in today's modern, civilized society. You, ladies and gentlemen of the Board, now act as the interpreters of the Second Amendment. In affirming our Second Amendment rights, I suggest you should consider two things. First, what was the legislative intent of our forefathers when they adopted this Amendment? And, second, does the Second Amendment still provide valuable freedoms for the private citizen in today's world?

"It's a primary rule of statutory construction that when you interpret a law you must give great weight to the intention of the legislative body which enacted it. To answer the first question we need to look at what prompted the recognition of our Second Amendment freedoms. Our government recognized early on, through this Amendment, the need to rely on its citizens to help defend our country and our government from external and internal forces which would threaten it. These United States were formed after long and bloody wars with France, England, and many Native American tribes. The citizens of our new country were widely scattered, and, in many instances, isolated from any protection their government might give them. These citizens, in order to survive, had to use firearms to protect and defend themselves and their communities.

"The key to the validility, the true meaning and value of the Amendment today is its second phrase, '. . . being necessary to the security of a free state . . .' The commonly accepted purpose behind this phrase is that our society must be able to protect itself by calling on its citizens to fight when threatened or attacked. Thus the term militia or citizen soldier.

"But I would argue the Amendment embraces a broader definition than that. The two words 'free state' mean not only the freedom of the political states, Virginia for example, but the natural state of freedom of each citizen of each of these states. Our Bill of Rights defines in detail what is included in this state of freedom into which we are born and have the right to expect to live. Included are the freedom to do many things and the freedom from many things, but the common thread is that they are all personal, individual freedoms, not freedoms that belong to the government.

"Much of our law has a basis in the common law of England and certainy there is no question that the freedom from violence against one's person or family and the right of self-defense are fundamental to us all. This Amendment mandates that each individual is and must be free to arm himself in order to protect that state of freedom guaranteed and defined by the Bill of Rights. These freedoms were necessary on the frontier two hundred years ago and they are just as important to each of us now as we face a new frontier.

"It may seem strange to call Rapidan County a new frontier. But it fits that definition. As our forefathers faced the wilderness frontier, we stand here on the fringe of huge metropolitan areas to our immediate northeast and southeast. A modern wilderness, if you will. These metropolitan areas infect our county with individuals who care little or nothing for the laws of this state and who daily sell illegal drugs to our citizens, to our children. And the crimes that are committed to enable others to buy drugs compound the problem. The dealers come into our county for this purpose and our local police, despite their best efforts, cannot adequately control them. Further with the present necessary concentration by law enforcement on the threat of terrorism, there has never been a period in our history when our government and our police have been less capable of protecting the individual citizen. Not because they don't make a valiant effort, but there are too few of them and too many criminals.

"Those who oppose the right of the people to privately possess firearms resort to the language in the Amendment that states 'a well regulated militia being necessary', arguing that in this day and time a militia is not necessary. They argue that we have the police and the National Guard. We have our Army, Navy, Marine Corps, and Air Force to protect us. That the cold war is over. All of these arguments are advanced to encourage legislative bodies to dispose of the Second Amendment. Yet, to those few I submit that we, as law abiding citizens, are in greater personal jeopardy today than any time in our recent past. Both from foreign terrorists and from the criminals within our own borders. It's only the face of our enemy that has changed, not the need of the citizen to protect himself as recognized by the Second Amendment.

"Each of us bears the responsibility of personal protection. Each and everyone of us must be ready, willing, and able to protect ourselves and our families from those who would take our freedoms. There can be no crime without a victim. If a citizen is unprepared to take the steps necessary for his or her own protection, then he or she is but a victim-in-waiting. And even in our rural society it is only a matter of time before someone takes advantage of that unprepared citizen, indeed of that unprepared society.

"In closing, Mr. Chairman, and I appreciate your indulgence, I would like to say that there is no question that criminals who care nothing for our laws or for the sanctity of our families and homes are and will continue to be well-armed. The terrorists who would bomb and kill us in mass numbers are well-funded and extremely well-armed. It is foolish to believe that stringent gun-control laws coupled with the abolition of our Second Amendment freedoms will lead to any significant reduction in crimes committed or the danger presented to our citizens. When an individual has a cancerous tumor it must be removed. In much the same way, we must operate on our society. The malignancy in this case, the tumor, if you will, is the criminal and terrorist who import, sell, and use illegal drugs, weapons, and firearms to perpetuate their criminal or terrorist enterprises. The elimination of these elements from society, the incarceration of those criminals, is the solution to the problem, not the removal of firearms from the hands of law-abiding citizens who need them more now than ever.

"Ladies and gentlemen, upon your studied reflection you will find that framers of the Second Amendment intended that we be able to protect not only the free state of our country but the personal state of freedom guaranteed by the Bill of Rights to each of us, as individuals, and our families. Protect them from all of our enemies, not just those from outside our national boundaries. Those citizens here tonight who urge this board to take a strict and narrow interpretation of the Second Amendment ask you to open the flood gates of gun control. That would do nothing but aid the criminal and terrorist elements and place our law-abiding citizens at what would ultimately become a fatal disadvantage."

Turning to walk back to his seat, Judge Collins was met with a standing, thunderous ovation. His presentation not only met with the approval of most of those in attendance but also had a significant impact on those on the Board of Supervisors not otherwise inclined to vote for the ordinance.

In spite of Chairman Monroe's use of the gavel, it was several minutes before order could be restored. While some of the spectators had been tempted to leave early, Judge Collins' speech had crystallized their enthusiasm and desire to remain and support the rest of the pro-gun speakers on the evening's agenda.

As Issac Porter walked toward the podium, many who knew him wondered what his comments would be. Most in the auditorium knew he had served in Vietnam and that he hunted primarily with primitive weapons. His comments, though brief, held everyone's attention.

"Thank you, Mr. Monroe. I apologize ahead of time if I'm a little nervous. The biggest group I've ever spoken to in the past was saying the blessing at Thanksgiving dinner. I can't speak like Judge Collins can, but I know what he said was right about the Constitution. I doubt any of you know this, but my great-great-grandpa was a slave over on Belleview. I went back and looked in the records in the clerk's office and found where he was sold on to that plantation. When the Yankee army came through in 1864 on the way to Richmond, they set him free and he joined the Union army. He fought at the Battle of the Crater in Petersburg and was there when Richmond fell. The Yankees told him to keep his musket, that he'd probably need it after the war. And the Yankees were right.

"My great-great-granddaddy died way before I was born, but I know from stories my grandpa told me that his daddy used that musket to feed his family and to protect his family when the Nightriders came. They didn't have the Klan up here after the war, but they had some just as bad. There were some folks around here who didn't like free blacks and especially didn't like ones that had fought for the North. But he survived all that and he was able to because of that musket. Over the years, he cut part of the fore-end off and shot so much game with it he wore the rifling out of the barrel so that it shoots like a shotgun now. I still got that musket. I don't hunt with it any but it would shoot if I asked it to. I know you're only talking about semi-automatic weapons now, but when you start taking, who's going to guarantee where you'll stop?

"All of you know that I went to Vietnam and stayed there a year. I've seen what semi-automatic weapons can do to other people up close and personal. I ain't never talked to anybody much about what I did over there or what I saw and I hope I never see any of it again.

"We did what we had to do in Nam, and, when we come back, what we had done wasn't acknowledged or appreciated. We weren't honored. People acted like we had done something wrong to be there. It seems like now people understand better, but for me it was always a question of going there to try and protect what we had here. Even in the seventies and eighties when people still didn't think that we accomplished anything there I always felt, deep inside, that all those boys who died over there died for something important. And they did. We fought over there and they died over there for the rights that Judge Collins was just talking about. Not just the right to own the kind of gun that we wanted but the right to live in a free society. To go and do and be what we wanted to be. My great-great-granddaddy fought for those rights and so did I. So are all those men and women in Iraq now. Those things were important enough for a lot of my friends to die for and we didn't do all of that to come back here and lose those rights here at home.

"All of us have got a lot of problems, a lot of things in our lives and in our families that we would change if we could. We have to take responsibility for ourselves and for our families. There's so much going on now, it's so easy to find excuses not to grow up, not to be a man, and there aren't any simple solutions. You have to look at yourself and look at your life and decide what kind of person you're going to be. You have to choose to be the kind person who takes on the responsibility, cares for his family, for his home, and teaches his kids right from wrong, how to survive, and if he needs to, to fight for those things. My great-great-grandfather had to do that. Everybody in my family, at some time or another, has had to do that, and we'll keep doing it. The freedom to own the firearms you want was given to the white man but it was a right that we blacks had to earn. We had to go through a long, dark time before that was recognized and you'd better believe that it's important for us to keep.

"If this law passes, then, in the future, the government will control who gets a gun and who don't. There'll be more gun licensing and registration. Well, let me tell you something. My people have already been through a lot of this licensing and registration business. How many of you here remember poll taxes and literacy tests? Well I remember them, and so does everyone in my family, everyone in our church. Those taxes and tests to be able to vote, to exercise one of our basic freedoms, were administered by governments too. And we all know why they were there—to keep us down. This gun control law is the same breed of animal!"

"Yeah," came a shout from the audience, "a skunk!"

"You tell 'em, Issac!" As a ripple of laughter swept the crowd.

Standing proudly at the podium, Issac concluded, "You can't take that right away from us. Too many people have died to make sure that we can keep it. We all know you'll do the right thing. Thank you."

Turning to walk back up the aisle, the audience was strangely quiet for a brief second. Then a few hands began to clap and, as Issac strode toward the rear of the auditorium, almost all of those in attendance rose. They were applauding not only his support of their position, but in admiration of his service to his country.

The speakers continued on until almost midnight. Adjourning at about 11:45, chairman Monroe indicated that the second session of speakers would begin promptly at eight o'clock the following evening and encouraged anyone who wished to to return and listen. While a vote on the ordinance would not take place until the board meeting on October 15, he was sure the Board would decline to enact an ordinance which so clearly violated the Constitution. It was so important to the vast majority of the local population that to cast a yes vote for the ordinance was tantamount to political suicide.

CHAPTER THIRTY-FOUR

THE PROPOSED ORDINANCE banning semi-automatic weapons in Rapidan County failed by a six to three vote—not a great surprise to most people in the county. Though the first night's remarks were more widely reported than the ones on the second, almost all of those who attended the public hearings were opposed to the ordinance. This was to be true not so much because so many of those people owned any kind of semi-automatic weapon, but because they realized this proposal was only a first step on the agenda of some to ban private ownership of weapons altogether.

John could not attend the actual meeting when the vote was taken, but when his friend Roy called him on Friday evening, he was relieved at the news.

"Yeah," said Roy, "I can't believe those three jerks actually voted for the ordinance. I can't wait 'til they try to get re-elected next year. Thank heavens Monroe and the other five have sense enough to see what's going on."

"Well," John said, "if enough people get active and involved and speak what's on their mind, the right thing usually happens. But I'll guarantee you this isn't the last time we'll hear from that committee or that Andrews woman. They've got more time on their hands than they do sense and I'm sure they'll come up with something else."

"I expect you're right. I just hope everybody else keeps their wits about them. You and Allen going bow-hunting Monday?"

"I can't make it. We have our regular board meeting at the bank Monday morning and the directors' meeting that afternoon, and I can't miss either one of them. Allen's been practicing real hard but hasn't said anything to Brenda or me about taking Monday off to go. I expect if he wants to go bad enough he'll skip school. Between all the practicing he's been doing and getting that old pickup truck running, I guess he's earned a day off."

"Yep, he's a good kid."

"That he is. Listen, I've got to run. Dinner's ready. I'll call you later on about bow-huntin', okay?"

"Okay, John. Don't spend too much time in the yard this weekend. Talk to you later."

That same day, Judge Collins was at the feed store and saw Issac loading some fertilizer into his truck. Grabbing one end of the bag to help, he said, "Issac, I didn't get a chance to talk to you after your comments at the hearing last week. I thought you did a great job. Your thoughts about what you and all the other boys fought for in Vietnam made a real impression on everybody there."

"Well, thanks, Judge. I just said what I felt. Until that ordinance came up I hadn't really thought that much about how much Vietnam meant to how we lead our lives here. It just seemed to me these people need to remember that many of us, black and white, have sacrificed a lot to make sure that this stays a free country. Your speech was real good too. You sure pointed out some things I've never really thought about."

"I appreciate that, Issac, but my arguments were more technical than anything else. Your speaking for the veterans who put everything on the line meant as much or more than anything anybody else said. By the way, you guys getting all geared up for bow season?"

"Sure are, Judge. We've got our stands all staked out and ready to go. You bow-hunt?"

"No, I'm a bit too old to be climbing up in trees. It'd be my luck to fall out on my head. No, I think I'll just wait 'til gun season and hope that you Robin Hoods don't kill all the deer in the meantime."

Laughing, Issac said, "No chance of that, Judge. I can generally come pretty close to hittin' what I aim at, but my cousins don't spend as much time practicing as I do. We usually get a few but it's a tough way to hunt."

"True enough. Listen, give me a call sometime so you can come down to the cabin during gun season. Looks like there'll be a pretty good acorn crop this year and the deer ought to be pretty thick on the farm."

"Thanks, Judge. I've really enjoyed hunting there in the past. Well," said Issac, climbing into his truck, "thanks for helping me load. You take it easy."

"You too," the judge said as he turned to enter the feed store.

Across town, Robert Carter walked through the front door of the NCAFV to meet Stacy Andrews. Though their efforts had been unsuccessful, there were other things he wanted to discuss with her, other plans which Sterling had for her involvement in this gun control effort.

"Good morning, Stacy," Carter said. "How are you this morning?"

"Well, all things considered, I'm okay. I don't guess I really expected the Board of Supervisors to enact that ordinance, but I was hoping that we could at least pick up one vote over and above the three who sponsored the bill. It's pretty discouraging really. I just feel sure that things would have improved if we could have gotten at least some of the guns off the streets."

"Well, we're not giving up, you know. Even though we didn't force a mandatory confiscation of semi-automatic weapons, we still made some progress."

Stacy glanced at Robert Carter, a question on her face. All of their efforts, she felt, had been for nothing. "What can we do? The Board of Supervisors has basically said anybody can own whatever kind of gun they want and as many of them as they want. It'll probably get worse before it gets any better."

Her frustration was apparent and Carter hastened to remind her of the second phase of the gun-control plan. Accurately predicting the failure of the ordinance, Carter had the committee plan a voluntary gun buy-back program that would follow the Board's vote on the ban.

Smiling, Carter said, "We may have lost a battle but we sure haven't lost the war. We have some additional funding available and our voluntary turn-in programs will get some of the guns off the street anyway."

At the thought of the plan to remove at least some of the firearms from public hands, Ms. Andrews' mood brightened considerably. "That's true! And with this program it doesn't make any difference whether they were semi-automatic pistols, rifles, shotguns—anything could be turned in. How much money have we got to work with?"

"Five thousand. More if we need it. We got an awful lot of good press out of the fight over the ordinance and we'd really like to keep the ball rolling. You know all these media types love it when there's a fight over gun control. Anything we can do to enhance our position is more than worth the money it costs to make it happen. Not only do we get good publicity from getting guns off the street, but we'd be providing necessary equipment to the school system here. It's a double-barrel winner." Grinning slightly, he said, "Sorry about that, no pun intended."

Early in the planning stages, she had decided to give up the .38 caliber revolver which her husband had left with her after the separation. She had been concerned about leaving it in the house with Mary Sue there anyway.

At Belleview, Sterling and Sam were also discussing the recent negative vote from the Board of Supervisors.

"Well, Sam, we stirred things up, didn't we?" Not waiting for an answer, Sterling went on, "It would have been a lot of fun to see somebody arrested for illegal possession of a semi-automatic weapon and all of the hoopla that a trial would've created. That'll happen sooner or later somewhere. For now, we've got everybody distracted enough so they couldn't care less about what's going on here."

"You're right. The little bit of money you've spent is worth the result."

"Don't forget the voluntary gun turn-in program. It's set for this Saturday and from what I hear, it's going to be done in a very public way. It'll sure get a lot of media attention. What we need to do is make sure to videotape everything. Do it very unobtrusively, but I want to make sure we have a record of who's giving up their guns.

You never can tell when it'll be helpful to know who's disarmed themselves."

"You got it," said Sam. "You know, you can't be sure that somebody's turning in all their guns but we've got records from a lot of different places where people have turned in firearms. It's been especially helpful in some of the metropolitan areas where we've got records of single woman and older people turning in their firearms. Generally those folks only have one gun and once we know they're unarmed, they're easy pickin's. None of that stuff means anything to us, but it's a nice little tidbit to be able to throw to some of our people on the street when they need some extra cash."

"Lambs to the slaughter. That's what it always reminds me of. It amazes me that people are so gullible. Christ, if the public knew how much of some gun-control efforts were funded by those of us who don't mind bending a few laws . . ."

"Bend! God almighty, Charles, you snap the hell out of them on a daily basis."

Laughing at his understatement and Sam's reaction, Sterling moved on, "I heard something about some deer season opening up Monday. Something about hunting for them with bows and arrows. Is there a lot of that going on around here?"

Nodding, Sam said, "There sure is. I've been listening down at the store the last couple of weeks and there are several primitive-weapons seasons here in Virginia. The deer hunting with bows and arrows starts on Monday and there are a lot of folks around here who hunt that way. Guess they think they're a bunch of fuckin' Indians."

"Do you think we may have a problem with any of them?" Sterling asked.

"We may. There are literally hundreds of bow hunters in the county and I think everybody knows that we have a large herd of deer here that nobody ever gets to hunt. I expect we'll have some poachers and I know we've got some people who've already set up tree stands on some of the land close around here."

"Hmm," Sterling said with a frown. "I don't like that worth a damn. Lester and Floyd can kind of keep a handle on things around here during the off season but if we're getting ready to have a real problem, we'd better put two or three extra men out on the perimeter. Get Lester and Floyd and three other men and make sure they understand that we have to keep people out of here. We're at a real critical time and we can't afford to have any problems. Our guns and D'Angelo's shipment of cash will be coming in soon. D'Angelo's surgery has gone well and I don't think his own mother would recognize him. Doc's still got a bit more work to do but he ought to be ready to leave here in the next month or so."

"Will do. I'll call them in this afternoon. I've already had them go all around the perimeter with new NO TRESPASSING signs and check all the fences."

"Good, that's a beginning, but tell them they really need to be sharp now that the season's opening!"

As Sam left, Sterling leaned back, swiveled in his chair, and looked out the large window from his office, across the grounds and over toward the woods and the river. *Beautiful place. Wish the hell we didn't have so much trouble with all the locals trying to get over here to hunt. That's going to be a real problem.*

The Dollars for Schools gun buy-back program set up by the local NCAFV was more successful than expected. Well funded, the ads ran in the local paper and on the radio station for several weeks before the actual event. For every firearm given up, no matter the condition, caliber, or age, fifty dollars went to the county school system's fund for new computer equipment.

On the morning of the event, a stage had been built in front of NCAFV headquarters and large tables arranged in front so everyone could see the take. Scheduled for 10:00 a.m. to 5:00 p.m. the Saturday before the opening day of bow season, the early crowd was larger than Stacy Andrews had hoped for. Speaking briefly to the crowd, she explained the purpose of the program. Then, taking a small thirty-eight caliber Smith & Wesson from a shoe box, she pushed the cylinder open to show it was unloaded. With a flourish, she handed it to the deputy and proudly proclaimed, "We, all of us who live here, are now just a little safer than we were a minute ago. There's one less gun to be turned on a loved one, one less gun to tempt the lawless. This is a small step, but it's a beginning!"

Unseen by Andrews, all of this was being video taped by two of Sterling's men from a second-floor window across the street. Even worse, Floyd Morgan caught a glimpse of Andrews as she made her donation.

What a dumb ass, he thought. *You may wish you hadn't done that one day, lady.*

Thirty-seven guns were turned in, and, while some were inoperable, the committee was well pleased, the school made eighteen hundred fifty dollars, and the media had a good story for the six o'clock news.

"Hey, Dad, Dad," Allen yelled. "How about Monday? You know I've been doing real good. One day isn't gonna hurt."

John had been expecting a plea to skip school Monday for bow-hunting's opening day. He knew Allen had already taken his tree stand and set it up on the oak ridge between the river and Belleveiw. He was proud of the way Allen had taken his time to scout the ridge, find the trails and crossings, and find just the right tree to set the stand up in. It had been a cool fall and the bucks, in preparation for the mating season, were already rubbing their antlers on small trees up and down the ridges. Allen had found a line of these rubs and thought he had even seen the buck that had made them several times.

"Well, your mom thinks that you need to go to school but we've talked about it, and I guess since you've done so well this fall, you can go."

"Yes!" said Allen. He had known his mom and dad would let him go, but it didn't surprise him that they made him ask. He didn't mind them giving him a hard time when he knew he had earned the day off.

"Just a couple of things though. You make sure you park the truck off the road far enough not to be a problem. And you make sure you use your safety belt. Don't pull the bow up in the stand until after you're up there and strapped in."

"Come on, Dad, I'm not a kid anymore. You don't need to tell me all that stuff. You drummed it into my head until it's tattooed on my brain."

"Allen, I don't care how old you get. You'll still be my son and I'm still going to tell you what to do. You just be careful. There's a lot that can go wrong in the woods. I know you've hunted a lot and if we didn't trust you, Mom and I wouldn't let you go. You just be careful."

Allen nodded and smiled without saying anything else. He knew that his mom and dad both loved him and cared for him enough to make sure that he learned how to take care of himself. He would miss hunting with his father on Monday as this would be his first hunt ever they hadn't shared.

Allen's excitement over the opening day kept him busy getting his equipment ready on Sunday and prevented him from sleeping very much that night. *I'm going to see that buck tomorrow*, he thought to himself as he turned out the light. *I'm gonna see him and I'm going to get him.* Allen lay in the dark for a long time, his eyes wide open, the only light the soft glow from his alarm clock set to go off at 4:00 a.m. "Yep," he said aloud, "even a bad day in the woods is better than a good day in school."

CHAPTER THIRTY-FIVE

THE BUZZING OF Allen's alarm clock woke John also. He lay there for a long time, listening to Allen get dressed and then go to the kitchen to fix breakfast. Once he smelled the coffee he got up and stumbled sleepily into the kitchen.

"God, you look terrible in the morning," said Allen. He had a smug smile on his face and didn't let his father forget that he was going hunting while John had to go to work.

"It must really be tough to be grown up and have to go to work instead of going hunting. I think I'll just stay seventeen years old for the next ten or twenty years. Think that would be okay?"

Pouring a cup of coffee and sipping slowly, John looked at Allen and smiled. "Sure, suits the hell out of me. If you figure out how to do that let me know. I'm not wild about getting any older than I am either. You got all your stuff together?"

"Sure do, it's all in the truck. You know where my stand is, don't you?"

"Yeah. You gonna stay all day?"

"I'm planning to. I think I've got enough sandwiches here to last me through lunch and on until dark if I need them."

Allen had set his lunch bag on the kitchen table. Peering inside, John said, "Looks like you've got enough in here for an army. Are you going for a day or are you going to stay a week?"

"Lay off, I'm a growing boy."

"Growing boy! If you eat all this you won't be able to get up in the tree."

Laughing together, they sat for a few more moments in silence, each lost in his own thoughts about opening day. John recognized the excitement in Allen's eyes and remembered when he was just old enough to go off on his own; how much of an adventure that always seemed to be. It was one thing to be hunting with your father when you were too young to drive; it was an entirely different experience to be old enough and capable enough to be let out on your own. John wanted to go with Allen badly but knew his obligations at work wouldn't allow it.

Might as well get used to this, John thought to himself. *Allen's getting older and there'll be a lot of things he'll be doing on his own. I hope he knows he can always come home.*

"Well, Dad, I'm out of here. It'll take me about twenty minutes to get to the logging road and another fifteen minutes to get up in the stand and I want to be in there at least half an hour before first light. Are you staying up or are you going to go back to bed?"

"I think I'll go back and try to catch a little more sleep. You know how it is when you get older, you just need more rest."

"Well, then, I guess you'll probably be in bed for the rest of the day, won't you?"

"Smart ass!" said John. "Good luck, Buddy, and take care of yourself. Good hunting."

Going out the door, Allen looked back and said, "By the way, if I get one, I'll come back and you can help drag it out."

"You got it," John said, as Allen closed the door behind him. John stood there in the kitchen for a moment and listened as Allen's truck went out the driveway. There was suddenly a hollow, empty feeling inside John. As the tail-lights of Allen's truck disappeared down the road, John realized that his son was no longer a boy but a young man who could only be expected to grow more and more independent.

Well, John thought, *we've done the best that we can and he's as ready as he'll ever be to be a man. I miss the boy in him already.*

The headlights of Allen's truck probed down the gravel road as he drove toward his stand. Slowing quickly, Allen turned into the logging road that intersected the gravel road by the river, his headlight beams swinging through the hardwoods and second growth. He pulled his truck about twenty yards into the woods and off to the side of the logging road. Though no one else would probably hunt in this area today, he wanted to leave room in case someone needed to get by.

Getting out of the truck he took out the garbage bag he had put his hunting clothes in three days before. He had put cedar limbs and oak leaves in and around the clothes in the bag and made sure no other scent had contaminated the hat, jacket, and pants he was going to wear. Pulling on his rubber boots that would eliminate any ground scent, he quickly finished dressing, grabbed his bow and day-pack, and started off toward his stand.

Using the small flashlight his mother had given him for Christmas he worked his way up the side of the ridge from his truck. After going about half a mile he turned sharply up the ridge, reaching his tree stand after an additional five-minute climb. Tying his bow to a length of black nylon cord he had left hanging from a limb, he began climbing the steps up to the stand which was about eighteen feet above the forest floor. Reaching the stand, he buckled his safety harness and quickly hauled his bow up after him. Untying the rope and tying that off to the tree, he took an arrow out of the quiver, nocked it, and sat back to wait for the sunrise.

A cool, clear mid-October dawn in the hardwoods of central Virginia is an extraordinary experience. At first, there's no light. Just the smells and sounds of the woods: the rustle of the leaves in a light breeze, the hoot of an owl along the river, every once in a while the snap of a twig or a limb, but mostly just the clean, clear, dark smell of the woods and the leaves. It wasn't so cold that his fingers and toes started to complain, but the air was crisp enough to make the flannel shirt and polar-fleece coat comfortable. There was no moon but the stars were clear enough in the sky to remind Allen of a late winter night. As he looked to the east, over the ridge, he could see the first streaks of light begining to pierce the sky.

He had spent many mornings in the woods with his father and a few by himself. He missed having his dad with him, but at the same time felt a sense of accomplishment at his ability to choose a spot where he felt his chances of success were good. Though he saw no game early that morning, he enjoyed watching the night turn to day, the orange glow of the rising sun finally hitting the top of his ridge about seven-thirty. There had been little frost so far that year and the leaves had not yet begun to change color. All of the foliage and second growth made it difficult to see further than about fifty yards from his stand, but he had a good field of fire, at least as far as his effective range with his bow.

Around nine o'clock a doe and yearling came slowly up the trail to within twenty yards of his stand. Though either sex was legal with his bow, he made no effort to shoot. He knew from his pre-season scouting that there was a nice buck that frequented his ridge and he was determined to get a shot at him. From the size of the trees the buck had rubbed with his antlers, Allen was sure the buck would be well worth the wait. Morning turned to afternoon and still, other than the two he had seen earlier, no other deer approached his stand.

Damn, he thought. *I was sure I would have seen something with horns by now. Oh well, like Dad always says, "It takes patience. If you can't be patient you've got no business being out here." I suppose I could have shot one of those little ones this morning, but I would have been ashamed to take one of those home. Dad wouldn't have said anything, especially if it was my first with this bow, but I want the first one to be special.*

Looking out across the woods over toward the sun, which was within several hours of setting now, he said to the deer he hoped he would see, "I'm waiting—I can be just as patient as you can."

As a whitetail buck will so often do, this one simply materialized in the woods in front of Allen's stand. One second there was nothing there but the trees he had been looking at all day and, the next second, a buck, all eyes and ears and coiled like a snake ready to spring at the first sign of trouble, was standing on the trail which led directly by Allen's tree stand. This was a better than average buck, with four points on one side and five on the other. Allen couldn't estimate the spread between the horns but knew that this was a deer he wanted to try and take.

As the buck moved slowly up the trail, Allen's heart began to race. *God, the buck must be able to hear my heart pounding even from up here! At least the breeze is taking my scent away from him.*

Whitetail deer are one of the wariest game animals in North America. Every few seconds the buck would throw his head up sharply, looking to his right and left, constantly testing the breeze, his ears swiveling to pick up any unnatural sound. The spasmodic switching of the deer's tail indicated to Allen that the deer didn't suspect his presence nor any immediate danger. It seemed as if it took the deer twenty or thirty minutes to cover the thirty yards between the edge of the woods where he had materialized to the spot below Allen's stand where he now stood, approximately twenty-five yards away from Allen.

Ok, Allen calmed himself, *don't stand up, just lean over and draw. He's twenty-five yards away. Use the second pin and don't forget to breathe!*

As he had done hundreds of times in practice, when the pin settled behind the buck's shoulder, he began to relax the muscles in his right hand which held the bow string back against the corner of his mouth. Almost unconsciously and without a specific command, the bow string rolled off his fingers, sending the shaft with it's razor-sharp broadhead hurtling toward the deer. Though he had placed spidery-looking, rubber silencers above and below the nocking point on the bow string, it made an audible twang as it snapped forward and the string attached to the string tracker peeled off the reel. Even at that distance, the sound of the bow string reached the deer's ears before the arrow sliced into his chest. The deer tensed and began to make a spring to its right, away from the tree where Allen sat. Before the deer could make that jump, the arrow struck directly behind his left shoulder. With a bow set at sixty pounds of draw weight and at that distance, the arrow sliced through the deer's rib cage, through his lungs and stopped, its point projecting several inches out the right side of the deer's chest cavity.

Allen saw the fletching on the arrow sticking from the deer's left side as the buck reacted to the shot and raced head-long back up the ridge.

"Wow, look at him go," Allen said aloud as he watched the string peel from the string tracker as the whitetail ran, mortally wounded, up the ridge toward the fields beyond.

After several minutes, the string was still and Allen's breathing almost returned to normal. He had not had buck fever before the shot, but immediately afterwards he had an almost irresistible impulse to climb down from the stand and run after the deer that had disappeared from sight. Allen knew he should wait at least half hour before tracking the deer, and it was almost that long before he felt calm enough to climb down from the stand. Knowing he had made a good shot he was confident he would find the deer quickly.

Man, I can't wait to get the deer home to show Dad. He won't believe this!

Retying the nylon chord to the side of the tree stand, Allen carefully lowered his bow to the ground and climbed slowly down. Retrieving his bow, he broke the string from the tracker, and, finding a young oak near where the buck's blood trail started, tied the string to the lower part of the sapling. The frothy, bright red blood trail indicated a lung shot and was not difficult to follow.

The quiver on his bow held six arrows when it was full. Before beginning to track the deer, he took the fifth one from the bow and slid it into place. While he was sure the deer would be dead when he found him, he didn't want to take any chances. The deer's path led up and along the trail to near the crest of the ridge. There the buck had turned abruptly to the left and headed down the short side of the ridge toward a creek which lay beyond.

Damn, I can't believe this deer is running this far, hit as hard as he's hit. But I've seen them go for over a quarter of a mile with a bullet right through the heart. I'm gonna find him, I know I am.

Allen moved slowly and carefully, even though the string provided an easy trail to follow. About a hundred-fifty yards from his stand, Allen approached the boundary line between the farm where he had permission to hunt and Belleview. As Allen approached the boundary line he could see, up and down the woods, the newly posted NO TRESPASSING—NO HUNTING signs along the boundary line.

"Shit," he said out loud. "This damn buck knew exactly where to run. He knew where he thought he'd be safe. I can't just let him go, I know he's dead." Looking at the reel on the front of his bow and recalling it originally held four-hundred yards of string, he estimated that over three hundred yards of it were gone.

That deer must be within two hundred yards of here. He looked up and down the boundary line and into the woods beyond and couldn't see anything or anyone. *I know I don't have permission to be on Belleview and I'll be trespassing if I cross the line. But from what I've heard about the owner, I won't get permission to go look for a wounded animal.*

"I'm not going to leave my first buck in the woods," he said aloud. "I can get him and get out before anyone knows a thing."

Tentatively at first, Allen stepped across the boundary line and continued to follow the string and blood trail in front of him. He was intent on the tracking job before him and did not notice, as he moved slowly through the woods, the two individuals standing on the edge of the field nearby. He was moving slowly and carefully, and, still dressed in camouflage, his presence was not noticed by either Lester Morgan or Sam. It was their conversation that first alerted Allen to their presence.

"Listen, Lester, you and Floyd and these other guys have got to keep all of these hunters out of here. Mr. D'Angelo is paying for privacy and paying for the privilege of getting out of this country without the authorities being any the wiser. We'll either be successful in helping him do that or we'll all end up six feet under. You got it?"

"Yeah, I got it. That guy must have more fuckin' money than anybody in the world!"

"He does, and he's bringing almost all of it here in the next week or ten days. We either do our job and earn a little bit of that money or die trying."

Allen had caught most of that conversation, and, while he didn't really understand what they were talking about, he did understand he was trespassing and one of the men was armed with an automatic assault rifle. He remembered the fear the man named Morgan had generated in both him and his father on their float trip last summer. Initially afraid of simply being arrested for trespassing, his fear grew as he continued to listen to the conversation. "Where'd this guy get all of his money anyway, drugs or what?" Lester asked.

"Yeah, mostly cocaine, I think," Sam said. "But I don't think I want to know any more. Sometimes knowing too much can be real hazardous to your health. You know what I mean?"

Lester, always the more intelligent of the two brothers, understood the implication of Sam's comment.

Allen, well concealed only twenty-five yards away, saw two other men approaching. He did not recognize them but knew they weren't local. They were also armed and Allen became more and more fearful.

As the two men approached Lester and Sam he heard one say, "What the fuck are we supposed to be doing out here? I didn't sign on to become a goddamn farmer. How come we've got to stand out here in the woods and keep people off the property? What's D'Angelo paying you rednecks for?"

"Listen," Sam said, "you're here because D'Angelo wants you here. We've got plenty of security all over the perimeter of this place. But your boss is the one who's in danger of going to jail for the rest of his life if anybody finds out he's here. I'll guarantee you if he goes to jail, your ass is going with him. I didn't put you out here, he did. I can't help it if you don't know your ass from a hole in the ground when you're in the woods. I guess the biggest pack of woods you've ever been in is Central Park," Sam said.

Lester, not quite willing to speak so directly to D'Angelo's two employees, simply squinted at them and said, "City boys," spitting a stream of tobacco juice toward a nearby oak tree.

One of the two, a dark-haired Hispanic, took a step toward Lester.

"City boys, my ass. I'll cut your fuckin' nuts off," he said as he pulled a pearl-handled switch blade from his pocket, the stainless steel blade shining in the late afternoon sun.

As he advanced, Sam stepped between them saying, "Hold it, hold it. We've got a job to do. You guys don't have to like each other. Let's just keep everybody else the fuck away from this place. Sterling and D'Angelo both are counting on all of us. Let's just do our jobs and get paid for it. Nobody wants to die out here."

Both men calmed down a bit and Lester asked the other man, "I hear your boss is a real hard ass. Somebody told me he had killed eight or ten guys himself. Any of that true?"

"Keep sticking your nose where it doesn't belong and you'll find out how true it is. What he's done and hasn't done isn't any of your goddamn business. You just stick to the job you're getting paid to do and shut the fuck up."

Allen didn't know who they were talking about. He only knew he was somewhere he wasn't supposed to be and hearing a conversation he wasn't supposed to hear. The four men started to break up and walk off in different directions. He knew if the one called Lester continued on in the direction he started he would come within ten or twelve feet of where he was hidden.

Shit, Allen thought, panic grabbing at his chest, *there's no way this guy's not going to see me if he keeps coming!* Making a split-second decision, Allen turned and ran as hard as he could back into the woods and second growth. He didn't notice that the string on the ground he had been using to track the deer caught on his ankle and trailed after him as he ran until it broke forty yards into the woods.

All four of the men heard Allen break and saw him run off into the woods. Realizing simultaneously that he must have heard everything they said, they knew he could not be allowed to escape.

"Get him, get that son of a bitch!" Sam screamed. Lester, who needed no instructions, was already running as hard as he could through the woods after Allen. The dark haired man fired three hurried shots at the fleeing hunter as the four of them spread out on either side of where Allen had disappeared into the woods. The silencer on the machine pistol muffled the shots, but, as Allen ran, he heard the whine of the bullets near his head and saw the bark of one tree explode in front of him.

"Where is he? Which way did he go?" They screamed to each other.

Allen, younger and faster than any of them, had managed to put seventy-five or eighty yards between him and the nearest pursuer. Lester had lost the track and veered off to Allen's right. The other man had gone even further off to the right and both were searching the underbrush for Allen. The third man, the dark-haired one, was off to Lester's left and was getting closer and closer to where Allen had hidden himself.

Allen, his bow still in his left hand, had found good cover behind a blown-down tree which allowed him to see anyone approaching from the field. Breathing heavily, he saw the dark-haired man coming toward him through the underbrush. This man knew nothing about walking in the woods and the sound of his feet in the leaves telegraphed every step.

Unfortunately, the man had chosen a course which would bring him right by Allen. Allen knew the man could not fail to see him and he was too close for Allen to run. He knew he had no choice. *Why?* he thought. *Why?* As he slowly raised his bow, an arrow was already in place.

The dark-haired man, with no experience in the woods and no eye for detail, was simply staring at the woods ahead of him, expecting to see a full human form standing upright in front of him. He didn't see Allen crouched in the blow-down only twelve yards away or Allen's bow raised to shooting height. Nor did he see the glint of the sun on the broadhead which was aimed at his chest.

God, please don't let him see me. I don't believe this is happening. His mouth dry and his heart racing, he only knew that if he was discovered he would be killed. He had never thought about taking the life of another human being. He hadn't drawn the arrow back but knew it was going to happen. Either that, or trust that these men who had already shot at him wouldn't hurt him. *I can't let'em get me! I can't!*

The dark-haired man took three more steps and stopped ten feet from Allen. Gazing at the forest ahead of him, he began to take another step when a movement to his right caught his eye. Looking swiftly to his right, the young hunter materialized in front of him as Allen drew the arrow back to full draw. As Allen's middle finger on his right hand touched the corner of his mouth, Allen saw the man begin to raise the pistol he had in his left hand. Allen could see the fear and hate in the other man's eyes as the muzzle of the pistol was pointed almost directly at him. As Allen's fingers in his right hand began to relax he saw the man's mouth begin to make a sound. It was a sound drowned out by the hum of the bow string slipping off his fingers, a sound that never escaped the man's mouth. The arrow sliced cleanly through the man's rib cage, through his heart, and exited swiftly out the left rear of the man's back. At that distance and from full draw, the arrow had a great deal of velocity left after it exited the man's body. Whistling silently through the air, it stuck an oak tree about four feet up and thirty feet behind the man who now had seconds to live. Covered with the man's blood, the arrow quivered slightly in the tree and then was still.

Allen remained on his knees with the bow held in front of him and his right hand still next to his right cheek. The scene appeared to unfold before him in slow motion. The dark-haired man in front of him still held the pistol in his left hand but he could raise it no further. The dark red stain on his chest was growing larger; his eyes were wide open and his mouth, though silent, was open. It seemed to take hours for the man to fall to his knees. As he fell, he lost his grip on the pistol. Falling face forward on the ground in front of Allen, a guttural moan escaped his dying lips.

He had been so close Allen could almost reach out with the bow and touch him if he had wanted to. *I've got to run! To get away! Where are the other three? Got to escape!*

His mind numb with fear, he looked quickly to his right and left, knowing there were others who would kill him if they had the chance. Taking the third arrow out of this quiver and nocking it, he tried to calm himself.

Stay calm, stay in control! Which way to go? What to do?

His breathing was heavy and rapid and he knew he had to make a decision, right or wrong, quickly. It was a decision he never got to make.

Lester Morgan was more of a woodsman than Allen had ever had an opportunity to become and he had not heard Lester sneak up behind him. As the dark-haired man was falling from the wound in his chest, Lester had been coming up behind Allen. He didn't know Allen, had never met him before. It wouldn't have made any difference if he had.

Allen felt a heavy arm around his neck. A tight, painful, squeezing around his throat. His head was pulled back sharply; he dropped the bow, its arrow falling to the ground beside it as he reached back to try and fight his attacker. Allen was a strong young man but he was no match for Lester whose long years in the woods had made him extremely strong. As Allen struggled, flailing with his hands against his sides and grabbing at Lester's clothing, Lester tightened his grip on Allen's throat.

The last thing Allen saw was a canopy of trees above him, a green and brown blur as his eyes closed, his left hand grasping a sapling next to him. He felt the excruciating pain in his neck; a bursting, exploding feeling in his oxygen-starved lungs. The last thing he smelled was the foul odor of the man who was killing him.

As Lester eased his grip around the boy's neck and let his body fall to the ground, Allen's hand stripped some leaves from the dogwood he had grasped. The small flashlight his mother had given him fell from his shirt pocket and was covered by the leaves as he fell.

"Sam!" Lester called, "Sam, get your ass over here." This wasn't the first person Lester had killed and he wasn't frightetend. But he knew Sterling wouldn't be happy.

"Goddamn it. Damn it!" said Sam when he saw Allen's dead body. "What the fuck are we gonna do now? Why did you have to kill him? Who is it anyway? Goddamn."

Sam took his foot and pushed Allen's shoulder so the body rolled over on its back. Leaning over and pulling up the camouflage netting, Sam saw a young white male. He didn't know Allen or Allen's parents. He only knew the body posed one hell of a problem.

"What about the other man?" Sam asked.

"Dead as a fuckin' mackerel. Look at that. Right through the chest. What are we doing to do now?"

"Go back to the manor house." Sam said to D'angelo's remaining man. "Don't use the radio. You tell Sterling what's happened and bring four or five men back down here. Don't bring a vehicle. We don't want to leave any tracks in the fields or in the woods. You just bring a tarp to put your buddy in. But what the hell are we going to do with this kid?"

"Well, I don't know who he is, but I expect he was hunting out of one of those two tree stands that are on that ridge on the other side of the property line over there," said Lester. "You stay here. Let me go back and see if I can find out where he was hunting. If he was hunting from a tree stand maybe we can make this look like an accident."

"Okay," Sam said. "I'll wait right here. You go see what you can find. But be quick about it. Whatever we're going to do we've got to do quick. Somebody's going to be looking for this kid if he's not home by dark."

Allen's stand was the closer of the two to Belleview, so it was the first one Lester checked. As he approached the tree he saw Allen's daypack on the ground near the stand. The nylon cord Allen had used to lower his bow was still hanging from the stand. Returning quickly to Sam he said, "I found it. As soon as a couple of the other guys get here we can take the body back to the tree stand. The stand's fifteen or twenty feet up in the tree. We can just make it look like he fell out of the stand and broke his neck. What do you think?"

Sam quickly agreed. "That'll work. You snapped his neck anyway. That oughta work fine."

A few minutes later Lester's brother Floyd and another man came running over the ridge. Floyd looked at Allen's body and looked at his brother. Grinning he said, "You got him, didn't ya, Bro? You got him real good! Yep, you sure did." Pushing on Allen's chin with his boot and noting with satisfaction the clean break, he said, "Yep, snapped his neck just like a chicken. That's what the little bastard gets for poachin' on our property. What are we going to do with him?"

The plan was quickly explained and Lester and Floyd picked up Allen's body and carried him back to the tree stand. Sam went along, carrying the bow and the arrow which had been nocked but never released.

"What do ya think, Lester? Do you want to haul him up in the stand and drop him head first?" That seemed like a pretty good idea to Floyd.

"Well, I don't know. I guess I could probably get him over my shoulder and at least up ten or twelve feet anyway. It would sure look more real that way. Help me with him, will ya?"

Lester, the stronger of the two, put Allen's body over his right shoulder with Allen's head hanging over his back. With Floyd pushing on Lester's back as far up as he could, he climbed slowly up the first eight steps to the tree stand.

"How high up am I?" Lester called back.

"You're about fifteen feet," said Sam.

"Okay, get outta the way. I'm gonna drop him." Lester leaned back away from the tree. Holding on with his left arm, he relaxed his hold on Allen with his right hand. Slowly at first, Allen slipped out of Lester's grasp until his knees passed Lester's shoulder. Then Lester released his grip altogether and Allen's body fell heavily, head first, to the ground.

At the sound of Allen's body hitting the ground Floyd smiled. "Nice shot, Bro. Right on his head. Nobody'll ever know it weren't an accident. Here, give me that bow and arrow. I've been wantin' one of those to hunt with," Floyd said as he reached for the bow.

"Floyd, you dumb shit. We've gotta leave the bow here. How's it gonna look like an accident if the kid's bow is gone?" Sam said.

"He's right, Floyd. We've gotta leave all this stuff here."

"Shit," said Floyd. "Waste of a good bow. All right, goddamn it. We'll leave it. Let's get the shit out of here."

"Lester, look around here real good. Make sure we didn't leave anything. We don't want anybody tracin' this back to Belleview," Sam said.

"You got it. We'll be along in a few minutes."

Lester and Floyd gave the area a quick once-over and turned to follow Sam back toward Belleview. The sun, now almost entirely down below the mountains to the west, seemed to cast a more reddish glow than usual that evening.

CHAPTER THIRTY-SIX

"JOHN, I'M GETTING really worried. It's been dark for over an hour and Allen's not home," Brenda said. The worry and distress in her voice was obvious. "I want you to go look for him and I want you to go right now."

John started to remind Brenda of how upset Allen would be at the thought of a search party being sent out after him on opening day, but he recognized the tone in her voice and knew it wouldn't do any good to argue with her.

"Okay, I'm going. But you explain to him when we get home why his daddy had to come for him. He's really not going to like this at all."

"I don't care what he likes and you use any excuse you want to. You tell him you were anxious to find out if he got one or you knew that he would need some help dragging it out of the woods. Whatever you want, but you just go look for him."

Slipping on his jacket and reaching for his cap, John said, "I'm going, but he'll probably get home before I get out there. If he's gotten one, he'll have found it by now and gone somewhere to check it in. Probably over to Oak Run. Matter of fact, before I go, why don't I call Frank and see whether or not Allen's shown up over there."

At that suggestion Brenda's mood lightened a bit and she stood anxiously by the phone as John called the store.

"Oak Run, can I help you?" the owner said.

"Frank, this is John Richter . . ."

"I know, don't tell me, you've got a deer you want to check in and you want me to stay open later to do that." Frank was always good-natured and usually willing to keep the store open as long as necessary for all the hunters to check in the game they had taken.

"No, Frank, I wish that was it. I didn't even get a chance to go out today. Allen went early this morning and we haven't heard from him. He was hunting on that ridge over between the river and Belleview and we thought that if he had gotten one, your place would have been the closest one to check it in. Has he been by?"

John was surprised at the concern which had edged into his voice.

"No, John. I haven't seen him all day. He didn't come down at lunch and he hasn't brought anything to check in this evening. I did have a couple of nice ones brought in. Rodney Porter, Issac's brother, brought a nice six-pointer over . . ."

"Frank, I don't mean to cut you off but I think I really need to run out to Allen's tree stand to make sure everything's okay. If he comes by before I get there have him call home, will you?"

"Sure, John. Be glad to. How's Brenda, by the way?

"She's fine, getting more pregnant every day. But she's really kind of worried right now, so I'd better run."

"Gotcha. I can appreciate that. I'll get him to call if he comes by here."

Brenda had heard one side of the conversation and could tell Allen hadn't shown up at the store. John tried to reassure her,

"Brenda, listen, you know what bow-hunting is like. He hasn't bow-hunted that much and if he hit a deer but didn't hit it in the right spot, he may still be tracking it. It can take hours to find one if you don't make a good shot. He's fine. I'll take an extra flashlight and I'll call you as soon as I catch up with him. Don't worry, Hon, he's just fine."

Brenda, only nodding, didn't trust herself to speak. *He's usually so reliable about letting us know if he is going to be late,* she thought. *He's okay, nothing could happen to him.* But there was a nagging doubt in her mind. A doubt that built every moment the phone didn't ring.

It took John about twenty-five minutes to reach the turn-off where he thought Allen would have parked his truck to walk up to the tree stand. The last several miles were typical unimproved Virginia gravel roads and, for some reason, there was more dust in the air from other traffic than he would have expected.

Must have been a lot of hunters out today, John thought as he continued down the gravel road toward Allen's stand. *I sure hope he didn't just wound one. He's always been so careful not to take bad shots. But this is his first opening day of bow season and if he saw that big buck, he may have gotten a little spooked.* Laughing to himself, John remembered several times in his hunting career when a buck with an unusually large set of antlers had jangled his nerves. *No one is immune to buck fever.*

Well, I've got my big flashlight and my whistle. If he's not in the stand, he can hear this whistle half a mile away. He'll have his in his daypack and know it's me if I whistle for him, John assured himself. Smiling inwardly, he thought about how proud Allen would be if he had gotten a nice buck on the first day out and how much he would enjoy helping his son drag it out of the woods. *Christ,* he thought, *if he's gotten a nice one the first day he'll may never let me live that down.*

Cresting the ridge that led down to the turn-off where Allen's truck should be parked, he didn't realize at first the lights below him were from emergency vehicles. In that split second of recognition, a tightness formed in the pit of his stomach like a giant fist squeezing harder and harder as he approached the sheriff's cars and the ambulance pulled up in the logging road near Allen's truck.

Though there were flares in the road and one of the deputies tried to flag John around the emergency vehicles, he ignored those hand signals and pulled his car over across the ditch and part way up in the trees. Seeing Allen's truck parked up the road with another deputy standing at the front door looking in the glove compartment, John slowly emerged from his vehicle, wanting to talk to someone but, at the same time, not wanting any answers to the questions that were racing through his mind.

Allen's body had been found by another deer hunter who had a tree stand about half a mile below Allen's on the same ridge. That hunter, leaving his stand for the evening, had come by Allen's stand about thirty minutes after Sterling's men had left Allen on the ground. He thought Allen was probably dead when he found him, but raced back to his truck and called the state police on his CB radio. Once the message was relayed to the sheriff's department and to the local volunteer rescue squad, help had been on the scene within half an hour of the call.

Fatalities were few and far between in Rapidan County and when Sheriff Longley heard that a hunter had died in what was apparently an accident, he went to the scene. Walking down the path from where Allen's body had been found at about the same time John pulled up, Sheriff Longley had recognized Allen as John and Brenda's son and was on his way to have someone sent to their home to inform them of the accident. Seeing John pull in, Sheriff Longley knew this was a task he couldn't delegate to someone else.

"Sheriff, that's Allen's truck. Where is he? What's happened?" John asked desperately. "Is he hurt? Where is he?" John's eyes were wide with fear.

"John, there's been an accident. We haven't finished the investigation yet but . . ."

John tried to focus on what the sheriff was telling him but, out of the corner of his eye, he saw the three ambulance attendants and the deputy carrying a stretcher down the trail. Trying to brush past the sheriff to see his son, Sheriff Longley grabbed John with both hands. "John, don't go over there. There's nothing you can do. He was gone when we got to him."

John would not, could not believe what the sheriff was telling him. Either that wasn't his son on the stretcher or, if it was, he wasn't dead. He couldn't be dead.

As he struggled against the sheriff, Longley continued, "John, John! We don't know what happened yet. But believe me, it's over. It looks like he fell out of the stand. John, the stand was almost twenty feet up in the tree and he landed on his neck. I know it's no help, but he probably never felt a thing."

John, still straining against the sheriff's hold, felt the tears welling up into his eyes, felt the knot in his stomach growing tighter and a choking sensation in his throat that threatened to strangle him.

"Let me go! I've got to see him. He's not dead—he can't be dead, I just saw him this morning. He's just knocked out, that's all."

"John, I wish that were true. They've tried, they've done everything they can. He'd probably been dead for an hour or so before we ever got to him."

"Sheriff," John said, pleading with the officer, "please let me see him." There was indescribable pain in John's voice. Not releasing his grip on John but turning to one deputy, he motioned for them to put Allen down before placing him in the ambulance. The harsh glare of the headlights, the twisting, revolving blue lights of the sheriff's cars, the flashing red-and-white lights of the ambulance all illuminated the still form of the stretcher. As John walked the few steps to the stretcher, the ambulance attendants and deputy stood back silently.

As John knelt down by the stretcher, he could see Allen's face. The ambulance attendants had taken off his cap and camouflage face-mask. Allen's head was twisted sharply to the left, facing away from John. His blond hair was matted to his scalp, some leaves and dirt clinging to the blond hair behind his left ear. Barely able to breathe, unable to speak, and almost unable to see, John knelt by his son and reached out slowly to touch his shoulder, as if touching him would bring him back. Gently placing his hand on Allen's shoulder, he saw Allen was not breathing, saw some of the bruising on the side of Allen's neck and knew his son was gone.

Reaching across his son's body he placed his left hand on Allen's cheek and turned the boy's face toward him. Allen's skin was still soft and smooth. The vision of Allen's first shave flashed through his mind. That had only been six months ago. He looked at his son's face, his closed eyes, his mouth that had lost its perpetual smile. As the world disappeared around him he slowly brushed the leaves from Allen's hair.

Taking a moment to find the words, he looked up at one of the ambulance attendants. "I want to ride with him."

The ambulance attendant started to say no, but looked at Sheriff Longley who was nodding it would be okay.

"John, one of my men will drive your car back and we'll get Allen's truck back to the house too. Don't worry about that. Is there someone you want us to call? What about Brenda?"

John had not even begun to think about how he would tell Brenda.

"No, don't call anyone. Don't tell anyone. I've got to tell Brenda myself. She's pregnant and this might . . ." Brenda was seven months pregnant and John knew he couldn't stand losing two children in one night. "I'll have to tell her myself."

"That's fine, John. Okay guys, let's go." Turning to one of the other deputies, Sheriff Longley said, "We can come back in the morning and look around again but this looks like an accident to me."

John held Allen's hand all the way into town, as if the physical connection would transfer some of his life to Allen's body. He couldn't take his eyes from his son's face. Every corner, every part of it reminded him of something they had said to each other. Something they had planned. Something they had dreamed. The reality of the end of all that was beyond his comprehension.

CHAPTER THIRTY-SEVEN

IT WAS NEARLY ten o'clock and Brenda had dressed and was within minutes of leaving to try and find Allen herself. She had no idea where his tree stand was nor exactly where to start looking, but she knew where the road by the river was and she knew that her son was out there and not home where he belonged. The ringing phone was a startling intrusion. She stared at the phone, unable to answer it as it rang twice more.

He's all right, she thought. This is John and they're on their way home.

"Hello?"

"Brenda, this is Frank Gibson over at Oak Run. Have those two men of yours gotten home yet?"

"No, Frank, they aren't here yet," she said, trying to sound angry instead of worried to death. "But I'm sure they'll be here soon. John's probably just had to help Allen drag a deer out."

"Well, I'm sorry to call so late, but I was a little worried and just wanted to touch base."

"No, Frank. I appreciate your calling . . ." Brenda saw headlights swing across the front of the house and heard a car pull up in the driveway. "Frank, somebody just pulled up. I'm sure that's them so everything must be okay. I'll have John or Allen call you in the morning and let you know what happened. Thanks again for calling."

"Great. Make sure they call. Bye."

Unintentionally slamming the phone down, Brenda hurried to the front door with a sense of relief and expectation. The front light was already on and when Brenda opened the door, she was ready to give both John and Allen a major scolding. In the split-second that she saw John standing there in front of her, she knew things would never be the same.

"John?" It wasn't just her husband's name, it was a question.

"Brenda, Allen's not coming home. He's . . ."

Brenda screamed, "No, don't tell me that. Don't you dare tell me that. He'll be home. He'll be home any minute!" As John reached for her, she began to sag to the floor in the doorway of the house. Catching her, he couldn't speak, only hold her as she began to cry.

"Where is he, John? What happened? I want to see him," Brenda said after a few minutes.

"He's at the hospital."

"I want to see him. Will you take me there?" The look in Brenda's eyes was a look he had never seen before. She was asking to go but at the same time begging him not to take her, not to make her confirm what she had been told. He led her to the deputy's car.

Death is a part of living, and the death of one who is loved is especially sad no matter what their age. But the death of a young person is impossible to reconcile and tragic in the extreme. The dreams, the expectations, the promise of a future generation, all of that lost.

Old people are supposed to die. One of their jobs is to die, and funerals for older people are fitting and proper. They can be a celebration of the accomplishments of a lifetime. But the funeral for a seventeen-year-old boy represents the loss of life never lived. All of the promise of life, all of the sunrises, the snow falls, the shy smiles, the Christmas mornings, all laid to rest at the cemetery.

To relieve stress on Brenda and her unborn child, she was lightly medicated and had to leave most of the planning of the funeral to John. It was a job he had never expected. He and Brenda had never talked about death with Allen and he had never spoken about it to either of them. John, through his grief, had to think about what Allen would have wanted, how he would have wanted something like this handled. They didn't want the casket opened. They wanted all of Allen's friends, all of their friends, to remember Allen as he was in life, not as he lay in death. The only service for Allen would be at the cemetery.

John had to bring clothes for Allen and almost without thinking, he started to pick a suit but realized almost immediately that wouldn't be what Allen would have wanted. Instead, John took a pair of Allen's most worn and comfortable jeans, his favorite rugby shirt that was only off long enough for Brenda to wash periodically, and his favorite loafers. *This is what he would have wanted*, John thought, *I know it is.*

Though there was to be no open casket, no church ceremony, John and Brenda had to see Allen one last time before the casket was closed. On Thursday morning, before the funeral that afternoon, they went to the funeral home for a final visit.

His coffin was in one of the corner rooms on the side of the building that was in direct sunlight. The shadows cast by the light coming through the blinds on the window made a sharp, stairstep pattern on the carpet in the middle of the floor. As they walked into the small room the door closed quietly behind them. They stood by the door a long time, holding each other, looking at the open casket but not being able to see Allen. It was as if, by merely standing there, refusing to cross the room, they could step back in time. Could step back to the last few moments they had shared with Allen.

John didn't know how long they stood by the door but when his eyes focused again on the shadows, the images had moved and now reflected on the side of casket. They walked together slowly across the floor, each step giving them a better view of the last thing they ever wanted to see.

Finally, standing quietly by the side of the coffin, his right hand laid softly on the wood and satin and his left arm around Brenda's shoulder, they looked down on the body of their son. Silent, quiet, handsome, his skin pale, cold, and firm.

"We brought some things for you to take with you, Son," John said quietly.

"Here's a picture of John and me. I picked it myself," Brenda said. "You know we'll always be with you." She slid the small picture of John and her under Allen's hands.

"And here's one of you and me on one of our first trips to our tree stand," John whispered. "You can't be more than four in this picture. You remember the hunter that came by and took this for us? He said we were laughing so hard over something he could hear us over 200 yards away. We did have fun that day. We always had . . ." John's voice faded away, lost in memories. Lost in the grief of a journey never to be completed.

Brenda was crying softly and steadily, leaning more and more on John. "Do you want to go? We can leave. I . . ."

"No," she said. "You stay with him for awhile. I just wanted to tell him I love him, that I'll always be there. If I could just hold him once more. If . . ." the impossible wishes disappeared into the mist of the pain engulfing her.

Reaching out, she touched Allen's hand once more and leaned over, her lips brushing his lifeless cheek. "I love you," she said quietly, surprised at the steadiness of her voice. "In my heart we'll always be together."

Standing, she looked at John. "I'm ready, but I know you need time. If you'll help me, I'll wait outside." Squeezing John's hand as he helped her out into the hall where friends waited, John said, "I'll only be a few more minutes." He knew Brenda needed him badly, but there was still some things left unsaid. Turning slowly, he returned to the side of the coffin.

He reached into his pocket and withdrew an old Remington pocket knife. Opening the longer of its two blades, he could see the edge was nearly a third gone—a victim of forty years of whet stones, Arkansas stones, and leather belts. But sharp!

"This is from Grandpa. He was going to give it to you for Christmas but now . . ." He had to stop again for a moment.

"He's here. He'll be at the cemetery. But with Mary gone, he just couldn't come here. Couldn't see you here. 'Never go without your knife.' He always told me that. You never can tell when you'll need . . . when something will . . . ." His voice again lost its direction. He closed the blade and pushed the knife gently into Allen's right front pocket.

"And your mom asked me to give you this too. It's your grandmother's wedding band. The one her mother wore for forty-eight years. She was saving it for you to give to the girl you would marry. To the daughter-in-law that would have her grandchildren. You know how sentimental she is. But she just couldn't leave it herself. She just loves you so much . . . we just love you . . . ."

His words trailed off into silence, into a void he knew nothing would ever fill. Standing by the coffin he looked at the child on whom he had pinned so many hopes and in whom he had so much faith.

He touched Allen's cheek with the back of his right hand then smoothed the blond hair across Allen's forehead. With that final touch John left his son and walked slowly with Brenda across the parking lot to their car.

How can anything be right again? he thought through the tears he could no longer control.

CHAPTER THIRTY-EIGHT

Family and friends overflowed the Richter home. They came, seeking comfort from one another, some understanding of how and why this could happen. The number of people who came to remember Allen was a testimony to the love the community had for him.

"Look at all this food," Brenda said to John. "I know how much time it's taken to fix all of this, but I just don't think I can eat it." They did eat, but couldn't recall later what they had. Sitting and talking quietly with friends that afternoon, both were appreciative of the support, but in a whispered voice when they had a minute alone, Brenda confided in John, "I wish all of them would go away—all of the food, all of the flowers, everything. I just want our lives back, our son." All John could do was hold her and dry the tears that coursed down her face.

Sheriff Longley was there and when he caught John's attention he motioned for him to step outside. Making sure Brenda had friends with her, John appreciated the opportunity to get outside for a few minutes, away from the crowds, away from the memories.

"John, I know this may not be the right time, but I thought you'd like to know what we've found." Looking at John but receiving no response, Sheriff Longley went on, "We went back to the tree stand Tuesday morning and looked around again real good. We can't really tell what happened. Allen had his safety belt around his waist but obviously it wasn't attached to the tree when he fell. There was a nylon rope hanging from the tree stand, but his bow wasn't attached to it. I guess the rope was there for him to lower his bow with. It's all speculation, you know, but what we think may have happened is that he had decided to get down out of the tree, unhooked the belt and in the process of turning around to tie his bow to rope, lost his balance and fell. It doesn't happen often, but it happens. I don't know what to say, John. It was just an accident."

John had no reason to disbelieve what the Sheriff was telling him.

"Sheriff, I want to thank you for everything you and your men did. I don't know, I . . . we always talked to Allen about safety. He and I and the Porters have been practicing, been shooting for months. We even had tree stands that we used over at Issac's place. I always told Allen, always tried to make him understand how important it was to keep that safety belt hooked until he was ready to climb down. I know he thought he had found a big buck up on that ridge. I don't know, maybe he got a shot at the buck, maybe he just saw it, I don't know."

"I don't either. It's just such a damn shame to lose a kid, especially a good one like Allen. I know you don't want to hear this now, but I put Allen's bow in his closet this afternoon. I figured you'd want to have it back. I hope you don't mind me going in."

"No, Sheriff, I appreciate everything you've done. I'd better go back inside now. Thanks again."

The last people left about six o'clock and John and Brenda were finally alone. They needed each other and time alone was the only thing that would keep them sane. They sat on the sofa in the den for a long time and held each other. They didn't speak, both lost in their own thoughts, silently remembering Allen, trying to come to grips with his death.

They slept together that night on Allen's bed, John's hand resting gently on Brenda's shoulder. Their love for each other and the new life within her was their only link to reality, the only sanity they shared. Just before he went to sleep, John remembered the way he felt the first time he had felt Allen kick inside Brenda, the wonder and joy that simple movement had brought. Brenda's gentle sobs had finally stopped and as sleep mercifully ended John's day, he called Allen's name.

Over the next weeks both of them went through life with robot-like precision. Each of them took the rest of the week off but the following Monday, those jobs, those requirements of the living resurfaced. Neither was able to focus adequately on their duties at work, though they made valiant efforts to block out everything except those responsibilities.

I've got to focus on this baby, Brenda thought, *and on John. I've got to have a reason to go on. I'll never forget Allen, but I've got to look to the future, look to the well-being of this child.*

John dealt fairly well at work; the difficult time for him was at home. The yard and house were neglected and he had no inclination to go hunting, even though several of his friends had called to encourage him to get out. Judge Collins had even called and offered the cabin for a weekend if John had felt like that would do any good. Respectfully declining, he didn't want any reminder of how Allen had died.

"You know," he said to Brenda several weeks after the funeral, "night time is the worst. I'm afraid to close my eyes, afraid to sleep, even to doze. When I do, Allen comes back. He's so real, so clear that I can hear his voice, see that wide smile and those hopeful eyes. He was so hungry for life. But then the dream ends and the reality comes crashing down, I . . ." His voice trailed off as he buried his head in his hands. He felt as if he was covered in an avalanche of sorrow so deep that he would never again see the light.

John was pulling his grief around him like a shell. One that would be so thick it would cut off all of those who sought to console him. It was forming a blanket which, if it had remained, would suffocate him.

Brenda would not let that happen.

"John" she said, "we have to share this loss, this grief, just like we shared the love, the joy, and the pleasure of Allen's life. If we don't, we lose the significance of his having lived at all." John only nodded. He knew she was right and he was trying. Sitting beside him, taking him in her arms, their tears brought them together.

"I know the pain will never disappear, I just hope I can learn to live with it." Looking at Brenda, he said, "You give me a reason to look forward again."

At dinner one evening about a month after the funeral, Brenda brought up a subject that both of them had been deliberately avoiding.

"John, we need to do something with Allen's room. We need to . . ."

John glanced quickly at Brenda, the look on his face showing clearly that he had no heart for the project she was suggesting.

"We have to, John. We can't make that room a shrine to Allen. He wouldn't have wanted us to do that," she said, pleading with her husband. John realized it was something she was going to do, with or without his help. He had to help her. Going through Allen's things was part of dealing with the loss.

"You're right. I don't have any plans for tomorrow. It'll be Thanksgiving in a couple of weeks and Dad'll be up. We really ought to try to get it done before then."

Just the agreement to begin a process that both dreaded so much seemed to ease the burden each of them felt, seemed to relieve both of them of part of the gloom that had followed them ever since Allen's death.

The next morning they went into Allen's room with boxes and bags and began sifting through his things—what they would give to Allen's friends, what they would donate to charity, or what they would keep for themselves. It was a long, painful process. No matter what item either one of them picked up, it brought back a flood of memories.

"What about the closet, John?" Brenda asked. They had, collectively, gone through everything in the chest of drawers and bookcase.

"Can't it wait until next weekend?" asked John.

"No, we've started. Let's finish this," Brenda replied. Opening the door to the closet and the world of memories that lived there, Brenda reached in and pulled out a dozen shirts on hangers. John followed, taking out pants and two suits that Allen had worn as seldom as possible. As John reached back into the closet for the last of the hang-up clothes, he saw Allen's bow leaning up in the corner where Sheriff Longley had left it the day of the funeral. The sight of that bow brought such an immediate and overwhelming flood of memories that John had to grip the door jam to steady himself. Looking back at John, Brenda could not see the bow, only the paleness of his face.

"John?" she asked.

"It's his bow," John said, reaching gingerly for the weapon. Taking hold of the top limb of the bow he pulled it slowly from the closet, carefully avoiding putting his hand on the hand rest where Allen would have been holding the bow when he fell. John couldn't bear the mental closeness that connection would have brought.

"Are you going to keep that, John?" Brenda asked. She was afraid he would and afraid that he wouldn't all at the same time. John was noticing things that now leapt with startling quickness into his consciousness. Brenda asked again, "Are you going to keep that?"

"Brenda, look at this. Look at what's gone. There are two arrows missing and almost all of the string on this reel is missing. Do you know what that means?"

Brenda didn't really care, but said, "I guess he shot at something, but what difference does that make now?"

It was such an obvious question John had no answer for it. Clearly, whether or not Allen had shot at and hit a deer would not change the fact that he was dead. But John felt he had to know. If Allen had killed a deer and John could find the animal, he could at least be close to Allen again in some way, for a little while.

"I don't know . . . I don't guess it makes any difference, but I need to know, I have to find out. It may help me understand how he fell, why he fell."

As John left the bedroom, Brenda called, "Where are you going? What are you going to do?"

"I'm going to go call Issac. If Allen did hit a deer and this string tracker worked, we may still be able to find it. If he did hit one, I owe it to Allen to go look for it. Issac's the best tracker in the county and I could use his help."

"John!" Brenda called after him. "Don't . . ." she never finished the sentence. *If,* she thought, *looking will help him get through this, if it will help us, he's got to go.*

CHAPTER THIRTY-NINE

AS ISSAC AND John drove toward the logging trail where Allen had parked, Issac looked at Allen's bow.

"Yep, it looks like there's about three-hundred-fifty to four-hundred yards of string gone off the reel. As much as Allen had practiced and as good a shot as he was, I'll bet you he did get an arrow in one. Funny, though. Allen didn't seem to be the type to get so excited that he'd forget all the safety rules you taught him. He was pretty level-headed."

"I know," said John. "I don't understand it either. We'd shot from tree stands dozens of times and this was one that he'd set up himself. It wasn't that high up and it was real secure. I just can't figure out what could have happened that would have made him fall like that."

Pulling into the logging road, John could still see the tracks made by all of the emergency equipment a month ago on the night Allen had died. Blocking that out, he and Issac left the truck and began climbing the ridge to Allen's tree stand.

"Did you ever come back to get the tree stand?" Issac asked.

"No, this is the first time I've been in the woods since Allen died. I just couldn't bring myself to . . ." John's voice trailed off. There were still many things too painful to express.

Issac understood and quickly changed the subject. "How did you tell Allen to use that string tracker?"

"Well, I'd never used one myself. But I read a couple of articles about using them and what Allen and I thought would be best was to tie the end of it near the first part of the blood trail if he hit one. I haven't been up here since Allen died and I don't know how far around the stand the sheriff's people may have searched. I guess we'll find out. Some of the leaves have started to fall, but things would still be pretty much the same as they were on opening day."

The pair were silent for the next ten minutes as they climbed the gently sloping ridge toward the crest where Allen's stand had been. Approaching the stand from the rear John found himself unable to look up at the stand.

Issac looked at John. "Are you okay? We don't have to do this, you know. If Allen did hit a deer and killed it, there's not much left now anyway. There won't be anything but bones and hide."

"No, no, I'm okay. I've got to do this. I've got to do it for Allen. I've got to know what happened."

They began to make ever-widening circles around the tree, each walking softly and carefully, looking for any indication of what might have happened just before Allen fell. They were looking not only for the white tracking string from Allen's bow, but for the fletching of either of his arrows sticking out of the ground or in any nearby trees. The blaze orange fletching would have been relatively easy to spot if the shaft were not buried under the leaves. About thirty yards out from the right front of the tree stand and up the slope, the way Allen's deer had run, Issac spotted a piece of string tied to the bottom of sapling within a foot or so of the trail leading up the ridge.

"John, John, get over here! I think I've found it!"

Running to Issac's side John bent down and pulled gently on the string which disappeared into some leaves by the trail. The string was tied with a couple of knots to the base of the sapling and was the same type of string that was on Allen's reel.

"I knew it! He did hit one! Come on, let's go."

"Slow down, John. We don't know what direction this goes in. Let's just take our time. We've got all day. If we're going to do this, let's do it right."

"You're right, you're right. It's just so important for me to understand, to know what Allen saw and did that last afternoon.

"I know, John. You probably want to run through the woods with the string in your hands and just trail it as fast as you can. But we've got to slow down, take our time so that we don't lose the trail.

"Allen could have followed the deer and tied off the string somewhere else. A lot of times deer will wrap one of these things around a tree while it's running and it'll break. We need to follow it as carefully as we can."

"I know, Issac. It's just that . . ." John's voice slid off into silence again. The thought that he might actually have a window into Allen's last day was an overwhelming possibility. They spent almost an hour going the first two hundred yards up the ridge. As the string ascended the ridge, both saw it was headed directly across the boundary line and on to Belleview. Bringing the string right up to the boundary line, they saw the posted signs still in place.

"What do you think, John? Would Allen have gone on over to Belleview?"

"Well, I expect he would have. He knew not to trespass, not to go where he didn't have permission to hunt. But, at the same time, he wouldn't have wanted to lose a deer, for the deer to be wasted."

"Do you know this Sterling guy? Do you think we ought to go up to Belleview and try to get permission?"

"Well, I was there once before and I've met him. But we couldn't be more than two hundred yards from the end of this string and we're right here. Besides, it's a Sunday. There won't be any other hunters in the woods. Let's go on."

John and Issac continued following the trail and were soon approaching the spot near the pasture where Allen had crouched and heard the discussion which led to his death.

"I don't understand this," said Issac. "Look how this string is doubled up and makes a left angle right here. And look at the ground. It's all torn up like a whole herd of deer ran through it."

Looking down the woods in the direction the string had been pulled into a sharp V shape, they could see where it had caught on Allen's bow and was strung three to four feet above the ground instead of on or near the ground where the deer had been dragging it. Following the string and the tracks for about a hundred yards, they came to the tree where Allen had hidden.

"This is really bizarre," Issac said. "This string stopped back there about twenty yards and angled back up toward Belleview, but these tracks keep going over toward that tree. I can't figure this out."

John didn't have any idea what these signs meant. Something was very confusing, very wrong about what had happened. Having lost confidence in the trail that the string showed them, John and Issac once again began making ever-widening circles from the point the string had slipped off the bottom limb of Allen's bow and made its sharp turn back toward Belleview. It was Issac who found Allen's small flashlight partially hidden beneath some leaves on the spot where he had been killed. There was no sign left of the struggle between Allen and Lester Morgan and there were no obvious clues to explain why Allen would have left his flashlight here.

"Maybe he hit the deer," ventured Issac, "followed it here with his flashlight, got to this point, lost the trail, and then lost the flashlight. That would explain why he went back to the stand and, since he didn't have a flashlight, couldn't see the edge of the stand and fell out."

"I don't know, Issac. Allen was a lot more careful than that. Let's keep looking."

The orange fletching on the arrow that had killed the dark-haired man caught John's eyes. It was about four and half feet off the ground, stuck in an oak tree about thirty feet from where they found the flashlight.

"Issac! Look at this. This is one of Allen's arrows! Look at it. Look at the fletching!"

"You're right. But . . ." Issac said, looking around. "This is crazy. We know the deer went over that way and all of a sudden the trail leads us here and then Allen shoots another arrow back in this direction. The deer he shot from the tree stand would have to have been way over that way," he continued, pointing toward Belleview. "This arrow was shot back toward the tree stand. He wouldn't have shot two deer in one day, would he?"

"No, I don't think so. He would have been so excited to have gotten one that I'm sure he wouldn't have shot a second without finding the first one."

"And why would he climb back in the tree stand? Didn't Sheriff Longley say that they found Allen's knapsack on the trail about fifteen feet from the tree?"

"Yeah, that's what Sheriff Longley said. And I know Allen wasn't planning on taking his tree stand down. There's something wrong here. None of this makes any sense."

"Well," Issac said, "why don't you pull that arrow out of the tree and let's see if we can find the deer."

Since the string had been pulled off course by Allen's flight from the men who killed him, it took Issac and John over an hour to find the deer Allen had killed on opening day. The carcass of the buck lay in the woods about a hundred and twenty-five yards away, in the thicket where the deer had fallen and died just minutes after Allen had shot it.

Making their way back to the tree stand with Allen's second arrow, Issac asked, "Do you want to take the tree stand down?"

"No, Allen put it up there and as far as I'm concerned, that's where it can stay. If you want it you can have it. Otherwise, let's just leave it."

"No, I don't want it. I just thought . . ."

"I still can't figure any of this out. I wonder if anybody at Belleview might have seen or heard anything. I've got to find out what happened. Maybe one of their people saw the deer or Allen."

John told Brenda what they had found but there were many questions left unanswered by the evidence discovered around the tree stand.

"What are you going to do, John? Do you really think there's any point in going any further?"

"Yes, I do. I'm going to call Charles Sterling and see if I can go talk to him. He seemed like a decent enough guy. Maybe he'll have somebody check out everybody on his staff. There's just something strange and I don't think I'm going to be satisfied until I find out what happened. I don't see any reason for Allen to have gone back up in the tree stand. His pack was on the ground. He had already shot the deer and tracked it. Why would he have gone back without the deer, after dark, with no flashlight, and climbed back up into the stand? It just doesn't make sense. Allen was a better hunter than that."

CHAPTER FORTY

"STERLING RESIDENCE, MELINDA speaking. May I help you?"

"Yes, this is John Richter. I work at the bank. Is Mr. Sterling in?"

"Well, he's tied up right now. Could I take a message?"

Sterling, sitting at the desk in front of Melinda, raised his eyebrows inquiringly. As Melinda spoke to John, she wrote his name on a pad and held it up for Sterling to see. Recognizing the name as the father of the boy his men had killed the month before, he made a sign for her to put John on hold.

"Can I put you on hold for a minute?" Melinda asked.

"Sure."

"That's John Richter on the phone?" Sterling asked.

"Yes, he wants to speak with you. Do you want to talk to him?"

"Yes, we don't need to raise his suspicions." Picking up the phone, he said, "Hello, Mr. Richter. This is Charles Sterling. How are you?"

"Well I'm getting along better, I suppose."

"I just wanted to tell you how sorry I am bout your son. I read about the accident in the paper. What a tragedy," he said, sounding sincere and sympathetic.

"I wondered if I might come out this afternoon and speak with you for a few minutes? There are some questions I had about Allen's accident and I thought maybe some of your people might have seen something."

"Certainly. Come out around three. I must tell you however that none of my employees have mentioned anything to me that would lead me to believe they know anything about your son's accident."

"Well, if it's just the same I'd still like to come out. There are a couple of things that I found and maybe you could check with your people. I really would like to try to find out what happened."

"I understand. I'll be glad to do whatever I can. I'll see you about three o'clock."

After hanging up, Sterling looked at Melinda. "Get Sam in here. We may have a problem."

Entering the office about five minutes later, Sam asked, "Yes, sir, what can I do for you?"

"John Richter just called here. He's coming out at three o'clock. This is the father of the kid that Lester killed last month. Are you sure we're okay on all that?"

"Absolutely," said Sam. "We went over that area a couple of times after we moved D'Angelo's man out of the way. There's nothing to connect us with that boy's death. He was just in the wrong place at the wrong time."

"Good. I want to talk to Richter and I want you here too. We want to show him that we're concerned. He says there are a couple of questions he has and he thinks somebody here at Belleview may know something. I don't know exactly what he's talking about or what he thinks someone here may know, but we have to make sure that he thinks we're trying to cooperate."

"Do you think we ought to let D'Angelo know what's going on?" asked Sam.

"Yes, that's a good idea. He's not going to be here that much longer, but I want to make sure that he knows we're not going to drop the ball at the last minute. Call and let him know I'm coming over in a few minutes to discuss this. He may even want to have one of his men here, just to hear what's going on."

Picking up the phone, Sam dialed D'Angelo's extension.

"Hello," Lynn said.

"Lynn, this is Sam at the manor house. Mr. Sterling would like to speak to Mr. D'Angelo. Would it be okay if he came over in about five minutes?"

"I think so, but hang on just a minute," Lynn said. Sam could hear Lynn asking D'Angelo if that was all right but had not expected Mr. D'Angelo to take the phone.

"What's the problem?" D'Angelo asked in an irritated voice.

"There's no problem, Mr. D'Angelo. Mr. Sterling just has a couple of things that he wants to talk over with you."

"Well, goddamn it, there better not be any problems. I've already had one of my men skewered like a shish-kebab by one of your fucking locals. We're too close to the end of all of this to have things screwed up now. When does he want to come over?"

"In about five minutes," Sam replied.

"That's fine," D'Angelo said, slamming the receiver down on the phone.

"Christ, he's in a worse mood than usual. I know all the surgery and everything has been rough on him and I know that he's paying you a bucketful of money to be here, but I'll be real glad to see him gone." Sterling's failure to respond was, to Sam, a confirmation of those sentiments.

Sterling's conversation with D'Angelo was short and to the point.

"Well, as soon as you find out what this son of a bitch thinks he knows, you let me know if we've got a problem. We can't afford to have anybody snooping around out here. I'm gonna be ready to get the hell out of here inside of a week and everything I need to take with me out of the country is going to be delivered here within the next forty-eight hours. If we've got a problem let's take care of it. I've got a lot of riding on this. And," he said looking fiercely at Sterling, "so do you. If any of this get screwed up . . . Well, I don't need to finish that sentence. You don't want to know what'll happen."

"There's no need for threats. We've known each other a long time and I'm telling you we've got everything under control. If you'd like, send one of your men over a little before three to sit in on our meeting. I can just tell Richter that your man is on the staff of one of our guests, and that I wanted the man to sit in to make sure everyone understands what it is he's looking for. Don't forget, I've got even more riding on this project than you do. We're in the middle of supplying all of our arsenals all over the country. You'll be gone in a week. We're here for the duration. Nothing's going to go wrong. I can give this guy enough answers to put him off the track."

"You better!" The threat implicit in what D'Angelo said was clear—he would let no one interfere with his plans to move his operation and the profits generated by it out of the country, not even his old and trusted friend.

At precisely three o'clock, John Richter drove up to the front gates at Belleview. The guard, phoning the manor house, was instructed to let him pass through the gate and direct him to the manor house.

It was with some reservation that John drove up the long drive to the manor house. *I'm not really sure what questions to ask. I just know the facts can't be reconciled with what happened to Allen. It's like pieces of a jigsaw puzzle that don't fit together. Maybe Sterling or one of his employees can shed some light on what happened.*

When he arrived at the manor house one of the staff came out to greet him. "Mr. Richter? Mr. Sterling is waiting for you. Follow me, please."

"Thank you." John followed the man up the stairs and into the large center hall. He had forgotten how exquisite the manor house was. The reception he and Brenda had been to early last spring seemed like a million years ago.

"Right this way, sir." Walking into Mr. Sterling's office, he couldn't help but again notice the quality of the renovations and the furnishings. Clearly, Mr. Sterling had spared no expense on this project. *What type of businesses generate the quantity of money necessary to sustain this type of facility?*

As John was ushered into the room, Sterling rose from behind his desk and walked around to greet him. "Mr. Richter, Charles Sterling," he said, extending his hand. "I know we've met before but it's been a long time. I want to tell you again how sorry I was to hear about your son's death. I'd never met him but had heard a lot of very nice things about him. I know you and Brenda must be devastated."

John could not believe Sterling remembered his wife's first name. Extending his hand, he said, "Thank you, Mr. Sterling. It's something I don't think we'll ever really get over. Allen was our only son. He and I were very close and . . ."

"I'm sure you were. Please, have a seat. Oh, excuse me, I forget my manners. John Richter, this is Sam Cross, my executive assistant, and this is Michael Billings. Michael is on the staff of one of my guests. They have half a dozen or so people with them and I thought Michael might want to sit in on our conversation and then talk with his people about your questions."

Shaking hands with the other two men, John was surprised by Michael's appearance. While Mr. Sterling had explained this man was not on his staff, he didn't fit into these surroundings at all. Much too uptown, almost Mafia-like. *Christ,* John thought, *what rock did this guy slither out from under?*

As the men sat down, Sterling asked John, "I know that Allen died a few hundred yards on the other side of my property line down toward the river. I understand from what I've seen in the paper that he was deer hunting in a tree stand and evidently lost his balance and fell. That's a real tragedy."

"That looks like what happened. I'd always been very clear with Allen about using his safety harness and taking a lot of precautions. Right after the accident, I didn't really look at things too closely. But in the last week or so I've seen several things that made me question what might have really happened."

"What things are those?" Sterling asked, his brow wrinkled with concern.

"Well, Sheriff Longley brought Allen's bow back to my house the day of the funeral and put it in Allen's closet. He didn't think that I would want to see it or have to deal with it at that point and he was right. But Brenda and I were going through some of Allen's things several days ago and I took the bow out of the closet and looked at it. There were several arrows missing from the quiver. I know it was full when Allen left the house the morning he died because I got up and had breakfast with him. There was also a device on the front of the bow—sort of like a fishing reel. It had string wound around a reel and the string was attached to the back of the arrow that he would've shot at a deer. It looked to me like Allen must have shot at a deer and hit it because most all that string was gone.

"Issac Porter, a good friend of mine, and I went over to the tree stand yesterday to look around. I just felt that if Allen hit a deer the day he died that I ought to try and find it. When we got to the tree stand and looked around we found where the end of the string had been tied on a small sapling about thirty yards from Allen's tree stand."

Surprised at this information and looking quickly at Sam, Mr. Sterling said, "And were you able to follow this string?"

"Well, yes, we did. It came up the ridge from the tree stand. In fact, it came over on your property. I know we didn't have permission to be over on Belleview, but yesterday was Sunday and there didn't seem to be anybody else around. I hope you don't mind that we followed the trail?"

"No, that was certainly fine. I had no idea that he had come over on our property. What else did you find?"

Not only was Sterling's curiosity aroused but there was a growing seed of doubt, tinged with some fear, that details had been overlooked which might lead to a further investigation of Allen's death. An investigation that could point directly to him and his operation.

"Well, we followed the string on over to your property about a hundred to a hundred and fifty yards. Then it made a sharp turn back into the woods for seventy-five yards. I found Allen's flashlight on the ground near where the string stopped and we found another arrow sticking in a large oak tree about thirty yards from where we found the flashlight. It took a while, but we found the deer that Allen killed about a hundred yards on the other side of where the flashlight was." John paused. "And that's what I don't understand."

"Well, I don't mind telling you, I'm more than a little confused. Can you simplify this a little for me?" Sterling asked.

"Sure, have you got a piece of paper?"

Sam went to Sterling's desk and got a legal pad and pencil.

"Here you are, Mr. Richter."

"Thanks. Here's what's so confusing to me." Drawing a diagram for Sterling, he explained again what they had found.

Sterling, trying to hide his concern, looked at the sketch and said, "Well, how do you know that's the deer that your son shot? I mean, if the string led one way and the carcass of this deer was way over here, how do you know it wasn't a deer that someone else shot and couldn't find?" Sterling asked.

"There's no question that it's the deer Allen shot. The end of the string was still tied to the arrow, and Allen had unusual arrows with uniqe fletching. He used two orange feathers and one light green one. I don't know anybody else in the county who hunted with arrows like that. We found one of those arrows still in the deer that we found over here. We just can't figure out why the string trail would have made the angle that it did when the deer was so far off in the other direction. And we can't figure out what Allen shot at that was in the opposite direction from where the deer that he was tracking actually fell."

"Was there anything on the arrow you found in the tree? I mean, could you tell whether anything had been hit with that arrow?" Sam asked.

"No. If there was anything on the arrow it got washed off in that hard rain we had several weeks ago. We don't know what he shot at nor whether he hit anything with that arrow."

"Well," Sam said, "he could have shot at another deer. I'm not a hunter but you can kill more than one deer a day in Virginia now, can't you?"

"You can, but I don't think Allen would do that. Especially if he was trailing a buck that he'd already hit. He was disciplined enough to try and find one animal before he would shoot another. Especially one the size we found. He had been trailing that buck for a long time and I'm sure he must have known how big it was and that he had made a good shot. No, I don't think he would have tried to kill a second deer before he found the first. The other questions I have are because of what we found around the tree stand."

Raising an eyebrow, Sterling asked, "What did you find at the tree stand?"

"Allen's day pack was on the ground about fifteen to twenty feet from the tree stand. That means that Allen had climbed out of the tree to track the deer and brought his pack down with him. We know that he trailed the deer three hundred yards or so and that he went back to the tree stand without finding it. What we can't figure out is why he would have gone back up in the tree stand after all this happened. Everything he would have needed to bring home was already on the ground. I know he wasn't planning on moving that stand. It just doesn't make any sense."

"I can understand your questions," Sterling said. "It doesn't seem to add up. Sam, have any of our people said anything about seeing or hearing anyone over on that part of the farm the day the young man died?"

"Well," Sam said, "we had our usual people out trying to keep poachers off the property. I remember someone said they heard several shots over that way, but when we sent someone over they didn't find anyone. If there was somebody hunting over there we didn't catch up with them. I'll check again, but nobody said anything to me about seeing a bow hunter or a wounded deer."

"I want you to personally talk with everyone on the staff and see if they remember anything at all that might help Mr. Richter figure out exactly what happened the day his son died." Looking at John, Sterling continued, "I don't know that we'll come up with anything that will help you, but I understand that it's important to you to try and piece this together. You've found the deer that he was trailing and you're certainly welcome to salvage any part of the animal that you want. While we don't allow hunting, I certainly would have let Allen look for the deer if he had come up to the house and asked for permission. He didn't do that, and, as far as I know, he didn't talk to anyone else."

"I would really appreciate your checking with your staff. I know you have a lot of people working for you and I don't want to cause any inconvenience, but I really need to know what happened to Allen. I don't know that I'll ever understand any of it, but any information might make it easier to accept. Thanks for the time you've taken and I really appreciate anything you can find out."

Standing, John shook Sterling's hand again and turned to leave. Michael, who had not taken part in any of the conversation, did not rise as John left nor did he make any move to shake his hand. He merely sat and stared at him in silence.

John tried to work his way through a swirl of thoughts as he walked down the front steps of the manor house toward his car.

I don't remember hearing anything about any shots before. I wonder who heard them? And who is that Michael guy? There's something wrong with him. I thought Sterling was an above-board sort of person. I wonder why he would have someone like this Michael character on his farm, even if he's with a guest.

Watching John drive down the driveway, Sterling turned to Sam. "I thought you said you went over the area where that boy was killed. What in the hell is this string that Richter's talking about? How in the hell did you miss something like that?"

"Christ, Mr. Sterling, we didn't see anything. I guess it would just have to be something you would know was there in order to see it."

"What about the other arrow? Didn't it ever occur to you to search the woods for the arrow that killed D'Angelo's man? I just assumed that it stuck in the son of a bitch and we buried the arrow with him!"

"We looked for it but didn't see it. I thought it must have gotten buried under the leaves. Jesus, I didn't know the damn thing was stuck in a tree!"

"Where did you bury that son of a bitch anyway?"

"He's so deep in a hole on the other side of the farm his bones will never surface. Nobody will ever find him. You don't have to worry about that."

"Goddamn it, it looks like I've got to worry about everything! You get Lester and Floyd in here, and the other guy who was with you. I want to go over everything again with all of you and make sure that we've got our stories straight. Michael, you tell D'Angelo that all of this is going to be handled. There may be a bit of confusion right now, but we'll take care of that. You just tell him that he doesn't have anything to worry about."

"He ain't gonna like this!" Michael said. "I'll tell him what you said, but you'd better be ready to do some more explaining. Overlooking these kinds of details gets people killed," Michael said, glaring at both of them as he left the room.

John reached the end of the driveway at the main road and turned right instead of left. He felt like going the long way around. Sometimes a drive in the woods along the river road would help him clear his mind. He just didn't feel like going home right then, and he was still too confused about what he and Issac had found to try and explain anything to Brenda.

As he headed north of the gravel road he saw one of Sterling's limousines coming down the road toward him. About a hundred yards before the cars met the limousine turned left in front of him and went up a woods road that John had not been on in many years. Passing the road's entrance into the woods, he slowed and looked to his right, just barely catching a glimpse of the disappearing limousine.

"*Why in the world would that car be going up into the woods that way? The last time I was down that road there was nothing there but scrub oaks. That road used to come up behind the old dorm, but I didn't think anybody ever used it anymore.* It was just one more unanswered question. Just one more piece of the puzzle.

John drove further, not really paying attention to the road but merely a spectator on this trip along the river. The cool mid-November air and several early frosts were beginning to turn leaves different colors. He noted how many dogwood trees alongside the road had already turned their burgundy fall color.

As with many things he saw, the dogwoods took him back to the day Allen died. A picture flashed through his mind of Allen being brought out of the woods on the stretcher. He remembered sitting beside him on the ground and picking up his left hand, a hand that was still tightly clinched. It had not seemed important then that there was a stem and a few leaves clinched in Allen's left hand. John remembered those leaves and only now realized they were leaves from a dogwood tree. Hitting the brakes of his truck as hard as he could, his vehicle slid sideways in the gravel and stopped in a cloud of dust in the middle of the road. "That can't be! That just can't be," he said aloud, his teeth clenching in disbelief.

Turning the pickup truck around in the middle of the road and almost getting stuck in a ditch, John sped back in the direction of

Belleview. *I know I'm right. That can't have happened the way Sheriff Longley thinks it did.*

Arriving back at the turnoff where Allen had parked, John jumped out of his truck. Leaving the door open and the keys in the ignition, he ran as hard as he could back toward Allen's tree stand. Racing toward the clearing where Allen's body had been found, John arrived breathless and too unsteady to verify his suspicions immediately. After several minutes, he began to look carefully at the area within thirty yards around Allen's tree stand.

It was as if shades had been drawn back from a darkened window. Staring in disbelief, his mind raced. *That's just what I thought. There isn't a dogwood tree within fifty yards of this stand. I remember when Allen and I came up on this ridge in the spring looking for a place to put a tree stand. The dogwoods were all blooming. We could see them up and down the ridge but there wasn't a single one anywhere near this tree. The doctor said Allen died instantly, that his neck broke, and he could never have moved an inch from where he hit the ground. If that's true, then how in the hell did he end up with dogwood leaves in his hand? He didn't die here! He couldn't have died here!*

The implications of what he was thinking, what he had discovered, were overwhelming. With the injury Allen sustained, he had to have died somewhere else and someone must have brought his body here to the tree stand. *Why ?* he thought, a rage building inside him. *Why would anyone have killed my son? What could he have done that would have justified killing him?*

CHAPTER FORTY-ONE

"SHERIFF LONGLEY, THIS is John Richter. I need to see you as soon as you can get over to the house."

"What's wrong, John? Is there some trouble?"

"No, but there're some things I've found out that I think you need to know. It's about Allen."

"Well, you know we've done a thorough investigation and . . ."

"Sheriff, I know you spent a lot of time on this, but we've found some things that your people overlooked. This is really important."

Sheriff Longley could tell from John's voice there wasn't going to be any way to satisfy him other than to listen to what he had to say.

"Okay, John. I can be there in about forty-five minutes. Is that okay?"

"That's fine. I really appreciate it. I think you'll understand how important it is once we talk."

Great, thought Sheriff Longley. *This guy's not going to let this thing go. I'd better call Sterling before I go out there.* Dialing Sterling's private number at Belleview, Sheriff Longley said, "Mr. Sterling, this is Sheriff Longley. I think we have a problem with this Richter fellow."

"What now? He was just out here and I thought things were okay. I didn't really have a lot of answers for him, but he didn't seem too suspicious when he left. What's he told you?"

"He hasn't told me anything yet, but I just got off the phone with him and he's insisting that he needs to see me. I told him I'd be out there in about forty-five minutes, but I wanted to touch base with you first. Is there anything that I should know before I go over to see him?"

"Well, there were a few things that my men missed when they cleaned up after our little problem."

"What do you mean 'missed'?" the Sheriff asked.

"Well, according to Richter, he and one of his buddies looked at the bow the boy was using and figured out he had shot at something and hit it. Evidently the bow had some sort of string device on it that led them over onto my property. They found the boy's flashlight, the arrow that took out D'Angelo's man, and the deer the boy hit. And all of 'em were pretty widely scattered. He's pretty damn suspicious."

"Goddamn it! I thought you said your guys had all of this taken care of. Well, at least now I know what to expect. What do you want me to do?"

"Go talk to him. See what he wants you to do and see if there's anything else that he didn't tell me. Once you've met with him, call me. I want you to come out here so that we can sit down and see what we need to do. You and I've got too much at stake here for this to get screwed up. You call me right after you leave Richter's house."

"Okay, but do you really think it's a good idea for me to come out there?"

"Yes, this needs to be handled in person. Besides, I think D'Angelo's going to want to know what's happening and be a part of this too. I'll talk to you later," Sterling said, hanging the phone up and rolling his eyes at Sam.

Sheriff Longley arrived at Richter's house a few minutes later and saw Issac Porter and Roy Combs were there ahead of him. Walking up to the front door, Sheriff Longley called through the screen door, "Anybody home?"

"Sure, Sheriff, come on in," John answered.

Sheriff Longley opened the screen door and walked softly through the living room. Brenda and John were seated on the sofa and Issac and Roy were standing next to the archway leading into the dining room.

"Hello, Mrs. Richter. It's good to see you. I want to tell you again how sorry I am about Allen," he said, taking her hand gently.

"Thank you, Sheriff. I appreciate everything you've done. John hasn't told me much about why he wanted to meet with you again, so I guess we'll find out together."

John hadn't given Brenda all the details. Not because he didn't trust her with them, but because he was still trying to sort out all of the facts in his mind. He knew how all of this was going to affect her.

"Have a seat, Sheriff. I'll try to be as brief as I can. You remember the day of the funeral you took Allen's bow and put it in his closet for me."

Sheriff Longley nodded. "Yes, I remember doing that. I knew you wouldn't want to deal with it just then."

"You were right. Brenda and I just started going through Allen's things several days ago and I noticed when I took the bow out that several arrows were missing and that most of the string from the string tracker was gone. I knew Allen must have hit a deer and since Issac is a hell of a lot better tracker than I am, I asked him to go with me to see what we could find. We went over to where the tree stand was and we found the end of the string where Allen had tied it to a small sapling about thirty yards from his tree stand."

"So he did hit a deer," Sheriff Longley said. "Well, I'll be damned. We went over that area pretty carefully and didn't see that. We may not have gotten that far away from the tree since Allen was found right under the stand. What else did you find?"

"Well, the trail led over onto Belleview and seemed to be heading generally north until the string took a sharp left and went about seventy yards. Near where the string stopped, I found Allen's flashlight, and, on the other side of that about thirty yards, one of his arrows was stuck in a tree."

At that point in the conversation, Issac stepped in. "Yeah, and we found the deer that Allen killed about a hundred yards off in the other direction. We just can't figure out how all of these things came to be where they were if Allen was the only person in the woods."

John said, "And I've been over to Belleview and spoken with Mr. Sterling. He said that none of his people had mentioned anything to him about seeing Allen but I've asked him to check with them again. He said he'd do that and get back to me. Did any of your men talk to anyone who heard any gun shots the afternoon Allen died?"

"The fellow that found Allen's body said that he heard several shots earlier that afternoon, but I didn't really think anything about that. Allen hadn't been shot and there didn't appear to be any evidence of foul play. I just figured it was a squirrel hunter or poacher. I didn't really see any connection between Allen's accident and a couple of random shots," Longley said.

"The other thing that I can't understand, the other thing that's probably as strange as anything else, is that I just remembered this afternoon what Allen had in his hand when they brought him out of the woods," John said looking at Brenda.

"John, you've never told me anything about that. What did Allen have?" Brenda knew that there was something wrong but she didn't understand it.

"It didn't dawn on me until I was leaving Belleview this afternoon. Allen had some leaves clutched in his hand when they brought him out of the woods. I didn't think that much about it then but now . . ."

"Yeah, I remember that," Sheriff Longley interrupted. "I just thought that it was a reflex that he had after he hit the ground. The medical examiner would have removed those if you didn't and if he had found anything unusual he would've given them to me."

"What was unusual was the particular kind of leaves they were. They were dogwood leaves. I remember that clearly."

"Why is that strange? The woods on the ridge are full of dogwoods," the sheriff said.

"Sheriff, I went back to that tree stand this afternoon after I left Belleview and searched for a long time. There's not a dogwood tree within fifty yards of that tree stand. If the medical examiner is right, if Allen died instantly when he hit the ground, he couldn't have grabbed a dogwood tree. There isn't one anywhere near there. Allen died somewhere else. I don't know how he got back to the tree stand, but I know he didn't get there on his own."

Brenda's hand went to her mouth and she gasped, her eyes wide. "You mean you think someone killed Allen?" That thought had never entered her mind. The idea was so foreign to her that she could barely comprehend it.

"What could he have done? Why would someone have done that to Allen? He was just a boy! He was only seventeen. He never did anything. He never hurt anyone." Brenda looked at John, at the sheriff, and back to John, looking for answers that no one had.

"Now wait a minute, John. We don't know any of that. How can you be sure that they were dogwood leaves? You were pretty upset that night and it was dark. Besides, I'm sure those leaves have been thrown away now. You must have been mistaken."

"Sheriff, I wasn't mistaken. I remember every second of the time that I spent with Allen that evening. I remember every detail. God, I wish I could forget! They were dogwood leaves. I've hunted all my life. I've spent years in the woods. Hell, I've even planted fifteen or twenty of the damn things here in the yard. I know a dogwood leaf when I see one. And there aren't any around that tree stand. Goddamn it, he was killed somewhere else by someone else and brought back to the tree stand. What I want to know is—are you going to look for them!?"

"Now wait just a minute. I'm going to do my job. I always have. We'll go back out and we'll look around again, and I'll talk to Sterling's people too to see whether or not any of them saw anything. We'll talk to the guy who found Allen's body again. We don't have any reason to suspect him, but I'll go back and do all of that again. If you're right, I'm just as anxious to find the person as you are. But I don't think . . ."

"Sheriff, I'm right. I know I'm right. If you go back and review all of this and dig a little deeper, I think you're going to find that it wasn't an accident. You know Sterling's got some pretty strange people out there with him. I've been there a couple of times and I've seen some things that don't mesh with his public image. He's supposedly moved here to get away from all the crime and all the guns in the metropolitan area, but some of the guys he's got out there look like bad guys straight out of a Steven Segal movie. There's more going on out there than we know about, and I think if we can find out a bit more, we'll find out what really happened to Allen."

"I'll get right on it, John. But you leave this to me. I'm the sheriff in this county and I don't need you out there poking around. Getting to the bottom of this is my job, so leave it to me."

"Just as long as you do, Sheriff. I just wanted you to know what we had found and wanted to make sure that you understand that we think there's something else going on. I'm more than glad to leave the investigation to you as long as you follow up on all this! We just want to find out what happened to Allen and catch whoever did this."

As Sheriff Longley walked down the sidewalk to his patrol car, John and Brenda looked at each other, more questions having been raised than answered.

"What do you think?" asked Roy. "It doesn't sound to me like the sheriff's got his heart in this. He sounds like he's already got his mind made up and anything else he does is just to keep you off his back."

"I agree," said Isaac. "I think if we're going to get to the bottom of this, we're going to do it ourselves."

"Well, there was something else that I saw today that I didn't tell Sheriff Longley about. As I was driving up the river road, one of Sterling's limousines turned into that old logging road about half a mile up from the entrance to the farm. I didn't follow it, but why in the hell would one of those two-hundred-thousand-dollar cars be driving up there into the woods?"

"You think we ought to go up and find out?" Roy asked.

"I sure as hell think we ought to."

"I haven't trusted that sheriff ever since he got elected. Seemed like he had a real well-funded campaign to be running for sheriff's office for the first time. You don't suppose he's on Sterling's payroll, do you?" asked Roy.

"I don't know," said John, "but I do know that we're going to find out what's going on out there. And the first thing I want to know is why that limousine was going back up into the woods. I think if we wait 'til night and go up that logging road, we may be able to get some answers. Neither one of you have to do this, but you're welcome to come along if you want."

"Count us in," said Issac. "What time do you want to meet?"

"How about seven-thirty tonight at the Oak Run Store."

"Sounds good to me. We'll see you there," said Roy. "Come on, Isaac, I think John and Brenda need a little time alone."

After they left, Brenda started in on John. "I don't think you ought to do this. The sheriff knows what he's doing. Why don't you leave it to him? That's what he gets paid for. That's his job."

"Hon, you heard the sheriff. His heart isn't in this. I don't know whether he thinks I'm just making all this up or whether he has some other reason. But he's not going to look very hard. I've got to find out what happened to Allen, why he died. I know he didn't fall out of that tree. It wasn't an accident. He did something, saw something, heard something that got him killed. And if there's somebody out there who's responsible for it, I'm going to find out who it is."

"But, John, this is dangerous. You're going on someone else's property. That man's got a lot of money and a lot of power. If you're caught out there, you could . . ."

"I'll be careful. Issac, Roy, and I have spent enough time in the woods not to let these city boys catch us. We're just going to go out there to look around and see if we can figure this out. We're not going to get into any trouble. And we're not going to hurt anybody."

"I'm not worried about anybody. I'm worried about you. Allen's gone. I don't know what I'd do if something happened to you. We've got so much to do and look forward to here," she said, looking down and caressing her stomach. Brenda was due in a little under two months. The pain in her eyes was almost more than John could bear.

"I'll be careful. You're going to have to put up with me for a lot longer. I've just got to find out what happened. I can't rest. I won't have any peace until I get these answers. You just take care of you and the baby."

CHAPTER FORTY-TWO

WHEN SHERIFF LONGLEY called Sterling and told him about the conversation he had just had with Ritcher and his friends, Sterling insisted the sheriff meet with him and D'Angelo that evening.

"Be out here at 8:30. We'll need to sit down with D'Angelo and go over all of this. I don't know what we're going to do, but we've got to make sure that this doesn't go any further. My operation and your job as sheriff depend on it. Be here at 8:30."

"Right," said Sheriff Longley. *Christ, what the hell am I going to do with these people?* he thought. *I have a feeling we're getting ready to jump out of the frying pan and into the fire and I'm in so deep with these guys that there's no way in hell I can get out. This is one meeting I'm not looking forward to.*

At about 7:30 that evening, John met Isaac and Roy at the Oak Run store. Leaving his car there, they drove to the old camp site on the river in Isaac's truck. They thought his vehicle would be less likely to be recognized than John's since he had been out there several times in the last week. Pulling the truck well down off the gravel road and into the woods, the three walked back out to the main road, crossed it, and started through the woods toward the logging trail where John had seen the limousine earlier in the day. All three were relatively familiar with the terrain along that stretch of the river and had no trouble intersecting the road they were looking for.

"Jesus, we all look like a bunch of commandos," Roy said. All three had dressed in different types of camouflage clothing which they routinely used for hunting.

"Yeah," said John, "but we've got to really take this seriously. I don't know what to expect or what we'll find but we've got to be careful. We don't want any confrontations. If they're involved and we tip them off, it'll be a lot harder to get any real evidence."

Walking carefully to the crest of the ridge, it felt a little like being in a movie, not something they would actually be part of. When they got to the end of the logging road they crawled carefully the last ten feet to the crest of the ridge. Seeing a light about fifty yards away, Roy took out a small pair of binoculars.

"What do you see?" Isaac asked.

"It looks like some kind of underground bunker with garage doors. One of the doors is up and there's a limousine parked inside. There's a driver by the door in front of the car," Roy whispered. "I can't see much more than that. Why don't we try to get closer?"

"Sounds good to me," said Isaac. "Let's go up the ridge about forty yards, cross the road, and come back down toward him. He won't be expecting anybody from above him."

In silent agreement, John fell in behind Isaac and Roy as they crawled to within forty yards of the bay entrance. Lying there in the leaves watching the guard, none of them knew what the bunker was or why it was there so far from the manor house. The lights of the old dorm were visible about two hundred fifty yards up the ridge behind the bunker, but there was no obvious physical connection between this structure and the main buildings around Belleview.

Close enough now to hear what was going on, they saw another man approach the right side of the bunker from the woods toward the manor house.

"Eric, Sam wants you up at the manor house right now. He needs to talk to you about that incident last month over near the river."

"Shit, I've already told him everything I could remember about that. Why don't they just leave me the hell alone?"

"Not up to me, Chief. Just get your ass up there."

"Okay, goddamn it. I'm going up through the tunnels. I don't like to walk all the way up there through the woods at night."

"No way. Sterling doesn't want anybody using those tunnels 'til the security cameras get fixed. Besides that, D'Angelo wants some privacy."

"Well, I'm just going to use the right-hand tunnel. Goddamn it, he's over on the left side. What does he care what tunnel I use?"

"Listen, I'm not going to argue with you. Sam wants you up there now and he doesn't want you using any of the tunnels. Get your ass in gear and come on. There ain't nothing out here in the woods that's gonna hurt ya. Christ, what a pussy!"

"You want me to close this down? Robert's supposed to be bringing in one of the largest gun shipments we've had so far. They were being flown in tonight and he should be here in the next half hour. The video cameras are off so there's no record of the shipment and if he gets up here and there's nobody here, he's gonna be pissed."

"Well, leave it open. This is the shipment with the shoulder-fired stinger missiles and we'll need those inside pronto."

"Yep. Besides, I should be back down here in a few minutes anyway, don't you think?"

"Damned if I know. But if you're not back down here in half an hour, I'll come back and wait for Robert."

As the two walked away from the open bay and into the woods toward the ridge that led them to the manor house, John, Isaac, and Roy stared at each other incredulously.

"I don't believe this!" John whispered. "This is no conference center for his business!"

"You got that right. There's something bad wrong with this place!" Issac said.

"What do you think, should we take a peek?" Roy asked. For a few seconds there was silence as each thought about the implications of going even further. They had no idea what lay behind the bay doors, nor anything about the tunnels that connected this bunker to the old dormitory.

"I've gotta go," John said. "This has something to do with why Allen died and I'm going to find out what it is. You guys don't have to go. In fact, stay here and wait for me. If anybody's going to get caught at this, it's gonna be me. Hell, if I get caught, I'll just plead insanity. Everybody else does and gets off. You guys wait for me here. If something happens and these guys come back before I get out, just leave me. I'll either get out on my own or get arrested, one of the two."

"Man, you shouldn't go in there alone. Let me go with you," Isaac said. "I've been in places like this before, been in situations like this. In Nam . . ."

"Issac, I appreciate that, but I can't let you do it. Allen was my son and this is my problem. Let me go in by myself and see what I can see. If I need your help, I'll come running. Just wait for me here."

"Okay, man, but you be careful. I don't want to have to go back and tell Brenda she doesn't have a husband either."

Smiling, John said, "You won't. Just wait for me here." Quickly sprinting the forty yards between the ridge where they lay and the open bay door, John moved quickly to the back of the bunker.

Remembering the guards' conversation about the right and left tunnels, he noticed neither was marked but that the left-hand door must access a portion of the old dorm which housed someone of importance.

From their vantage point forty yards away, Isaac and Roy could see John as he slowly opened the door and disappeared inside. "Shit, I knew he was going to go in there. He don't know where he's going or what he's getting into," Issac said.

"Makes me wish I'd brought my .357," Roy said. "Well, let's just wait here. For better or worse, he's in."

The tunnel led uphill with steps and ramps at intervals. The relatively narrow concrete corridor was lighted with bare light bulbs spaced closely enough to provide minimum lighting between each. The hand rails on the right-hand side going up were cold to the touch and hadn't been cleaned often since the tunnels had been completed almost a year before.

As John slowly climbed the steps he thought, *Why would these tunnels be here? Why would they park all of these cars so far away from the main buildings? It's not a bomb shelter. There's no place down here for people to hide or take cover in any kind of emergency. Somebody went to a lot of time, trouble, and expense to make those cars accessible without being seen from the main buildings. There can't be any legitimate use for . . ."*

His thoughts were interrupted when he reached the top flight of stairs, terminating at the back of the old dormitory building. Stepping up onto the landing there were two alternatives open to him. Through a door directly in front of him he could see a small vestibule and another door which led to an unknown location. To his left was a second, steeper set of steps leading further upward. Deciding to go as far up as he could he took the steps to the left. He was going much more slowly now, realizing he must be closer to the main buildings.

Holding onto the hand rail to steady his footing up the narrow and dimly lit concrete steps, he came to a right turn leading to another flight of steps going even further up. Slowly peering around the corner and looking up toward the second landing, he tentatively reached around the corner, grasping for the hand rail he assumed was there. Just as his fingers touched the cold metal of the hand rail he felt a sharp scratching sensation on the top of his hand and wrist. Believing he had been discovered, he swung quickly around to his left, his left hand reaching, swinging forward, to strike whoever had touched him.

The teeth of the largest rat he had ever seen were a wicked, pale yellow. As the rat jumped from John's right hand and ran up his right arm toward his shoulder, John's urge to scream was almost uncontrollable. Just before the rat reached his neck, John knocked it from his right shoulder. The rat, landing heavily on the concrete steps, righted itself and ran back down the tunnel. It was all John could do to resist the inclination to turn and run headlong down the stairs. His heart racing and his breathing double its normal rate, he sank slowly to the steps, his head resting on his arms which were folded over his knees.

Holy shit, he thought, *I can see the headlines now. 'Local Banker Dies After Rat Induced Heart Attack.' I make a rotten criminal. What the hell am I doing here?* Resting for a few more minutes he remembered the guard had said he would probably be back at the bay within half an hour. Quickly checking his watch, he realized he only had about fifteen minutes left if he was going to get out before the guard came back.

His nerves now steady enough to allow him to continue, he rose and climbed to the landing at the end of the flight of steps. At the top of that landing another door confronted him. This one was unlocked and, like the door below, led to a small vestibule with another door on the opposite wall.

Crossing to this other door, he put his ear against it to see if he could hear any conversation on the other side. Hearing none, and seeing no light under the door, he turned the handle very slowly to see if the door would open. While there was a lock on the door, the handle turned and, when pulled gently, opened about an eighth of an inch. Looking through the small crack in the door, John could barely see the outline of another door with a light beyond it. As he opened the door more fully, the light from the single bulb in the vestibule showed he was entering a utility closet where there was a water heater and cleaning and toilet supplies were stacked on shelves. Checking to make sure the door into the vestibule would not automatically lock when he closed it, he walked quietly over to the inner door, again putting his ear against it to see if he could hear a conversation on the other side.

"Mr. D'Angelo, this is Sheriff Longley. Sheriff, this is Raphael D'Angelo."

"Good evening, Mr. D'Angelo. It's nice to meet you," said Sheriff Longley.

"Sheriff, it's good to meet you. Mr. Sterling has told me a lot of good things about you. You'll forgive my not getting up, but Mr. Sterling's doctors have put me through quite an experience and today is not one of my better days."

"No problem. I understand. You just take it easy."

"I'm told we have a little bit of a problem with one of our locals?" D'Angelo said. In a better mood now, it was still clear D'Angelo required more than just answers. He was looking for solutions. "What's going on? I want to know everything."

John Richter, his ear still pressed against the door, stood silently as he heard Sterling and Sheriff Longley lay out the entire story. All of the facts surrounding the death of his son were stated in cold, simple terms. They spoke of his son as if he were a side of beef that had to be thrown away because it rotted. As the details of the murder unfolded, he could barely contain his rage. His impulse, every part of him, wanted to throw open the door and revenge his son's death. He knew he couldn't do that now and forced himself to listen further.

"Well, Sheriff," D'Angelo said, "it looks like you have quite a problem on your hands. This Richter guy seems to have enough evidence to at least make people suspicious. What are we going to do about him?"

"It's not as bad as it seems. The fact that the boy was over on Belleview property doesn't make a whole hell of a lot of difference. There are a lot of reasons he could have came over here and then gone back to his tree stand. As far as the shots that someone heard, there aren't any bullets, there aren't any shell casings, there are no ballistic reports, and nobody even knows who fired the shots. He's not going to be able to come up with any hard evidence. Besides that, the guy who shot at the boy a couple of times is already dead, right?"

"That's right. And once we leave here we won't be coming back, so that's not a problem."

"As far as those dogwood leaves go, that's just his word against everybody else's. The medical examiner isn't going to remember what the hell kind of leaves the boy had in his hand, and I know that he didn't keep them as evidence. There's not enough probable cause for me to get any kind of warrant against anybody."

"What if Richter doesn't stop with you? What if he goes to the state police?" D'Angelo asked.

"That's no problem either," Sterling said. "In addition to the fine services of the sheriff and several of his men, I have several well-placed friends with the state police. They won't let any investigation get very far. Besides, no further investigation is justified by what little evidence Richter has been able to come up with on his own. As long as he doesn't get hold of anything concrete, nothing is going to come of it."

"It better not," D'Angelo threatened. "You know how much money I've got coming in here in the next couple of days and how important it is for me to be able to move it. If there's a problem it's going to be a major problem, and not just for me either. And what about this Lester and Floyd pair? They sound like a couple of real losers. You got them under control?"

"Absolutely," Sterling said. "I pay those guys well enough that they'll do anything I ask them to do and forget anything I ask them to forget. But if they do get to be a problem, I certainly won't have any trouble getting rid of them. What's a couple of woodchucks more or less? Hell, probably nobody'd even notice if they did disappear."

"Which one of them did you say did the Richter kid?" Sheriff Longley said.

"Lester did," Sterling said.

"Well, he sure did a good job of it. That broken neck was just the ticket to make it look like an accident. By the way," the sheriff said, "do either one of those clowns know that I'm involved with this outfit?"

"Sheriff, you're safe there. The less those two guys know the better off we are. They don't have any idea that you're part of the operation," Sterling said.

"Okay, let's keep it that way. I know all I need to know and I'll take care of making it look like we're still investigating this. You won't hear anything else from Ritchter. I can satisfy him with just a little more paperwork."

"Thanks for coming by, Sheriff. Call me if you have any problems," Sterling said as the sheriff left D'Angelo's bedroom.

"Charles," said D'Angelo, "other than our little problem here, things are going pretty well. I got all of my papers up from the printers a couple of days ago. With this surgery, the makeup jobs that your people are giving me, and these documents, I can go anywhere in the world I want to and nobody will have a clue about who I am. The makeup and hairpieces are particularly good. I make a pretty good little seventy-year-old, don't I?"

"Absolutely! That get-up will sure as hell get you through customs to anywhere you want to go. And with Lynn as your nurse, it's more believable. They gave you one female and two male personalities, didn't they?"

"Yep, and all the papers to go along with each of them. I can be me or I can be any one of three different people all on the same day. Passports, visas, social security numbers, hospital and dental records, everything I need. I've got to hand it to you, this is one hell of an operation. When I heard about what you were doing, I thought I'd be lucky to just have you help me get out of the country, but to be untraceable is perfect. With the cash and other goodies, I shouldn't have to worry about anything for the rest of my life, your bill notwithstanding. And getting in on the ground floor of your little firearms and weapons operation is just the icing on the cake."

The two men laughed heartily at the progress of Sterling's escape operation. He had had successes before D'Angelo came, but this was the most impressive yet.

Almost too stunned to move, John realized he had to get out of the tunnel and back to Isaac and Roy before he was discovered. To be found here would mean instant death. Turning quietly, he walked back through the inner door to the vestibule. Opening it slowly and closing it quietly, he rushed through the outer door and down the steps toward the bunker. Glancing at his watch as he hurried down the ramps and steps leading to the bunker, he realized his time was almost up. When he got to the door which led into the bay itself he was not sure if he could open it safely or not.

Roy, watching from his vantage point forty yards away through his binoculars, could see the knob on the door begin to turn. As he leaned over, Isaac punched him in the ribs, pointing down the logging road toward a pair of headlights swinging rapidly up the dirt road toward the bunker. At the same time, Roy and Isaac heard voices coming from the trail in the woods to the right of the bunker.

John, not hearing any of this in the bay, opened the tunnel door slowly, exited, and crouched down behind the limousines, closing the door behind him. Still crouching, he moved as quickly as he could to the front of the nearest limousine. At the same time the incoming vehicle pulled into the lot in front of the bay, its headlights nearly catching out in front of the parked limousine. As the car pulled up, Eric and the other guard stepped off the trail from the manor house and into the low light surrounding the front of the bunker.

Frozen at the front of the limousine, John couldn't stand up, go forward, or retreat. To go back into the tunnel would mean he would be trapped there for the night.

Isaac and Roy knew they had to divert everyone's attention long enough for John to get out of the bay and into the shelter of the woods.

"Pick up that rock over there and when I tell you, throw it as far over into the woods on the other side of that car as you can," Roy said.

"What then?" asked Isaac.

"Just do it. I know what'll work."

Fingering the baseball-sized rock in this hands, Isaac got up on one knee and waited for Roy's signal.

"Now," Roy whispered and Isaac let the rock go, sending it forty yards into the woods on the other side of the car. Two men had gotten out of the truck and were talking with the guards in front of the bunker. When the rock went through the branches and hit the side of a large oak, all four of the men spun to face the noise, two of them pulling semi-automatic pistols from their shoulder holsters and looking intently into the woods.

John, seeing all four of the men turn their backs to him, took the opportunity to sprint the four or five yards from the front of the limousine into the darkness of the woods next to the bunker. Getting six or eight yards into the woods, he dropped quickly to the ground, and lay still with his face in the leaves, his camouflage clothing covering the rest of him and blending into the darkened forest floor. As he lay there he could hear the last echoes of Roy's owl hoots echoing down the ridge.

Jesus, saved by a five-foot-eight-inch owl, John thought. *Never figured I'd be so glad to hear that.*

"What the shit was that?" asked the driver of the vehicle.

"Just a dumb-ass owl. There's more fuckin' wild animals out here than you can shake a stick at. Every time you turn around something's gone off running in the woods. Spookiest damn place I've ever been. If I shot at every sound I heard, Sterling couldn't afford the ammunition."

"Yeah, whatever. Get these crates unloaded. Sooner you get that done, the sooner we can all have a drink."

"Sounds good to me. How about help with these boxes?"

"Fuck you. I brought the bottle, you unload the boxes."

"Smart ass!"

The two guards, walking into the bay, passed within yards of John who was still lying quietly on the ground nearby. John was sure they would be able to hear his heart beating; it seemed as if the ground shook every time his heart hammered. But they were more interested in a little relaxation than anthing else.

After the crates of guns and missiles were unloaded and taken inside, the bay door swung down and John was able to crawl back over to Isaac and Roy. As he moved up beside them they looked at him, wide-eyed and questioning.

Before they could ask, John said, "Come on, let's get the hell out of here. You guys aren't going to believe what I found out. I can't believe it." Isaac and Roy followed John back out of the woods and down the road to Isaac's truck where he told them everything that he had heard.

"What the hell are you going to do? We can't go to the sheriff. We can't go to the state police. What the hell are we going to do?" Isaac said.

"I know what we're not going to do," John said. "We're not going to let them get away with it. I've got an idea. I need you guys to meet me over at Judge Collins' cabin tomorrow afternoon. I'll have some other folks there. Isaac, I need for you to bring your brothers too. I'll tell you what I've got in mind, but nobody needs to get involved who doesn't want to."

"Well, what about . . ." Roy started to say.

"Tomorrow," John said. "I'll tell you all about it tomorrow."

CHAPTER FORTY-THREE

"MR. STERLING?" SAM said, as he knocked gently on the office door. "Mr. Sterling, can I see you a minute?"

"Come in, Sam. What gets you up this early in the morning?"

"I wouldn't bother you this early if I didn't think it was important, but I think you'd better hear what Lester and Floyd have to say," Sam said, looking toward the hallway where the Morgan brothers stood, hats in hand, waiting for an invitation to enter the office.

"Is there a problem?" Sterling said.

"There may be. Lester, Floyd, come on in here. Tell Mr. Sterling exactly where you were last night and what you saw, and don't leave anything out."

Lester and Floyd entered the office hesitantly. They had been in his employ for over a year, but seldom had an audience with him, much less in his office.

"Well, what is it?" Sterling asked. "If you've got something to tell me, tell me. Don't just stand there." Sterling got irritated with the Morgan brothers very quickly. They seldom were able to express themselves as concisely as he wished and their mere presence was generally offensive to him. They, in turn, sensed Sterling's dislike of them and, despite his command to speak, both remained silent.

"Come on, godamn it! I don't have all morning. If there's something I need to know about, let's hear it!"

"Well," Lester said, "we was out ridin' around last night like you told us to do, like you pay us to do. We didn't see nothin' for a long time, nothin' suspicious that is. But about eight-thirty or nine we was down on the river road and saw a pickup truck parked down by the old clearing off the road. We didn't think nothin' about it at first because people park there all the time. But when we circled back around about forty-five minutes later it was still there. We went down and looked at the truck and scouted around. There wasn't anybody down there. Usually folks either park down there to fish or fuck, but there wasn't nobody doin' either last night."

Floyd, tickled his brother would speak to Mr. Sterling that way, started to laugh. Sterling cut the laugh off quickly, saying, "So what did you see? Is there anything that I really need to know about?"

"Well, there is. We couldn't figure out why anybody would leave their truck down there so we pulled down the road a couple of hundred yards, and then walked back up and hid in the bushes about fifty yards from the truck. We hadn't been there fifteen minutes when a truck came by and turned up the old loggin' road to them garages you got built behind the old dormitory. About five minutes later three guys, two white guys and a nigger, came runnin' back down through the woods and jumped in the truck. There wasn't anything else for 'em to be doin' except snoopin' around that garage up there."

Lester and Floyd had Sterling's full attention now. While they didn't fully comprehend what could happen should his operation be exposed, Sterling could see his problems getting worse and worse.

"Why didn't you stop them? Why didn't you keep them from driving away?" Sterling asked.

"Well, we started to do that and we could have stopped them if we wanted to, but we didn't know what they seen or whether you'd want us to jump 'em. Their truck wasn't on your property and it could have been messy if they'd put up a fight."

Thinking for a minute, Sterling said, "Lester, you're right. You're exactly right. To do anything other than what you did would have made the problem worse. Did you recognize any of them? Do you know whose truck it was?"

Lester, grinning because he knew that Sterling would be appreciative of his efforts, said, "Sure do. I 've seen that truck around town a lot. It was that nigger's, Isaac Porter's. I've seen his truck down by the river a lot when he was fishin' and in spring turkey-huntin' season. Besides that, that Ritcher fella was with him too. He turned me down for a loan four or five months ago. It was him all right. I'm not sure who the other white guy was. You got any idea what they were snoopin' around for?"

"Don't worry about that, Lester. We'll take care of it. You boys did a fine job. There'll be a bonus in this for both of you. Don't mention this to anyone else and make sure that you're both available for the next couple of days. There's going to be some activity around here and there could be some trouble. If there is, I'm going to need both of you. You can go now. Sam will get in touch with you when we need you. You still have your radio in your truck, don't you?"

"Sure do, Mr. Sterling. You can count on us. You just call us whenever you need us," said Lester as he and Floyd backed slowly out the door. Both were surprised and pleased at Sterling's friendly manner and the promise of a bonus was an unexpected reward.

Closing the door behind the Morgan brothers, Sterling said, "We've got to find out what Richter was doing there and what he knows. I knew that we were going to have trouble with him. There are just too many unanswered questions about his son's death and he isn't going to stop until he gets some answers or we stop him. Do you know where he lives?"

"Sure do. What do you want me to do?" Sam asked.

"I want you to send somebody over there in a car that nobody will recognize and just have them watch the house for right now. If Richter goes anywhere have him followed. As soon as it gets dark, get somebody over there in a position where they can hear what's going on. Maybe we can pick up something that will help us. Another shipment of guns is coming here this afternoon and we'll ship them out to the warehouses tomorrow afternoon. We can't afford to have any slip-ups. This is the largest shipment we've gotten in and will put us well on our way toward fully stocking our arsenals in New England and the mid-west. We have to be able to deliver on these first contracts of automatic weapons if this operation is going to succeed. Especially the missiles! Make sure whoever you send has a cell phone so he can stay in touch with us and let us know what's going on."

"Will do. There'll be somebody on the house within half an hour. Anything else?"

"No, Sam, I think that'll do it for now. We just have to find out what's going on. If he goes to the sheriff or the state police we're okay. If he does anything else we may have a problem."

John was the first to arrive at Judge Collins' cabin at the far end of the county a little before two o'clock the next afternoon. Shortly after John arrived, Isaac, his brother, and his cousins pulled in, as did Roy. Within half an hour there were almost a dozen cars and trucks in the yard of the cabin. Once everyone was inside, John stood up to speak. As he stood, the swirl of conversation in the room ceased, and, with questioning eyes, all of them looked at John.

"Guys, all of you here are my friends. We've known each other for a long time. We've all hunted together and fished together and I think we've gotten to know each other about as well as people can. I've got something to tell you that I think is going to shock you. Then I'm going to ask all of you to help me do something. What I'm asking you to do may not be legal and it sure as hell will be dangerous, but, once you hear what I've got to say I hope that you'll all agree that it's something that has to be done."

John quickly looked at each man and could see the questions in their eyes. "All of you thought you knew how Allen died back in October. I thought I knew too, but Isaac, Roy, and I found out last night that what we thought and what actually happened are two entirely different things. Allen didn't have an accident. He didn't just fall out of that tree stand. He was murdered."

"What do you mean? Who'd want to kill Allen? John, that can't . . ." said Rick.

"I know, I couldn't believe it either, but it's true. There were a lot of things that made me suspicious and what I heard at Belleview last night confirmed it."

John went into detail about the things that he and Isaac had discovered about Allen's hunting trip the day he died.

He told them what they had done the night before—about his entry into the bay, the tunnel to the dormitory, and the conversation he had overheard between Sterling, D'Angelo, and Sheriff Longley. His description of D'Angelo and Sterling's plans left all of the men stunned.

"Guys, this isn't a joke. It couldn't be more serious! Sterling and the people that he's got up there are some of the worst people in the world. What they're planning is bound to kill lots of innocent people. It's already killed Allen. The way they're underwriting the gun control groups, they're going to be the only ones with weapons before it's all over with. We've got to get in there and not only stop this shipment of automatic weapons and missiles from getting into the country, but we've got to expose what they're doing.

"D' Angelo and one of the men who was there when Allen died are leaving within forty-eight hours. I won't let the men who killed Allen just walk away from this. We can't go to the sheriff's department or the state police either. We don't know who we can trust there."

"What do you think we ought to do, John?" asked Rodney Porter. "How are we going to stop them?"

"Well, that's where your brother comes in. He and I have talked about this, and I think we've come up with a pretty good plan. Isaac, why don't you tell them what we've got in mind."

"Well, it's like this. What John overheard last night isn't enough to go to the FBI with," said Isaac. "It's just his word against Sterling's. We've got to get more evidence against these guys. What John wants to do is to get into Belleview and videotape what he finds in there. If we can get some good tape of a stash of illegal weapons, we'll be able to go straight to the FBI and they can bust this up before it goes further. And, since we aren't the police, we don't need any kind of search warrant. But John ain't gonna get into Belleview without one hell of a diversion. That's where all of you come in." The men listened quietly as John and Issac carefully explained their plan.

Having heard the plan and speaking for everyone, Rick said, "John, we understand how important this is. You know how we feel about Allen's death too. Sure, it'd be better to let the law handle this, but we can't until we get some evidence."

Rodney agreed, saying, "We're all with you, John. It ain't right, what happened to Allen, and we sure as hell can't let it happen to other folks. If we don't stop these guys, lots of folks all over are gonna be killed."

"Well, that's what I was hoping all of you would say." John looked around the group. "We can't do this without you and I know you have the skills that we need to accomplish this. I wish I could tell you it wasn't dangerous, but it is. But we've got to stop these people and it's got to be done in the next twenty-four hours. Isaac and I have drawn up a list of those we think would do best in the three different groups of hunters. We'll pass that around, and if any of you think you really need to be somewhere else, just holler."

The list circulated through the cabin. Isaac's cousin Scott questioned the assignment of the second line of men, the turkey hunters. "Come on, Isaac, you know I'm a good bow hunter. I'm as good a shot as you, maybe even better."

"Well, that may be true, Scott, but you always bow-hunt from the ground and we want all the bow-hunters up in tree stands. Your fat ass isn't going to fit up into any tree stand we've got."

Laughter filled the cabin as Scott agreed it would be a bit difficult for him to get up into a tree and remain there unobserved. "Well, I guess I don't mind being at the base of the ridge. I do look more like a stump than an eagle."

"Listen up," said Isaac. "We all need to meet here at three o'clock in the morning. You know what gear to bring and make sure you bring plenty of ammunition. We don't know how this is going to turn out, but you sure as hell don't want to be out there and run out of ammo. And don't say nothin' to nobody about this. As far as the families are concerned, you're just going hunting in the morning."

After everyone else had left the cabin, John and Isaac stood on the front porch for a few minutes. Neither said anything for some time, each thinking silently about the course of events that had been set in motion.

"This is something we've got to do, isn't it, Isaac?" John asked.

"Yeah, John, it is. Some things you know in your heart are right, you know they have to be done. Your son died because he was in the wrong place at the wrong time. Because these guys decided to bring all of this bullshit to our home, we've got to do this. Not just because of Allen, but to protect all the other people out there who aren't able to protect themselves. Damn, man, I haven't felt like this since Nam."

"We'll be okay." John smiled. "These city boys don't know their ass from a hole in the ground once they get off the asphalt. You just keep your head down, okay?"

"You got it. I'll see you here at three."

John didn't notice the pickup truck parked down the block from his house as he returned home that evening. As soon as he turned in the driveway, Sterling's man was on the phone back to Belleview advising him Richter was home.

"Well, as soon as it's dark enough for you to do it, get up as close as you can to the house and see what you can find out. We need to know what he knows and what they plan on doing. You stay there as long as you have to to find out what's going on. You understand?"

"Yes, sir, Mr. Sterling. I'll call you as soon as I have anything."

"Hi, Brenda, how are you doing?" It was a question John asked, though he didn't expect an answer.

John's father had come back up to spend Thanksgiving week with John and Brenda. Though this was usually a festive week and one full of family activities, it was a particularly sad holiday this year. It was the first one since Allen's death and his absence was having a profound effect on Brenda. Except for John's father's visit, there probably wouldn't have been any special plans for Thanksgiving at all.

"Hey, Dad, did you have a nice day?"

"Sure did. I love coming up here. I get a lot more rest up here than I do at home. What have you been up to?"

"Oh, just went over to the cabin to see a few of my buddies," John replied. John went into the den and sat down without saying more. Both John's father and Brenda realized there was something going on. It was unusual for him to be as quiet and pensive as he was.

Should I tell Brenda and Dad about what I found out? I know they need to know, would want to know that Allen's death wasn't an accident. But once I tell them that, how could I not tell them the rest of the story? How could I not tell them what was really going on at Belleview? About our plan for the morning and how dangerous it is? She wouldn't want me to go, to expose myself to the kind of danger there will be in order to prevent Sterling's plan from succeeding.

In the long run it was John's father who made him realize he needed to tell them his plans.

"John," he said, "I know how hard this is on you. You and Allen spent every opening day together for ten or twelve years. You never missed hunting together during Thanksgiving week. I've never lost a child so I know there's no way I can tell you that I know how you feel. But you have to understand that things are going to get better. With the new baby, maybe that will . . ."

"Dad, there's something I have to tell you and Brenda, something really important. Brenda," John called into the kitchen, "can you come in here for a minute? There's something we've got to talk about."

They sat in stunned silence as John recounted what he and Isaac had uncovered at Belleview. Brenda couldn't believe her husband had gone into the facility, exposing himself not only to criminal charges but to injury or death. The information about the corruption of the local sheriff's department and the inside connections within the state police were particularly unnerving. That information did help them understand why John, Isaac, and the other hunters had come up with the plan they had.

"John, I want to go with you in the morning. Allen was my only grandson. If you're going to do this, I'm going to be a part of it," John's father said.

"Dad, I appreciate that, but it's too dangerous. I need for you to stay here, to take care of Brenda. I don't think Sterling has any idea that we know what he's up to, but I want to make sure that nothing happens to Brenda. We've already lost one child and I . . ."

"I understand what you're saying, but I'm going with you in the morning. If for no other reason then moral support. If you don't want me to go over to Belleview, I won't. But I'm going to go with you in the morning. I'll come back here after you all leave."

"Okay, Dad. I'll take all the moral support I can get. But don't worry about me. You taught me pretty damn well. I can hold my own against these guys."

"John," Brenda said quietly, "I know you have to do this. I just wish there was something I could . . ."

"I know, Hon. You and Dad stay here and take care of each other. This is all going to work out and we're going to get the people who killed Allen. They're not going to get away with it."

The three of them sat quietly in the den, John and Brenda holding hands. John's father leaned forward with his clasped hands held up to his lips. Each thinking about the events that would unfold the next morning and each reluctant to face what might be lost.

Outside the house hidden behind the shrubbery beneath the window, Sterling's man was only able to hear bits and pieces of the conversation. He picked up enough to understand Richter knew something was wrong at Belleview and the people there had had something to do with Allen's death. He heard something about meeting at the Judge's cabin in the morning, but not the time and he knew Ritchter and some others intended to try and stop Sterling.

After watching John and Brenda go back to their bedroom and the lights go off in the house, he called Sterling and relayed the information he had.

"That's all you could hear? You don't know any more than that?" Sterling asked.

"That's it, sir. I did the best I could. He knows something's going on and he knows that somebody at Belleview had something to do with his son's death. They're going to make trouble and they're going to do it in the morning. That's just all I could hear."

"Okay, get on back as soon as you can."

"Shit! Sam! Sam!" Sterling yelled. "Get in here. We've got a real problem!" He told Sam what his informant had overheard and ordered him to have ten extra men brought down that night from Northern Virginia to help with Belleview's security.

"I don't give a damn what time it is. You get those assholes out of bed and get them down here in the next hour. We've got too much at stake to have a bunch of rednecks screw this up for us. You get them down here, and you tell them to bring everything they've got. If those guys think they're going to just waltz in here, they've got another think coming."

After Sam left, Sterling swiveled in his chair to face the window. Looking out the bay window in his office across the grounds and over the woods toward the mountains, Sterling thought, *If these guys want a fight they've sure as hell got one. We've got the best weapons money can buy. If these rednecks want to match themselves up with the finest weaponry in the world, let 'em! We'll chew 'em up and spit 'em out. And it'll all be self-defense. As soon as they set foot on my property their asses belong to me*

CHAPTER FORTY-FOUR

THE TUESDAY BEFORE Thanksgiving was a clear, crisp autumn day in central Virginia. A Canadian high-pressure system brought unseasonably cool air and clear weather with it. If this had been an ordinary day the men gathered at the cabin would be thinking of which stand they would take that morning, whether or not the deer's mating season had started yet, whether or not they had enough clothes to keep warm, and a hundred other things that hunters think of during deer season in Virginia.

But that morning was anything but ordinary. All of the hunters who had been at the cabin Monday afternoon were back again by 3:15 a.m. Tuesday morning. Rick, the cook, had gotten there at two o'clock and had built a fire in the cookstove and a roaring blaze in the fireplace. As the others arrived they were met with the sounds and smells that would ordinarily have been welcome early in the morning—the twenty-cup coffee pot was warming on the back of the stove, a second pan full of bacon was just finishing, and hot biscuits were coming out of the oven.

Those who were hungry helped themselves but everyone was quiet, lost in their own thoughts of what was about to happen. While a few of those present had served in the military, it had been many years since any of them had fired a shot at another human being. Most of the men at the cabin that morning never had.

All of them, however, had thought a great deal about what was being asked of them. To a man, they all realized their obligation, not only to John because of Allen's death, but to their community. It was their responsibility because under these circumstances, normal channels of law enforcement couldn't be trusted.

All of the men were confident in their abilities as outdoorsmen, as woodsmen, and as hunters. They could do what had to be done. They had come from families where generations had been raised to appreciate the value of taking care of themselves and their families, to protect what was theirs, and if necessary, to be deadly.

Issac and John looked around the cabin with satisfaction as they noted that the three distinct groups of men had each chosen the appropriate camouflage for their particular assignment. Those who were to be armed only with bows were dressed in several different patterns which mirrored the bark of trees common to the Rapidan area. With gloves, headnets, camouflaged tree stands, and camouflage bows, each of them would have the ability to climb twenty to forty feet up in their chosen trees. There, remaining motionless and virtually invisible in the early dawn, they were confident no one would suspect their presence unless it became necessary to fight the men from Belleview.

Those who were to take their places along the base of the ridge had chosen camouflage patterns which would blend into blinds they would build on the ground in the second growth and brush on the forest floor. While the bow-hunters had chosen Advantage and All-Purpose Realtree patterns, those who were to be on the ground favored the Predator and Mossy Oak patterns. These patterns, coupled with some judicious trimming of branches from trees and saplings nearby, would make the turkey hunters practically invisible to any oncoming men.

The weapons carried by the turkey hunters were ten gauge and twelve gauge, three-inch magnum semi-automatic and pump shotguns and were also camouflaged. Each of the men had removed the plug from the magazine, enabling them to load five shots instead of the three they were restricted to when hunting turkeys. Most of the men had chosen the largest, deadliest buckshot size available. With the thirty and thirty-two inch full-choke barrels on these guns, the buckshot would stay in a tight, close pattern that could easily kill a man out to eighty or ninety yards.

The best marksmen in the group carried the widest variety of weapons. The six men who were to be the stationed on top of the ridge approximately three hundred yards from the edge of the woods had chosen flat-shooting, bolt-action rifles with a maximum capacity of five rounds. All of the rifles were equipped with variable power scopes with large objective lenses to take maximum advantage of the low light early in the morning.

All of these men had chosen their favorite bullet for their particular rifle and all of the bullets had one thing in common. They had been developed for expansion and penetration. Each of the men were grateful for the quality of the firearms they possessed and the ammunition available to them. While none of them had ever anticipated these weapons would be used against other people, they realized that fate and necessity dictated that their lives depended on their skills and the quality of the weapons and ammunition they had chosen.

Just as John and Isaac were getting ready to review the plan once more, a truck drove up in the yard and footsteps were heard approaching the front door of the cabin. Reflexively, John placed his hand on the Smith & Wesson .357 he carried in a holster on his right hip. Unsnapping the strap he tried to prepare himself for whatever might come through the door.

The door handle turned quickly and as the door opened the light fell on Judge Collins' surprised features as he saw all of them assembled in front of him. Seeing John standing in front of the other men, with his hand now relaxing its grip on his pistol, Judge Collins asked, "John, what in the hell's going on here? This looks like a war room."

"Judge, we didn't want you to get involved in this. We didn't want you to get into any trouble. The best thing you can do right now is just turn around and leave. I'll explain all of it to you later."

"Well, John, I appreciate those sentiments, but I can't leave. You guys are going to have to tell me what's going on. I've spent my life trying to make sure that laws were upheld and you're damn well going to have to explain all of this."

John could see Judge Collins was in no frame of mind to accept any other alternatives. Quickly briefing him on everything they had discovered, they told him what their plans were and why they felt it was necessary to carry them out.

"Well, John, I think you're right about the search warrant and the FBI. Just on the facts that you have, I don't think there would be probable cause for a search warrant of Belleview. What you found with respect to Allen doesn't point the finger at anybody there and what you overheard when you went into the tunnel is hair-raising, but probably not enough to get a warrant. And you didn't actually see any of these illegal weapons, just crates. I don't approve of your going to Belleview. That's trespassing, at least, and breaking and entering at worst. You've got to know that you can get into a hell of a lot of trouble doing what you're doing."

"Judge, I appreciate that, but you have to understand that Allen was murdered and I know the men who did it are at Belleview. I don't care what kind of trouble I get into, we're going to get to the bottom of this. I'm going to find the men who killed Allen and we're going to stop Sterling."

"And Judge," Isaac said, "we may not even get into it with these guys. We've got a pretty good plan and what we really want to do is just distract them. Hell, these city boys may get to the edge of the woods and not even come after us. We really hope they don't. All we want to do is divert their attention for a few minutes so that John can get in there, take videos for evidence, and get the hell out. We'll be off Belleview property and only fire if they come off Belleview and into the woods after Issac and William. They'll have to put us in a position of protecting ourselves before we fire. But I'll tell you something, based on what we know, if these guys want a fight, they've sure as hell got one. Everybody here knows how important this is and what's at stake."

Judge Collins looked around the room slowly. He looked into each man's eyes. He knew all of these men personally, individually. He had spent many years getting to know their capabilities and their commitment to their families and their community. He could tell, to a man, that each of them was committed to this effort.

"Well, I can see that there isn't any talking you out of this. Give me about three minutes and I'll be ready to go . . ."

"Judge," said John, "we can't let you do that. We all trust you and respect you too much to let you put yourself in this position. You spent your whole career on the bench upholding the law and we're getting ready to bend the hell out of it. That's not something we expect you to do. What we need for you to do is to use your connections and get an FBI agent down here as fast as you can. If you can have an agent and a federal magistrate at the courthouse by eight o'clock this morning, I'll be there as soon as I can with a video of whatever I find at Belleview. If they can have a TV and VCR set up so the magistrate can see what's going on there, he can be ready to issue a search warrant. If we get in trouble because of the way we've gone about this, then we'll answer for that. You can help us most by making those contacts. At the same time, you don't run the risk of getting into trouble with us."

"I guess you're right. I know the people to call and I'll have that set up. We'll be waiting at the courthouse for you at eight o'clock and we'll wait as long as we have to."

"Okay, guys," John said, "it's time to go. It'll be daylight in about an hour and a half and it'll take us about thirty to forty minutes to get to our positions. Sun up today is at 6:15. Isaac, if you can kick up a fuss over on that side at about ten minutes after six, that should give me the time I need to get in there, do the taping, and get out. Dad, why don't you stay here with Judge Collins for a while? Maybe he'll need some help with what he's doing. Okay?"

"Okay, son. But I'd rather be going with you. I may be old but I can still shoot."

"I know you can, Dad, and I appreciate that. But I need to make sure that if something goes wrong, you're . . ."

"Don't talk that way, boy. Nothing's going to happen. You'll be here to see that baby born in January and don't you think otherwise. You just keep your head down, do what you've got to do, and get the hell out of there."

John nodded. He and his father were as close as a father and son could be. They had spent a lifetime together and had developed a love and a trust that neither time nor distance could break. As John started out the door, his father touched him lightly on the shoulder and, as he turned and looked in his father's eyes, his father said softly, "I love you, Son."

"I love you too, Dad. I'll see you soon."

The cabin seemed very quite and empty after the trucks pulled out of the driveway. For a few long moments John's father and Judge Collins sat in silence, thoughts of what could happen in the coming hours racing through their minds.

"What do you think, Judge?" asked John's father.

"They're doing what they've got to do. This is a bad bunch of folks we've got here and there's nothing else they can do to stop them. I just hope all of them come through it."

Looking at his watch, Judge Collins continued, "It's early yet, but I think I know this one district chief well enough to call him at 4:30 in the morning. This guy can have twenty agents here by eight o'clock in the morning. Especially for this kind of bust."

As Judge Collins made several phone calls, Samuel sat anxiously by the window looking out into the darkness. The sky was still clear and the stars bright in the crisp air. *A dangerous day*, he thought as the tail lights disappeared down the lane.

CHAPTER FORTY-FIVE

CHARLES STERLING DIDN'T calmly await the unfolding of the plan he had learned John Ritcher had set in motion. As soon as he had his investigator's report, he met with Sam, some of D'Angelo's men, Lester, and Floyd.

"This has gone far enough, he's got to be stopped! We know that Richter and some of his buddies are up to something and we can't afford to have it go any further than this. Lester, Floyd, Michael, get and three or four others and be at Judge Collins' cabin at first light. You make sure that nobody sees you and when you think you can, take all of them out. I don't care what you use. I don't care how you do it, but just take everybody out that's there. Sam, go downstairs and bring me one of those keys of cocaine and four or five dozen rocks of crack. When you get done over there, hide the cocaine somewhere so it can be found, and scatter the rocks around in a few drawers and stuff them in some pockets of what's left of whoever's over there. We've got to give Sheriff Longley an excuse to publicize this as a drug-related shoot-out."

Floyd, delighted at the prospect of carrying out these orders, snickered. "Won't that be a kick in the ass for all of those do-gooders? All shot up because of a drug deal gone bad. I can hardly wait!"

"Mr. Sterling, do you think six or eight of us will be enough to do the job?" Michael asked.

"Remember who you're dealing with," Sterling said, cutting his eyes sharply at Michael. "These guys are using guns out of the dark ages. You take whatever you need out of the armory. There's a bunch of fully automatic machine pistols, or anything else you need. If you can't take out a bunch of rednecks with this arsenal you better get the hell back to where you came from!"

Michael, not caring for Sterling's characterization, shot back, "We'll get the job done, don't you worry about that. I'm just saying we don't know how many of them there'll be. Some of these country boys can shoot pretty good."

"We'll, if you're too scared to go, Lester and I'll take care of 'em," said Floyd.

Michael would take any amount of criticism from Sterling because of his position, but he was not about to let Floyd Morgan question his bravery. It was only through considerable effort that Lester and Sam kept Michael and Floyd from settling the matter right then and there.

"Calm down you two. You'd better save all that hostility for whoever's at the cabin tomorrow morning. I have a feeling you're probably going to have your hands full," said Sam.

By the time Sterling's men began to approach the cabin, John Richter and the other men involved in the plan had long since gone. Only the judge and John's father remained in the cabin by sunrise that Tuesday. Just as it became light enough to see, Samuel, still sitting and staring out the front window, noticed the headlights of several vehicles approaching the cabin.

"Hey, Judge, they're coming back. Something must have happened."

Judge Collins, moving from the fireplace to the front window, looked at the approaching vehicles. They had stopped at the edge of the woods and their occupants were jumping from the vehicles. Not recognizing the cars or the men and seeing they were armed, the judge yelled, "Get down, Samuel! Get down!"

As the men dove for the floor, automatic rifle fire began to rip into the cabin. Sterling's men, seeing seven or eight vehicles in the yard around the cabin, assumed they had caught everyone still there.

"Lester, Floyd, you guys go around back. Don't let anybody out that way," Michael yelled. "We'll keep 'em pinned down here. You pick 'em off if they come out that way!"

The Morgan boys circled the cabin, firing steadily through the windows of the cabin. Inside, Judge Collins and Samuel crawled as rapidly as they could to the gunrack on the inside wall near the front corner of the cabin.

"Christ, how in the hell are we going to get out of this?" Samuel yelled.

"Can you shoot?" Judge Collins yelled over the sound of the rifle fire and bullets splattering against the walls of the log cabin.

"Damn sure can. Taught John everything he knows. Besides, I'm too old and fat to run!"

"Good. Grab that twelve gauge and two or three boxes of buckshot and let's see if we can't give these assholes a dose of their own medicine."

As Samuel grabbed the Remington Model 870 twelve-gauge three-inch Magnum and began stuffing in loads of number-one buckshot, Judge Collins reached up and grabbed the Ruger Mini-30 by the stock and pulled it down beside him. This semi-automatic rifle was chambered for the 7.62x39 military round, and, though not a rifle the Judge had hunted with yet, was a good brush rifle for deer in this part of Virginia. Pulling several boxes of shells off the shelf below the gun rack, Judge Collins began filling the magazine with 125 grain power points. Within a minute he and Samuel were, at least, able to let their assailants know they were not helpless.

Most all of the windows on the ground floor of the cabin had been blown out by the initial bursts of fire from Sterling's men, so Judge Collins and Samuel were able to return fire easily. Since the walls of the cabin were at least eight inches thick and solid wood, they had excellent protection. The ammunition used by their attackers would have been devastating against a normal, modern home with vinyl siding and sheetrock walls, but they made little impression on the thick treated timbers which made up the cabin walls. The judge and Samuel were able to stand in relative safety to fire at the attackers and were only in danger from a well-aimed shot at the little part of each of them that was exposed when they leaned out to fire.

Lester and Floyd were the only two country boys in the group attacking the cabin, and the individuals firing into the front of the dwelling didn't aim. Their method of marksmanship was to quickly pump as many bullets in the direction of the target as possible and hope they hit something. The judge and Samuel, on the other hand, knew the value of one well-aimed shot. Judge Collins was the first to draw blood. Having taken time to locate four of the attackers in front of the cabin, he spotted one who had taken refuge behind a large sycamore tree about forty yards from the front of cabin. This one was periodically stepping out from behind the protection of the tree and spraying the front of the cabin with eight to ten rounds per burst. Estimating accurately, he brought the rifle to his shoulder and leaned out the broken window. The stock came naturally to his shoulder and his head rested comfortably on the cheekpiece, the sights lining up quickly on the left edge of the sycamore just as the man leaned out to deliver another burst of fire. The sight settled quickly on the man's chest and Judge Collins sqeezed the trigger. The recoil from the rifle pushed the Judge's shoulder sharply back as the single round struck the man full in the chest. Falling backwards into the leaves, his M16 lying uselessly beside him, the man took two shallow breaths and died.

Samuel was watching out one of the side windows and saw Floyd run quickly from the woodpile toward some of the larger trees in the back of the cabin. Raising the twelve-gauge, he fired two rounds of buckshot at Morgan. One load went high and the other one buried itself in a large oak. But for the presence of that tree, Morgan would have taken a lethal dose of nearly a dozen buckshot at about fifty yards.

"Damn, missed his ass," Samuel said as he reloaded the Remington. "That's all right, Godamnit, he'll keep his head down for a few minutes anyway."

Michael, seeing one of his men fall and recognizing the small volume of fire coming from the cabin, yelled, "Let's go, there are only two or three of them in there. Pour it on!"

At Michael's urging, the remaining attackers increased the volume of fire toward the cabin. Advancing, several of Sterling's men got to within twenty yards of the front of the cabin, and, from a vantage point behind one of the pickup trucks, began a steady delivery of fire which kept both Judge Collins and Samuel pinned down.

"We've got to get those guys out from behind the truck. If they stay there we can't move, and the other guys out there will move up to the windows and pick us off. Cover me while I get back over to the gun rack."

Samuel, not questioning the judge's request, fired three quick, unaimed rounds of buckshot out the front window in the general direction of Sterling's men. While none of the three rounds struck home, it gave the judge a few seconds to get back to the gun rack.

"Wait till they see what this does," Judge Collins shouted as he reached for the Winchester Model 70 .416 Remington Magnum. "I've killed a couple of Cape buffalo in Africa with this rifle. Those guys behind the pickup truck think they're safe. I'll show 'em how safe they are!"

Pulling the bolt-action rifle off the shelf and grabbing a box of ammunition, Judge Collins loaded two in the magazine and one in the chamber, and, with Samuel firing more buckshot out the front, crawled back to one of the front windows.

"Where are they, Samuel? Can you see them?"

"They're still out behind the blue pickup truck, right where they were a couple of minutes ago. You want me to give them another round?"

"Yeah, but hold on a second. Let me take a quick peek first," Judge Collins said. Easing up slightly, he could see the back edge of the pickup truck and just the tops of the heads of the two men closest to the cabin. "On the count of three, you fire everything you've got at the guys in the woods and I'll take the two behind the pickup truck. Ready?" Seeing Samuel nod his head, Judge Collins began a silent count with his fingers. When the third finger went up, Samuel fired three more rounds at Michael and the other two men in the woodline. Samuel's first shot put several buckshot into one of the men who had left his shoulder exposed behind the tree; the other two shots merely served to keep Michael's head down.

Judge Collins rose up behind the front window. As he stood, the rifle came smoothly to his shoulder as it had many times in the past, his right thumb flicked the safety off, and his cheek came down on the stock. The open sights quickly settled fourteen inches below the double sidewall of the truck and directly beneath the top of one of the heads he could barely see. Satisfied, he squeezed the trigger.

A .416 Remington Magnum is one of the most powerful cartridges in the world. It's 515 grain solid shot will stop a charging Cape buffalo or elephant in its tracks. This round went through the inside and outside walls of the far side of the pickup truck, and, having been flattened out by its passage through those metal walls, smashed into the throat of the man closest to the cab of the truck. By the time the bullet reached its man it had expanded to almost three quarters-of-an-inch wide and still had plenty of power behind it. The well-aimed round severed the man's spinal cord. The impact hurled him onto the gravel of the parking lot, his head hanging by only a few threads of muscle and skin.

The other man looked down at what was left of his friend and realized the truck provided no protection whatever. He dropped his rifle and turned, sprinting across the parking lot toward what he hoped was the protection of the woods.

Judge Collins had been in many situations where a quick second shot was necessary for survival. Having immediately bolted another shell into the Model 70 after the first round had been fired, he was ready to deliver a second shot before the other man got four steps away from the truck. As the bead on the front sight settled between the man's shoulder blades, Judge Collins squeezed off a second shot which literally tore the man's heart from his chest. The slug entered the middle of the man's back, pushed through his chest and separated his sternum into two pieces. The man was thrown ten feet by the weight and velocity of the slug which killed him. As the bullet exited the man's body bits of flesh, bone, and blood splattered against the trees and vehicles in front of him, some of it striking Michael in the face. Recoiling with horror at the damage done by this single bullet, Michael watched as the man's body fell toward the driveway. The man lay spread-eagle in the dirt and gravel of the parking lot, blood oozing rapidly from under his body forming small pools in the depressions in the ground. In the chilly November air, steam began to rise slowly from the blood pouring from the exit wound.

These two shots had been taken in less than three seconds. By this time Lester and Floyd had worked their way around the back of the cabin. They could hear all of the firing from the front of the cabin, especially the two thunderous reports from Judge Collins' 416. Recognizing this would be their best opportunity to rush the back of the cabin, they sprinted forward, jumping on the back porch and quickly stepped up behind the rear windows.

The judge and Samuel heard the steps on the back porch of the cabin too late. As Lester and Floyd leaned in the back window, their weapons at waist height, the Judge and John's father turned to meet this new threat. Though Lester and Floyd were more comfortable and accurate with their hunting rifles, they had become fairly proficient with the automatic weapons supplied by Sterling. As they began spraying bullets at the two old men in front of them, Judge Collins got off the only remaining round in the Model 70. The slug from the rifle smashed into the window ledge near Lester, showering him with splinters but not doing any harm. Samuel's one remaining round from the twelve-gauge sailed harmlessly out the window as the bullets sliced into their bodies.

Judge Collins was struck three times in the body by Lester's bullets. Samuel was hit four times by those rounds Floyd fired; both men slumped to the floor of the cabin, apparently dead. Lester and Floyd looked with satisfaction on the results of their attack, gave each other a high five, and walked around to the front of the cabin.

Crossing the parking lot toward Michael, Floyd went over to the second man Judge Collins had hit with the .416. Taking the toe of his boot and turning the man over, he looked with grisly curiosity at the damage done. "Lester, come here and look at this goddamn hole! Jesus Christ! What a shot! I had heard he was a good shot but, Christ, look at this!"

Lester glanced over at what was left at the man's chest. "Shit! Sure as hell am glad that wasn't me."

Michael, angered at having lost three men and having another one wounded, threw the bags of cocaine at Lester and Floyd, saying, "You guys are really fucked up. Here, put the cocaine in the cabin somewhere where the police are sure to find it, and scatter these baggies around in a couple of drawers. Put some of it in their pockets in there too. Shit, I sure didn't expect this kind of a reception."

Turning to the two other men Michael said, "Come on, let's get these guys in the truck. Find a tarp or something to cover them up with. We'll bury 'em back at Belleview."

As two of the men picked up the body behind the truck the head separated from the torso and fell with a soft, moist thud on the gravel. The disembodied head, its eyes staring widely and blindly, blood coming from the corners of its mouth, rolled slowly over on its side.

"Goddamn! Fuck, get something to put his head in and get it outta sight. Jesus Christ!" Michael had seen many men die but few as violently as that.

As Lester and Floyd went up the front steps of the cabin to plant the cocaine, Floyd looked back at the corpse, punching his brother in the ribs. "Sure knows how to get ahead in the world, don't he?" The two brothers, laughing at Floyd's sick humor, entered the cabin. Judge Collins was still alive but unconscious. Samuel, pretending to be dead, remained silent and still as Lester and Earl finished spreading the drugs around the cabin. As he heard the vehicles pulling out of the driveway, he slowly began crawling over to Judge Collins to see if he was still alive.

In the lead car leaving the cabin, Micheal dialed Sterling's number and said to the driver, "Step on it! We've got to get back to Belleview! God knows where the rest of these bastards are."

CHAPTER FORTY-SIX

WELL BEFORE DAYLIGHT the truck carrying John Richter rolled slowly down the gravel road which paralleled the river and skirted the edge of Belleview. When it reached the closest point to the old dormitory, John jumped out, rolled once, and lay still in the brush beside the road as the tail lights of the truck disappeared into the dark. It would only take him ten minutes to get into position to enter the building and it was well over a hour until first light.

Better to move off the road another thirty or forty yards and wait a few minutes, he thought as he began to creep slowly up the hill toward the distant dormitory lights. *It'll take Isaac and the rest of the boys half an hour to forty-five minutes to get where they're going.*

Crouching in the woods about half-way between the road and the buildings around Belleview, John had time to think about what he was doing. *I've been in the woods this time of morning so many times . . . but never to do anything as desperate as this. God, I wish that Allen and I were here together, that we were in the woods heading out to stands to deer hunt, rather than me here alone trying to expose the men who killed Allen.*

He looked up for a moment. The sky was dark, the air crisp and cold. There was no moon and each individual star seemed to be close enough to reach out and touch. Taking a deep breath of the clear, dry air he sensed, as he had many times before, the intensity of the fall woods near the river. It was a smell that was musty, earthy, oak-like. Closing his eyes, it seemed he could almost touch it.

As John lay in the woods near the dormitory, Isaac and the other men made their way slowly down the river road, the vehicles spaced about five minutes apart to avoid suspicion. Moderate activity on this road during hunting season was normal but a pack of vehicles might have raised an alarm, even in the city boys at Belleview. Parking one of the trucks nearly half a mile from the logging road where Allen had last parked his truck, everyone climbed into the two remaining vehicles for the final four-minute ride to the logging road. Pulling quietly onto the road, they drove far enough into the hardwoods so they couldn't be seen from the road.

All of the men got out and gathered around Issac who said, "Okay, guys, this is it. You bow-hunters grab your stands and go on. It'll take you longer to get where you're going and you've got more to carry. Just remember, spread yourselves about sixty yards apart, starting on low ground down near the bottom where the woods stick out closest to Belleview, and then come on up the ridge. When William and I come back, we're gonna be hauling ass and we're going to run right under you. Make sure your stands are on the west side of the trees and if anybody follows us into the woods, let 'em go on in behind us. Don't shoot at them unless you have to, and if you have to, try to get them coming back out of the woods. If we have to shoot, they'll be using the trees for cover and their backs will be to you."

Four of the men shouldered their portable tree-stands and started slowly up the trail which led through the open woods toward the brushier areas near the edge of the field where they would be stationed. As they disappeared into the darkness, their footsteps were muffled by the thick carpet of leaves on the ground.

Isaac turned to the remaining nine hunters. "All right, you five with the shotguns follow the bow-hunters up. Spread yourselves along the base of the ridge about a hundred and fifty yards from the edge of the wood line. Dig in good and face Belleview. If we get the kind of response that I think we're going to get, some of these assholes will probably be right on top of you if we have to cut loose on them."

Looking at each of the men, he continued, "Your life may depend on your camouflage. You guys have never hunted turkeys that shoot back, so make sure you do this right."

"Okay, the rest of you guys listen up. William and I are going to cut through the woods and across the field toward Belleview. When we see some people stirring around, we're going to kick up a fuss and then come hauling ass back here. William and I can run faster than anybody else, so I guess we're the bait. When we come back we're going to run under the bow-hunters, through the turkey hunters, and up on the ridge. We'll fix us a couple of spots on the ridge before we go down.

"Crank your scopes all the way up and watch close. I don't want any of you guys putting a hole in either one of us. If anybody chases us, they may stop at the edge of the woods. If they do, don't shoot at them. If they come in the woods they'll be off Belleview and on our territory. But if they keep coming and get up close to the line of turkey hunters, be on your toes. If they come that far into the woods, the chances of us getting out of this without having to do some shooting are slim to none. And let me tell you something—if we have to shoot, put the crosshairs on 'em and don't pull any punches. From what I've seen of these guys, they'd just as soon kill you as look at you. Pick your shots and be careful of the guys down there in front of you. Issac looked each man in the face. "Any questions?" No one answered. "Everybody okay?" Again, there was silence. "Okay, let's go."

This last group of hunters had the shortest distance to go. Walking quietly and in single file to the ridge about five hundred yards from the parked cars, the group knelt again in the darkness. "Okay, William and I are going to fix up a couple of spots right along here. I'm going to go over the ridge just a few yards that way. William you go about a hundred yards further down. Two of you guys go with William and go down below him. Space yourselves about a hundred yards apart. You two guys go on down about a hundred to two hundred yards a piece and do the same thing. We can cover almost half a mile of this ridge with our rifles. It's pretty open up here and well down into the bottom. Try to put yourself where you have at least a two-hundred yard field of fire.

"William, you and whoever's down below you will probably be able to shoot all the way to the edge of the woods if you need to. That's about a four hundred yard shot so Charlie, you got that .264 magnum and William has his 7 mm. Those are good, flat shooting rifles that can reach out to four-hundred-yards, no problem. You two take the positions where you can see all the way to the field. William, as soon as you get a spot set up, come on back here and you and I will go down together."

No further words were necessary. Everyone knew what to expect and what was expected of them. As each man did when hunting deer or turkey, he searched out a position he was comfortable with, taking into consideration the possible targets and the directions from which they would be coming, his own capabilities, and the capabilities of his firearm. Scattered along this hardwood ridge over a distance of about six hundred yards, each man could see some of the lights of Belleview in the distance and knew that soon, men from there would probably be trying to kill them.

As the four other hunters settled in their spots, William came back along the ridgeline finding Isaac ready to go. He looked at his cousin and said, "How do you want to play this?"

"Well, you brought your .44, didn't you?" Seeing William nod, Isaac continued, "Let's head on down the ridge and across the field before it gets too light. We can hole up behind that barn over near the main house. As soon as we see some activity at the dorm, we'll throw a few rounds at the house, wait until they figure out where we are, and then take off. How's that sound?"

"Well," said William, "it sounds fine to me as long as they don't have any kind of decent rifles to shoot at us with. I expect I can outrun a pistol bullet at that distance, but I sure hope there aren't any real shooters in that crowd."

"Guess we'll find out," Isaac said as he and William started slowly down the ridge. In a crouch William followed Isaac, both tense and nervous at the prospect of what lay in front of them. The eastern sky was just beginning to turn a faint blue as Isaac and William reached the base of the ridge and started across the narrow flat of woods between them and the fields. As they passed a stump and brush pile, they were startled by a sharp but soft "Boo!" Laughing quietly, the stump turned out to be Rick, who said to William and Isaac, "You boys be careful down there, ya hear?"

William, his heart now going twice its normal rate, looked over at the stump which had come to life so suddenly and hissed, "You dumb son of a bitch! You almost made me break the trigger off my pistol and crap my pants. You just take care of that white ass of yours and don't worry about me. And don't shoot me when we come back through here either."

"You got it!"

Isaac and William drew up at the edge of the woods. Stretching to see above the hay in the field, they could spot the dim outlines of the buildings at Belleview about six hundred yards away. Looking up into the trees on the inside of the woods up and down the ridge, Isaac was satisfied he couldn't pick out any of the bow-hunters he knew were there. *Good,* he thought to himself, *I know they're there and I can't see them.*

"Well, let's get this over with." Silently and as swiftly as possible, he and William ran at a crouch through the knee-high hay, reaching the back side of one of the outbuildings at Belleview in only a couple of minutes. Looking quickly to his right and left, satisfying himself there was no one else out, he and William sat down, leaning against the back of the building to catch their breath. "Well, I guess now all we can do is wait."

"And pray too," said William.

"I heard that!"

As the fighting at Judge Collins' cabin was underway, twelve miles away the sun began to show itself between the trees east of Belleview and activity increased around the manor house. Sterling was up earlier than usual because of the shipment of arms due to leave Belleview that day and the imminent departure of D'Angelo and his entourage. Opening the French doors which lead onto the terrace, Sterling found D'Angelo and Sam already seated at the table.

"Good morning, gentlemen," Sterling said. "What a beautiful morning! I think we'll accomplish a great deal today. How are your departure preparations going, Raphael?"

"Very well, my friend. I'm almost sorry my stay here has come to an end. It's been everything you told me it would be. Not only have you given me a new lease of life and an avenue out of the country, but a new business venture which promises great things. With my connections in Russia, China, and South America we'll have an unlimited supply of automatic weapons and missiles for you. With your network of armories already established here in the United States, we'll be the premier supplier of these weapons to your customers. All this despite the best efforts of our friends, the gun control groups, and the government."

"It does seem very promising," Sterling said. "And actually our little gun-importing business wouldn't be possible without the help of all of our gun control friends." Looking at Sam, Sterling asked, "Are we having our little problem taken care of this morning?"

Sam, looking at his watch and having confidence in his men's ability to carry out their orders said, "By now, Mr. Sterling, we don't have a problem anymore. There'll be some extraordinary headlines in the morning, a brief investigation, and then back to peace and quiet."

"Wonderful!" Sterling said. "Pass the eggs."

From their position about a hundred yards from the side of the manor house, William and Isaac could see the three men on the terrace. While Isaac had never met Sterling, he recognized him and thought he knew Sam too.

"See that guy on the left, William? That's Sterling. That's the son of a bitch who owns this place. I'm not sure who the other two guys are. I think the one on the right is the guy that works for Sterling. And I know how to stir things up a bit. Let's do this," he said, leaning over and whispering in William's ear.

The plan Isaac proposed made Williams's eyes widen with surprise. "Christ, Isaac, you think that's a good idea? We might get in there and not be able to get out."

Isaac said, "Look around. Outside of those three jerks on the patio, none of the other people are up and around yet. We can go in there right now and get a head start before the odds get too serious. What do you think?"

"You remember that old joke about bear hunting?"

Isaac looked at his cousin as if he had gone crazy. "What the hell are you talking about?"

"You know, the two guys who was out bear hunting and surprised a big ol' grizzly and the bear takes off after them. As the two hunters run through the brush, one of them yelled at the other, 'Go, we gotta out run this bear!' And the other one yelled back at him, 'The hell we do, all I gotta do is out run you!'"

"I see what you mean. How fast do you feel this morning?" The cousins looked at each other and grinned. The joke helped relieve the tension but both knew they were about to take a desperate chance.

"Ready?" Isaac asked.

"Right behind you," William said. "Lead the way."

Looking around the grounds one more time to be sure there were no other security people visible, Issac and Willaim stood up and walked purposefully across the yard toward the patio. Knowing their exit from the grounds around Belleview would need to be made as rapidly as possible, they elected to leave their rifles in the woods and take their pistols instead. With their pistols held down by their sides and slightly behind them, the two men approached the patio unobserved. Stepping up onto the flagstone steps near the table where the three men sat, Isaac said, "Good morning, gentlemen. How are y'all this morning?"

Surprised, Sterling, Sam, and D'Angelo began to stand up, but Issac and William pointed their pistols at the trio and said, "That's all right, gentlemen. Just stay in your seats. It's too early in the morning to get shot."

"What do you want? Who the hell are you?" Sterling asked. "You better get the hell out of here. Sam . . ."

"Now just a minute, no need to get peevish. Me and my cousin live in Rapidan County and we know exactly what you boys are up to here. We just wanted to drop by and introduce ourselves and let you know you aren't going to get away with it. There's a bunch of us that know what's going on here and this game ends today."

"I'm sure we don't know what you're talking about," Sterling said. "This man," pointing at Sam, "works for me and Mr. D'Angelo is a house guest. We . . ."

"Save it, you piece of shit." Issac cut him off. "We know all about the guns and missiles, the fake I.D.'s and passports, and we know about Allen. We know it all!"

Realizing the full extent of the problem, Sterling settled back into his chair and smiled. "Let's assume that there's some truth to what you think you know. What makes you think we're going to let you leave here?"

"Well," said William, looking around the table, "my cousin and I have a couple of friends here who may have something to say about whether we stay or go. Unless you plan on stopping us with that glass of orange juice, I guess we can go whenever we want to."

"Yeah," said Isaac, laughing. "Tell me something, is that croissant loaded?"

"You son of a bitch," Sterling said, starting to rise from his chair, "I'll see that . . ."

"Now, now, don't get upset. You just stay in your seat and we won't have a problem," Issac said.

While the discussion on the patio was going on, Melinda, Sterling's secretary, had stepped into the office to see if there was anything he needed her to do. From across the room and through the French doors, she saw the confrontation in progress. Slipping quietly back out of the office she ran to the phone, calling the security office in the basement of the old dormitory.

Hitting the silent security alarm which alerted everyone at the manor house, Bill responded to the call for help. As he came around the side of the old dormitory building, running toward the manor house, half a dozen other security people were converging on the manor house from other areas.

Not knowing the alarm had sounded, Isaac and William knew they had pressed their luck far enough and were backing off the patio. Keeping their pistols pointed at the still-seated trio, William said, "It's been a real pleasure. Wish we could stay for strawberries and cream, but we've got to get back to our friends. We just wanted to let you know that you're in some deep shit."

William, stepping off the patio before Isaac, could see around the side of the house where three security guards were running toward the manor house, each carrying an assault rifle. Yelling to Isaac, William said, "Here they come, man! Run!"

Both men jumped from the patio and sprinted back across the side yard to a vantage point behind the garage. Catching their breath William said, "You ready, cousin?"

"Yeah, let's get the hell out of here!"

The security men converged on the patio and looked to Sterling for orders.

"Don't just stand there, you bunch of dumb-ass mother-fuckers! Get those guys! Bring them back here in a bag!"

By this time there were eight security guards around the patio, all armed with fully automatic M-16's. Looking to the west, the men could see Isaac and William sprinting across the field about two hundred yards away. Several of the men raised their M-16's and fired bursts at the running men, but those shots only made William and Isaac run faster.

Running side by side, stride for stride, Issac yelled to William, "Stirred the shit out of that beehive, didn't we?"

"Yeah, and they're buzzing all over the place!"

The eight men had left the yard and were following rapidly through the tall grass in the pasture.

"Man," William said as he reflexively ducked the bullets singing over their heads, "they run pretty good for white guys!"

All of the men waiting in the woods heard the initial burst of shots from Belleview and knew the situation could soon be critical. A few seconds later, Isaac's and William's heads appeared above the pasture grass, then their torsos and legs as they ran madly toward the woods. As they entered the edge of the hardwoods, the bowhunters in the tree stands could see the eight security guards fanned out across the pasture in a ragged line, firing and running as hard as they could.

As William and Isaac ran underneath one of the bow hunters, William yelled, "Here they come, Chief. If you have to, give them one for me!"

Continuing on through the woods, past the line of turkey hunters, William and Isaac sprinted up the ridge, split up, and dove into their prepared positions. Breathing heavily, they grabbed their rifles and leveled them at the edge of the woods. Issac, looking back toward Belleview, thought to himself, *Now it starts!*

CHAPTER FORTY-SEVEN

BILL RAGLAND, THE head of Sterling's security force, and three of the other men ran up to the edge of the woods and stopped, waiting for the slower men to catch up. As all eight men approached the edge of the woods, Ragland signaled them to gather around him. "Listen, I've sent four other men around to the road to cut off the back side. These two sons of bitches are in here somewhere and we've got to get them. We want to carry them out feet first. Let's spread out, but stay close enough so we can see each other. Watch what you're doing. These rednecks can be pretty fucking tricky. Okay, spread out and let's go."

Fanned out at about sixty yard intervals up and down the edge of the woods they began walking slowly forward. The woods close to the field were fairly open and each man, as he advanced, kept his eyes on the ground in front of him. None of them were woods-wise enough to think about danger from above. Even if they had been cautious enough to look up into the trees as they reached the denser brush, the four bowhunters hidden there would have been very difficult to spot. Their combinations of camouflage made them practically invisible against the trees.

The bowhunters, each with an arrow nocked and ready, stood tensely in their stands, several of them having Sterling's men pass directly beneath them. *Christ*, Roy thought, *I can spit right on this asshole's head. That's okay, baby, you just keep going. We got a real surprise for you up front if you start something.*

Rick Bannister, one of the turkey hunters positioned in the center of the line at the base of the ridge on the ground, could clearly see one of Sterling's men, about seventy-five yards away, coming straight for him. Rick himself was virtually invisible from almost any distance. One of the better turkey hunters in the county, he had found a slight depression with an oak tree growing out of the back of it and small, bushy scrub oaks growing in front. Clearing away the leaves under him and trimming a few branches so he could swing his shotgun without hitting them, he was confident the man approaching would not see him. Like Rick, each of the riflemen on the ridge had picked a target and followed that man's advance through their scopes.

Isaac, who was near the center of the line, had his rifle trained on the man directly in front of Rick. Periodically, the cross hairs on his scope would settle on the man's chest. *An easy shot,* Isaac thought. *I hope I don't have to take it. Maybe these guys will give up looking by the time they get to the base of the ridge and just turn around and leave.*

As the man next to Ragland walked slowly forward, he made a common mistake for people unaccustomed to being in the woods. Instead of looking for specific parts of his target, he starred blankly ahead of him at the landscape, waiting to see the entire form of a person in front of him. Because of Rick's skill with his camouflage that wasn't going to happen, but he knew if the man continued on his present course he would all but step on him. Rick had already trained his twelve-guage Remington semi-automatic on the man's chest. The shotgun was fully camouflaged and it wasn't necessary for him to move anything other than his right index finger if and when the time came.

The man was only four steps away from the end of Rick's gun barrel when he finally looked into Rick's eyes. As their eyes locked Rick's index finger began squeezing the trigger as the man's arm began to swing his pistol toward Bannister. Before the barrel of the M-16 could even be pointed at Rick the explosion of the twelve-gauge round reverberated through the woods.

The three-inch magnum load of twenty-four number-one buckshot had only spread open a few inches when they struck the man full in the chest. The force of the blast knocked the man upward and backwards about ten feet, his rifle flying unused through the air, landing about twenty feet away. To Rick, the man seemed to fly backwards in slow motion as the sound of the shot echoing back and forth through the trees. A small, blue cloud of smoke from the shot hung in the air between Rick and where the man had stood only a second before.

Before the body of the man had come fully to rest on the ground, all of Sterling's men took cover and began firing blindly into the brush in front of them. Ragland, only sixty yards to the man's right when he was killed, had looked sharply to his left at the first shot and had seen his man flung backwards through the air. Although he couldn't see Rick, Ragland sprayed a dozen rounds in Rick's general direction. Within two seconds of Bannister's shot one of Ragland's bullets had found its way through the brush and into the side of Rick's head. Killed instantly, he slumped backward against the tree behind him, his twelve-gauge falling across his legs.

With his Winchester Model 70, .308, William Porter searched the woods through his scope for a target. The scope, turned all the way up to twelve power, seemed to bring the base of the ridge right up in front of him. One of Sterling's men had taken refuge behind an old oak stump which rose about four feet above the forest floor. The stump, approximately thirty-inches wide, gave the man good cover though, while protected by it, he couldn't pick a target on the ridge. From William's vantage point a hundred-sixty yards away, he caught the flicker of movement down below him as the man craned his neck to find a target.

There you are, you son of a bitch. Stick your head up there one more time, he thought as he settled the cross hairs on the top of the stump. Several times, the top of the man's head showed briefly above the stump, but was gone so quickly William couldn't pull the trigger. *Damn! That bastard isn't going to give me a shot!* Moving slightly, William felt a bulge in his right coat pocket and remembered the turkey call that had been left there from the prior spring. It was one of those calls that could be operated with one hand by shaking it vigorously to imitate the call of a tom turkey. *We'll see how smart you are.* Resting the rifle across the log in front of him, he centered the cross-hairs of the scope on the stump again, took the safety off and put his finger on the trigger. Holding the call in his left hand and looking through the scope, he shook the call violently for a second.

The thunderous gobble that reverberated through the woods made everyone within two hundred yards look toward William's position, including the man behind the stump. Not recognizing the noise and afraid of an attack from that direction, the man rose up on one knee, his head from the nose up visible above the stump. *That's all I need to see, asshole.* The recoil of the .308 and sharp report of the rifle caused William to lose sight of his target for a split second, just long enough for the hundred-eighty grain bullet to strike the man between the bridge of his nose and left eye. The bullet penetrated and expanded, as it was designed to do, and exited the back of the man's head, carrying most of the brain tissue with it. The man, dead long before his body hit the ground, lay spread-eagle behind the stump. His right foot twitched convulsively and then he was still.

At the report from William's rifle, the firing from the remaining security guards increased. The rest of the riflemen on the ridge picked targets through the trees. The turkey hunters at the base of the ridge opened up on the men closest to them. While the fire from Sterling's men was much louder and of considerably higher volume, it was ineffective. Sterling's men couldn't see their targets on the ridge; they only knew that bullets were slamming in very close to them from unseen positions. Bark flew from the trees they took cover behind, and, while they fired hundreds of rounds up the hill toward the crest of the ridge, they could not tell whether any of their shots found their mark.

As one of the men backed around a large beech tree, his backside came in view for one of the turkey hunters about seventy yards away who had not yet fired. Seeing a target he felt would be hard to miss, he swung his ten-guage Magnum to the left, lining up the front bead sight on the man's beltline. Miscalculating slightly, the load of double O buckshot tore large pieces out of the beech tree but only a few of the pellets struck the man. They did, however, hit a very sensitive area, sending the man rolling in the leaves, screaming in pain. Grabbing his left buttock and abandoning his rifle, he began half-crawling and half-running back toward the pasture.

With three of his eight men out of commission and unable to see his attackers, Ragland began to backtrack toward the field. He wasn't sure what he had run into, but he knew it was more than just the two men who had accosted Sterling and the others.

"Back to the house, back to the house!" he yelled, waving to his remaining men to begin backing up. As they began to retreat toward the wood line, Isaac was able to draw a bead on one of the men as he crossed a small clearing two hundred-fifty yards away. Isaac had not killed a man since he had left Vietnam in 1968, and he had always hoped he would never have that experience again. However, Isaac could see this man aiming his M16 back toward the base of the ridge where his friends were and there was no hesitation as the cross-hairs settled high on the man's chest. At the report of the 7mm Magnum, the man crumpled, his M16 useless on the ground beside him.

Seeing the fourth man fall, Ragland turned to run toward the wood line. As he did, his path led him directly beneath one of the four bow-hunters still stationed near the edge of the woods. As he took a step toward the tree line Roy drew back his arrow, the thirty-yard pin sight coming to rest on Ragland's chest. Just as the string was released and the arrow sent on its way, Ragland stopped suddenly. The arrow passed about six inches in front of him and buried itself harmlessly in the ground to his right. Ragland looked down and saw the arrow buried near his feet. Startled and confused for only a split second, Ragland quickly followed the path of the arrow indicated by its angle in the ground up to the tree stand where Roy was hurriedly nocking another arrow. Before he could, Ragland swung his M16 upward in an arch, pressing the trigger and firing a burst of eight rounds at him. This burst emptied Ragland's clip and two of the bullets hit Roy, knocking him out of the tree stand. Having secured himself to the tree with a safety strap, and, hit in both the left arm and left side, Roy hung helplessly from the tree, his bow lying on the ground under the stand.

Ragland, seeing his victim helpless but alive, reached for another clip for his rifle. Ejecting the old one and slamming a new clip home, he worked the bolt to throw a live round into the chamber. As he brought the muzzle up to a firing position, Ragland said "Kiss your ass good-bye, you fucking redneck!"

As his finger tightened on the trigger, other men started to act. William, from his position three-hundred yards away on the ridge, had seen his friend fall out of the stand at the first report from Ragland's rifle. Swinging his rifle toward the base of the tree, he had picked up Ragland's form as Ragland reloaded. The closest turkey hunter, approximately eighty yards away, had also seen the shots that had struck Roy and was swinging the barrel of his ten-gauge toward Ragland. One of the best bow-hunters, Issac's brother Rodney had also seen Roy fall, and though the shot would be almost sixty yards, was drawing his compound bow, preparing to release an arrow toward Ragland.

As Ragland continued to swing the muzzle of his M16, William was squeezing the trigger on his rifle. At the same time, the turkey hunter was squeezing his trigger on his ten gauge and Rodney Porter was relaxing his fingers on the string of his bow. Ragland's M16 went off first, firing two rounds.

Rodney's arrow was the first to arrive at its target, the graphite shaft with a razor sharp broadhead burying itself in Ragland's left side, the point penetrating and protruding from his right side. Staggering and glancing quickly down at the shaft, he had little time to appreciate the wound. The load of ten gauge buckshot, though fairly spread out, struck him in the back at almost the precise moment William's bullet ripped into his chest from the right side. Ragland, spinning and being thrown forward by the force of these blows, reflexively held his finger down on the trigger of the M16 which fired ineffectively into the air and the ground around him. He had only seconds to live after he fell, the woods around him shrouded by the blood and pain. The last thing he saw before his eyes closed forever was the shaft of the arrow extending from his side and the last words that he uttered, "Oh, fuck," were drowned out by the firing of the surviving members of his team, now rapidly retreating toward Belleview.

Running to cut Roy down, Issac stopped several of the others who had started out into the field to chase Sterling's men.

"Hold on—Hold on! We can't go back in there. They brought the fight here to us, off Belleview. We can't go back in there. We just have to hope we gave John enough time. Let's get Roy to the hospital."

CHAPTER FORTY-EIGHT

FROM THE TIME Isaac and William had entered the woods until the survivors of Sterling's security team ran back out of the woods toward Belleview, only ten minutes had passed. At the first burst of automatic weapon fire, John had moved quickly to the back of the old dorm and seen Sterling's security men running in the opposite direction.

Entering the unguarded operations room, he moved quickly down the corridor from room to room until he came to the large storage room in the left rear of the basement of the building. There, in a thirty by fifty foot room, were nearly a thousand automatic rifles, cases of automatic pistols stacked up on the floor, twelve cases of shoulder-fired missiles and dozens of cases of ammunition. Videotaping the room quickly, he was almost ready to leave when he heard voices in the corridor.

"Mr. D'Angelo, I don't know what's going on. There's a lot of firing over to the west of the house. I don't know if it's the police or what."

"Go find out, asshole. We're too close to being ready to get out of here to get caught now. Get over to the manor house and find out what the hell's going on. Take one of the rifles with you."

As the voices came closer to the door, Richter heard the other man say, "Listen, goddamn it, I ain't getting caught here. I didn't kill that kid but I was with 'em when they did. They're not gonna put that on me. I'm gettin' the hell out of here as soon as I can."

"We'll all get out of here. Just get over there and see what's going on. If it's that bad, our car's ready and we can be gone in three minutes. I've got all my stuff ready to go anyway. You go check it out and I'll meet you upstairs at the tunnel out of my room."

"You got it," the man said as he opened the door to the armory.

John had the evidence he needed, but hearing the man admit that he had been part of Allen's death was more than he could ignore. D'Angelo's man didn't realize he was in danger until John cocked the hammer on his .357 Magnum single-action revolver. The man looked quickly in John 's direction.

"Don't even think about it! From this distance I'll turn you inside out."

Realizing he was trapped, the man stopped reaching for the rifle in the rack. Instead, he put his hand up and took a step or two back. "Wait a minute man, wait a minute. I ain't done nothin'. I just work here."

"That's bullshit, you son of a bitch. I heard what you just said. That was my son you killed," John said, extending the pistol further and aiming it directly between the man's eyes. "I want you to tell me what happened. I want you to tell me who killed my son and why."

"Okay, okay, I'll tell you. But it wasn't me. Just don't shoot, okay?"

"Tell me, you son of a bitch, or the muzzle of this gun's going be the last thing that you see."

"Okay, okay. We were walking down by the edge of the woods and Lester and the other guy were talking to us about some of the stuff going on here. About D'Angelo and what he and Sterling were planning. We didn't know the kid was there. He had all this camouflage stuff on. If he hadn't moved, we wouldn't have known he was there. When he jumped up and ran, one of the other guys took a couple of shots at him and missed. When were looking for him he put an arrow into the other guy.

"It was Lester Morgan, Lester snuck up behind him and got him in a choke hold. I've never seen anything like that. He just twisted his neck and the kid fell over. Christ, we didn't even know he was a kid. He had that net over his face. Honest, I didn't know who he was. I didn't do it."

The pistol John held only had a two and a half pound trigger pull. Just a gentle squeeze and Allen's death would be partially avenged. John's finger tightened on the trigger, the gentle squeeze beginning. The man could see the hate in John's eyes, could see the tip of John's index finger curling tightly around the trigger, and realized he was about to die.

"Wait a minute, man. Wait a minute. I'll tell anybody you want what happened. Just don't kill me!"

John had never felt this kind of rage. Flashes of Allen lying on the stretcher kept returning to him—the bruises on his neck, his eyes closed forever. John's finger tightened further, no more than two or three ounces of pull away from committing a murder himself.

The muscles in John's finger began to relax. "I'm not going to kill you. But you're damn sure going to help me. Get in here, turn around, and get on your knees."

Realizing how close he had come to dying, the man complied quickly. John grabbed a role of tape from a shelf and quickly bound the man's hands behind him. Pushing him in the back with his right foot, the man fell heavily against a stack of weapons against the wall. With the man lying on the floor, John bound his feet with tape and put several long pieces over his mouth.

"You're a lucky son of a bitch! D'Angelo's in suite three, isn't he? Goddamn it, you better tell me or I'll kill you!"

The man, unable to speak because of the tape over his mouth, turned on his side and held up three fingers. Looking down at the man, re-cocking the pistol, and placing it flush against the man's ear, John said, "You better be right, you bastard, or I'll be back. And if I have to come back, there won't be any second chance." The man closed his eyes and nodded.

John shut the door behind him and, putting the videotape in his jacket pocket, ran up the stairs toward D'Angelo's suite. As he reached the second floor, John could hear the firing continuing on the ridge six-hundred yards west of Belleview. *Hold 'em boys, Hold 'em. I'm almost done here.*

John Richter was no cowboy. He wasn't a martial arts expert or even an expert marksman with a pistol. He was a man who had grown up with guns and whose son had been murdered. He knew who, why, and how and he was not going to be denied. Easing down the hall he approached D'Angelo's door carefully. It was open about a inch and he peered in. Seeing no one in the foyer or the front rooms, he eased through the dining room, looking down the hall toward the master bedroom. Of all the doors down the hall only the last door on the left, the door to the master bedroom, was open. He had moved about halfway down the hall and was between doors when an old man in a maintenance uniform opened the bathroom door and stepped out into the hallway.

Holding the pistol down by his side, John approached the man carefully. Carrying a mop and bucket, the man was startled by John's sudden appearance.

"Who are you?" John demanded harshly, holding the pistol in plain sight.

Stepping backward, the man said, "The plumber. Goddamn shitter is always backing up. They must think I'm the fucking maid. Who the hell are you and what's all that shooting? I didn't know they had a target range on this place."

"Have you seen a man named D'Angelo?"

"There was a man here a minute ago. Come to think of it, he went in the back closet and ain't come out yet. Must be packing to leave."

Richter, believing the man's story, was sure D'Angelo was escaping down the tunnel. As he started toward the man he realized the plumber was wearing a very expensive pair of lizard-skin tassel loafers.

It all happened so quickly that John barely had time to react. D'Angelo did not hesitate, pulling his small stainless steel .380 from its concealed positon behind his back as John raised his .357, cocking it as he elevated the muzzle. Both men crouched and fired at the same time. John's first shot slammed into the wall next to D'Angelo's head. D'Angelo fired three quick shots, narrowly missing John. As John cocked the hammer and fired a second round at D'Angelo, D'Angelo stepped backwards into his bedroom, pushing the door closed at the same time. John's second round tore into the door frame only inches from the man. Not taking time to lock the bedroom door, D'Angelo fired two rounds through the door hoping to slow his attacker down. Moving quickly to the closet, he passed through it and into the tunnel, running as rapidly as he could down the narrow, dimly lit concrete steps.

John knew the tunnel system and where D'Angelo was going. Listening briefly at the bedroom door to the footsteps retreating down the stairway, John opened the door to the bedroom and ran to the closet. Arriving at the top of the first flight of stairs just as D'Angelo got to the bottom, John saw him stop and turn toward him, the pistol still in his left hand. As two more shots rang out, John ducked behind the framework of the door. The two bullets passed harmlessly by, burying themselves in the wall behind him. Swinging quickly around the corner, John fired the .357 at D'Angelo. That round struck the side of the concrete wall at an angle, ricocheted off, slammed into the opposite wall, spraying bits of concrete and dust. The sound of the .357 exploding in the confined area of the tunnel was deafening.

D'Angelo got to the garage about thirty seconds before John and, in those thirty seconds, was able to alert the driver and bodyguard and jump into the back of the limousine. Speeding quickly out of the garage, the tires smoking on the concrete floor, the limousine turned as quickly as it could in a confined space and started down toward the river road and freedom beyond.

As the limousine straightened out and started down the hill, Richter ran out of the tunnel and into the open garage bay. As D'Angelo screamed "Kill him, kill that son of a bitch," the bodyguard leaned out the window and sprayed the garage with a dozen rounds from his rifle.

John's pistol, already cocked, came up swiftly to eye level. As the sights on the revolver came to bear on the bodyguard, John squeezed the trigger.

The bullet hit low, striking the back of the the limousine just below the center of the rear license plate and pushed forward through the gas tank. Sparks generated by the bullet slashing through the metal ignited the forty-gallon gas tank and the car erupted in a ball of flame. The explosion ripped the back half of the car off, engulfing

D'Angelo and the bodyguard in a mushroom cloud of fire. The front half of the limousine, also in flames, careened down the road for over thirty yards before veering off into the woods, smashing into one of the large oaks near the end of the logging road.

The explosion of the gas tank only forty yards away had been so powerful it knocked Richter back several steps. He could feel the intense heat from the burning rear half of the vehicle fifty yards away. Secondary explosions erupted from the flames as the ammunition stored in the limousine began to burn.

Though John couldn't see it and D'Angelo was beyond caring, the flames consumed the fortune D'Angelo had amassed. As the millions burned, the plastic disguise D'Angelo had thought would lead him to freedom blistered and blackened on his face, locking it into a bizarre and twisted death mask more gruesome than the man himself. Through the smoke of the fire, John thought he saw several other vehicles down the logging road, but none of them came any closer to him than the bottom of the hill.

As all of that happened, Sterling received the reports of the fight on the ridge and Michael's report on the unsuccessful attack on the cabin, Sterling knew it was time to leave Belleview.

Yelling to Sam, Sterling said, "Get the helicopter over here now. You know what to load, make sure you clear all the computers. We've got to get the hell out of here! Get in touch with the airport, have the jet ready."

Sterling, never one to let details escape him, had previously planned for an emergency exit from Belleview. All important documents and records were kept on computer disks and could be packed in seconds. All other records could be destroyed or erased from the computers almost instantaneously. Though Sterling's investment in Belleview was huge, it was not so substantial a portion of his assets that he would risk prison or even death to keep it.

"Sam, let's go! You got everything?"

"Got it," said Sam, and both ran toward the helipad. Sam carried the two attaché cases of records and reports which Sterling would need to continue operations from a different location. Melinda, Sterling's secretary, and Lynn were already in the helicopter. Lynn had made a quick and life-saving decision to board the helicopter, planning to meet Raphael at the airport. Throwing the cases aboard, Sterling and Sam climbed in the helicopter as it lifted off the ground. As the helicopter passed over the manor house, D'Angelo's limousine exploded into flames below them.

Sterling arrived at the Culpeper airport well before any effort to stop him could be made. As he, Sam, Melinda and Lynn boarded the jet Sterling took one last look at the Virginia landscape and muttered, "Beaten by a handful of country boys! Who would have figured that?"

At the same time, Lester and Floyd were pulling in behind Michael and the other men from Bellview on the road leading into the garage. Both had heard the radio conversation between Michael and Sterling and knew everyone else was bailing out. Seeing the helicopter pass overhead and the front of D'Angelo's burning limousine slam into a tree in front of them, they knew they had to run. Lester shoved the truck into reverse and backed out onto the river road in a cloud of dust. Putting the truck into drive and flooring the gas pedal, they flew down the road, throwing clouds of gravel and dirt behind them. Michael's truck, the bodies from the fight at the cabin still in the back, disappeared in the dust behind them.

"What the hell are we gonna do, Lester? We're in some deep shit. Goddamn! What are we gonna do?"

"Well," said Lester, "I'll tell you one thing we ain't gonna do. We ain't stayin' the fuck around here. We're gonna stop by the trailer and grab a few things and then get our asses up into the National Park. Once we get up there, won't nobody find us."

Even Floyd could see the sense in that. The George Washington National Forest and the Skyline Drive composed some of the most rugged wilderness areas in the eastern United States and it was only thirty miles away. If they could get to the park their chances of being apprehended were slight.

"Right, right. That's what we need to do. But we need to stop in town too. We're gonna need a bunch of shit up there in the park."

Stopping briefly at their trailer, Lester wouldn't tell Sandy anything about what was going on. "Shut the fuck up, Bitch. You can have the trailer. Take care of the kids. We're outta here. And don't expect to see me anymore."

Not one to look a gift horse in the mouth, Sandy stood back as Lester and Floyd loaded sleeping bags and a few other camping items in the truck.

As they sped down the road toward Clarkton, she said, "Good riddance," smiling at her good fortune. They had just made the last payment on the other truck they had left behind.

By this time the FBI had been alerted to the attack at Judge Collins' cabin. Judge Collins had told Samuel, prior to the attack on them, that he had set up a meeting with the FBI at John's request. He had the name and phone number of the agent he had called in his pocket, and after Sterling's men left, Samuel crawled over to the judge and took the slip of paper out of his pocket. Though tinged with blood, he was able to read the number, and, with great difficulty, called the agent. Ambulances were soon on the way to the cabin. Though Samuel knew of the basic plans at Belleview, he did not know the status of the plan, only that his son and his friends would need help. He had passed out before he could say much to the first agents to arrive, but the information he had given was enough to set the men into in motion. Accompanied by several squads from the Virginia State Police, more than a dozen vehicles raced toward Belleview and Judge Collins' cabin.

A few of these vehicles happened to pass Lester and Floyd's truck heading toward Clarkton, unaware of their involvement.

"We need money. You got any money?" Floyd asked Lester.

"No man, I ain't got shit."

"That's okay, we can just rob a store," Floyd said.

"No good," Lester responded. "If we rob a store in town they'll be on us in a heartbeat. We gotta go somewhere to get some money."

As they sped toward Clarkton Floyd remembered the gun turn-in program and the Andrews woman. He especially remembered the jewelry the woman wore and the expensive car she drove. He remembered too how proud she had been to let everyone know she was giving up her revolver. How much safer she felt now that there wasn't a gun in the house.

"I know where we can go. Take a right up here at the third light. I know just the place to get some money."

CHAPTER FORTY-NINE

PULLING UP IN front of the Andrews' home on Park Street, Floyd was disappointed there were no cars in the driveway. "Damn, she's not home."

"Well, that's okay. All we need is some money. We don't need you gettin' into any more trouble. Just get in there and get some cash."

"Well," Floyd said, "I don't know if there'll be any cash there or not. I just know she don't have no gun no more. Let's split up. You drop me off here and come back in thirty minutes. You go try somewhere else and I'll just meet you out here at nine o'clock."

"Okay," said Lester. "but you be here at nine o'clock. I don't have time to wait for your ass. We gotta get the hell outta here!"

Lester drove off as Floyd walked around the back of the Andrews' home. Lester drove aimlessly down the street. He didn't pick a target for a few more minutes, not until he saw Brenda Richter walk in front of her living room window. As he drove slowly by their home, he noticed the name on the mailbox and recognized it as the name of the people whose son he had killed a month before. *Well, fuck, I might was well take out the whole family.* Parking his truck around the corner, Lester walked toward the back door of John and Brenda's home.

By this time, Floyd had forced his way into the Andrews' house through the kitchen door and was helping himself to the contents of the refrigerator. Slicing several slabs of ham, he made a thick sandwich. *Damn shame I gotta live like I been livin' and this bitch has got all this stuff.*

Finishing his sandwich, he wiped the knife on his pants and stuck the blade of it between his belt and blue jeans. "Well now," he said aloud, "if I was a rich bitch, where would I hide my money? Bedrooms. They always keep their shit in bedrooms."

Walking down the hallway past an open bathroom door, Floyd first came to Mary Sue's bedroom. Not immediately recognizing it as the daughter's and therefore unlikely to hold any valuables, he walked in and looked around.

The room was typical for an eighteen-year-old high-school senior. The stereo and TV in the corner would have made a nice haul if they hadn't needed cash immediately. *Damn, I could probably get a hundred bucks for that at the pawn shop. But we ain't got time to pawn shit.* Rifling through the headboard of Mary Sue's bed, he found only two one-dollar bills and some loose change in a coffee cup. "Shit!" he said, throwing the cup up against the wall, fragments flying out across the room. At the other end of the headboard was a picture of a girl in her gymnastics outfit, attractive and physically well-developed. Picking up the picture Floyd stared at it. *Damn, wouldn't mind some of that! I haven't had anything that young in a long time.* Lingering over the picture he tried to remember what it was like to have sex with someone who was young, pretty, and sober. A frown crossed his face as he found his memory wasn't that good.

Tossing the picture down on the bed, Floyd went quickly through her closet, finding nothing of interest. Taking the drawers of her dresser out, one by one, he dumped the contents on the bed. The only items of interest were the girl's underwear. Picking a particularly fancy pair of briefs, he hooked them over his index finger and spun them around. *Boy, I sure would like to get hold of what's wrapped up in these!* Remembering that he had only a limited amount of time to try and find cash, he threw the underwear into the pile on the bed and hurried down the hall.

He looked briefly into what apparently was the guest room and saw nothing there of interest. It was too unused. Opening the last door at the end of the hall Floyd walked into Stacy Andrews' bedroom. Neat and clean, he saw with a glance that there were several possibilities here. Going to the chest of drawers, there were necklaces hung over the corner of a mirror and several jewelry boxes on top. He began sifting through them for anything of value.

Ms. Andrews, who was always at work by eight o'clock, had followed her usual routine that morning. A little before nine, a mishap with a full cup of coffee had turned her dress into a disaster area. "Ruth," she said, as she tried to wipe away the stains, "I've got to run home and change clothes. I've got an appointment at the bank at eleven o'clock and I sure can't go there looking like this. I should be back in a half hour or so. Okay?"

"Sure, take your time. I'll hold down the fort."

Grabbing her purse and running out the door, she got into her car and quickly drove the mile and half from her office to her home. Pulling up in the driveway she turned the car off, taking the keys with her. Walking hurriedly up the sidewalk to the front door she thought, *Of all days, why today? This meeting at the bank is so damn important.*

Looking for the front door key, she fumbled with her key ring and dropped it on the sidewalk. "Damn it," she said aloud, "get with it, girl." Unlocking the front door and entering the house she walked quickly by the kitchen, glancing at the crumbs and opened mayonnaise jar on the kitchen table.

What in the world? Mary knows better than to leave a mess out like this. Quickly capping the jar of mayonnaise and putting it back in the refrigerator, she hurried toward the back of the house, not noticing the back door still slightly ajar.

Floyd hadn't heard her pull up but had heard the keys when they fell from her hand to the sidewalk. Glancing quickly out the bedroom window, he saw her car in the driveway and stepped quietly into the bathroom connected to her bedroom. Leaving the door slightly open and wrapping his fingers around the handle of the knife still stuck down between his belt and blue jeans, he thought *Well now, this may get real interesting. I may get a little more out of this than just some loose change.*

Ms. Andrews opened the bedroom door and walked over to the bed, unbuttoning the back of her dress as she went. Slipping out of the dress she tossed it onto the bed and walked over to her closet. Floyd, watching from the bathroom, could feel his excitement growing. She had always been an attractive woman, and, since her divorce, had paid even more attention to her physical appearance. Compared to the female companionship he was accustomed to, Ms. Andrews represented a quantum leap forward. He almost never got laid unless he got the woman he was with really drunk, so drunk she couldn't make a conscious choice not to have sex with him. Now, here in front of him, was an attractive, well-to-do woman.

Damn, she ain't been rode hard and hung up wet.

In the meantime, Ms. Andrews had picked out another dress and laid it across the bed. Glancing down, she saw her slip was also stained. *God,* she thought, quickly pulling her slip and pantyhose off and throwing them in the corner. *I'm never going to get out of here.* She turned her back to the bathroom door as she walked toward her dresser, now clad only in her underwear. She never heard Floyd as he opened the bathroom door, took four steps across the bedroom and pinned her violently between himself and the chest of the drawers. The impact of his attack from behind her knocked perfume bottles and a small jewelry case from the top of the dresser onto the floor. Trying to scream, she felt a thick, heavy forearm around her neck and saw the ten-inch blade of a kitchen knife in front of her eyes.

Floyd, pressing himself against her from the rear, made contact with her from the knees up. Her struggling caused her buttocks to move back and forth across his crotch, and, already aroused, he said, "Go ahead, bitch! That feels good. You and me, we's gonna have some fun. And you ain't gonna yell, are you?" He held the knife closely against her throat.

She could not answer verbally. Floyd's left hand was clasped tightly across her mouth. Held firmly against the bureau, the pulls on the dresser drawers were making imprints on her torso and left leg. She tried to shake her head back and forth, hoping her attacker would not hurt her further. Feeling the woman's resistance decreasing, Floyd relaxed his grip, grabbed the back of her hair, and violently turned her around to face him.

Up until then, she didn't know who her attacker was or what he looked like. Coming face to face with him, his eyes, nose, and mouth only inches from her, she realized how much danger she faced. The rage and lust in his eyes couldn't be mistaken for passion.

As he pressed himself more tightly against her, a fresh wave of fear and nausea came over her, giving her a strength she didn't realize she had. With desperation and a primal urge for self-preservation, she pushed Floyd backwards, kicking at him with her right foot. He stumbled backwards several steps, but held the knife firmly in his right hand. Touching his right cheek where Andrews had raked her fingernails across his face, he glared at her, his lust combining with a hatred he would not try to control.

As he stepped backwards, Stacy Andrews stumbled to her left, toward the nightstand next to the bed and the drawer where she had kept her pistol. She grabbed the drawer and pulled it open and only when she saw the empty drawer did she remember the gun turn-in program. The vision of her holding the pistol up to the crowd, their cheers and applause, and her sense of pride and high moral position at having relinquished possession of such a deadly weapon flashed through her mind. A guttural snarl from Morgan brought her back to the deadly reality she faced. Looking quickly from the empty drawer back to her attacker, she saw him straighten the knife in his right hand, his left hand beginning to unbuckle his belt.

"You give it up, didn't ya? I know you did. I was there when you put that pistol in the pile with all the rest of the guns. You didn't see me but I saw you. I thought to myself, 'Lady, you're crazy as shit. If I ever get a chance at you, you're mine.' Well, you got no protection and it's time."

She was in a corner of the bedroom where there was no window, no closet, nowhere to go. As Floyd removed his belt from his blue jeans and walked slowly toward her, she retreated the few steps she could to the corner of the bedroom. As he got within several feet of her she attempted to kick him again but was blocked by a vicious slap on the thigh with the leather belt he held in his left hand. The blow made a loud snapping sound and instantly left a wide red mark on her leg. The buckle of the belt cut across her inner thigh causing a trickle of blood to flow. The sound of the blow and the sight of blood heightened his twisted desire for her.

Screaming in pain, she put her hands up in an effort to block his advance. Morgan grabbed her by the hair and threw her over the bed. She landed face down, unable to move. Morgan walked up behind her, straddled her legs, and made a noose out of the belt he had just taken off. Slipping it over her head and around her neck, he tightened his grip on the belt, strangling her.

She felt the belt around her neck, the tightness in her throat. Gasping for air and clutching at the comforter on her bed, she felt his hand in the waistband of her panties as he pulled them down around her ankles and off one leg. She heard him unzip his pants and felt him struggling to push his pants down around his knees. He stood behind her, his left hand tightly wrapped around the long portion of his belt, the noose pulled even more tightly around her throat. The knife flew across the room, hit the wall, and fell to the carpet ten feet away. It might as well have been on the other side of the county. She felt his right hand reach under her stomach, pulling her buttocks higher and she felt the first savage thrust as the rape began.

The noose that Floyd had placed around her neck was a good one. During his attack, as his passion increased, so did his grip on the belt. She had lost consciousness less than a minute after the attack began. As it continued over the next seven or eight minutes, all of the oxygen to her lungs would be cut off and she would die long before his attack was over.

It was only after he finished with her and relaxed his grip on the belt that he noticed her open, unseeing eyes, the scream frozen on her lips. His attack was an act of primitive, self-centered savagery and he neither knew nor cared whether she was alive or dead. Pushing her body away from him onto the bed, he bent over to loosen the belt from around her neck. Looking into the face of his victim, he said, "Was it as good for you as it was for me?" He laughed out loud.

"Damn, that was pretty good. It's a shame I only get to use it once. Oh well, let's see what the bitch had in her pocketbook." He picked up the knife and left the bedroom.

Walking back down the hall, he replaced his belt and began searching for Ms. Andrews' pocketbook. She had left the front door open slightly and he closed and locked it. Seeing Ms. Andrews' pocketbook in the living room, he picked it up and dumped its contents on the sofa. Putting the knife down he pawed through her things. "Mastercard, Visa, American Express. Gees, this bitch had it all. Cash, what about cash?" Looking through her wallet he found almost a hundred and fifty dollars and an Exxon credit card. *Well, this'll get us started anyway.*

As he stood up to leave he saw another car with the two people in it pull into the driveway behind Ms. Andrews' Volvo. Looking through the curtains he could see a young man driving the vehicle and a pretty young woman getting out of the front passenger seat. It was the same girl in the photograph in the other bedroom.

"Great, Mom's home," she called back to her boyfriend. "I'll just be a second. I know I left that report on the dresser in my room."

"Well, hurry up," the boy said. "We're late for first period already!"

"Okay, okay!" she said as she searched through her pocketbook for her keys.

Picking up the knife off the sofa where he had laid it, Morgan stepped quickly behind the front door. At the same time he could hear the storm door opening and the girl still searching through her pocketbook for the keys.

"Why do things always have to get buried at the bottom of this thing? Finally!" she said as her hand located the small set of keys she carried. Looking back at her boyfriend she waved and smiled, "I found them. I'll just be a second."

The young man, already impatient, was looking through Mary Sue's notebooks and merely waved. As Stacy's daughter inserted the key in the lock, Floyd's hand closed on the knob on the opposite side of the door. Holding the knife in his right hand, he could feel the knob begin to turn in his hand.

"Mary! Mary! Here it is! Here's your report. You had it all the time!"

"You're kidding! I thought I looked. Oh well, let me just slip in and say hi to Mom and then we'll go" she said, turning the knob further.

"No, come on, we're late already. You'll see her this afternoon."

Mary Sue, always very close to her mother, looked quickly at the door, her watch, and her boyfriend. Making a decision that would save her life, she released the knob, locked the door, and ran back to the car. Getting in she said, "Mom's gonna be mad. She doesn't like me running in and out without speaking to her. But that's okay. I'll make it up to her tonight."

Inside the house, Floyd relaxed his grip on the knife handle and peered at the young woman running back to the car. *Next time. I'll save you 'til next time.*

CHAPTER FIFTY

ONLY A FEW blocks from where Stacy Andrews lay brutally murdered, Brenda Richter sat at her kitchen table. Nervously awaiting word from John, she tried to talk herself out of a fourth cup of coffee. She understood why he had to do it, even wished she could be part of it. Now she only wanted to know he was safe.

She was, however, more than seven months pregnant this Thanksgiving week. The doctor had told her the baby was due in early January. While their focus was on a strong, healthy child, both of them really hoped the delivery would take place before Christmas. They knew the child, while they would love it for itself, would help both of them through this first Christmas without Allen. They had talked at length about this baby not being a substitute for Allen, not being a surrogate for the son they had lost. "This baby is going to be its own person," Brenda told John. "We're both going to have to be very careful not to try and shape this child into a replica of Allen."

Allen's death, the dangerous situation in which John had placed himself, the birth of this new child were all like photographs that swam through her mind like the colors of a kaleidoscope. It was hard for her to focus on one thought, one hope, one fear, before a whole new set of emotions rolled in and over those thoughts.

"God," she prayed, "I just want to have this baby. I wouldn't care if it came early as long as it was healthy. Just bring John home and let the baby be okay."

Brenda heard the storm door at the front of the house open. *John's home!* Rushing from the kitchen to the front door, she would usually never have opened it without first looking to see who was there. In her haste she removed the chain, unbolted the door, and opened it, expecting her husband to be standing there.

Lester Morgan was a large man—tall, broad-shouldered, and imposing. Dressed roughly in clothes that obviously had not been cleaned in a long time, his appearance startled Brenda. Letting out a slight gasp, she clutched the top of her robe with her right hand and started to try and close the door on this man she didn't know.

Putting his right hand against the door, he held his right foot up on the door jamb, preventing it from closing more than about six inches. "Mrs. Richter, I'm Lester Morgan. Your husband had made me some loans down at the bank. I hate to disturb you, but I was on my way over to do a tree job down the street and my truck's broke down. I happened to notice your mailbox when I went by and wondered if I could use your phone to call my brother. You know these damn 'ol pickup trucks. There's always something fallin' off of 'em. My brother's got the tools to fix it with and if I could just give him a call . . . I won't take up any of your time."

Brenda would ordinarily never let a stranger into the house. But Lester, contrary to his brother, could at least feign some social graces. Standing there in his work clothes, hat in hand, he seemed a simple hard-working man with a broken pickup truck. In a moment of indecision, she began to say, "Well, I don't . . ."

"Please, Ms. Richter. I promise it won't take but a second. I don't know anyone else out here and it's over a mile back to the 7-11 where there's public phone. If I don't get over to the folks' house, somebody else is going to beat me to the job, and then I won't be able to pay back the loan your husband made me." He said this with a smile and a gentle laugh. That made Brenda relax her grip on the door.

"Well, I guess it'll be all right. Come on in. The phone is over on the wall in the kitchen," she said, pointing through the kitchen door where Lester could see the refrigerator, stove, and sink.

"I really appreciate this, ma'am. This job's real important." As Lester walked toward the kitchen, he continued looking back at Brenda over his shoulder. "I see you're in a family way. That's nice. That's real nice."

Brenda, more at ease, began to smile and say something to Lester about what they hoped the child would be. The sentence never left her lips. Spinning quickly to his right and extending his right arm, the back of Lester's right hand caught Brenda fully in the right temple, knocking her across the living room floor and against the sofa. Dazed, she half-sat, half-lay on the sofa, her left hand under her right hand across her stomach. Blood quickly began to trickle from her right nostril and from the right corner of her mouth.

Stunned, her vision blurred, she saw the man walking slowly toward her. "You stupid fuckin' bitch. Your asshole of a husband's fucked everything up. I thought this was his house. Well, I'm gonna fix his ass. He'll wish he never heard of the Morgan boys." Lester knew from what Sterling had told him John Richter was the father of the boy he had killed and it was Richter who had organized the encounter at Belleview which ended his job and the steady stream of money it had brought him.

Standing in the middle of the living room floor, he glared at Brenda and growled, "I already killed your bastard son. Looks like I'm gonna get number two today."

At first what the man said didn't register. Crying, the pain still raging through the side of her head, she stared in disbelief at Morgan. "What do you mean? What are you talking about?"

"That was your kid that died last month up on the ridge, right?" Not waiting for an answer Lester continued, "Well, I'm the one who done him. Snapped his neck like a chicken. The boy put up a good fight though. Skewered one of those other guys just like one of them fancy meals on a stick. But he never heard me come up behind him. Once I got my arm around his neck, it was all over."

Laughing, the recollection of Allen's death brought to the surface the sickest humor Lester could conjure up. "Yep, you shoulda seen his eyes buggin' out. But he didn't hurt for long. I mean, it only took a couple of seconds. Now you, on the other hand . . ." he said taking another step toward Brenda, "you gonna feel this for a long, long time. Don't make any never mind to me that you're pregnant. Just means that maybe you got a little more experience, that's all."

Brenda, wide-eyed with pain and fear, stared at Morgan. "You, you're the one who killed Allen, killed my son? Why, what could he have done to you, what could he have taken from you?"

Moving swiftly, much more swiftly than Lester could have imagined, Brenda rose and, in one motion, grabbed a heavy lamp from the coffee table next to the sofa and threw it. The cord ripped from the wall as the lamp sailed toward Lester. Deflecting the lamp, the glass base shattered, cutting a deep gash in the meaty part of his forearm. Stumbling toward the rear of the house Brenda screamed as loudly as she could. Morgan, while blocking the lamp, had lunged toward Brenda. Falling forward, he reached out his right hand, barely making contact with her ankle, but tripping her in the process.

Brenda fell heavily against the small end table in the hall. As she fell, she turned sideways and the left side of her rib cage took the brunt of the impact. Sharp pains stabbed through her body as three ribs separated from the cartilage connecting them to the rest of her rib cage.

Lester, bleeding profusely from his left arm, got up on one knee and reached forward to grab her leg and pull her back toward him. Kicking with both feet, Brenda stumbled toward her bedroom. There was no plan in her mind, no time to form one, only a need to run and separate herself from this nightmare. Getting to the bedroom door, she reached up, braced herself against the chair railing, pulled herself upright, and stumbled into their bedroom.

The small .38 caliber snub-nose revolver was hanging in its holster hidden behind the headboard of their bed. Wanting it to be accessible if it was needed, she and John had felt that was the best place to keep it unless they had company. Stumbling toward the bed, reaching behind the headboard for the pistol, Brenda could hear Lester scrambling behind her, coming closer every second. If she was lucky, she would have time to turn and fire.

She fell on the bed at the same time her right hand reached around the headboard and gripped the small handle of the .38. It came easily out of the leather holster, and, rolling over on her left side, she began extending her right arm, cocking the revolver and pointing it in the direction of her attacker.

Lester, confident he would soon be able to do whatever he wished with Brenda, had regained his footing and, as she rolled over on the bed, was only two steps away from her. The sight of the revolver pointing directly at him stopped him in his tracks. He could see the pistol was cocked and that its chambers were loaded. He was close enough to even see the small, dark hollow cavities in the end of each of the four hollow-point bullets that were visible in the cylinder.

Putting his hands up near his shoulders and taking a step back, he said, "Now wait a minute, wait a minute, I was just kiddin'. I weren't gonna do nothin'. I just needed a little money to get out of town. That's all I wanted," he said, taking another step back and to his right.

Brenda, still pointing the pistol at the center of the man's chest, screamed, "You killed my son! You destroyed a life I brought into this world. I loved him. We loved him. He would have done so much . . ." Every muscle in her body was tense, making her begin to squeeze the trigger. Morgan could see her fury was about to take over and end his life.

"Now wait a mintute, wait a minute. That wasn't my fault. I didn't even know the boy. He was somewhere he shouldn't a been and heard stuff he shouldn't a heard. Christ, I didn't even know he was a kid when I killed him. If he had just stayed still, if he just hadn't moved, we wouldn't even have known . . ."

"Shut up! Shut up! You took him, you didn't have to . . ." she said, standing up with difficulty by the bed, tears of rage and pain welling up in her eyes. She had to concentrate to keep the images of Allen in the funeral home, in the casket, from overwhelming her.

A car braked suddenly on the road outside the window to avoid a neighborhood dog. The tires made a grinding, loud noise and the horn blared. In the instant Brenda reacted to that noise and looked briefly to her right, Lester saw his opportunity.

Always strong and agile, Lester leapt from his position toward Brenda, his right hand reaching out for her. Lester was two feet away from her and the pistol that stood between them. Sensing his movement, her head snapped back to the left toward him, her right index finger tightened on the trigger. With no time to aim, she only knew the pistol was pointed at his body when she fired the first round.

She did not hear the report, did not feel the recoil. She saw the muzzle jump, the small light blue cloud of smoke that followed the stabbing orange flame. She saw the impact of the bullet in the man's right shoulder. The force of the first round spun Lester back around to his right but did not put him on the floor. Grabbing the bedpost with his left hand he continued toward her, realizing his only chance was to keep moving.

Brenda, her savage, primal scream piercing the air, leveled the pistol at the largest, broadest part of the man and, for as long as he was standing in front of her, continued to pull the trigger. As the second, third, and fourth shots tore through his chest, he staggered backwards, finally falling over a chair in the corner of the room. A smaller man, one less fit, would have collapsed after the second shot, but Lester absorbed four rounds before dying.

Brenda continued to back up, ready to pull the trigger again until she realized he no longer posed a threat. Crying uncontrollably, she slid down the door jamb to a seated position, her left hand across her stomach, the pistol held loosely in her right hand.

It was many minutes before she felt she had the strength to stand and reach the nearest phone. Her 911 call was received at just after 9:30 in the morning—roughly an hour after the end of the fighting at Belleview, but several hours before Stacy Andrews' body would be discovered by a concerned co-worker who went to her home looking for her.

The authorities would want to question John Richter more about the events at Belleview, but for now he was released from their custody. As he turned the corner onto his block, he saw the deputy's car and a ambulance in front of his house. Getting closer he saw the ambulance attendants removing a body from the house on a gurney, covered with a sheet drenched in blood.

No, not Brenda. It can't be. He rammed the car up over the sidewalk and into the front yard. Running from the car to the stretcher he jerked the sheet back and came face to face with the corpse of Lester Morgan. The front of his shirt was saturated with blood, a crooked, agonized, twisted grimace frozen on his face.

"Thank God," he said. "Brenda!" Forcing his way past a deputy and into the living room he saw Brenda lying on the sofa being attended by several EMT's. Running over, he knelt beside her, taking her right hand in his and asked,

"Are you okay? The baby?"

Through the oxygen mask and tears, Brenda could only nod and murmur, "Okay . . . we're okay."

But neighbors weren't the only ones watching what was happening at the Richter home that morning.

CHAPTER FIFTY-ONE

"DAMN, WHERE IN the hell is that sonofabitch?" Floyd muttered under his breath. *He was supposed to pick me up fifteen minutes ago! We got to get outta here.*

Shaking his head, he walked toward the Richter home until he spotted their truck parked only half a block from the Richters. *Well, at least he left the keys in it. I can always count on him for that anyway.* Hearing a siren coming up fast behind him, he tightened his grip on the pistol in his belt. As the police car passed by he breathed a sigh of relief, but wondered again where Lester was.

Several other police cars quickly pulled up to the front of the Richter home as well as another ambulance. Curious, Floyd sat slouched down lower in his seat and waited impatiently for his brother. A crowd soon gathered outside the Ritcher home and it wasn't long before word spread there had been a killing there.

A teenager Floyd didn't recognize came running by, yelling to a friend across the street, "Hey, hey, the police said Mrs. Richter killed one of the Morgan boys. Shot him a bunch of times!"

Floyd's his first impulse was to take his rifle from the truck and get whatever revenge he could, but even he realized that any attempt at vengeance would be futile because of the number of police on the scene. Sitting in the truck for several long minutes, his hatred built and his grip on the steering wheel tightened, but he finally convinced himself to leave.

"This ain't over," he said aloud. "That fuckin' family's gonna pay. Before I get done with 'em, they'll wish Lester had killed all three of 'em instead'a just the kid." He turned the key in the ignition, put the truck in drive, and headed out of town toward the Blue Ridge Mountains. As Clarkton disappeared behind him, he glanced in the rearview mirror. *I ain't done with you yet. I ain't done!*

The emergency room at the small hospital in Clarkton looked like the triage area in a combat zone. By the time Brenda's ambulance arrived at the hospital, John's father and Judge Collins had already been brought in. Judge Collins, much more seriously wounded than Samuel, had been taken almost immediately to surgery. The bullets that had pierced his body had done tremendous damage and his wounds were initially considered fatal. John's father, while struck by more bullets than the Judge, was not in mortal danger.

Walking beside Brenda's gurney as she was wheeled into the emergency room, John heard Dave, one of Rapidan County's deputies not on Sterling's payroll, call over to him, "John, John!"

John was not going to leave Brenda's side and shouted back, "Later, I've got to see how Brenda is."

Several nurses and a doctor took charge of Brenda's gurney, wheeling her into an examination room. "You'll have to stay out here, Mr. Richter," the doctor said.

"The hell I will. I'm going . . ."

"Listen, John, let me do my job. You're only going to get in the way if you go in there. We'll find out if there's anything wrong a lot quicker if you stay out here."

The doctor's firm hand on John's shoulder told him it would be useless to argue. *Besides,* John thought, *the doctor's probably right. Brenda seems okay. She was conscious and alert, and I could only see a small cut on the corner of her mouth.*

Grabbing her hand briefly as she was wheeled away from him he looked into her eyes and mouthed the words, "I love you." Brenda, unable to speak back because of the oxygen mask, blinked her eyes, nodded her head, and gave his hand an extra hard squeeze. *God. She's gotta be all right!*

Turning from the examining room, he saw Dave again. The deputy was still looking in his direction and waved John over to the other side of the emergency room.

"John, how's Brenda? I heard what happened over the police radio."

"I think she's going to be okay. She said her side is really hurting, but it doesn't seem to involve the baby. I know she's going to be okay."

"I'm sure she will, John. Listen, did you know your dad's here?"

"What's wrong? What happened?" John looked around, further panicked.

"You hadn't heard anything about what happened at the cabin after you left this morning?" Not giving John time to answer, Dave gave him an outline of the events of the cabin, including how Samuel and Judge Collins had defended themselves. The bodies of the men they had killed were found in the back of the pickup truck when Michael was arrested at Belleview. One of the other men who had been captured told the deputies what had happened at the cabin. "Yeah, your dad and Judge Collins shot the hell out of 'em. It sounds like the Morgan boys snuck up behind the cabin and caught 'em from the rear. They're both lucky they aren't dead."

Peeping into his father's hospital room, John started to close the door, thinking his father was asleep or so heavily sedated he wouldn't know he was there. Samuel saw John and raised his right hand, motioning for him to come in. John walked slowly across the floor and took his father's right hand in both of his. His father had an oxygen line in his nose and IV's in both arms. The bandages on his stomach, chest, and shoulder were all stained red. "Christ, Dad. You look like a piece of Swiss cheese."

Samuel Richter had a great sense of humor and trying to control his laugh was extremely painful. He smiled and caught the laugh about mid-way, causing tears to run out of both eyes. "How's Brenda? How's the baby?"

"She and the baby are both fine, Dad. And we got a lot of those bastards out at Belleview too. I don't know how many got away, but when they chased Isaac and William off Belleview and into the woods, they really put it to them."

It had been a long time since John looked at his father's hands. He could see the scars, the wrinkles, and calluses that age and hard work had brought him. Realizing how close he had come to losing his entire family that day, John held his father's hand and said quietly, "You and Judge Collins kept them off us today, Dad. If it hadn't been for you, if those guys had gotten back to Belleview, none of us would be here. I just wanted you to know that."

"Listen, you don't need to thank me for anything. You're my son and I'd do anything for you. If you feel obligated to me, how about this. Doc tells me it's going to take probably a month or more for me to get well enough to get around on my own. Think you and Brenda can put up with me long enough for me to stick around and see the baby born?"

The thought of something positive in the future brought a light to John's eyes and a smile to his face. "You got it, Dad. You stay as long as you want. Listen, you get some rest. I'm going down and check on Brenda. I love you."

"I love you too, son. You go take care of that wife of yours. Don't worry about me. It takes more than a half-dozen jerks and four bullets to kill me."

John smiled and walked softly back out of the room. Closing the door quietly behind him he said a silent thank-you for his father, the man who had been there for him when he needed him.

Roy too would survive his injuries. Four days later, John would go to Rick Bannister's funeral along with everyone else who had participated in the raid on Belleview except Roy.

Judge Collins would remain in intensive care for nearly three weeks and have four major surgeries to repair the damage to his liver, colon, and left kidney. To the amazement of all of his doctors, he would be released from the hospital in less then seven weeks.

Brenda would come home from the hospital after two days, but her ribs would be stiff and sore for well over a month. John's father was released from the hospital after twelve days and remained at John and Brenda's through Christmas.

Neither John nor Brenda would get their wish for the delivery of their second child before the holiday season. Christmas that year, cold, gray, and snowless, would come and go as would New Year's Day, before Brenda felt the labor pains that took her to the hospital on the tenth of January. Contrary to popular practice, John stayed in the waiting room for the delivery of their child. He was a bit old-fashioned and had no desire to be in the delivery room during the actual delivery. He and his father would not see Brenda until both she and their new baby son were back in her room. When they entered, Brenda was lying there, their new son wrapped in blankets and lying cradeled in her left arm. As John crossed the room and sat on the edge of the bed, Brenda smiled. "He's perfect, John. He's a perfect little boy. Just like . . ." Brenda caught herself in mid-sentence.

"Oh, he sure is, Brenda. I can't believe it. Tiny little hands. Tiny little feet. Thank God he looks like you!"

"Christ!" John's father said. "How can you tell who he looks like, all shriveled up and red like that. I haven't been around that many babies, but he sure does remind me a lot of you when you were born. Your mother was all proud and I think it kind of hurt her feelings when I looked at you and said something like, 'Looks kind of puny to me'."

"Well," said John, "I got over that, didn't I?"

"You sure did. How about if I hold him for a minute?" Samuel said. "Kind of nice to hold that third generation." John's father cradled his new grandson in his arms, looked into his eyes, and said quietly, "What you gonna be, huh?"

"Well," he said, looking up at John and Brenda, "I guess we have plenty of time to find that out, don't we? What's his name?"

"Samuel Collins Richter. Kind of has a nice ring to it, doesn't it?"

"Sure does, Son," Samuel said as tears began forming in the corners of his eyes.

"Come on, you two," said the nurse. "Brenda's got to feed the baby and she needs some rest. You can both come back at nine o'clock in the morning."

"But," John protested, "it's only three o'lclock. Can't we have a few more minutes?"

"No, I'm sorry," she said, shooing them out of the room.

"Wait a minute," he said, turning back to Brenda's bed and leaning over her. "I love you, Sweetheart. You take care and I'll see you in the morning."

"I love you, too," said Brenda. John softly brushed the wisp of light silky hair back off the baby's forehead. He was reminded so strongly of Allen that he turned and left the room quickly, not trusting himself to speak.

"John, are you okay?" his dad asked.

"Yeah, sure, Dad. Just a little overwhelmed by it all, I guess. Do you mind driving home on your own? I think I need a little time to myself."

"No problem. Where are you going? Can I fix dinner?"

"I don't know, Dad. Don't worry about dinner. I'll get something if I get hungry."

"Okay. You just take care. This is all gonna work out okay." Samuel stood quietly in the hall as he watched his son walk away. He had seen this look in his son's eyes before. He had, in fact, felt this way himself in the past.

I wish I could help you, Son, Samuel thought to himself as John left the hospital. *But you're finding out some things you just have to work out for yourself. Some things you can't change. You just have to accept them and do the best you can.*

John got in his truck and, before he realized he had a destination, he was driving down the road toward the judge's cabin. He hadn't been there since the day of the fight and wasn't really sure he wanted to see the place where he had come so close to losing his father. The farm, though, was magnetic. He approached the clearing slowly, pulling up in the driveway in front of the house. The windows had all been boarded up with plywood and John could see workmen had already been there to begin repairing the damage.

He got out of the truck, walked up to the front porch and tested the door. It and all the others doors and windows were locked, not that he really wanted to go inside anyway.

Turning back toward the parking lot, he took several steps down off the front porch and sat slowly, leaning against one of the front pillars.

"God," he said aloud, "If I could just speak to Allen one more time. If we could just go for one more walk in these woods together. There are so many things I wanted to teach him, to tell him, and to show him. So many things that he never got a chance to do." He buried his head in this hands. "Why couldn't it have been me? I'd change places with him, if I could."

The answer came back to him in the words Brenda had spoken quietly and softly when he had gone into her hospital room that afternoon. "You have a son, John." There, in those words, were the answers to all the questions he had been asking. *I have another son. Allen's gone and there is nothing I can do for him. But I have memories of him, of that love, that I can pass on.* He rose from the porch and walked to his truck. Taking a pad out from under the seat and a pen from the glove compartment, he turned and walked up the path that led to the ridge behind the cabin.

Just as he had done at the end of the hunting season the January before, John went to the large oak in the grove a half mile from the cabin. It was several hours before sundown and it was a cold, steel-gray day. Deer season had ended the week before, and the woods were peaceful and quiet. Sitting on the heavy carpet of oak leaves under the tree and leaning back against its ancient trunk, he began to write.

> January 10, 2005
>
> To Samuel Collins Richter
>
> I held you for the first time today, taking you from your mother for just a few moments. I cradled you in my arms, looked into your eyes, touched those few small strands of hair on your head and then handed you back to her. You will never remember that I did that and I will never forget. We don't know each other yet. I don't know what you'll be like. The only thing I know about you right now is that you're my son and I love you.
>
> I'm writing this letter today to share some things with you, in case, when you're older, I'm not here for you. You have to understand that life is a gift. You only get one

and in that life there will be few things that are constant. One of the things that will be is my love for you. There will never be anything that you can't tell your mother or me. Nothing that you can't bring to us that we won't try to understand and help you with.

You'll learn later on that you had a brother. His name was Allen. You'll never know him because he died last October. But you would have loved him too. He was a fine young man. A great son. He would have made a great brother. You'll find out later how he died and what happened and all of that is important for you to know. To remember.

There are a few material things I want to leave you that are very important. One is your great-grandfather's wood-framed slate writing tablet that he used to practice his ABC's and his times tables on when he was a child. Not because I expect you to use it but because it stands as a constant reminder of our struggle to learn and to educate ourselves. Always remember that, with effort, we become better people. Each generation in turn surpassing the last. Never become too old to learn.

I leave you your grandfather's sixteen-gauge Sterlingworth shotgun. It's been in the family since 1926 and is one of the finest shotguns this country has ever produced. The finish is worn by three generations of Richters carrying it in corn fields and oak woods. It remains a symbol of how our family has been prepared to provide for itself and a reminder that you must always be able to do so. This shotgun was Allen's. I've cleaned it, wiped the barrels with an oil cloth, and put it away. It won't be fired again until you're ready to use it. It's been a good friend of our family for nearly eighty years and it deserves a rest.

I leave you my albums with pictures taken over the last sixty years. Photographs of my father and his brother; of your grandfather and me; of Allen and a host of other friends and family. People who have spent lifetimes in the woods and on the water because they chose to. I ask you to look at each and every one; examine them not for the evidence of the success of the day in the field or on the water, but for the proof of the satisfaction and peace a day like that can bring.

You will see many pictures of game and fish taken but just as many more of people whose friendship grew stronger; of fires that warmed not only their hands but their hearts; of smiles that never faded and days that never ended. Friends who depended on each other, not just in times of trial or need, but who loved each other for the love of this world they shared. Proof that the bonds forged between those who share this heritage are stronger than time.

I have been blessed, my son, to go and see and do many things. Some of these experiences I hope you and I will share, for they are truly wondrous. But if I am not here know that my heart and my spirit will be with you. When you have seen these places, a part of you never leaves. Our footprints on these trails are quickly covered by falling leaves but a memory in the heart never dies.

I leave you the simple pleasure of the crisp winter air on an early January morning as you prepare for a day in the Virginia hardwoods. The chilling, toe-numbing cold of the Rappahannock River in late March when the ice forms in the guides of your fishing rod as you wait for the first run of hickory shad up from the Bay. The thick, soft ooze of mud between your toes and the velvety soft, warm touch of the summer waters of the Rapidan as it tumbles gently out of the Blue Ridge on its journey to the sea.

I leave you the excitement of the whistle of a brace of doves over your head as they pass so quickly that there's no shot. Only the admiration of their twisting, diving, whirling, seemingly out-of-control flight. And I leave you the heart-pounding excitement of that first whitetail deer as you see him briefly through the frost and haze of a mid-November morning. A step, a glance, a moment frozen in time—a trophy for the mind.

Indeed, son, I leave you the world to see and to explore. To love, to cherish, and to preserve. But in the largeness of life, in your awe at the wealth of natural wonders, do not neglect the ordinary, everyday beauty of it. There is nothing so small in this world that you should not marvel at its beauty; at its place in your life and your place in its.

I leave you your heritage. You are a product of all of your ancestors, of all of their actions. And though there may be some that you disagree with or do not understand, you are responsible for remembering them, for making sure their sacrifices and their contributions are not lost on future generations. A family, a country, that cannot come to grips with its past, all parts of it, good and bad, is doomed to failure.

I leave you your rights as a human being and an American. Our ancestors recognized certain rights which were inalienable, untouchable; rights which could not and should not be tampered with. We live in a society today where many think that some of these rights are no longer important. If you find these rights threatened, then it is incumbent on you to do everything you can within the framework of our government to see that these rights and liberties are protected. If you, either through neglect or failure to act, lose any or all of those rights, then it is only you whom you must blame.

We, each of us, must decide in our own lives what is important to us-what we will love, what we will cherish, what will endure in our minds as we get older. I want you to know that I already treasure the time we will spend together. Some journeys are short. Some seem to go on forever. Yours, my son, is just beginning. May it be long, happy, full of love, and may I be blessed to be a part of it for many years to come. With all of the love it is possible for a father to have for his child, I leave these things to you.

> Keep them in your heart and in your mind. For, no matter what time or distance may separate us, in my heart, we will always be together.

He folded the letter and slid it inside his jacket. As he did he leaned back against the rough bark of the tree and looked up through the bare branches toward a sky that was just beginning to show a little blue.

"We go on, don't we, Son?" John said. And in the wind swirling through the leafless branches of that tree which had sheltered him forever, he was sure he heard Allen's answer.

THE END

Edwin F. Gentry was born in Durham, North Carolina. He now lives in Culpeper, Virginia, with Faye, his wife of 36 years. He is currently a lawyer in private practice and a substitute District and Juvenile Court Judge. Also the owner and head chef of Gentry's Catering Service, LLC, he enjoys being "camp cook" on his hunting and fishing trips with friends.

An avid, life-long hunter, fisherman and outdoorsman he has been privileged to travel to many destinations in the lower 48 states, Canada, Alaska and Mexico in pursuit of these interests. His son Eddie, has shared many of these experiences with him.

As a former U.S. History teacher, he has been very active in many aspects of the preservation of Civil war battlefields and history. He is a former museum president and founding member and former Captain of Company B., 19th Regiment, Virginia Volunteers. He has been in charge of staging many large civil war battle reenactments one of which was filmed by ABC as a special for television. This show was narrated by the author.

Writing extensively for his own pleasure all of his life, this is his first novel.

Author photograph: Stephen D. Dudley, Culpeper, Virginia
Cover Art: Lou Messa, Fine Artist, Madison, Virginia
Cover Photograph: Garland C. Gentry, Jr., Culpeper, Virginia

BVG